The Mission

BY

Richard O. Benton

The Mission
© 2010 by Richard O. Benton

Notice of Rights
No part of this book may be reproduced, stored in a retrieval system or transmitted by any means, electronic, mechanical, photocopying, recording or otherwise, without permission, excepting brief quotes used in connection with reviews written specifically for inclusion in a magazine or newspaper.

Disclaimer
This is a work of fiction. Names, characters, places and incidents are the products of the author's imagination or are used fictitiously. Any resemblance to actual events, locales, persons or groups, living or dead, is entirely coincidental.

For information, write:

Storycraft Publishing
Post Office Box 1647
Litchfield, CT 06759
    or
Email: Storycraft.publishing@gmail.com
www.richardObenton.com

ISBN 978-0-9822424-2-1

This book is printed on acid free paper.
Printed in the United States of America

This book is dedicated to my wife Holly

Acknowledgements

The author wishes to acknowledge the assistance of Peter Aziz, Bantam Fuel Company, for scientific knowledge of Diesel fuel I lacked, Jennifer Gangloff, Jay Worsham, Amy and Tim Nicholson, mother and son duo, for taking the time to read the original manuscript and make suggestions, and especially for Christina Schoenknecht, who treated her reading as a homework assignment and offered some invaluable comments that made the story stronger. For encouragement, there has been none more dedicated than the following members of The Litchfield Writers Guild, past and present in keeping me working hard for excellence in the writing. They are Barclay Johnson, Adrienne Barbe, Dora Cox, Barbara Francis, Carolyn Carosella Martin, Sharon Annable, Barbara Fincken, Rob Pizzella, Maletta Pfeiffer and Bea Murgio. Encouragement doesn't make the writing easier, but it brightens every day in between.

Finally, special thanks to author and computer guru Dan Uitti, who kept me on the right side of the digital divide.

Prologue

The world had changed beyond the ability of any mind to comprehend. It had gone through a cleansing process, but the few people who lived called it apocalypse and wondered for what reason had they been spared. They felt desolate and hopeless, and terribly alone.

For those with a deep faith in God, it was a calamity of greatest proportion. What had God allowed humanity to do? For those without faith, it was much simpler, because simple calamity sufficed. In the end, the faithful retained their faith out of habit because they couldn't conceive of an alternative. The nonbelievers shook their heads and held their tongues.

Twelve years before, the world had spun on its axis into chaos. Earth became in one horrifying day and one lethal night a smoking ruin. Four hundred and ninety seven thermonuclear explosions flashed and thundered across the planet. Of the thousands of missiles that remained in caches around the world, it only took four hundred and ninety-seven to destroy civilization. The bomb that wiped out San Francisco set off earthquakes along the North American and Pacific tectonic plates, as did the bomb that hit Tokyo along the Japan Trench. All of Earth's major cities died immediately. Everything else died slowly.

The bombs that hit Europe eradicated political boundaries. How can there be politics without people? In Asia, the vastness of Russia and China and all of its varied peoples became instant wasteland. Some ICBM guidance systems failed and bombs exploded in every ocean Man had named. Tidal waves destroyed millions. They avoided the slow death.

How lucky!

Dormant volcanoes along the Aleutian trench reactivated, adding their noxious gasses and dust to the poisoned atmosphere. Oahu died in a cataclysmic blast. The shock wave fractured the Mona Loa and Mona Kea lava shields. Both erupted simultaneously and covered the Big Island with molten lava. There were no people to see it.

Exactly four hundred and ninety seven multi-megaton hydrogen bombs wiped out civilization. Teeming billions died. It took only a small step to believe that the animals and insects and fish followed them into oblivion.

Malevolent forces brought all the world's nations and peoples to their knees on that day, first in lightning war and then in the slow death. Apocalypse. The end. Nighttime for humanity!

But it wasn't the end of all. By some fluke, one hundred survived. Deep inside a mountain in the Canadian Rockies in a completely self-contained biosphere, one hundred scientists and technicians stood in shock and horror and waited and listened to their one radio as the world died. They were appalled, disgusted, afraid, but they were not stupid. They realized immediately that the murder of more than six billion souls along with countless trillions of other life on Earth had indefinitely extended their underground experiment.

They must live for as long as it took in cramped surroundings designed for a two-year stay on bottled and chemically recycled air and water. They grew what they lived on. Additional plantings took up every otherwise unused space deep within the mountain. Thus they lived on the thin edge for twelve long, almost impossible years, fifty men and fifty women, a pitiful number.

They who had deliberately and willingly allowed themselves to be buried under the mountain faced their uncertain future. In a cave filled with bright souls, men and women with specialties in refrigeration, atomics and atmospheric reprocessing, and the agronomists and chemists amongst them went to work. They learned how to extend their resources well beyond the biosphere's planned timeframe. They developed the means to recycle air and water indefinitely. Plants and animals helped one another in a thankless symbiotic exchange of oxygen and carbon dioxide.

They had animals, five cows and a bull, five sheep and a ram, a male and two female goats, several dogs and cats and a few rabbits. They carefully husbanded their animals and the population grew slowly. As they expanded their living area for plantings, they tinkered with the walls of their prison, exploring and widening small cracks here and there. In the sixth year it paid off. They unearthed the caves.

With relief they discovered that their tight surroundings had expanded. At first they feared greatly, but quickly discovered that the caves were also closed off to the surface. Nothing of the radioactivity above could leech into their environment to poison them. They made a decision to grow into the caves.

In the sixth year they ended their moratorium on children. With ample space they began to think about repopulation as a necessary feature of re-growing the race. Some resisted it, thinking that perhaps the Earth ought to spin along empty; that humanity had had its chance and blown it. Hot debate ensued. There existed surprising support for letting the race die, but in the end, they decided they owed it to themselves to try again and to do it better this time. The will to live ran strong.

Chemical inhibitors designed for recreational sex were removed and the resultant couplings began to produce children. They renamed Biosphere I and their home became New Beginnings, a hopeful name.

Chapter 1
Out of the Caves

Arthur Mavis, Chief Scientist and oldest resident, now sixty-seven and a kind of grandfather to them all asked the hundred to meet. Recruited in their early twenties, all but Arthur were now in their mid thirties. They and forty children ranging in age from one to five congregated in the large, strongly stone-pillared main hall.

Arthur stood alone on a natural dais, a flat table of rock perhaps three feet higher than the surrounding cavern floor. He wore a loose fitting one-piece fatigue of canvas white and a pair of the sneaker-like rubber shoes that velcroed over the arch of each foot. Woven cloth peppered with grommet holes invited things to be hung from hooks as appropriate. The belt buckled above the waist and completed the ensemble. Two sets of deep pockets were fitted in the hollow formed by the anterior aspect of each hip, one set near the belt area and the other lower down to provide easy access and maximum carrying capacity. It was part of the standard clothing allotment, and what little the styling did for the inhabitants, fatigues available in bright colors rectified.

Although the outfits were not designed to promote attractiveness, they *did* in the manner of each individuals desire—depending on the emotional state of their day—promote or ward off contact with their fellows. Living close, clothing that could be adjusted to reflect each person's mood acted as a kind of barometer that others could read at a glance. After years together, it served to regulate conduct without confrontation. It was part of the psychology of the long dead and it worked.

Arthur addressed them.

"The world remains a dangerous place, my friends, the southern latitudes especially, but my instruments tell me that radioactivity levels above us have diminished to a point where we can safely break the plug that seals us in and climb the tunnel to the surface. We can breath the world's air again."

His next words were torn away by shouts and tumult. He stood, mouth open, wondering if these were the same people who had moved quietly about their tasks with hardly a smile for twelve long years. He consciously closed his mouth and with a quirk of his lip stood and waited for quiet.

Perhaps, he thought, *I should have offered hope much earlier. But how could I,* he argued, *I was prepared to wait twenty-five years. I couldn't believe in hope before that. The rapidly falling levels in the past year might have been fortuitous.*

Still, he was gratified.

Finally he held his arms up high. A few noted his gesture and began to quiet the people around them. Sanity returned and Arthur spoke again.

"The world above may be unlivable even though the air is clean, but I think we must find out. This has been our cocoon." He stopped and waved his hand in a circle. "It has served our needs for twelve years. In these depths we have books and equipment and knowledge. Very possibly, we are all that's left of Earth's intelligent life, if indeed, *any* other life still exists. I want to bring our life back to the surface."

More clamor. Arthur waited patiently. It died quickly now.

"We can drill through yon cement plug." He gestured. "Who's game to start now?"

A hundred voices shouted joy!

Men and women hugged and cried in each other's arms. They began to excavate immediately. The cement plug at Bio-cave level turned out to be ten feet thick. It took two days of drilling and fifteen tiny, carefully placed, shaped charges to break it up. After that a shower of sand and small stone dribbled into the cave. To their surprise, pulverized rock still blocked them. The material was much like process gravel, the stuff used to make highway roadbeds. Some insightful individuals on the surface had foreseen the coming cataclysm and realized that a world going as wrong as it appeared might leave the hundred alone.

As a final act of charity, the topside construction people had backfilled the entire tunnel to preserve the life within. Arthur marveled that no one had reported hearing scraping or muffled thuds when this happened. Seven hundred feet of material had to be removed. They put it in the caves.

Arthur knew when they were sealed in that the builders required there be no communication with the surface. They must live unsullied by contact with the rest of the planet. Arthur learned the night before in a special and very secret meeting with the company's principals of the dual nature of their interment. He was sworn to secrecy and he had never broken that trust. The builders wanted to discover if one hundred men and women could survive and thrive deep underground. If they could, perhaps they could also live in space.

In the final meeting with his superiors the night before they were closed in, they told Arthur the biosphere must sink or swim. They could not and would not be monitored. They would not be saved from calamity. They would do or they would die. Arthur understood the psychology of the requirement. He knew that to alert the colony would change the nature of the experiment and that must not happen.

They had a few computers for recording experimental data, but no connection to the Internet. Arthur confiscated the one radio they were allowed to keep. He refused to use the radio and didn't retrieve it from its locked cabinet until tremors rocked the cave on the day the Earth died.

They'd crowded around him, barely contained, demanding!

"Please, I don't know any more than you. I'll get the radio," he'd said. They heard uncommon fear in the older man's voice.

All who lived below were frightened. Only cataclysmic forces on the surface could cause such shuddering. He hooked it to the one wire that ran the length of the tunnel, the one that allowed him to conduct limited experiments he'd insisted on before being sealed in. It became their antenna. Arthur turned the radio on and the biosphere's scientists and technicians heard their worst fears realized. For long after, the hundred wore haunted expressions.

Discovery of the caves gave a few of the biosphere's souls opportunity to be adventurous. There were spelunkers amongst them and they mapped the tunnels. It helped direct potentially dangerous energy. Unused parts of the caves, dangerous holes, unsafe shelves and the like served as repository for the tremendous amount of material they took from the tunnel. Sixteen days later they came to another plug.

The workers labored feverishly. With the possibility of release, home became claustrophobic. A day later they broke through.

Arthur breathed a sigh of relief. Cuts from rock chips and skinned knuckles and broken fingernails expressed the enthusiasm of their mission, but no serious injuries occurred. So many things could have gone wrong. He chided himself for worrying.

The day they broke through Matt Duncan had control of the drilling machine. As he drilled for the placement of yet another charge his drill broke through. Warm air blew back through the hole. He put his nose to it and smelled the unfamiliar odors of an outside world. Turning, he yelled to those behind him. "Call Arthur!"

The call filtered down to the biosphere.

Built into the mountain, the biosphere only required a modestly engineered incline and workers had finished the tunnel at the height of a tall man. The Chief Scientist made his way up with little difficulty.

Arthur's standing order to notify him at the point of breakthrough met, Duncan consulted before blasting the remaining plug out of the way.

"The site map shows a forty foot natural tunnel beyond the plug that opens out into the valley, if you remember," Arthur told Matt. "No bombs hit near us—nothing up here worth blasting, I guess. We're a hundred miles from the nearest volcano the war activated, so far as I can tell. You should be clear to punch through."

"Okay, Arthur, stand back." Arthur retired behind the mickey-moused blast screen, several boards in a frame held nearly vertical by a two by four attached top center. It was heavy enough to keep shards from bloodying the workers, light enough to move easily. Matt set the charges and carefully connected the posts to two wires they had used many times before. He ran back fifty feet and twisted the wire ends to the battery-powered switch.

"Now!" Matt closed the switch. People blocked their ears.

A thunderous blast, magnified by the circular tunnel shook the walls. A few pieces of cement rattled up ahead of them. Arthur looked at the ceiling.

Matt laughed. "No problem, Arthur, we check the integrity of the ceiling after each blast. The boring machine that carved the tunnel did good and the operator knew his job."

Arthur laughed, too. "For years I have not worried about our Bio, but here it's different."

"Sure. Anyway, that should do it. Arthur?" Matt motioned to the scientist.

"Thanks, Matt. C'mon gang, Let's all see what's out there."

The entourage moved forward as one person, anxious to see, to feel, to smell, anxious to be out of their womb. They were nervous, but nothing could stop the moment. They crowded out of the blast dusted narrow opening into a wide, broad cave and picked their way through cement debris. Daylight streamed in. The fresh smell of life, so unlike the bottled, recycled, antiseptically clean air they had breathed for years crept up their nostrils. Noses wrinkled and one or two sneezed, but they pressed forward and then they were outside.

They knew the earth hadn't trembled in years and any radioactive dust must have settled and been carried away by Earth's rains and rivers. To their glad eyes, they faced a green valley filled with trees and grasses. A small stream cut through it. The water ran clear and sparkled as it tumbled over water-smoothed rocks. One who sipped without testing it first pronounced it fit and wonderful. The survivors poured out of their self-imposed prison and fell to the ground, rolling and laughing like children.

They came out into a warmer world than the one they had left. The cold whiteness that covered the mountains surrounding them was mostly gone. Only the tips of the highest peaks held a mantle of hoarfrost and snow. Arthur Mavis smiled and said nothing to the rest. Let them enjoy their newly reborn world for as long as they liked—for today, anyway.

Arthur knew something else, something he hadn't told *anyone*. It would keep.

Chapter 2
Contemplation

Matt Duncan and Mike Peters came up and stood by Arthur. Matt and Mike wore blue coverall fatigues. On both, the knees were worn nearly white. Into 'cavin', Mike was fond of saying.

Both men stood tall, Mike having an inch on Matt. Both were muscular and fit. Matt had fine, wiry, well muscled hands where Mike's were larger, not quite outsized, but prominent.

Mike spoke. "Have you noticed what I have, Arthur?"

"No animals?"

"None."

"Perhaps somewhere else?" Arthur said hopefully.

"In the lower forty-eight I would guess there are none, but here, shouldn't there still be animals in the north?"

Arthur sighed, "I don't know, Mike, I just don't know. One bomb could devastate an area much larger than the blast area depending on prevailing winds. The bombs they used would make the majority of the Earth unlivable. There's an old term, "nuclear winter."

"I know the term. Surprises me we came out so soon."

"I can't believe there is a mechanism operating we haven't thought of."

Matt, a molecular biologist, said, "I have quietly entertained a theory that the earth is a living thing that heals itself in ways science has failed to grasp. All the rest of my knowledge tells me it ain't so, so where I get off saying that, I don't know."

"Matt," Arthur said, "only a fool thinks he has all the answers."

"I know, Arthur."

Mike, who had been listening with one ear and reveling in the sounds of the crowd down the hill with the other spoke up. Mike often diddled with mathematical formula's, searching for answers to realities within rock, sea, and fire. His colleagues considered him brilliant, fine praise from his peers, who were no slouches in the brainpower division.

Like all brilliant people, Mike had his foibles. Within his specialty no one could argue his points, but that didn't run to the day-to-day use of his time on earth. Generally quiet and a willing follower, he surprised Arthur, who believed that Mike lived with mathematical certainties and had little imagination beyond. Nonetheless, Arthur knew Mike looked up to him and despite the age difference; they were friends.

"Arthur, I think we should move up here, out in the open. If the radioactivity has gone below the danger level we could start a town right over there," he pointed. The long valley opened out in the distance. A relatively flat part a mile away and half a mile wide looked inviting. Tall pines covered much of the valley's sides. "We could set up a lumber mill beyond, build roads, the whole magilla."

"I think you're right, Mike, but we'll go slow. The first thing we need to do is to create an impervious door to the bio-sphere, just in case."

"Of what?" Mike asked.

"Storms that may carry radioactivity. Still a lot of it in the south."

"But it got better quicker up this way, right?"

"Why throw caution to the wind? Maybe there *are* animals. We don't know."

"Okay."

"Beyond that," Arthur said, "a few of us will have to turn into scouts and range beyond the mountains to see how safe it really is."

Both men spoke up. They could do that.

"We'll outfit you, get you compasses, counters and better radios than you fellows used in the caves. We have maps of the ranges. I think George and Roddy should go, too. You four seem the most daring. The rest of us will start a village up here. It's summer. I want to get the group together again and talk it over. There is something else, too."

Matt and Mike looked at Arthur expectantly.

Arthur said, "I'll break it to you all at the meeting."

"Mysterious," Matt breathed.

"Not really, but I want to promote pure democracy in our group. Everyone with a voice and everyone must be willing to contribute. I've thought about it and that's the direction the new civilization should take, I think."

"Sounds good to me," Mike said.

"Matt, why don't you and Mike go down the hill and bring the group up. I can talk from here."

"Sure, Arthur." The two picked their way down the ledge leading to the grassy valley and started rounding up the people below. In the couple of hours they'd been outside they'd scattered considerably and dark shapes could be seen dotting the gently sloping hillside.

Arthur thought, *No, they shouldn't know yet. Let's make our mark on the surface before I tell them.*

Chapter 3
Twilight Meeting

The rock face in front of the cave entrance made another natural stage, kind of like the one in the bio, but somewhat higher. Arthur surveyed it and sighed. *I'm leader,* he thought, *but that's the last thing I want to be. Better say nothing until I come up with the formula I think will work best. When I know exactly what I want to present to the group, I'll get everyone involved.*

New Beginnings Clan! Arthur smiled. *Good name for the lot of us,* he thought, as the closest part of the group began to arrive a few feet below where he stood. It took considerable time to get everybody together. The sun had reached the western sky, one extended fist above the mountains, ten degrees. Shadow would start changing the landscape in less than an hour.

The last straggler arrived. Several of the women kept the children near the outskirts of the crowd and did their best to quiet them, so that they, too, could hear Arthur's words. Modesty was a commodity few concerned themselves with and two women with newborns suckled them comfortably, their attention and eyes on the leader.

Arthur cleared his throat. "My friends and co-workers—we are both—we need to consider a few things before the sun sets today. First of all, I have led in the Bio as a matter of duty and I don't mind leading for now on top, but I want all of us to participate in running this new civilization it appears we are about to create. We must not *recreate* what we had. That's gone and good riddance. What I propose is that we all think on what was good about humanity, get into little groups and list those attributes. Do the same for the bad. Good. Bad. Assets. Liabilities. Pro. Con. However you think of it.

"I know it's all laid out in books we have in the Library, but old ideas aren't what I hope for. Of the volumes available, exactly what we have come away with and what we practice daily is what we should focus upon. Some kind of government will be necessary, but the founders of America had to write about their new beginnings and evolve them. We do, too.

"There is much more. Security, for one, will require that we explore well beyond our mountain valley. I have spoken to Matt Duncan and Mike Peters and they are willing to outfit for an extensive time away from us to find out what's out there. Humanity is likely entirely gone and likely the animals, too, but until we know this as fact, it is not fact. Scientific method has guided us for most of our lives and we know it works. If George Handy and Roddy Brown are willing to join them, I think they'd make a good team."

Roddy piped up from the crowd, "Good for me, I'll go."

"Me, too," George called out from near the back.

"Good! Fellows, meet with me after the meeting here and we'll decide where to go and how to do it."

"Wait a minute," Sue Dorchester yelled, "Not so fast. George is my man and father of Duncan here. I think I should have something to say about this." Sue stood about middle height for a woman and was fit and comely. Her flowing brown hair and fitted yellow fatigue left little doubt about her sex and hands on her hips settled the notion. At the moment her expression bordered on quizzical and irritated.

"Yes of course, Sue," Arthur replied.

"Why George, then?" Sue asked. A space opened around her so she could be seen as well as heard.

"We're at the very beginning of all this, Sue," Arthur said. "George is adventurous..."

"You can say that again!" Sue interrupted, and everyone laughed. Everyone knew about *their* chemistry. It made her smile. Sue's job lay in animal husbandry. A veterinarian by training, she was a mainstay of the animals program she kept in the caves.

Arthur laughed, too, but soon became serious again. "I agree that George has some responsibilities around here, but he is most physically fit, as are Roddy, Mike and Matt. All of you have mates, to greater or lesser degree. These four, in my opinion, have the best chance to climb the mountains and deal with whatever they have to face and to come back with what we need. We need information."

Sue was silent for a few moments and then said, "Okay, selfish of me. I understand."

"Not selfish, I think, but a singular concern that needs to be addressed and is only one of many." Arthur smiled at Sue. "One thing we will not do is to go off half-cocked. Nor will we move forward on anything until it's been discussed and voted on. Okay?"

"That's fair."

"Now," Arthur said, "our haven beneath the mountain is our ultimate safety net and a place we can run to if it ever comes to that. I hardly expect anyone to do it, though. I'm sick of the place."

More laughter.

Mary Beth Holiday, a former Haitian woman who'd gotten her degree at Princeton and whose work in the biosphere ensured them of light and heat—her job was to care for the mini atomic pile situated two hundred yards into the mountain beyond the main living areas—waved a hand for attention. A tall, childless but hopeful woman of thirty-five, her current attachment went to Roddy. Mary Beth was no one to fool with. She said, "Believe we'll all have to do a few things we don't want to. Roddy, if you want to go exploring, go."

Roddy stood near the front of the crowd, a six foot-two inch muscular black, also thirty-five, a husbandman who worked with Sue Dorchester. He looked over at Mary Beth.

"Got a feeling there's plenty else to do around here in the meantime," she continued.

Roddy nodded. "I'll take care, Mary Beth."

"Know you will."

"Back to our subject," Arthur interjected. "We're all going to work hard, just like any pioneers. That's what we are, but we're going to try and save what the world gave to us before it was destroyed by hatred and stupidity. Here are some things we have to do. Explore; make sure we'll be safe outside of our cocoon. Next, build us a town. That won't be easy. We don't have that kind of equipment. We can make lots of stuff and we'll manage. We've plenty of knowledge in our storehouse and plenty of raw materials. Next, come up with a viable code of conduct. I expect that will be a simple extension of how we've been living for the past twelve years. Write a new Constitution to fit our new realities. Exercise our minds as well as our bodies. Invent. Come up with better mousetraps. Any questions?"

A hand went up near the back of the assemblage. Arthur couldn't see whose it was.

"Millie here, Arthur." Millicent Bainbridge, Agronomist, University of Michigan, part of the scientific soil and planting programs said, "I've checked the soil out lower down and we'll have no trouble growing crops to sustain ourselves. Any idea how much warmer things are at this latitude?"

"The world temperature, based on preliminary information has risen four degrees."

"Whew, bet the North American coastlines don't look the same anymore."

"No bet."

"We'll do very well, then. Thanks...oh, one more thing."

"Yes?"

"Why not get a few of us to scout the inside range and the valley to see what we can pick up on. Maybe the dear departed left us some stuff somewhere. You never know."

"It's a good idea and our explorers will start there, but I think we should get back to the bio-sphere for tonight and take a new view of what we can spare down there to bring up tomorrow."

That got a few grumbles. Arthur waited for calm and added, "We have animals to feed and chores to do. Think on our move and bring me any suggestions you have. I'll be liaison. Let's head back."

More grumbles, but the shadow of the western peaks had already crept halfway down the mountains and they could see the efficacy of Arthur's suggestion. The needs of plants and animals living deep inside the mountain didn't cease because they had broken out. With a last look behind, they filed back.

Chapter 4
The Last Dream

Throughout the night excitement ran high. Those who worked had no trouble staying awake. Those who needed sleep didn't get much. A lot of loving went around during the night, nature's release for deliverance. They left the tunnel open to the surface, but blocked it at biosphere level to prevent the dogs and other freely roaming animals to escape.

Early next morning Arthur checked his calendar. Twelve years, four months and eight days, he realized. February 17, 2011, the day the biosphere experiment was buried. Twelve years, two months and nine days from apocalypse. *Amazing*, he thought, *the world has ended and June 25, 2023 may be the actual start of our new beginnings. New Beginnings, the reality. How good that sounds! Should I suggest we start with the year one? 1 NB?* He picked up the list he had accumulated through the night. Suggestions came from the thin stream of people who came to his bedside table where he sat thinking. He wrote them down religiously until he decided he was exhausted. It would have to wait until morning. He closed his curtain then and tried for sleep.

The dream came back, the dream he'd never told to anyone in all the time they'd been underground. In it he saw the horror of apocalypse. Maybe others had dreamed, too, but this he never shared. He floated somewhere out in space, unsupported, unable to breathe in the vacuum of space, yet he lived. He saw the crescent Earth, brilliant blue, shining below. He saw the night side, too, great cities, great spots of light, the culmination of man's dominance over all things. Earth, a unique place in all the universe, a jewel of breathtaking beauty.

Then a shadow passed over his eyes and everything changed. Suddenly he saw a brilliant flash of light. America! Yes, right about where Washington should be. A bright flash followed on the dark side right about where Israel would be. Then another bright blossom, and another and another and the flashes escalated alarmingly. Flares of brilliance began occurring all across the temperate belts of the world. Dazzling, blinding light! Horrible circular clouds began to appear on the dayside and they took the form of mushrooms. As he watched the blue Earth turned gray and white, clouds obliterated the entire globe and lightning flashed within them. Then volcanoes awoke and spewed their titanic clouds of poison into the atmosphere. Arthur watched the world die.

A feeling of great loneliness came over him. He lived that way for long, long years, neither here nor there, but everywhere and nowhere. Finally, something strange and wonderful happened. The sky slowly brightened. The clouds thinned and became hazy remnants of what they once were. Again he could see the world. The oceans were blue again and the land varied in colors of brown. In the northern latitudes he saw green, forests beginning to return. Earth was healing. Then the dream faded and was gone and somehow he knew it had gone forever.

A remnant would stay in his conscious mind all of his days and he welcomed it, because he didn't ever want to forget man's ultimate inhumanity to Man, becoming the instrument of his self-destruction! Now it became a distant event and with the happenings of yesterday he knew the distance would increase day by day. The bilious taste he'd lived with for twelve long years disappeared, soothed like a swig of Pepto-Bismol. He felt energized!

Arthur got dressed and stood and stretched, pulling out some of the kinks in his sixty-seven year old body. It felt good. The smells of cooking on electric hotplates wafted into his cubicle. He pulled back the privacy drape and stepped out into a new day rife with excitement. It occurred to Arthur that everything had been running smoothly before he made his announcement the day before, a hopeless, waiting smoothness. Today it felt electric! Today his skin prickled. *We must never again feel the way we did yesterday morning*, he thought, *never again!*

Chapter 5
Preparations

"What's cooking?" Arthur asked the kitchen staff. A rotating chore, cooking was shared by all, based on a simple roster. Bethany Howell, normally the Veterinarian's assistant, Maude Nash, Plant Life Specialist and a member of Arthur's own team, Frank Billings, general maintenance and all around handyman and Amy Fox, chemist and part of the water and air purification staff were the cooks today.

Bright smiles and affirmative "hellos" and "good days" assailed him. He returned them with a laugh.

"Ready for another day topside?" he said mischievously.

"Can't wait," said one and another said, "Me, either. Think we can package some of this stuff and take it topside?"

"Absolutely! Why don't you put together enough food to feed a party of fifteen for a week?"

"Sure...uh...what's going on?"

"We're going to do some exploring and some building and we'll need to feed some hungry people. We're also going to look over that place Mike suggested for a town site. A few of us will scout it out *after* we have covered the valley end to end and made certain there are no dangers we need to think about."

"Dangers? From what? Animals? Thought they all died," Maude said.

"We think they did, but at least one of us has suggested that in the north and probably in the extreme south it might have been possible for relatively protected life to continue to exist. We're going to make sure. Personally, if there is no other life on Earth save us, I'm going to feel very lonely."

"Oh...yeah, me too. No more horses." Maude lost her smile thinking about that.

Arthur said, "Yes." His mind flashed to memories of a beautiful herd racing across a golden-grained plain.

Frank spoke up. "Thinking about our cattle and thinking about radioactivity and thinking about mutants, Arthur."

"I am, too, Frank. I'm putting the brakes on a wholesale move upstairs until we are really certain, not just hopeful. You agree with that?"

Billings was a cautious, thoughtful man. His methods got the ire of the impulsive few, but Frank stuck to his guns and wouldn't be baited. Eventually, deciding that they weren't going to get a rise out of him, they subsided and Frank worked his time at his pace. Ultimately, no one could fault his work.

"Yes, that's what I would do."

"I'm passing this thought around in meetings. Individually, wherever I can. We are going to be totally democratic about everything we do. We will find ways to slow some down and to speed some up, but everyone will have a say in what we do. If we are to build a new civilization, I want it to be as clean and pure as we can make it."

The four nodded and Arthur heard an "Amen."

"Now, how about some breakfast?" Arthur smiled.

"How do you like your steak and eggs, moving or dead?" Bethany said.

"Dead is fine. If it moves it's probably a new life form I don't want to meet."

"Not a chance," she tittered. Canned goods were kept at a temperature just above freezing in a basically humidity free storage facility. The biosphere planners had postulated canned foods would last one hundred years in that condition, minimum. Low temperature, low humidity storage in a special containment facility was one of the original biosphere experiments. They hadn't enough cattle to tap as a resource, so they'd rationed cans and only used them as an adjunct to the food they grew. It was a joke anyway, as the entire group had become vegetarian, after the less than adequate supply of canned meats had run out. Talented individuals learned to form and flavor said vegetables and meals remained attractive and thus mentally tastier. No one thought about it anymore.

Arthur took his tray and retired to a table in the small dining area. He wanted to get above again and see how the exploring parties were doing with their preparation. He wanted to hear their plan before they set out. They really didn't need him, but he wanted to remain visible in case disagreement in the "how to" or the "where to start" part led to a needed intercession. Arthur felt a little old now and then. He wanted to contribute, but didn't want to be looked on as the end all. He sighed. He'd have to start thinking about government soon. This move to the outside encompassed more than the rules they followed in the biosphere.

He finished his meal and got up. Amy came over and took his tray. Arthur said good day to them and returned to his room for a moment to pick up one of the few pairs of binoculars they had. Then he made the hike up the tunnel.

Chapter 6
Heading Out

Matt, Mike, Roddy and George were already in the upper cave with their hiking equipment. Backpacking had become a little cottage industry when the caves were discovered and the four were well versed in their uses. They altered their food compartments and made them large enough for an extended trip. They acquired sufficient clothing from the Bio's storehouse. They were all imbued with good dexterity skills, something everyone rapidly picked up on when the extended two-year experiment caused a lot of rethinking.

As Arthur walked into the upper cave, Matt held up a small boxlike piece of electronics.

"Ernie made up these little beauties," he said, and smiled at the older man.

Arthur took it and looked it over. Much smaller than the big jobs they used in the caves.

"Long distance radios. We'll each have one and there will be a larger model here. We'll be able to communicate with each other and keep home base in the loop at all times."

"Excellent!"

Ernest Tibbets, Ernie to all, communications man and electronics engineer turned farmer twelve years before had had an opportunity when the caves opened to work up some walkie-talkies for use in exploring the then recently discovered caves. They were fortunate that the bio-project's movers and shakers had left much raw material with them for their use in fashioning whatever they might need. Hundreds of feet of fine wire, modulators, tool making equipment, cloth, canvas, anything that a totally isolated community might call for had been stored in various places. The rest of the equation rested in the minds and will of the people.

Matt said, "We've been discussing an itinerary. We want to explore close by for a couple of days, check out the valley and the side hills. Map it, like we did in the caves. We plan to leave shortly. Just waiting on you."

"Thanks, Matt. You don't need my help."

"No, we do. You have been the leader for all the time we've been here and we want to make sure you know what it is we are doing. We may face no danger worse than a rockslide, but, as you said, this is a changed world. Anything could be out there."

"Are you going to split up?"

"Mike and I will take the north side of the valley and hug the cliffs. Roddy and George will take the south side. We'll meet at the end and come back through the middle, separated by a quarter mile or so, to gather what data we can. We'll compare notes on our return. Then we can plan the next phase."

"Good." Arthur remembered the binoculars he wore. "Matt, take these. George, you are younger than I. In my trunk you'll find another pair. Seems to me there are a couple more of these down there, the storehouse, I think. Check it out and see if you can come up with them. I should have thought of this before I came up."

"No problem, Arthur. I'll run." George said. George was about Matt's size, but thinner and wirier. He moved toward the entrance.

"Wait, George," Matt called. "We have to pick up rations for two days away. I want to get more and bring it to the upper cave for easy re-supply. It'll take an hour. Then we'll be ready to go."

"The kitchen should be ready. I asked them before I came up to package meals for you fellows."

"Great. We'll all go down. Want to say goodbye to Millie."

"Another good idea," Roddy said. He thought of Mary Beth. He'd given her a mighty good goodbye last night, but another wouldn't hurt. Not a bit.

Arthur said, "You have everything under control. I'll stay up here and look around. Since you're going down, I'll take my binocs back for a few, Matt."

Matt handed them to Arthur and the four walked into the darkened tunnel.

Arthur put the ten by fifty Bausch and Lomb binoculars up to his eyes, focused them and started panning left to right. Crisp images of distant mountains drawn closer by the twin objectives yielded detail only hazily seen by eye. *And my eyes aren't what they were, either*, he thought.

The surrounding mountains rose nearly ten thousand feet. A major reason the valley had been chosen by Bio-Corp's search committee, Arthur knew, was because of its mountain locked privacy. The remoteness of Canada's Yukon Territory removed their project from notice. Being away from air travel lanes and in a virtually uninhabited area equaled project secrecy and the fact that the least precipitous pass was sixty-five hundred feet above their valley had been considered before focusing here.

All equipment, personnel and construction materials came in by sky-crane helicopter. Workers were sworn to secrecy by contract and alerted to the heavy penalties that would assess against any loose-lipped employee. It had been an immense project, but Bio-Corp kept its existence low key, and somehow, in an information starved Internet world, it had preserved its secrecy.

The project had been under way and hush-hush for several years before a surreptitious advertising campaign for "pioneers" filtered into the college scene. One thousand were screened and one hundred chosen. They came out of top colleges; recruited not only for their specialties, but also for certain psychological attributes the founders wanted in their recruits. Save for Arthur, who had worked with Bio-Corp for ten years before as a consultant and later as an employee, they were all students. The recruits were also put under contract and sworn to secrecy. They were told that their removal from the world for the two-year experiment would give the company final insights into a far-reaching plan that would help America help the rest of the world, but that it would be interesting, very important and likely fun. Above all, they were told that they would be making a real contribution to the human race.

Lights went off in Arthur's brain. He squinted and then closed his welling eyes tight against tears of depression. No one must see him respond to destroyed dreams. He blinked the thoughts away. He stood, drew in slow, silent breaths, and began to look again.

A few chairs and a table had been brought up on the second morning. Sitting on the table Arthur saw a contraption he took to be the communications device Ernie had concocted. It had a battery pack. He looked it over. The unit was off at the moment.

Most of the Bio's people were below, tending to chores. Arthur took a chair and set his elbows on the table so he could continue his sweep of the hills and valley without tiring his hands. Intent on finishing the southern side, he didn't hear the four return.

"Ready, Arthur."

Arthur turned. "Quite a lot out there, gentlemen," he said.

"See anything interesting?"

"Sure, but I'm interested in what you fellows are going to report when you get up close and personal."

"Well," Matt said, "we have enough food for a couple of days and a short run around the valley will be a good exercise toward a bigger hike. We're ready."

"Go ahead, men. I'll man the radio awhile. We'll get a few to do shifts on it to spread the workload. Why don't you try your units out so I can hear them?"

"Sure." Mike unhooked his from his belt, went over to the equipment on the table, turned it on and spoke into the mike. "Testing...testing..."

His voice came out tinny but clear.

"Great!" Arthur exclaimed.

The four hoisted their backpacks and headed out.

Chapter 7
A Discovery of Note

The weather couldn't have been finer. Blue sky, a few wisps of captured cloud hanging near the closest peaks advertised the direction of prevailing winds near ten thousand feet. No breeze here. The valley lay in muted shadow, as the sun at this time of year rose behind Keele Peak, the highest point in Canada's Mackensie mountain range.

The terrain sank slowly toward the center of the valley. Matt took the lead. They were all very competent in their chosen fields and in the twelve years of their internment each one had contributed to the biosphere community in significant ways. Nonetheless, some people are born to lead and some are born to follow. They pulled in behind Matt as they made their way lower.

Roddy spoke to the air. "It's great to be outside again. Must have convinced myself below was good. Now it feels like a coffin. Almost don't want to go back."

"I feel like that, too," George said.

Matt picked his way down a five-foot embankment but said nothing. Mike looked around, appreciating the day. He said, "A whole world out there, waiting just for me!"

"And a few others." Matt finally broke silence.

"You know what I mean," Mike said.

"Sure. Just don't want you to forget we're all in this together."

"Duh."

Matt changed the subject. "That point we picked as a shoving off place is a couple hundred yards ahead. George and Roddy, you can head south and Mike and I will try to put up with each other going north."

Mike laughed. "Like it's a problem," he scoffed.

Matt turned and smiled at him. "See what I mean?"

Mike made a rude gesture and then clapped Matt on the back. In a few moments they arrived at the debarkation point.

"Split time," Mike said.

"Yup. You two guys try to stay line of sight, okay?" Matt said.

"Why?" Roddy asked.

"Untried equipment. Question of range, other stuff."

"Yeah."

"At least to home base. They can relay if there's trouble."

"Good enough."

"Okay, bucko's," Matt said, and held out his hand. They each shook. "Good luck. Keep records."

"Right, Matt. Mike's pretty lucky," George said. "Want to wager on the first find?"

"Not for me. Not a betting man," he said.

"I'll bet," George laughed.

The other three gave him a grimace.

They turned and filed away. George and Roddy had easy going for quite a while. They ploughed through tall grass, then hit thinner soil and soon came to rocky ground. They looked closely for bugs and small life, but saw nothing. The other half of the party stayed in sight for a while, but dips and turns and their footing required all of their attention. Soon they arrived at the south side foothills.

Thick undergrowth hampered their way. Tall trees and older growth stood stately and looked ordinary, but a lot of the smaller stuff didn't look quite right. Bulbous on the bottom and having straggly leaf-like needles, the two stopped and scratched their heads, got out their bags and collected samples.

"Never saw anything like this, not ever," Roddy said. "Think we ought to call it in?"

"No," said George, "It'll keep. Samples and records for now. Looks like mutated trees. Everything we feared would happen. Definitely under twelve years old. Damn!"

"Glad we have plastic bags."

They picked their way through the stand of pines. Some of it seemed all right, but they knew if mutations were occurring here they would be everywhere.

"This could change things." Roddy got a worried look. George could read his thoughts. Go back into the biosphere? Live there again for how long? Would the mutations increase or would Mother Nature, horribly brutalized by Man, be able to heal?

"Wonder how Matt and Mike are making out."

Chapter 8
Second Discovery

Matt and Mike made better time to the foothills on the north. Outcroppings were few and the land remained relatively flat. Shortly after they left the other two, they topped a small rise and came upon what appeared to be the remnant of an overgrown dirt road. It led somewhere. The road took them out of the line of sight to home base, but they took care to visualize the scene behind them, and they had a compass. They knew that if the way became confusing, they would find a way to mark their route.

"Looks like we may get the first big break, Matt," Mike said.

"Doesn't surprise me. There were several roads up top at the time of the construction phase. What surprises me is that we haven't seen anything, no structures, no metal lying around, no debris, nothing."

"Maybe we'll find out."

The road turned out to be under a quarter mile. They rounded a corner and it petered out, ended.

"What the hell?" Mike whispered.

Matt stood looking at the side of the hill, his hand on his chin. He got out his Geiger counter and checked it. Background within limits. He hung it back on his belt and then went right to the side of a pile of loose rock ahead and started throwing hefty-sized pieces to the side.

"Give me a hand, Mike."

"Okay. What you got?"

"Looks like an avalanche, but it didn't come from far enough up the hill. I think somebody dynamited the rock above something, maybe a cave, and closed themselves in."

They dug at the pile. Matt kept looking up and gauging the angle of the hillside. Then he'd pull off some more red rock and toss it aside. Mike followed suit. After about fifteen minutes, Matt called out, "Mike, something metal."

Mike scrambled closer and pulled shards of rock from around the area close to Matt. Between the two, they uncovered the lid of a fifty-five gallon drum. It had a twist lock, a little rusted, but it still turned easily. Matt released it and the cover fell with a resounding clang. Matt peered at the cover and then into darkness.

"Look at that. It's designed to open from the inside, too. There's another one attached to it and maybe a couple more. Those are open ended. Can't see well. Give me the flashlight."

Mike handed the flashlight over and Matt shined it into the blackness.

"It's a regular tunnel, Mike. Goes somewhere. Let's go!"

Mike looked over the pile of rubble and hesitated, but Matt said, "It's made this way. It's a way in, to somewhere." He sounded excited.

"Should I call it in?"

"Not yet."

"Maybe I'd better stay outside and you take a look."

Matt considered. "Yeah. Good idea." Matt crawled into the first drum. His legs quickly disappeared. He called out between grunts every few feet. Then Mike heard a muffled bang.

"Well, what do you know!" and then Matt said, "Poo! Bad stench! I'm coming out."

He crawled out legs first. "Metal door at the other end, too. Some people died in there. But the big news is, it's a big cave and it's filled with heavy construction equipment. It's a find!"

"Fantastic!" Mike said.

"*Now* let's call it in!"

In a huge forest of pine trees about an hour into their hike, George and Roddy heard Mike's message to base.

Chapter 9
Evolving a Plan

From the elevated cave entrance Arthur watched the men descend toward their break point and he smiled. He understood the kind of charisma that affects others and puts one individual out in front. The hikers followed the new path downward for a couple of hundred yards and then veered north to follow a ridge that started there.

They gradually became smaller. Arthur finally took up the binoculars and surveyed the valley again. A thin hiss came from the communicator. It tempted his pique. He wondered if Roddy and George would be the first to break the silence.

An hour passed. Arthur began to think of his other duties. A couple of men arrived armed with handsaws and a few pieces of lumber from the storage bin below. Meant for repairs to existing structures, it clearly had new purpose.

"Hi. Arthur," Al Parks called. "What's doing?"

"The first party is out. Hanging around waiting to hear something."

"We'll be around for a few hours. Want us to spell you?"

"I have been thinking about going below to get some work done."

Just then, Mike's tinny voice came through the radio.

"Arthur, we've found something. It's big!"

Arthur jumped for the transmitter button. "What'd you find?" The two construction men stopped and listened.

"We found a road that ended at an avalanche. It looked man-made, so Matt got to digging and found a tunnel made of fifty-five gallon drums. He went in and discovered a cave filled with construction equipment."

"Really? That's fantastic."

"That's what I said."

"Can we get to the stuff?"

"Have to move a lot of loose rock. Lot of big stuff."

"I'll send five strong men out to work on it. Gil," Arthur spoke to Al's companion, "would you run down and scare up Hal Hastings and four other strong guys and have them come up as soon as they can break from their chores?"

"Sure, Arthur." Gil Castonguay turned and disappeared.

The Chief Scientist returned to the mike. "Good. That stuff runs on diesel. If there's fuel there, too, it should be fine. Great going guys! Roddy, George. Did you hear?"

Roddy's voice came back immediately. "Good thing we didn't bet, huh?"

Mike's voice, "Sore loser!"

"Put 'em up, Mike!" George returned.

"Get closer and say that!" Mike called.

Arthur laughed. "Gentlemen, you have too much energy! George and Roddy, continue what you are doing. We still need the area mapped and you have two days. Matt, you and Mike wait on the "rescue" crew and when they get there, you take off and complete your mission, okay?"

Matt keyed in his radio. "Right, Arthur. There'll be a lot of work getting the opening freed up. It'll take several days, I think. We ought to be back before they break through."

"Good enough."

One of the men behind Arthur said, "If they could get in through a tunnel and could get one of the big payloaders going, couldn't they push everything out of the way?"

"Good question, Al," Arthur said. "Matt, did you hear that?"

"What?"

"Al Parks asked if you could get inside and start one of the big machines and push the rockslide out of the way."

"Good question, Arthur," Matt replied, "but there's hundreds of tons of stuff here and I wouldn't want to damage anything we might need later on."

"How about dynamite?" Al asked.

Arthur passed it on.

"Limited value, I think. Likely bring down more of the rock above. If we have a bonanza here, we shouldn't take a chance."

Arthur passed the mike to Al.

"Hi Matt, Al here. I just realized we have the rest of our lives to get it all done. I withdraw my suggestion. Slow and easy."

"Okay, Al. You coming out with the crew?"

"No, Gil and I are making a door for the cave entrance. Hal Hastings and Mark Cohen will certainly want to come. A couple more guys don't have much to do right now can, too. Gil's chasing after them. We'll have a crew for you shortly."

"Thanks, Al. Let me talk to Arthur again," Matt said. Al handed the mike back to Arthur.

"Go ahead, Matt."

"I don't think the air in the cave is healthy, Arthur. Might want to send the Doc out to test it."

"He's busy delivering a baby right now. I'll talk to him later. We have time."

"Yeah, true. Okay, look, this place is going nowhere and it's easy to find. Just have the men come down to our debarkation point and turn left. The road is over a rise and you can't see it from there, but it's easy enough to find and it leads right to the cave. I think Mike and I will head out *now*."

"Okay."

"Let's go, Mike."

"Matt," Roddy came in. "We're taking samples and we've found some mutated trees over on this side. Keep an eye out, okay?"

"Yeah?"

"Yeah. Pine-like and leaf-like at the same time. Weird! Radiation slightly higher than at base, but in limits."

Arthur and Al listened in, but said nothing.

"Roddy, we're not close to trees yet. The grasses look fine and normal, but we haven't analyzed them. We'll keep an eye out. We're up fairly high right now."

"How high?"

"Maybe five hundred feet."

"Okay."

Silence for a few seconds. Mutations should be expected. Any area bathed in radiation for several years would...should...cause significant changes in hardy grasses and in the trees. But they had not seen evidence of it when they came up and they'd hoped that the surface, at least deep in the northern mountains was pure and unaffected.

Fifteen minutes later Gil led a group of five sturdy men into the upper cave. With him were Hal Hastings, Mark Cohen, Hans Liszt, Don Smythe and Jerry Ells. Arthur repeated briefly what Gil had already told them. Three carried shovels and all five had heavy leather working gloves.

All five were pale, robust, and muscular, in good physical shape. The northern sun would take a while, but they'd tan in time. Most of them worked with animals or the cave's plants. They had come to the surface the day before with everyone else, but had gone back to their chores, waiting for the call.

Arthur gave them directions and they set off, shovels on shoulders, striding purposefully. Hal, the man in front, started to sing. He had a strong baritone voice. The others took up the tune and sang along, their voices fading with distance.

"Hi Ho, Hi Ho, it's off to work we go..."

The remaining men laughed gleefully, euphorically.

Al Parks said, "You can't keep a good Welshman down. Arthur, we don't have enough song in New Beginnings. There's power in music. I think we should make it a priority for our future."

Arthur said, "You're right, Al. I'll put it on the list."

"We'd better get to work."

"Doorway," Gil said, looking at Al.

"Now," Al countered. They marched off in an unintended step that reminded Arthur of Tweedle-Dee and Tweedle-Dum.

Arthur realized he'd been smiling a lot lately.

Chapter 10
George Disappears

George and Roddy tried for a while to stay pretty much at the same level on the side hills, but couldn't. The land undulated naturally. More and more they found themselves in some hollow and out of sight of either the mountain cave or their co-explorers across the valley. And as they moved they got farther from each.

George spoke into his unit when they were at the bottom of a waterless ravine. "Base, can you hear us? Testing...testing."

"You're about four by right now. Can't see you. You all right?"

"Fine. Trying to find out the range of these units and how much oomph they've got. We're in a hollow and there's a lot of hill obstruction. My best guess is that we are two miles from the main camp and maybe about the same distance from Matt and Mike. Mike can you hear me?"

"I read you."

"Good. Stay in touch."

"Will do."

Grunting with exertion, the two climbed over a huge fallen pine and made their way further down the gully, looking for a place to exit. The sides of the gully were fifteen feet over their heads. Finally, around a bend they saw a tree that had toppled into the dry streambed and they were able to climb up to the other side.

"Bet this place is dangerous during the spring," George said to Roddy.

"No argument."

They plunged into thick undergrowth. Mutations in the trees appeared more frequently now and Roddy drew an imaginary line across the passes that he could see. Although they saw a lot of underbrush, it was treelike and not grass-like. Something stirred in his mind and he grasped for it. Something odd about the way the hills came together. He thought it might be significant. What was it?

"Hey, Roddy, look at this!"

"What you got?"

"A hole. Cold breeze blowing out. Can't tell where it goes."

"Careful."

"I will be."

No sooner than he said that then the edge crumbled away and with a frightened yell, George disappeared.

"George!" Roddy panicked. "George, where are you? You okay? George...?"

No answer. After the first yell, George was simply gone. Roddy grabbed whatever he could and held on because the ground had started to crumble around him, too. He got hold of one of the small aspen saplings that grew abundantly nearby. He remembered they were pretty sturdy, but he shouldn't totally rely on that. He backpedaled until he felt rock under him. By this time the hole had enlarged to about seven feet across. Whatever went in didn't shine back at him. The hole was *deep*.

Roddy stood, not knowing what to do for a second. Little impulses went through his brain in all directions. *Calm*, he thought, *calm*. Roddy got control and called George again. No answer.

"Base, Roddy here. Ground opened up and swallowed George. Called to him. Getting no answer. Worried."

"Base. Arthur here. You got any rope with you?"

"No. We didn't think a short trip around the valley would require it."

"Hang on. I'll get a few opinions."

"Okay." Roddy thought furiously. He looked around him. Lot of downed stuff, some of it recent enough to still have strength.

"Base, going to dump some pine remnants over the hole and get over it to see what I can."

"Roger, Roddy. Be careful."

"I didn't need that." Roddy moved into the woods, found a fairly recent fall. He went to work. Matt had insisted that they carry a small pruning saw with them. Roddy had objected to the extra weight.

"I won't object to anything like that again," he breathed. He took the saw from its sheath and quickly began to denude the main trunk, leaving a few four-inch nubs for grasping surfaces. Ending up with a fifteen-foot log, six inches in diameter, he muscled it over to the hole and carefully dropped it across. A little debris fell into the hole but it didn't enlarge any more. Moss and tree roots now rimmed the hole. Searching again, he found another dead tree twenty feet into the woods and did the same. He sweated with the labor, but some of the sweat was fear.

"Roddy."

"Busy," he keyed briefly.

"Roddy, where are you, exactly?"

He didn't want to answer, but paused to look up and give a landmark.

"Okay, we have the general direction."

"Going back to work."

"Roger."

Returning to the hole every two minutes or so, he called to George. Still no answer.

Finally he searched out two thinner logs and laid them crosswise. Twenty minutes. He was dripping and beyond worry.

"George!" No answer.

With two strong "planks" across the hole and the thinner ones to make his construction stable, Roddy told Base he would crawl across and peer into the hole.

"I'm sending some men your way," Arthur told him.

"Negative, Arthur, hold until I find out what we're dealing with."

"This can't wait. They're on their way."

"Whatever. Going across," he said. "I'll need both hands."

"Okay."

Roddy tested the impromptu bridge gingerly and decided it would easily hold his weight. With more confidence he crawled over the hole and peered in. Blackness and a sound of running water, far below. Roddy closed his eyes to get them used to the darkness, and after awhile he opened them. Now he could see dimly into the darkness. The sun slowly approached zenith. *Another hour*, Roddy thought, and then addended his thought, *could be too late.*

"George," he called, "George, can you hear me?"

From below he could hear water sound. He also thought he heard moaning.

"George...George, can you hear me?" Now he shouted.

Another moan, stronger this time. Roddy waited. George was certainly still alive. Roddy looked around from his perch. Any vines? He hadn't been looking for vines. He focused on vines. Some grew not far from the place where he lay. He got out his radio and called Base again.

"He's alive, but I can't get his attention. I'm going for some vines. Maybe I can rig something."

"Al and Gil are on their way, straight to you," Arthur said. "They've got a couple hundred feet of rope. Give me your best locator. They should be there in half an hour if we can pinpoint you. They've got a radio."

Roddy looked up and around, trying to visualize what a rescue party might see. "That rock nub just south of me I told you about, you should be able to see it all the way. It's unusual enough. We came down a steep hill to the gully we just passed. There's a small stand of forested pines there, greener than the surrounding ones, for some reason."

"Good. I can see what you are talking about. Where are you relative to that?"

"Just about in the middle, best I can guess."

"Okay, we've got you. Do what you can."

"Will do." Roddy put his radio back in his belt and opened his eyes again.

"George, answer me!"

Thinly, from well below, another groan, and then, "Roddy...I...can see...you."

"You okay?"

"Broke...something. Bleeding. Don't feel...uhh...good."

"Where are you?"

"You're...a long way...up. On my back. Ledge...I think. Water...uhhh...long...way..." he groaned again. "Back hurts. Can feel...legs...good sign."

"Yeah, George. Help is on the way. Can you hang on?"

"Think so. Cold...down here...see my breath."

"Yeah, well, keep talking to me, buddy." Too far, no point in trying for vines.

"Yeah."

"Can you tell me what's down there?"

"Can't turn...much. Maybe fifty feet across...to the other side...where I am. Don't dare try...to move. Loose stuff...pine needles, moss...under me...angle...nothing...to grab..."

"How bad you bleeding?"

"Not too much...but steady...starting to feel...lightheaded."

Roddy worried. He called base again. "It's bad."

Al Parks broke in. "We're halfway, Roddy, Gil and me. Fast as we can. We're pushing."

"Make a guess. How long?"

"Don't know, fifteen minutes, maybe?"

"Just hurry. George is bleeding."

"We know. We're hurrying."

Roddy keyed off the radio. "Hey, George, Al is on the way with Gil. We'll get you out. Hang on."

Georges voice came back, weaker. "No problem, I'll...be here."

Roddy thought quickly. "George, do you remember that time I got stuck in that little side cave down below?"

Slower. "Yeah."

"You saved my hide that day. Going to return the favor, okay?"

"Sure...Roddy."

Keep him talking, Roddy thought, *don't let up; make him stay with us.*

"And the time you and Matt and I went into the lower caves, remember that?"

No answer.

"George?" Silence.

"Hey George," he said, suddenly panicked again, "Talk to me."

Weakly, but still there, George responded. "Hey friend...need a little...rest. Still here. Don't...worry."

Roddy keyed his communicator radio again and whispered into it, "Guys, hurry man, he's getting weaker."

"We're running, Roddy. Ten minutes, maybe less. Getting thicker now. Tough going."

Roddy was scared, scared for his friend. He felt helpless.

Time stretched. George stopped talking and Roddy couldn't raise him. He stayed where he was, but changed position so he could see over the little ridge that separated him from line of sight to the base cave. In a few minutes he heard crashing sounds and finally he saw a little movement amongst the scrub brush in the area.

"Hey, you guys," he yelled, "over here." He waved and continued to shout. The crashing changed direction and headed right for him. Al and Gil came puffing out of the scrub.

"Roddy, how is he?"

"Haven't been able to raise him for ten minutes. I'm really worried."

Al made a quick appraisal of what they had going for them and decided that Roddy's trees would work as a hoist anchor. He quickly took the rope he carried and knotted it around both stripped logs. He made the rope fast and fashioned a slipknot at the bottom.

"Roddy, we're bushed. Want the honors?"

"Sure."

Al fed the rope over the side and let it down to seventy feet. He tied it off and handed Roddy some leather gloves. Roddy put them on. Twisting the rope around his leg, he began to let himself down. The rope slid through his gloved hands slowly. He knew if he built up too much friction he'd wear them out, followed by his hands. Just like spelunking, no different. He quickly disappeared from sight.

Roddy found George nearly fifty feet down. He was unconscious and breathing shallowly. He lay on the edge of a short ledge. It had a stable surface further in toward the sheer wall, but Roddy was amazed that George hadn't slipped off and fallen to his death. At the angle he lay...!

Roddy shook his head. He looked down. The sound of running water came from below, but he couldn't tell how far below. He took the flashlight out of his pocket and shined it downward. The beam fanned out and he couldn't catch the glint of water.

"Whew!" he breathed.

He got to work. Carefully raising his body slightly above the unconscious man, he started a swing to carry himself over the man and land behind him. At the right moment he let himself down onto the ledge. From there he grasped George's belt and dragged him carefully away from the edge. Roddy worried about hurting George further, but he had no options.

Now on a stable surface, Roddy poked and prodded George gently, feeling for broken bones, dislocations and other wounds. He found a lot of blood under him. The major wound involved his right arm, gashed from elbow nearly to wrist, but not deep enough to allow him to bleed out. Still, he had lost a lot of blood and he needed attention immediately. Multiple other wounds from striking surfaces on his way down had left George battered but still intact. He thought, *you should be dead.*

Roddy called up to those above. "Al, he's alive, but not by much. You'll have to haul him up first and then get me. I'm on a stable ledge. He's in bad shape. I'm giving the best first aid I can from here, but base will have to have the Doc available immediately. Matter of fact, maybe he'd better grab a bag and head this way right now."

Al broke in, "Roddy, we anticipated that and he's on his way, with more help and a stretcher. Should be here anytime."

"Good, Al. Okay, got to work on him."

Roddy keyed out. Within five minutes he had George fixed up the best that he could. "Guys, I've tied him around the chest and under the shoulders. Take him up but easy does it."

"Okay, Roddy."

"Pull away."

The rope tightened and George swung like a pendulum out over the abyss, then rose slowly toward the light. Seven minutes later Al called down, "Got him. Give us a minute, Roddy."

Roddy waited. Gil had made a level place to lay George out. The two above transferred him gently and came back. The rope snaked down. He grabbed at it as it wiggled by and missed. The period of the ropes' motion slowed and it hung straight, seven feet beyond his reach.

Roddy called up. "You guys, can one of you swing the rope back and forth until I can get hold of it?"

"I'll do it," said Gil. Soon the rope started moving side-to-side, parallel to Roddy's position on the ledge.

"Gil, can you start that again perpendicular to the rope's current motion. I can't nab it."

"Okay." The rope came to rest and then began its motion again.

"That's better, a little more...more...more...ah, got it! Give me a little slack."

Gil fed out another seven feet.

"Great." Roddy tied it around his chest as he had done for George and called up.

"Ready."

The rope tightened slowly.

"Okay, guys, you've got my weight now. I'm coming off the ledge."

The two men above began to pull him up. Roddy weighed forty pounds more than George and the strain on the men above was evident. It took ten minutes for Al and Gil to pull him out.

When he got to where he could grasp the trees above, Roddy helped them. Gil grabbed one of Roddy's muscular shoulders and Al grabbed him by the belt. They hoisted and pulled him over.

Roddy smiled. "Thanks guys. Much obliged."

"You did a good job down there, Roddy."

"Thanks. How did George make the trip?"

"Not well," Al said, "Still out but he's alive and resting comfortably."

"Base," Roddy called, "What's the doctor's ETA?"

"Why don't you ask me yourself, Roddy?" the Doc's voice came over another voice radio.

"Doc...how you making out?'

"Following the lumbering carpenters trail. Should be there in a minute or two."

"Did you bring blood?"

"Yes. Got a couple of units. Have to do."

"It'll help."

Nothing to do but wait. They heard more crashing and the Doc appeared over the near ridge and descended. He went to work on George immediately. Seems he'd brought everything he needed. He took pulse, respiration, gave him an expert exam, administered both units of blood intravenously.

"Good job on the arm, Roddy," the doctor said.

"Thanks."

Half an hour later George moaned. His eyes fluttered and finally opened. "Where am I?"

"A question asked by millions," Doc said.

Roddy spoke up. "You had a fall. You're going to be okay."

George turned his head slightly. "Hey, Roddy. Yeah, I remember. I really didn't think..." His shoulders began to shake.

Roddy sat on his haunches and gently grabbed George's hand. "Over now, buddy. Got a new cave to play in when we get bored creating a new world."

He smiled down on his friend.

Chapter 11
Completing the Circle

"George, are you comfortable?" Arthur asked the injured man as he lay in the one bed infirmary.

"Doc gave me something. Don't feel much now."

"I need to ask you who you would recommend to go with Roddy and finish up the circuit?"

"That's easy enough, Arthur. How about Jules?"

"Jules? Never thought about him. Is he strong enough?"

"Call him in and see for yourself."

"I will."

Arthur went looking for the skinny chemist. He scratched his head. He knew Jules. He knew everybody. Well, he'd ask.

Jules Beggin majored in Chemistry and minored in Graphic Design, two unlikely bedfellows in a college curriculum, but Jules remained strong-headed about his choices and found a large eastern college that offered both courses. He graduated with high honors. His credentials from M.I.T. were impeccable. He'd been recruited right after graduation.

Fortunately for the selection committee, Jules had the ability to get along, and along with his stubborn streak, he had a sense of adventure. He was disaffected from his divorced parents. He convinced the selection committee that he wanted what they were offering, to get away and to make a contribution.

Arthur approached Jules in his lab. The man wore a white lab coat, mask and clear plastic glasses. He was mixing air purification crystals with a desiccant and pouring them into large glass containers. He set the container down as Arthur came in.

"You busy, Jules?"

"Hi Arthur. No, I'm just finishing this up for Amy."

"You heard about what happened to George Handy, didn't you?"

Jules came out of his chair. He looked thunderstruck. "No, what happened? I've been in the middle of this for hours. I'm alone."

"He went out with the exploring party and fell into a subterranean cavern."

"Is he...?" Jules face filled with dread.

"No, but almost. We brought him in on a stretcher an hour ago. Doc worked him up. He's got broken bones and he's barked up quite a bit, but he'll make it."

"That's a relief. I count George amongst my closer friends. I'll go and see him. Is he in the Infirmary?"

"Yes, but before you go, I want you to know that he has recommended you as his replacement. Cover the lower hills and valley to the end and then back, study the land and take copious notes on what you've found. Do you want to do it? You'd be going with Roddy."

Jules sat back down and thought about it. "Yes, I'll go. Yes, I want to go. Thanks, Arthur. Should I get ready now? I'm finished here."

"Are you up to it? I hate to ask, but I've never thought of you as a powerhouse."

"I can handle it, Arthur."

Jules liked people and got along well with Roddy and the other explorers. He didn't do much spelunking, but he had a small, wiry body and a great deal of stamina. His agility could aid Roddy's method of muscling his way through. The two would make a good team.

Arthur and Jules made their way to the Infirmary. Jules stood by George for a few minutes. The injured man had been given a heavy sedative and was sleeping. Jules shook his head several times.

"Tough break," he said.

"Yes, it was. Are you ready to go?"

"Yes, I'll see him when I get back."

"Let's find Roddy."

Brown sat in the cafeteria drinking a cup of herbal tea. He looked up when the two stopped in front of him.

"Your new partner," Arthur told Roddy.

"Hey, Jules, welcome," Roddy said. He held out his hand. Jules took it.

"Really sorry about George, but I'm looking forward to this. Gets me out of my little lab."

"Yeah, know what you mean."

"What do I need?"

Jules had to make up a new pack. George's fall had ruined his and in concert with moss and pine needles no doubt helped break his fall. They started out immediately. The mid afternoon sun shone moderately high and bright in the clear air, although relatively far to the south.

They cut across to the point where the original team had stopped, easily following the new trail carved first by Gil and Al and later the doctor and stretcher-bearers. Roddy brought Jules up to speed on George's accident, his rescue and then on the things they had seen along the way. He showed Jules some of the mutated samples of pine trees and some of the grasses they had sampled that had no visual evidence of mutation. He explained how he saw the charge given them by Arthur and warned Jules to keep a sharp eye out for pitfalls as they stood over the hole.

"The one George fell into was a doozy!" Roddy said, looking down.

"I'll say," Jules replied.

The two trekked around the lower hills and made several significant discoveries. In one in particular, a miniscule fold of the hills on the south side, they discovered a natural paddock. It spread out about fifty yards or more and ran along sheer cliffs for a quarter of a mile, abruptly ending in a cleft only a bumblebee could pass. The floor was level and heavily grassed in, well protected. The entrance wouldn't take a fence more than eight feet in length to contain cattle or horses.

"Horses," Roddy said.

"If there are any."

When they came upon the steam vent at the very end of the valley, Jules became very excited.

"Roddy, another source of power. This is great!"

"I don't know, Jules. I thought volcanic activity was far to the south. This worries me."
"We ought to call it in."
"Yeah, let's."
"Jules to Base, come in."
"Got you," Base replied. "You're a little thin, but readable. Where are you?"
"Almost at the four mile mark, I think. Near the end of the valley in a little side chute."
"What've you got?"
"Steam vent. Kills the idea of no volcanic activity in a hundred miles, that's sure."
"Okay. No new lava, right?"
"Right. Hot, though. Blistering out pretty good."
"No shortage of power sources anyway. Atomics, waterpower and steam. Excellent! What could be wrong with that?"
"Base," Roddy cut in. "It's pretty late. We're going to find a place to hole up for the night. We'll wake you in the morning. Matter of fact...hold on," he clicked off.
"Why not stay right here, Jules?" he said.
"Sure. I'd love to look this vent over in detail."
"Base, we're going to stay by the vent for the night. Our chemist just turned rock hound."
"Good for him."
Roddy continued, "You know, these radios don't have much range."
"We know. Ernie is working on it."
"That's good. Out."
"Okay, Roddy. Base out." Roddy hung his radio back on his belt.
"We'll head down the interior valley in the morning. It'll be easier going. Should be home by noon or a little after, maybe."
"Sure. Getting chilly. Nice around this vent. No fire, not in this underbrush. Sleeping bags will do. We'll be fine."
"Right, but I've got an idea. Got a little light. I'm going to look around."
"Knock yourself out."

Jules searched the underbrush and around a slight bend he discovered an aspen grove. He called to Roddy. "Give me a hand with some stuff over here."

Roddy went over. Jules had pulled out a couple dozen thin stake-like pieces from the surrounding woods. He took out the short woodsman's axe they'd added to his pack and hacked down four thin trees.

Retaining the "V" split at the top, he hefted them and said, "There's more around here we can use. This would make a great way station. Help me fashion a lean-to."

"Should have thought of that," Roddy said. He grabbed a dozen dried pieces and began dragging them back nearer the vent. Jules trailed behind with the four green pieces he'd just cut. They made several trips, piled the stripped aspen saplings to one side and quickly cleared a flat area about twenty-five feet from the vent.

"In case it spits during the night," Jules said to Roddy's raised eyebrow.

The four "V'd" saplings they carefully pushed about eight inches into the ground.

"They'll stand fine when we get 'em tied together."

The two facing the sheer hillside he put in so they stood four feet above the ground. The ones he cut for the front of the lean-to he inserted five feet high. Two heavier stakes he found amongst the brush and trees he cut to eight-foot lengths. With the form Jules decided on it ceased to be a lean-to and became more like a saltbox.

"Don't think anyone will care if we use a few feet of our rope, do you?" Jules asked Roddy.

"Doubt it."

Jules removed some braided nylon rope from his pack. He deftly cut a couple of strips three feet long and then separated them into lashing strands. While Roddy held the pieces, Jules tied them to the "V" stakes. Soon a very respectable, strong frame stood awaiting crosspieces. Forming the roof took a half hour. Jules lashed down every sixth cross member for strength. When the roof was completed, he took two spare pieces and laid them over the ends to hold the loose stakes down in case of windstorm.

The backside of the saltbox they finished with horizontal pieces lashed in a weave and they did the sides the same. By the time they were through, darkness had come and they had to use the flashlight to finish the work.

"Good job, Jules."

"Thanks."

"Won't need to seal the roof tonight," Roddy said, "but the next people who come this way should bring plastic for roof and doorway. Make it nice and cozy."

"You don't want it to blend with the woods?" Jules asked.

"You mean thatch?"

"Sure. In some ways we're bound to get pretty primitive. Might as well get some practice."

"Suppose, but not me, not this time. I'll do it when I have to."

Jules yawned. "A little early, but we don't have any light to work by. How about we turn in and get an early start?"

"Okay by me."

They opened up their bedrolls and laid them out. They sat outside the aspen construct cross-legged and watched the stars come out. They talked about the biosphere and their work some, but mostly they dreamed and talked and dreamed more.

Later, with a start, Jules looked at the luminous dial of his watch and said, "After eleven already. Going to turn in."

"I'll sit up awhile, Jules. This is the first night in over twelve years I've watched the stars wheel across the night sky. I need this!"

"Okay, buddy." Jules went under the lean-to and crawled in.

Roddy sat in the absolute stillness of a destroyed world and his eyes glistened as he contemplated the fable of the Phoenix.

Chapter 12
Digging Out

Five men, led by Hal, turned left as ordered. The barely recognizable old road stretched in front of them, two sparsely grass filled ruts in which harder packed soil had resisted growth for fifteen years or so. They spread out, two taking one nearly nonexistent track and three the other. Mike and Matt's passing had made little impression.

"Might as well start beating a path for future trips," Hal said to his companions.

Mark Cohen piped up, "Got a feeling this is the easy part."

"Probably."

"How much farther?" Hans asked.

"No more'n a quarter mile, what Matt said."

They trudged along, not singing now but feeling light and content in the fresh piney air. Beyond a rocky outcropping they saw it.

"Yup, manmade," Mark Cohen said.

Hal said, "This is going to take awhile."

"I want to take a look at the fifty-five gallon tunnel," Jerry Ells said. He'd studied Civil Engineering in college and had a secondary skill in refrigeration, the reason the Bio builders chose him for their project. He walked over to the side where the tunnel lay open and bent down to inspect it.

"Smart."

"What?" Hal asked.

"They piled a lot of big rock against the sides and top of their tunnel before bringing the rest of the hillside down on it. Hardly dented."

"C'mon guys, it'll take forever if we don't start."

They all gathered at the front of the huge rubble pile, donned their gloves and began removing rock. Some pieces weighed several hundred pounds and required several men and considerable effort to move, but with enough sweat the avalanche got smaller. They worked in two-hour shifts, took fifteen-minute breaks and an hour for lunch. A half hour before nightfall, they packed up and returned to the biosphere.

In the morning they started early and worked through the day. The pile got smaller still. It took more work to pull the stuff to the sides and make a path into the cave, but they figured the potentially useful equipment they'd find would be worth it.

When one or two griped, Hal said, "Stupid to have to move it twice."

About two p.m., Matt and Mike came through. They looked tired and didn't stay long.

"You guys are doing great," Mike said to the workers.

Hal told Arthur later that night, "One more day and we'll be clear,"

"Any of your men," Arthur said, acknowledging that Hal had taken leadership of the work crew, "know how to run heavy equipment?"

"I can, and Jerry and Hans, I think, have some experience with heavy equipment. We'll figure it out."

"Good."

"We're all beat, Arthur. Going to bed."

Hal left Arthur's cubicle with a tired wave.

Morning in a biosphere is a matter of chronology. The sun does not shine, although there is light, but alarm clocks work everywhere. The men were up and ready at six a.m.

"One more, gentlemen," Hal said.

They filed out silently. The morning air held a chill, but it didn't bother. Matter of fact, it felt good. They were all glad to be back on top. Fresh air didn't smell just good, it smelled *wonderful*! A few minutes later they were at the dwindling rockslide, picking 'em up and laying 'em straight.

By noon they had cleared the top, tossing pieces any which way to get a look into the cave. In another hour the sun would shine directly into the opening. It would help them see inside better than any flashlight.

A bad smell grabbed their nostrils, but some didn't even want to stop for lunch. Hal insisted. They took their break but were back at it in half an hour. The stench from decomposed bodies hermetically sealed for twelve years wafted out to the working area and the men tried hard not to gag. Their sandwiches didn't taste so good.

Hal called Arthur shortly after they broke through. He declined to make the trek over to the equipment depot.

"Air it out for a day or so, Hal."

"You're right, Arthur. We're all anxious."

"I know, I know."

"Okay, you've got it. Mark and Don, would you be the burial detail while Hans, Jerry and I get the rest of the debris out of the way?"

Mark gave Hal a dirty look. "Okay, but you owe me a drink."

"A drink of what?"

"Whatever. Does it matter?"

Arthur came over the radio again. "Why don't you quit for the day as soon as the entrance is clear? Let the place air out tonight and we'll all go over in the morning? Give us a whole day to figure things out."

Hal thought about Mark's offhand demand. "One condition."

"What's that?"

"Time we had a party," Hal said with a big smile. "About damn time!"

Silence. Arthur laughed. "You know," he said delightedly, "you're right. All work and no play…"

Hal changed the subject. "How's George?"

"Pulling through. Nasty fall. Some heroics by Roddy. George is lucky to be alive."

"You can say that again."

"Yes."

"Well, I want to go and see him. Then we'll party."

"Sounds like a plan."

Chapter 13
The Party

"I have an announcement to make." Arthur stood in the main cavern waiting for the last people to come in from their chores. "I asked all of you here because of a request from Hal Hastings. He insisted that I tell you all that he got his idea from Mark Cohen. Didn't want to take the blame."

A few in front laughed. They all knew Mark and wondered why Arthur was beating around the bush.

"I called you all in *after* your chores were completed, so no one could make up an excuse to miss this. We're going to have a party, a real ripsnorter. I made a few preparations with today's kitchen staff and I am pleased to show you their work. Let the party begin!"

With that, four women walked out of the kitchen area—sashayed—platters filled with all manner of hot and cold hors d'oeuvres. A shout went up. The menu consisted of a variety of vegetables and cheeses, but they were attractively made up and everyone began to crowd around.

Arthur held up his hands and projected over the crowd, "Plenty for all. Maybe a line would help."

Sue Dorchester was on kitchen duty this day and shouted, "Wait a minute. Us girls cooked up an even better one. You-all stay where you are. Spread out a little and we'll circulate like the hors d'oeuvres ladies used to do at classy shindigs. Don't worry about us. We'll get ours. Maybe we have already."

More laughter.

Somebody yelled, "We just bet you did!"

Sue pouted good naturedly, "Well, we had to get it right."

The throng spread out, overjoyed. Sue, Jane Potter, who normally assisted Mary Beth Holiday in running the power station, Babs Monigan, who cared for the original three sheep, now fourteen and Nancy Spiller, another plant life specialist moved through the crowd, trays held in front at waist level.

"Delightful," Arthur said as he reached for a cream cheese and carrot morsel.

The ladies circulated and the choices quickly depleted. They went back to the kitchen for more. Just then Amy Fox came out of the kitchen wheeling a metal table normally used for preparing vegetables. She bent over and locked the wheels on the flat stone surface, putting a narrow shim under one leg to level it. Then John Knudsen, another water purification specialist came out of the kitchen carrying a tall stainless steel coffee urn. He gently muscled it onto the table and clapped his hands.

"Attention, everybody!" he waited until the mass of milling people turned his way and then he said, "I've been waiting a long time to do this. This is *not* coffee! I repeat, this is *not* coffee! You may call it punch if you like, but whatever you call it, keep in mind that it has a lot of it. Punch, I mean."

John stopped and faced the audience.

"Do you mean...?" Mary Beth called, and waited breathlessly.

"I mean..." he let the sentence drag.

"Party! A real party, with real...oh my!" Mary Beth yelled.

Isabella Gratinelli bellowed, "Hot damn!"

Sue and Millie let loose with a simultaneous whoop and then laughed.

"Stereo," Somebody yelled.

Half the assemblage laughed. The party had begun!

Arthur was startled. Alcohol in Biosphere I? He thought about it; *water purification people. They have the means of distilling. Why not? It wasn't exactly forbidden. They had gotten used to not smoking and not drinking, but most of them had done so many years before socially.* He approached the urn and drew off a half glass of the sweet smelling brew.

Others watched him and decided; many came over and soon a line formed.

John gathered the low stone stage and yelled out over the crowd. "Everybody take it easy. We're all years away from this. Need I say more?"

Someone called out from the middle of the crowd, "Hey, I'm not driving."

Everyone who heard him laughed, a raucous sound filled with released tension.

Arthur sipped his drink and found it delightful. He opined silently that there wasn't much alcohol in the punch and thought that John and Amy had acted very responsibly with both the concoction and the warning. He moved into the crowd, raising his glass to those around. And he smiled and smiled.

Around eight p.m., Bio-time, Arthur noted that things had gotten louder. Mary Beth, Sue Dorchester, Nancy Spiller, along with Maude Nash and Isabella were round-housing a conversation on men, a subject never very far from most women's hearts. One would make a comment and then another would say something and they would laugh, or groan or just talk excitedly. A little liquor went a long way with this crowd. Isabella, especially, imbibed and became quite loud, but no one took offense. This was a long time a-coming.

Arthur moved on to another, quieter group of about fifteen. They were talking sports and Packers, Rams, and the Forty-Niners were mentioned. Some seemed morose and Al Parks sat with tears in his eyes.

"Never again," he said sadly.

Doc Simmons had joined the group minutes before and said, "No more Packers or Jets or Lions or any other team, but maybe we can build a new world. How about that! In it we can sow the seeds *we* want. We can bring as much of the past with us as *we* want. We can discard what we *don't want*, freely. I see wiping the slate clean as an opportunity."

"Can't do anything else, can we," Frank Billings said bitterly.

"No, we can't, Frank. It's all onward and upward from here."

Arthur joined with his comment. "I like to think of us as the seed of a new civilization, too. Diversity will follow, but what if we pick the right path? How great could that be?"

"Arthur's right as rain, guys," Roddy Brown said. "We have the biggest chance ever."

From near the back, Hal Hastings began to sing. His beautiful baritone captivated them and conversation slowly died. In the first silent moment during the party, Hal sang "Danny Boy." At the end of the first stanza, tenor Mark Cohen and Doc Simmons, who could also reach into the first tenor range, began the second verse. Those two were part of the sports group. Don Smythe, a bass, joined the harmony from a corner where he'd been gabbing with three women. Hans Liszt began to sing from the other side of the hall. His good second tenor smoothed out the harmony and the sweet song of death and love wafted gently through the hall.

Walking slowly, like magnets attracting in slow motion, the four arrived in a tight group facing Hal and their harmony pervaded the hall. None could see the other, because of the tears, but it didn't matter. Most of the crowd stood in mute astonishment as the voices coalesced and every one present realized they were experiencing a magical moment.

At the end, Arthur called to all. "Please, let's do it again. Everyone join. Please." Tears streamed down his cheeks and blurred his sight. He felt drained and uplifted at the same time.

Hal started again and this time everyone joined, good voice or not, and sang as sweetly and gently as Hal had when he started it. A long, teary silence followed the last strain. Arthur couldn't see, but he heard sniffling from all directions surrounding him and he knew there were very few dry eyes. He also knew there was nothing so right as this moment.

Then someone clapped and with a thunderous roar the rest of the audience joined in, paying tribute to Hal, to the harmonizers...and to a lost world. Like a hot toddy, it did more for their psychological loss than any psychologist could have done in many sessions. They'd established yet another connection. Soon after, the party broke up. Those who must stayed up and those who could went to bed. Arthur told a few people around him to pass the word to sleep as long as they wanted tomorrow.

Chapter 14
Sowing Seeds

Only those with absolutely imperative chores dragged out of bed. The rest slept in. Good party. No! *Great* party. Arthur had been awake for three hours, but out of deference to those sleeping it off nearby he stayed in his cubicle at his desk and wrote, occasionally crossing out and rewriting something above it. Several notes became a part of the greater work and the scraps found file thirteen easily enough. He organized his work and at about ten-thirty, grabbed a few who were up and asked them to wake the rest for a meeting.
"Gently, please."
They chuckled and went about Arthur's business.
Eleven o'clock. The milling crowd created a low composite sound, voices and movement. They stood again in the main hall waiting. With party history fitted into all things past, it had become a shining and beautiful memory. As he had before, Arthur stood at the lectern and held his arms up for quiet.
Isabella called out from the crowd, "I thought we could stay in bed as long as we wanted."
A few laughed. Arthur ignored her and began.
"We broke out of Biosphere I only four days ago," Arthur said to the audience, "and I am more than impressed with our progress to date. And our luck, too. Yes, I know, I don't believe in luck, but except for George's accident, all other things have been fortuitously positive. It has happened this way because everybody pitched in and did what they needed to do without complaint.
"I learned long ago that showing our young by example is the best way to bring them up and the example of hard work, willingly given, is amongst the greatest of the virtues and values

we can offer them. In other words, my friends, we should keep doing what we are doing.

"Now to the present. I have gone over everything gathered to date. I have distilled it to two pages." He waved the sheets in the air. "These pages are what I will term the outline of our beginning. It is all good. Even George's fall might be turned to some good purpose. Happily, he will recover and I think will be none the worse for wear. And what a story he can tell his grandchildren!"

Everyone laughed.

"Seriously, we will need a steady source of power. Waterpower is a prime option. From what I was told, there is a strong stream running below the hole George fell into. Hydroelectric power is therefore an option. We have a meandering stream across the valley. We can use that. Roddy and Jules discovered a hot steam vent. There are no plans to remove the mini-atomic power plant below. You may agree with me that the atomic pile is safest remaining where it is."

Half the audience grunted approval.

"I am going to suggest that our bio-home be kept active and available for the foreseeable future. You can all see why, I believe. I will suggest, however, that once our town is established we name it New Beginnings and revert to calling our subterranean home Biosphere I again, if that is all right with everyone. To be true to my original statements on running this as a democracy, let's make that our first vote. How about a show of hands."

Arthur looked out over the group and nearly every hand went up.

"Any opposed?"

No one said anything. "Hector, you didn't put up your hand. Do you have a comment?"

Hector Bertrand, Husbandman, said, "I don't care, Arthur. More important things to do."

"Hector, I absolutely agree with your right to abstain, but if we are going to form a new civilization based on the precepts of democratic action, could you please indicate a yes or a no or an abstention and your reasons for it. Not caring is an answer, but if you didn't like something and said nothing, it might sow seeds of discontent."

Arthur addressed the full audience. "A few other hands didn't go up, I noticed. I'm not picking on Hector. If we are going to do things differently in the future we need to be of one mind on this. Does everyone not agree?"

"Arthur!" Isabella Gratinelli raised her hand. Isabella commanded attention when she spoke, though she only stood five foot one inch tall. Her voice compared favorably to a foghorn. She didn't speak often, preferring the company of her goats to people, although it could no longer be said that she wouldn't enjoy a party if offered. She'd made quite a spectacle of herself the night before at the "Coming Out Party" as it was already referred to by most. Now she had something to say and her previous conduct didn't faze her.

"Arthur, politics don't interest me. I've always been happy with political choices in the past, or I got used to them. Now you're telling me I *have* to be involved, whether I want to or not?" People around her made a space for her. Arthur could see into the crowd now and Isabella had hands placed defiantly on her hips.

"Isabella, I understand what you are saying." Arthur shifted and looked out, encompassing everybody in the room. "Too many people gave up their right to make themselves heard twelve and twenty and fifty years ago simply by going along. Nearly seven billion people are dead because of it."

"Arthur..." Isabella started.

"No! Listen first!"

Isabella nodded and subsided.

Arthur began again. "I desperately want to introduce pure democracy into the new world we will try to create. In that hitherto never before seen society, everybody will know the issues and everybody will be responsible for having an opinion based upon reason and interest. Everyone may not agree with any majority decision, but they will accept the will of the majority and get behind it. To do that will let our whole society grow in the best directions, those mandated by intelligent reasoning, but of the majority.

"Disagreements will be the order of every day, but divisiveness cannot be allowed. One hundred and forty one people represent a tiny number when you consider the monumental job ahead of us. That includes baby Josh, who just became a member of our colony yesterday.

"As for you, Isabella and Hector and you others who didn't desire to be involved for whatever your reasons, would you go along with the majority if we bring that to a vote? Hate to put you on the spot, but now's the time."

Isabella jumped in. "Hang on, Arthur. I want a powwow with those who didn't vote and I invite anyone who has any hesitation on this subject to join the discussion. Is that okay with you?"

"Absolutely, Isabella. Let's take a break for...how long, Isabella?"

"We ought to be able to hash this out in a half hour or so is my guess."

Arthur looked at his watch. "All right, then. I will voluntarily suspend the meeting for one half hour to get this important issue discussed. We'll reconvene at eleven-forty."

He looked around for something like a gavel and finding nothing that would serve, shrugged and stepped down from his makeshift podium. He made his way to his cubicle. Matt Duncan followed him in.

"Arthur, this worries me. Isabella isn't exactly anti-social, but she has strange ideas."

"Matt, I couldn't have asked for a better start to the new order. This is what the doctor ordered and it's coming much sooner than I could have hoped. I absolutely encourage it."

"Really? You're not worried that somebody will decide that they would make a better leader than you?"

"Not in the least. I'm no great shakes. I don't want power. I want our colony to start out right, and that means involving everybody. Don't you realize that everybody who didn't vote on the innocuous subject of bringing our town name out of the mountain and giving it to the new town we are about to build is now totally involved. I couldn't have done this better if I'd tried."

Matt looked at Arthur and he smiled. "You're sure you didn't plan this?"

"No, Matt. I'm not that clever, not in that way. Manipulating isn't my style."

"Yeah, I guess I see where it's leading."

"All we have to do is wait."

"And you're really not worried?"

"Not in the least, as I said. They are all bright people. They will talk themselves right into my plan, just wait and see. And they'll do it because they want to."

Matt shook his head. "Arthur, you are a lot more political than you think you are."

"Heavens, I hope not." He laughed nervously.

At the end of the half hour Matt and Arthur returned to the short stone stage and surveyed the assembly. The group of fifteen hadn't returned as yet. Arthur was in no hurry. A chair had been placed near the podium and Arthur sat, leg over knee and waited. He tried to look bored, but no one believed it.

Another five minutes went by and the fifteen filed back into the main hall. Arthur stood and waited.

Isabella spoke. "Arthur and everybody, the group has asked me to be spokesperson, mostly because of my big mouth."

A lot of people chuckled.

"Anyway, we talked about this democracy thing of yours and the upshot is, we don't want to be left out of anything, so I guess you've got your wish. If the majority wants, we will participate fully."

Arthur took the podium and said to all, "All right then. There is a motion on the table to transfer New Beginnings in the mountain to our new town. All in favor raise your hands."

Everyone's hand went up.

"Opposed?"

No one stirred.

"Motion carried. Thank you all."

A shout went up that reverberated on the chamber walls. No one saw Arthur's eyes cloud up.

Chapter 15
Future Plan

It could be said that the members of New Beginnings—save children who would act like children no matter what—were all serious minded. After all, everyone had come from well-known and highly touted colleges. They had been hand picked by specialty. Intelligence and drive were needed, but sociability had concerned the founders a lot more than it would seem on the surface.

To know the one hundred, one would have thought them a diverse group. Not so. Even that had been planned closely, given the need. Science and psychology chose them. Brilliant minds now long dead decided who would fit in a group of a hundred people who could remain underground for two years without mental damage. They'd left nothing to chance.

Inadvertently, the old choices had produced as fine a group of people as might give the human race its second chance. Perhaps the psychologists would have smiled.

"Ladies and gentlemen, let's move on," Arthur said. He tapped the gavel he'd fashioned while waiting for Isabella's group to conclude deliberations, "We're here to consider our future plan. I have compiled some ideas and taken suggestions from a few who have showed up at my cubicle. There will be many more, I am certain. Feel free to break in any time if something hits you."

"First things first. The equipment area could be a bonanza. We should start there. We'll go in tomorrow morning, after the cave has aired out overnight. Some of our men have at least a limited knowledge of heavy equipment. If we find a supply of usable fuel, we will plan out a town. Jerry Ells trained to be a civil engineer in his past life. I know he's still interested. We have gone to him for advice on subjects other than refrigeration. I propose to name Jerry "Project Manager" for the building of our town."

"Should we vote on that?" Sue Dorchester called from the assembly.

"Certainly. I make a motion to name Jerry Ells Project Manager for the construction of New Beginnings."

"I'll second that," Gil Castonguay yelled out.

"Hang on, everyone," Arthur said. "We're going to need someone to take notes on these meetings, I can see. Volunteers?"

Regina North spoke up, "I majored in English at Tufts and I've done some writing. I'll volunteer to be Secretary."

"Thanks, Gina."

"How about a vote?" Mark Cohen laughed.

"Funny!" Gina retorted, "Are you volunteering? Can you even write?"

Everyone snickered. Most of them knew of Mark's sweet spot for Gina.

"Just trying to be democratic," Mark said innocently.

"Gina, would you please come up here and we'll end this subterfuge." Arthur smiled.

The woman walked through the crowd. A thirty-three year old now, recruited rather late in the selection process for the biosphere project and the only college junior the company had recruited; she was of average height and weight. She had long brown hair with a tinge of auburn in it. Her features were soft and the years underground had done little to undermine her natural beauty. Her gray-blue eyes were kind. Everyone liked her. Although she was a very bright woman, her current work involved tending the vegetable gardens. She enjoyed turning the earth and getting her hands dirty.

Arthur brought a few sheets of blank paper with the material he had taken from his cubicle. He handed them to her. She stood to the left of Arthur, waiting for his first request.

"I think the founders left some spiral notebook pads in the stock room. We haven't had much use for them, but I think we will now. Besides the daily log we kept on the computers before they failed, I can't think why I didn't consider the need to take written notes on everything we were about before this. I suppose it's because we were so deeply in the groove by then and nothing was spectacular enough to warrant writing it down. Now we'll have a big need to keep track of decisions and actions, disagreements we can't resolve and other things we might need to refer to as we grow our new community."

"I'll be your Official Recording Secretary then," Gina said.

"Somebody get her a chair. And how about a table?" Arthur said.

A chair appeared from the one side of the hall, a table from the other.

"Everybody set?"

Murmur from the crowd.

"Gina, if you could jot down what we've done to date..." She nodded.

"Now, next order of business, exploration. I've spoken to Matt, Mike, Roddy and Jules. After Georges fall and rescue, as most of you know, Roddy got a new partner, Jules Beggin. More on that later.

"Anyway, the four of them—with George's bedside input—spent several hours compiling the information they had gathered and will present it in a separate forum for us to hear.

"Next, our town. Jerry Ells got into the explorers discussions as a listener. The map that Matt and Mike drew is pretty explicit and Jerry has it now. He wants to look the town site over personally and survey it out with a couple of people as best he can. For our consideration, I turn the meeting over to Jerry."

Ells jumped up onto the stone platform. "Hi gang. Everyone hear me okay?"

A murmur from the crowd told him he had reached the back of the hall easily enough.

"Okay. From what I can see, we have about three square miles of area that can be easily turned into a town. That's plenty big enough for this group, but it's pretty small for a city. We'll start here and deal with cities later on, not to worry. To date we haven't found animals of any kind. That is not to say they don't exist. Worse case, they have mutated and who knows what we might have to face then.

"So, on the theory that it's better to be safe than sorry, I propose widely separated housing units to give us space to grow food and places in which to expand as we grow. Beyond that we will have a central location, almost equidistant from all outlying dwellings in which we can all congregate in the outside chance something is still out there that doesn't like us and can do anything about it."

Some people in the hall fidgeted and looked around.

"The central location will essentially be a fort. Initially that is what I envision. If it turns out we actually have something to fear, we can consider enclosing the entire town, but that amount of labor is not indicated at this time. Any questions?"

Mary Beth spoke up, "We have no guns. Do you think weapons of some type will be necessary?"

"I don't know, Mary Beth. My plan doesn't include maximum security. Just haven't seen the need for it."

"But you want to be prepared, right?"

"Of course."

"I took up archery as a young girl. I can fashion a bow and make arrows. I'll offer that in case it's needed."

"Okay, Gina can make a note of it. Any questions pertaining to the building of a town?"

Silence.

"Arthur, it's all yours."

"Thanks, Jerry. Well, folks, the list goes on, but it occurs to me that we've all had a busy day and I don't see any point in dragging this out. I think the three major areas we've presented today is enough, don't you? Let's stop here for now. Jerry can pick a couple of you to help him survey the new town. Hal and his group and anybody who doesn't have to be here for chores, and who is *interested* in heavy equipment can go to the depot this afternoon and look things over. I think it would be a good idea for one person to be in charge up there, though. Any takers?"

Hal raised his hand. "Might as well."

"No objection?"

All looked attentive and no one spoke.

"Guess that's the answer. We'll have a meeting tomorrow night to record progress. Meeting adjourned."

Chapter 16
Gina

"Arthur bent down to Gina and said casually, "Come see me after you put your notes together, okay?"

"Sure, Arthur. They're almost done now."

"Good. I have a couple of ideas on compiling and storage."

"I wondered about that."

Arthur left to straighten his cubicle so Gina and he could work. As Chief Scientist he rated two chairs in his private space. The extra chair had become a repository for a miscellaneous collection of papers and other things that now reached almost two feet high. He thought, *better cull the stuff I really don't need and get rid of it. So hard, though.* He laughed at himself. *A packrat, that's me.*

Gina came in. Arthur motioned her into the chair. She looked around and smiled. She'd never had a need to be in his cubicle before.

"You live close, don't you, Arthur?"

"Yes," he said, "and it embarrasses me for the first time. Just a moment ago I decided that I'd better recompile everything I have and get rid of a lot of junk."

"I didn't mean..."

"No, it's all right. Things are changing and I'll have to change with them or be left behind."

"You're a smart man, Arthur."

He ignored the praise.

"Ever since the computers crashed and we ran out of spare parts, I've been collecting this way. I should have guessed that we'd have to take a few steps back, but I always held out hope that Ernie or a couple of the others would work some magic and get them running again. Ernie gave me a sour look when I suggested that seven years ago. He was right."

"We were all affected by that. Pause and regroup, what else to do?"

"You are right. Getting to it, we still have a supply of paper. I thought we were overstocked at first, but the company had more vision than I did. Anyway, we can use what we have while we're getting started above. Soon enough we'll have to start manufacturing paper. One of probably dozens of new industries we'll start or restart just to keep a semblance of our current level of civilization."

"I see where you're going. On the other subject, what do you want me to do with my notes?"

Arthur reached over to the back of his little desk and handed her a spiral, blue-lined notebook. Gina remembered the old college edition with the beige cardboard covers.

"Please transfer all of your notes into this. We have a dozen more so we won't run out soon. I'd like to ask you to draw up an outline for use with future meetings and use it each time. Try to consider the most logical order of things and I will attempt to run the meetings along those lines. It will be extremely important that we have a running record of everything we are doing."

"I understand."

Arthur hesitated and then said, "Gina, would you be willing to be our Town Crier?"

"Just like old times?" She smiled.

"Yes, just like medieval times. Ernie is working up some more radios and you would perform like an information minister. You'd be responsible for keeping everyone up to date on all the major projects. Eventually I think we could manage to set up a radio station that will serve. What do you think?"

"I like the idea. I like it a lot, but what about my work in the gardens?"

"For the time being you'll do double duty. There won't be much note taking for now. Later, when most operations are above, we will probably retire the gardens down here. If not, we'll assign someone to maintain the Bio gardens at a minimum level."

"Why not move everything up wholesale?"

"I think the world will remain too dangerous for that for many years to come. We need a place to run to if something goes badly wrong."

"What?"

"I don't know, radiation storm...I don't know, but I think it's wise. Maybe I'm being foolish."

"No, probably not, Arthur. Cautious is best. I'll take the notebook to my quarters and draw up an outline for meetings."

"Thanks, Gina. Let me know what you come up with. Tomorrow is fine."

"Sure. Goodnight, Arthur."

"Goodnight." Arthur looked at the retreating back of the pretty little lady and wished for a tiny moment that he were thirty years younger. He sat at his desk chair and stared at the now empty second chair. Then he got up and piled everything he'd put on the floor back on the chair. *Tomorrow morning*, he thought, *I'll start tomorrow morning*. How tired he felt.

Chapter 17
Slowing Down

Hal Hastings crew sort of naturally stayed together. They sang or hummed some of the time, looked around and breathed deeply of the surface air.

"Them as plays together, stays together," Hal said twenty times if ever once.

He got a groan from a couple of the men barely disposed to answer the old chestnut. They pointedly ignored him after that. Evidently he got a kick out of it. The workers were too happy with being outside and performing, "honest work" as Arthur termed it, to ask him to cease and desist. They did work well together. None could wait until morning of the day after they'd opened the cave to see what was there. Since discovery had been saved for this bright and sunny day, all five relished getting inside and looking around.

"Jerry, Don and Mark, would you mind getting started inside clearing out the old bones? I'll work with Hans getting the rest of the small stuff out of the way."

The workers acknowledged their chores and filed into the cavernous opening. An overnight airing had worked wonders with the stench.

Jerry said after a couple of deep breaths, "I see bones and clothes, but decomposition is complete. The lingering odor is easy now."

Don said, "Not bad at all. Hand me one of those bags, Mark."

Cohen handed him a black bag from several he carried. Don took the square dung shovel they had brought with them from his shoulder and went to the nearest pile of bones. There were several.

Jerry said, "Look, the bones are a two man job. I'll scout the inside and I'll make a list of what I find."

"Go ahead," Mark said. "Better mark where the bones are, in case we can identify them somehow. And describe the clothing."

"Actually, that's a good idea." He took his pencil and sketched out the general area. "Okay, done."

With a backhand wave, Ells walked deeper into the cave. Each had a small notebook and a pencil. Jerry flipped to a blank page and headed into the gloom. When twilight deepened to where he couldn't be certain of his footing, he stopped. He figured the cave would be flat, but walking blind was stupid. He unhooked his flashlight and turned it on. The concentrated beam shone dimly on some equipment, but he didn't stop to examine it. He decided to walk to the very back of the cave and work his way back toward the light.

At two hundred feet, the cave ceiling began to slope toward him and he realized it would end soon. There, his flashlight shined ahead on a solid wall. He'd counted a hundred and twenty paces, nearly three hundred feet in. Still quite high, it extended across the cave, whose sides had by now also pulled in toward his position. He flashed his light around. To his right he saw another much smaller and still blacker opening. Before exploring, he turned out his light and faced front.

The opening spread out in the distance, a brilliant crouching hemi-circle of light. It reminded him of his one trip to Hawaii during summer break. He'd bummed Oahu, pretty safe at the time. Just before Kee Beach a large cave face beckoned. It formed a dark, wide turndown smile, kind of like the famous tragedy mask. He walked into that cave's mouth to savor its mystery. He went straight to the back wall without turning or looking, as he had done here.

Jerry thought he was past all the horror, but felt his throat constrict at the memory. Hawaii, beautiful island paradise, the ads said. He'd managed to see Honolulu and a few outlying areas. Now Oahu and Hawaii were only memory and beyond retrieval, and so with the other beautiful places of Earth. Anger welled, but he put it down.

Glancing briefly one way and another inbound, he noted many vehicles parked on both sides of the cave. Whoever ran the show liked things neat. He'd catalogue them on the way out. No evidence of a fuel dump, cans, barrels or otherwise so far. Jerry put down disappointment. The search had only begun.

What he saw on his quick trip in were borers, graders, traxcavators, payloaders, and a miners belted oar carrier. There were also three heavy-duty hi-boy trucks and they looked like seven-yarders. He tried to picture those heavy pieces carried over the mountains by helicopter during the construction phase. Skycranes, without doubt. Even so, they had to come in pieces and that made for a lot of trips. Jerry guessed the government was a lot more involved than they'd ever let on.

He saw two pretty good-sized diesel-powered generators. They weren't connected to anything. Must be standby units. Lots of stuff here. Hal has the radio. *I'll jot until I get back out,* he thought. *Now for that opening on the right.*

He walked over and shined his light around. Manmade, as he thought. The smell that had dissipated near the front of the cave became strong again as he walked in. He'd found the construction crew's quarters. Jerry wanted to gag, but swallowed the urge. He moved back twenty-five feet and grabbed several breaths. Holding it, he went for a comprehensive look-see.

A long, narrow hall greeted him. About ten feet wide and, he guessed, maybe fifty feet long. Carved out with miners' equipment, not blasted. Beds lined one wall, with adequate space for walking at the foot of them. On the right wall were cabinets similar to high school lockers with doors but no locks. He quickly counted twenty beds and then ran out to grab more untainted air. All but seven beds were occupied. Suicide? Jerry shuddered.

In a couple of minutes he was ready again and plunged back in. Past the corner of the room on the left he saw a desk. On top lay a financial register, and it sat out begging someone to pick it up. He grabbed the ledger, tucked it under his arm and got out of there. Now he headed for the cave front and didn't stop until he was outside.

The workers looked up as Jerry materialized out of murky darkness.

"What'd you find?" Hal called.

"Lot of stuff in there. Found the rest of the workers. But this," he patted the diary he held, "this may have some answers."

They crowded around. Jerry opened the book to its first page. It said, "Diary for a Dead Planet." It was written over in ballpoint ink several times. The dates began on the second page with March 15, 2011. On the first page they read twenty names. Below it was a short sentence with a February date and a dash followed by "Bio sealed in."

"These guys, the ones in the cave," Jerry mused.

They read the first diary entry.

Chapter 18
Seth Hollister's Diary

My name is Seth Hollister. I am in charge of the construction crew. I have twenty guys working for me. Things have been going from bad to worse in the last two weeks. Now it's getting crazy and I am starting this book. I don't know why I'm even doing this. I just think I should. The company called on the radiophone last night and told me to seal the bio people in tight, not just the plug top and bottom, but all the way. I'm to do it softly so they don't hear me filling their tunnel. How in blazes do I do that? Much as said the world's going to hell in a hand-basket and we've got to stay topside. The news is telling us that the UN finally gave up and it's trying to appease that idiot dictator Faustonelo. He stole the bomb and he's got no sense at all! And he's allied his country with insurgent elements in China, India and Pakistan. They're pretty unlikely bedfellows, but that's the news. Never thought that could happen, not in a million years. Got to get my crew working. Going to have them widen our construction cave, too. Later.

"This is a find," Jerry said to Hal.
"Yeah, it is," Hal replied.
Hans said, "How far does it go?"
Jerry turned to the last written page, about three quarters of the way through. "The last entry is dated June six, same year."
"Radioactive cloud got em', I bet," Don Smythe guessed.
"Maybe," Jerry said skeptically, "but there are fourteen skeletons lying in bed in the back, there. I think they did for themselves."

Hal said, "We found five up front."

"Might have been in charge of dynamiting the cliff face."

"We counted nineteen."

"Maybe one of them bought it, accident or something."

"Book says twenty."

"You find any fuel?"

"No, but there are lots of places to look yet."

"C'mon, you guys, we're done here. Let's get this back to the 'sphere and let Arthur take a gander at it. Tomorrow we'll come back with some spotlights and clear out the darkness. Then we'll see what else we can find."

"Check out a couple more pages before we go, okay?" Don said.

"Okay, then back we go. I'm calling this in," Hal said. He unhooked his transmitter and let whoever manned the command console know. "We're coming back," he said.

"Roger."

The day wasn't quite done, but they'd worked hard and readied the cave for full exploration. Big lights would help a lot. Jerry turned to the third page. It read March 16, 2011.

I haven't told the men. Some are suspicious of the new order. I'm going to tell them after the tunnel is filled. Then, what can they do? I hope I'm not being a coward about it. Some of the men are hard to control and I don't want them to think they can break in and stay safe. That would upset the balance and I can't let that happen. I decided last night to hide this journal. I'm no martyr, but what I'm hearing on the radio scares all of us. I'll push them hard; give them no time to think.

Jerry turned to the next entry, March 17, 2011.

The men all know. I'm not fooling anybody. The pansies amongst us are complaining. The tough guys, most of them, are riding the hell out of them and telling them to shut up. Jake Freeholder, our Comanche bloodied Rob Smart's nose when Smart's whining got to him. Don't blame him. Had to stop it on principle. At least Rob quit talking. Less said the better. Today they worked like fiends. The rock crusher is working overtime. Hope it holds together long enough to finish the job. Place'll look like a chain gang if it doesn't.

Jerry turned the page. March 18, 2011.

Drills got another ten feet into the left wall today. Ronnie's crew packed about forty feet up against the lower plug quietly, as I said. At that rate it'll be sixteen days before we can plug the cave entrance. Hope we've got the time. Had a meeting after shift today. Told the guys what I knew. Told them it didn't look good and we had to protect the bio-people quick as possible. Smart knows there's no way any of us are going to get down now. He apologized to the men and me today. Said he was just scared. I said who isn't. Don't think he'll be any more trouble. Couple others subsided, too. Eases my burden some. Let them know we're going to pull our own cave in around us. Maybe we'll have a chance if the whole thing doesn't come apart. I think it helped.

Hal put his hand over the book before Jerry could turn another page. "Come on, you guys, let's head back. We can read more later. Let Arthur go through it. We've got inside chores."

"Yeah," Jerry said. He closed the book. The five men turned their backs on the cave and headed for home in silence.

Chapter 19
Finding the Pace

Arthur stood in his usual place on the low stage. The lights rigged around the perimeter of the cave dimmed, leaving one bright spot to shine on the speaker. On Al and Gil's newly constructed podium a hooded light also shined on Arthur's tastefully hidden notes. Arthur didn't look all that comfortable, but that he didn't come across like a politician endeared him. No one in the audience wanted to be there, either. With a visible sigh, he tapped the microphone and a sound like a woodpecker knocking on a street sign reverberated within the hall.

"First," he said, as the low conversational din subsided, "let me thank Al and Gil for their fine carpentering efforts. The shelf under the podium is very useful. This is definitely better than dragging a table up here whenever we had to in the past. I like to think of this as one of the visible changes we'll be making around us for years to come. Let's get started. Almost everyone is here. For those who couldn't be, members of their groups please fill them in. Any questions after any meeting please see me."

Gina sat at the small table she'd used the other night. A cloth now covered the table, no longer drawing attention to her lovely crossed legs. She opened the spiral binder and handed Arthur a single sheet of paper. He looked at it and smiled. He set the paper on top of his notes and began to read from it.

"Gina has come up with a meeting outline to help us cover everything with a minimum of strain. It's excellent. Thank you Gina."

Gina blushed a little, but smiled up at him.

He lifted the paper with a hand and put it on the undershelf. "Tonight I'll not use this because I only want to give a progress report. I won't take much of your time and I hope to keep future meetings short, too. Our exploring party, Matt, Mike, Roddy and Jules have devoted today to reading maps of the surrounding mountains. They have planned out a two-week hike. They will go together and will start in two days time. Tomorrow they will pack and spend time with their loved ones.

"Hal, Jerry, Hans, Don and Mark, the singing quintet," he paused for the laughter and a few snickers, "will return to the equipment cave tomorrow with floodlights. They will bury the dead and then scout out the rest of the cave. Jerry tells me there are lots of nooks and crannies he couldn't take time to delve into on his first run-through. We'll have a report on that tomorrow night.

"Of particular note is a diary Jerry found written by Seth Hollister, the construction supervisor. It is a clear account of their last days on the surface. I have read it and I want to share it. It is meaningful and those men were heroes. They are probably responsible that we stayed alive through the end, an end that began with a day I want to call Black Saturday.

"I don't want to relate it today. Rather, I think we should pick an evening when no other big things are going on and devote the time to this record. We may want to honor them as the first heroes of the new age. We can talk about it later."

Sue Dorchester spoke up. She'd heard the rumors and curiosity got the better of her. "Couldn't we hear a couple of pages now?"

"I can't deny anyone that," Arthur said. "Let me finish with the update and I'll read a little."

"Okay."

"Finally, I want Jerry Ells to get right to surveying our town site with a couple of other volunteers. Whether we have heavy construction equipment to use or not, we still have to build. That will be the next priority. Now I'm through for the evening. Any questions?"

A lot of people shook their heads. Nobody offered, so Arthur read the first three entries to the assembled. "I'll pick a better time for more, soon," he promised, and closed the meeting.

On his way back to his place, Gina followed him out. "A computer would make this much easier, Arthur. Couldn't Ernie do something?"

"There are no parts to replace ones that failed. Sorry."

"Too bad." Gina's face fell.

"Yes, I know," he replied.

Gina turned to go. Arthur called after her. "Gina, are you busy?"

"No, why?"

"Would you join me for a cup of tea in the Café, take pity on an old man?" He smiled.

"Of course," she smiled brightly, "but you're not old."

"I feel that way some days."

"So do I!"

Arthur laughed, "Well, that's perspective."

They walked side by side to the common kitchen and dining area. Before they got there they heard a voice behind them.

"Hey, Gina!"

They turned to look and saw Mark Cohen catching up with them. "Hi."

"Hi yourself," Gina said.

"Where you heading?"

"Arthur and I are going for a cup of tea. Want to join?"

"Sure," he said, "but what I wouldn't give for a cup of coffee."

"Me, too," said Arthur.

"Poor planning not to include unroasted and still viable coffee beans in the biosphere," Mark said.

Arthur laughed and said, "It was, wasn't it?"

Gina nudged Mark. "So we're addicted to tea, instead."

Both men laughed. Arthur thought back to his youth when he smoked and how glad he was he kicked that habit. The three arrived and took a table. Hot water on the counter and pulverized tea next to it in a small bowl soon combined. The aroma of something close to Olde Earl Grey wafted up their nostrils.

"Umm..."

They sipped slowly. After awhile Mark looked around, as if he'd never seen the scene before. When he spoke he sounded a little troubled.

"Arthur, do you really think we'll do it? There is so much to do."

"Mark, I haven't always been an optimist," he said, "but I am convinced that we will not only do it, but we will do it far better than our predecessors. I believe that. You are the seeds of a new civilization, all of you younger people. You're smart and tough and you have other qualities you probably wouldn't recognize in a crowd. You'll do well."

"There would be fear...of course. There would be tragedy...of course, but upward was the only way they could go." He spoke like a man possessed.

"You will win the day," he said, "and do you know why?"

"Why?" Mark asked.

"Because..." Arthur looked searchingly at both, "because we are all that's left. We'll take it slow and make few mistakes. We'll learn from them. We'll do it better and we'll give our race and Mother Earth another chance...a last chance. There is no way but to go up. By the way, why don't you two get married?"

The question startled them and they stared at him, slack mouthed. Arthur roared. A few people close by in their cubicles complained loudly about wanting to sleep and how could they with all the racket!

Mark looked at Gina. "Good idea!"

Gina colored. "You through running around?"

"Running around...me?" Mark looked shocked

"I'm kidding," Gina said sweetly. "Seriously, I'd consider it if I knew you'd be around to be a father to our children."

"Is it my aftershave?"

"Ha, ha," she said. "That's the other thing, Mark. How about being serious once in a while?"

That stopped him. He looked at her and then at Arthur, who tried hard not to look amused and failed.

"I can be serious," he said to Gina, "but I don't like it much. You know I care about you. Would you trade happy-go-lucky for just happy?"

Gina looked at Mark intently and seemed to weigh her next statement. "I think I could do that."

"Well, look, I don't want to marry you until I can show you another side of me I must have hidden too well. Okay? How about a date?"

"I think I could do that."

"Tomorrow night, after the meeting, okay?"

"Sure."

For a moment, Mark looked like he'd fallen into a trap. Then he chuckled. Gina batted her eyes.

"I've been mulling something over," Arthur started. The two focused on him. "Everyone knows that my wife died of cancer several years before I agreed to head up the biosphere project. At least Molly didn't see the end of civilization. I think, had she lived, I would never have chosen to join the experiment. We were happy together..." Arthur stopped and turned inward.

Gina's felt her heart wrench, but after a moment he continued.

"I need to get some fresh opinions on monogamy and marriage. Our new civilization needs to be based on certain precepts. I want us to be as free as possible, but still willing to adhere to general rules of conduct that we can teach our future children. Would you and Mark talk that over and share it with others, like one on one. Seems kind of basic to me, but it's important that everyone ratify whatever rules we decide to keep and toss the ones we don't."

Gina said, "Pretty heavy, Arthur, but I agree with you. Mark, why don't you and I sit down tonight? You have anything else you need to do?"

"No. Arthur, if you're fed up with our company, we'll go."

"Not at all, Mark, but I'm fine."

After they left, he thought, *slowing things down. Yes, time and finesse. Lot of work ahead. And law. Old law won't work and pioneer law is too hit or miss.* He put his cup into the sink and returned to his cubicle.

Chapter 20
Depot Revisited

Mark met with the five-man detail after breakfast and they headed out, Hal in the lead, into the mountain-shadowed valley.

"Serious chill!" Hal said.

"Maybe winter's not through with us," one of the others said.

Mark was quiet, preoccupied. He recalled the dilemma Arthur had presented to Gina and him last night. He'd said nothing since, but it weighed on him. He'd have to say something soon before he got cold feet. Oh well, the best time was always now, wasn't it?

Gina is one smart gal, he thought as he relived the previous night.

He'd spent the first few minutes of their meeting looking her up and down, appreciating her fine good looks. Not long after, Gina said, "If you're through looking, could we get down to business. Mark?"

"Huh?" Snapped him right out of it. "Oh, sorry."

"See, Mark, you're not taking this seriously."

"You're right. Go ahead, I'm listening now." They spent two hours talking about what they believed, what they carried with them from childhood, their influences from school, strength of family bonds, strength of family religious beliefs, their own. They held back nothing. A couple of times Gina took on a surprised look, but put it down and said nothing out of the context of their session. Mark, for his part, recognized Gina's momentary squint as she filed the new perception away. Later in their discussion, Gina posed a few questions and Mark answered them honestly. In the end, they felt closer than ever to each other.

Now Mark walked along with the other four and when Hal started to sing, he couldn't join in. Something had gone out of him. His sense of freedom to think and act as he pleased felt tempered. *I was a happy-go-lucky guy, wasn't I?* They neared the gaping cave entrance. *Didn't want to face issues. Did what I was told. Did what I had to do. Did well enough in the bio. Pretty structured, pretty secure, safe. Up here, I can go anywhere. Even leave people I've known for twelve years and longer. Fact: we need each other more now than ever.*

He'd avoided it. *I knew I'd have to get serious sometime, but the day never seemed to come. Always something funnier around the corner.*

He gave up thinking about it as they arrived at the depot. The five opened the battery packs and set the floods. Three hundred feet of cable, light stands, heavy-duty portable flashlights, pads and pens connected efficiently.

Hal called them together.

"The batteries will last twelve hours. That's running time. We can stretch that a long way by turning off what we're not using. First thing we bring out the bones. If you find anything to identify them, make a note and we'll bury them with honors, but I don't think that was what they were thinking at the time."

They nodded and got started. Inside of an hour they had hauled all of the dead out into the sunlight. They had bagged the bones and labeled the men as best they could. Each bunk had a nameplate, so the "bunkhouse" group was easy. That took care of all but the five out front and the missing man. Jerry told Hal that the men should be buried up on a knoll off to the side and he pointed.

"Why?" Hal asked.

"It'll be in view of the new town and I don't think we should ever forget these men."

"Right." Hal called base and told them what they planned to do. The five carried the bones almost reverently to their final resting place. Hans Liszt wanted to put a cross up to commemorate the spot. Hal looked troubled and asked the group if it wouldn't be better to just raise a generic stone to the men instead.

"I'm not strong on religion," he said, "and I've never been pushed to lay my beliefs on the table. I'm going to do it now. I feel if you want to believe, that's okay, but religion has, in my opinion, been the cause of a majority of the world's ills and may have led directly to its fall. Doesn't mean we can't have values. We should have values, but let's not drag religion back into it, okay, guys?"

"I feel as you do," Jerry said.

Don Smythe nodded. "I've no problem with that, but, you know something, we'd better hash this out with the rest of us, and damn soon."

"I've had trouble with the idea of church, synagogue, temple or whatever all my life, I think," Mark said. "I was brought up in a Jewish household. My family always talked about the Holocaust and the way Jewish people have been pushed around all the time. They went to synagogue, but even with them, I never felt it was anything more than habit. I'm for not bringing it in."

"Hans?" Hal faced the younger man.

"I'm okay, I guess. When I said that, it was just me reacting in the old way. I've got to tell you, though; the women are more likely to object. I can see this becoming a big issue."

"Yeah, you're right, Hans. Better take this up with Arthur."

"Listen, crew, it's nine o'clock and we've got a lot to do before we go home today. Let's get at it."

Hal took out a folded piece of paper. "Jerry gave me this, this morning. He sketched a map of what he was able to see and figure out. Look..."

They gathered and stared at the paper. The map showed the approximate depth of the cave and was a good freehand job.

"I suggest Don take the left side. Mark, you take the right. You two gather all the info you can on the equipment parked along there. You guys okay with that?"

"Yeah, sure," they replied. They left.

"Hans, examine the left cave wall behind the equipment and shout if you find anything."

"Okay."

"Jerry, take the right side, okay?"

"Okay."

"I'll hang out here. Radio doesn't work well inside."

The men spread out and disappeared into the cave. The lights were heavy duty, but the cave was huge. Gloom started just beyond each circle of light. Hal watched flashlights bob and dip on the periphery. Five minutes later they heard Hans shout. "Hey! Come a-runnin'." He waved his flashlight back and forth.

Lights began to converge on Liszt. Hal trotted in. About two hundred feet inside, Hans motioned to a tall crack in the cave wall. The crack came together fourteen feet up, but it was six feet wide at its base. It had a flat floor of familiar red gravel and they could see small tire marks that led into a pitch-black interior. They didn't need eyes; their noses told them what was in there.

As they converged, Hans said, "Look at what I found." He led them into the side cave and there, lined against one wall they saw scores of fifty-five gallon drums stacked four high pervaded by the heady smell of Diesel fuel. The cave opened out to maybe twenty feet and continued into the dimness.

"Bang a few drums, Hal," Mark called. Obligingly, Hal went over and thumped several near him. The two above rang with a hollow sound, but the two lower ones gave off a dull thud, full! Elated, the men whooped. An echo came back strong enough to make them grab their ears.

"You guys thump a few. Let's get a count." The men went to work and the counts came in.

"Seven full in my group."

"Ten full here."

"Three over here and a couple of partials."

"I've got fifteen good ones here."

"Okay," Hal said, "Inventory shows at least thirty-five full barrels. There are eighty barrels in all. Somewhat less than half. It's a find, gentlemen. Let's go and tell our brethren. Arthur will be pleased."

"Not to mention me," Jerry said. "Building our town just got easier."

"Better not say that until we start some of these monsters." Jerry nodded.

"I'll report. You keep looking."

Jerry returned to his spot on the rough cave wall he'd left when Liszt yelled. A few feet deeper into the cave and behind the big bucket of a Payloader he'd spied a doorway with an actual door. He tried it and it opened easily. Inside, the beam of his flashlight showed four desks. Three of them held computers like the ones they had down below. *Good, good,* he thought, *they might still work.*

The room was not large, but it had one other interesting feature. His heart gave a thump. A long-range communications device? Of course! The construction crew had to be in touch with the home office, didn't it? Actually, probably the other way around, but who cares? This was a *big* find, big as diesel fuel.

He found the door substantial, fitted with heavy edge seals. That'd keep dust out. Good job. Wiping a finger over the flat desk surface, only the thinnest film could he feel. Obviously whoever worked in there made sure the door got shut in a hurry every time someone went through. Even so, something got in sometimes. He inspected the hinges. As he thought, they were spring-loaded. *Don't let the door hit you in the ass on your way in or out. Bet Seth Hollister got on the men about that.* The thought made him smile.

Jerry left the office and yelled to the others. "My turn! Come a runnin'!" He waved his flashlight.

Hal jogged over, followed by the others. Jerry motioned them in and they looked the place over.

"Nice," Mark said.

"Wonder if those computers still work?" Hal said.

Jerry nodded. "Thinking the same thing. Tell Ernie and have him come over and check them out."

"I'll do that. Okay, this is good. Anybody got any more looking to do?"

"Yeah," Jerry said. "The place has to have a working generator somewhere."

"Right. Okay, if the rest of you are done with your stuff, let's all look for it. Can't be far," Hal finished.

"Wait." Going behind the communications console Jerry found a big, black junction box. Behind it his light traced the spot where heavy cables disappeared into the rock wall.

"Generator's got to breathe, right?" he said.

"Right."

"Generator makes ozone and carbon monoxide, right?"

"Right."

"Then it has to be outside."

He walked out of the office and headed for the cave entrance. He knew exactly where to go. Outside he paused to get his day vision back, squinting until the light no longer hurt his eyes. Then he made a left turn and followed the hillside for a couple hundred feet.

"Found it!" he cried.

The others, who had waited while Jerry nosed it out, ran over.

The generator was big. It fit nicely into a rocky alcove. A slanting rock shelf three feet above it kept most weather off. Behind it, against the rock wall sat a five hundred gallon tank on stilts. A blasters drill hole through which heavy cables ran directly into the rock behind the machine.

Jerry banged the tank. "Mystery solved."

"Empty as my stomach," Don called.

"It's that time." Elated, they broke for lunch.

"What do you think, men?" Hal asked.

"We're most done exploring," Mark said. "Not much else. Wouldn't hurt to get back into the bunkroom and check out the open locker bins they each had."

"Why?" Hans said, "Who you going to send the stuff to?"

"Nobody. Creepy anyway." Bad idea.

"How about the equipment inventory?" Hal asked.

"All done." Mark handed Hal a list. "Here." Hal looked it over.

"Good. Anyone want to try to start one of these monstrosities?"

"Considering the fuel reserve, why not wait until we know exactly what's going into the town and how to get the best mileage out of the big stuff?" Mark said.

"Yeah, you're probably right. We'd play hell trying to get another tanker full of the stuff. Probably lots of diesel in the radioactive south. For all intents, close as the moon."

Jerry spoke up. "We're pretty much done for now and we've got half a day left. I don't want to go to the bio. Who wants to walk down to the town site with me? I'm starting to itch."

"Hey, I'll go," Don said.

"Why don't we all go," Hal suggested.

"C'mon guys," Jerry said, as he walked away from the cave mouth.

Chapter 21
New Beginnings

The hillside descended gradually for several hundred yards and abruptly dropped fifteen feet, leveling out again ever more gently. Several small streams fed by snow melt cascaded over the rocky face of the drop-off. The men picked their way down easily.

The valley's central stream flowed a quarter mile away, running north to south about mid valley. The land that Matt originally suggested be used for the town site had been walked some by the original explorers on their return from the periphery, but no one had taken time except through binoculars to really look it over.

Hal notified base.

"While you're down there, look for evidence of mutating grasses," the operator said.

"Will do." They immediately spread out and grabbed a few slender grasses and grains and eyeballed them.

"Looks okay to me," Hans said.

"Me, too," Don returned.

"Didn't Mark and Mike collect some of this stuff for microscopic exam?" Jerry asked.

"Yeah," Hal said, "but it's inconclusive so far. Chances are they are changed a little, at least. If so, can we use them or will we have to clear out the entire valley, turn the earth under and plant seeds from down under?"

"It's a question." Mark said.

"We'll figure it out."

He drew in a big lungful of sweet north Canada air and now Mark felt like singing. With news of more good discoveries and after his session with Gina the night before, he felt differently about her. He decided to throw the monogamy thing out to the men.

"Hey, you guys, what do you think about marriage?"

"Where'd that come from?" Don laughed.

"Gina and I were talking about...things...last night. Arthur asked us to discuss our views on monogamy and marriage. We really got into it."

"Oh?" Don said.

"Anyway, I'd like to hear some discussion on the subject."

"God and marriage and hanging tough with one partner, huh?"

"Always been tied together in some way or other. My attitude is that we don't need to have faith in a deity if we live our values."

"Makes sense. What do you think, you other guys?" Don said to the others.

Hans spoke up. "What about the Ten Commandments?"

"What about them? Do we need to say "God" in front of them to make them any more sensible than they are. Let's look at them. But first, is everybody willing to talk about this?"

"Do we need to?" Hal said.

"Listen," Mark said, "this is going to be an issue. Arthur isn't just smart like we think of smart, he's canny, too. He foresees that every one of us will have to be on the same page about a lot of things before our children are old enough to get our ideas. We need a united front. Gina taught me that last night. Her ideas are different. She approaches things from her personal point of view and also from a female point of view and I can tell you, it's not how I see it."

"I don't have strong feelings. Never did," Hal said, "but it's live and let live, the way I look at it."

"True, all of us think that way. Problem is, it's the tip of the iceberg. All of us are highly educated and we don't just buy into the old trappings automatically. What and how much to believe, in whom, those are all valid questions. They need valid answers. Like I say, answers we can give our kids, stuff they can grow with."

They trudged toward the town site. The going was easy now, the land undulating gently here and there, but relatively flat.

"Some of them you could let go," Mark continued. "I know them all. You guys probably do, too. I'm saying that the first, second and third and fourth we don't need. They deal with setting up a religion. It's a control thing. The fifth, honoring or respecting your father and mother is socially responsible. The sixth, not to kill, the seventh, not to commit adultery, the eighth, not to steal, those are socially good ones. They're responsible ones. Not to bear false witness is totally civilized and the tenth, not to covet is a modification of number eight. They deal with social mandates and plain common sense. They make *sense*. They are rational. We don't want to live in a community of fear and control, but of reason. Am I right?"

"Right," Hans said a little petulantly, "but my parents believed and they brought me up that way, too. I don't have any problem with the subject and I'm not about to try to push my beliefs on anybody else. I could no more throw out the first four than I could the last six."

"I'm not trying to push anything on anybody, Hans," Mark said, "I'm only asking that a bunch of smart guys walking around on a destroyed world think about what we're about and how we should deal with it. My take on your thinking, which I respect, is that everyone should believe what they feel in their hearts and live the example. What would you guys think about suggesting that we create a rule? Everyone lives the values they have and keeps it inside, never speaking about it publicly?"

"Sounds like something we could do," Don said.

"The problem is," Mark continued, "what do we teach our children and how soon after that will some of us decide we have to leave New Beginnings and set off on our own, because we're surrounded by a bunch of people who don't see eye to eye on things the way we do? What happens then? Same thing that happened before! We get nowhere," Mark finished.

"That's a problem," Hal said. "That's a real problem."

"Arthur hit on that last night," Don said. "We *all* have to agree on the course we take and we have to set off in the same direction. We have to teach the right things to our children and they have to be the same things. We have to be of one mind. Otherwise, the world will become what it was all over again. When we die, everything has to be in place. Our new beginnings have to kick off our new civilization right."

"Damned if you do, damned if you don't."

"That's how I see it," Don said.

"Hal, this is bigger than all of us. Suppose we decided, all five here, right now, on one course of action. We go back to the sphere and announce our plan? We call a meeting? What? We'd still have to convince every one of the rest of us down below. Seems to me that the spirit of compromise will be essential when we get into it. My guess is everybody is going to have to give up *something* to the ideal."

Mark picked it up. "I think that's the answer. This will have to be negotiated."

"Yeah, I guess," Hal said. "Now, let's get off the subject. You're giving me a headache."

Mark muttered under his breath, "Gina said it wouldn't be easy."

Jerry was closest to Mark. "What did you say, Mark?"

"Nothing," he replied.

Jerry looked at him. "Can you imagine a world without churches, Mark?"

"If it was the right choice."

The men traversed the town site through waving grass and wild grains. They looked around and got a feel for the place.

On the way back to the cave, a light wind passed five silent, introspective men.

Chapter 22
Atomic Glitch

Mary Beth Holiday glanced at the atomic clock from which all others picked up its Cesium beat. Accurate to one, one-hundredth of a second in a hundred years, it left virtually no margin for error. She wanted to run a wire up to the new town so that everybody would have the same time.

"You never know when coordinating up and down might become critical," she told Arthur one day.

"I know, and that's something I've meant to bring up with you."

"Sure. And I have an idea."

"Yes?"

She suggested running a wire to New Beginnings and wiring a central broadcaster. Ernie Tibbets offered her one better, a signal based upon the atomic clock, transmitted through the one thin cable that ran to the surface, the one Arthur had used as his antenna during the world-shattering news of twelve years before. He would omni broadcast the signal by radio from there.

"Save us a lot of wire, Mary Beth."

"You're the man, Ernie."

"Nice trade-off. You keep us alive and I putz and putter."

"Sounds fair." She smiled, waved and marched off down the narrow rough-cut tunnel to her atomic pile. Ernie looked at her as she disappeared. *Fine hunk of woman*, he thought, as he returned to his workshop.

He subsequently fashioned a tiny radio transmitter that would broadcast a time signal to all parts of their rapidly expanding world. Then he incorporated a discriminator circuit into all the walkie-talkie type radios he could grab from everyone who'd started to carry them around, instantly making Base time universal.

Mary Beth ran one hand gently against the tunnel's side as she walked and wondered how many thousands of years it would take for her hand to wear a groove in the wall. She continued in silence, but her heart was full and for a serious woman who carried the weight of responsibility she had, she felt quite happy. Her man, Roddy was out adventuring and she was home cooking her atomic pile. So long as he remained safe, she could deal with the home fires—atomic and otherwise. More than that, she knew that Roddy had found release with his friends. Roddy needed it. His kind of challenge...good for him.

When he came back to her, he'd be bright and fresh and she anticipated they'd be spending a lot of time alone together. That felt like something she wanted, too.

Two hundred yards is six hundred feet. Mary Beth never thought about it. She considered the tunnel part of the furniture, a long doorway in to work. As she rounded the last corner Jane Potter, her assistant, ran into her.

"Mary Beth!" she was a little breathless. "I was coming to find you. We have a problem, I think."

"You think?" The dread that lives under the surface for people working with atomics came up like gorge.

"We're getting some heating in the reaction core. Slightly high right now, but rising. I tried to reach you a couple of minutes ago by phone, but you must have been in the tunnel and you don't have your pager on."

Mary Beth looked down. It hung on her belt, but she'd switched it off to save power. They started to run.

"You checked the rods?"

"Of course." Jane sounded a little hurt.

"Jane, I'm running system check to save time. Coolant water flow?"

"No. Gauge nominal."

They arrived at the control console. Mary Beth double-checked everything. All gauges and dials were nominal except the core temperature gauge. The two women walked into an adjoining room and inspected the equipment. Nothing. Then Jane walked around the back of the evaporator/recycler.

"Mary Beth, come quick!"

Mary Beth rounded the corner and stood in horror, looking at a slowly growing puddle of steaming hot water. She immediately returned to the console and rapped the water flow gauge hard. It dropped by two-thirds.

"Jane, call Al and Frank immediately. I'll start the damping process. As soon as they are on the way, sound the general alarm for shutdown."

"Okay, Mary Beth." Jane ran to the phone. Mary Beth heard her pick up and call for the two maintenance technicians who were familiar with the pile and its equipment. After a minute, the alarm sounded.

Jane returned. "They're on the way. What can I do?"

"Get a counter from the desk and check for radiation back there. I think it's the purified water, but if it comes directly from the core, it will be too hot for either of us. Radiation suits for the guys and we get the hell out of here!"

"Gone!" Jane made quick work of it. This problem had never surfaced before, but it was one of twelve dangers they learned to deal with first hand at their initial training. They practiced from time to time and both women knew the score. Don't take atomics for granted. Ever!

Jane returned quickly, eyes wide. "It's hot," she said.

"Out of here. Now!" Mary Beth stayed long enough to be sure the automatic shutdown she'd started was working properly and then she left.

"Hit the showers!" she called to Jane, already fifty yards ahead. The echo of her voice reverberated along the tunnel. She heard Jane's yell and continued running. Soon she came across a shirt and bra, then shorts. Mary Beth started to undress, too. As she rounded the final "S" turn with its broad blast protection, a flat wall truncated toward the rear and meant to absorb a pressure wave, she was naked. She met Al running towards her with Frank hard on his heels.

"It's the core! We've got a breech. Suits, guys! I'll call for backup!"

They looked grim and barely glanced at her. A hundred feet in from the reactor room they jumped into the suit room.

The Mission

Dressing quickly they went carefully over each other checking suit integrity and moved purposefully into the reactor room. The automatics had done their job and the bio was now on batteries. Floodlights bathed the entire reactor area. Al and Frank went immediately to work.

Using short-range suit radios to communicate, Frank checked the shutdown process. It needed another minute. He put Al in the loop. They prepared expertly, as though they had rehearsed daily for twelve years. When the clang chimed, they went to work. Puddling evidently had reached the site drains.

"Al, the core is dead. We can do it."

"Good."

They teamed and found the leak.

"Right there," Frank pointed. "See that thin discoloration. Crystallized."

"I see it. Surgery indicated."

"Let's get busy"

Inside the long radiators a seam had begun to split. They cut out the bad section, checked the integrity of the rest and arc-welded the repair. Four hours later they flushed the area thoroughly and then spent another two minutely inspecting every square inch of the reactor.

"Good to go," Frank announced, as they finished.

"Radiation residual?"

"Counter says within limits."

"We're done." He wrote it up, describing in detail what they had found and done.

Al called Mary Beth. She thanked them both and told them they could leave, clean up and return to the bio.

Tired, they jumped into the showers, suits and all. The needle jets washed the suits down. They de-suited and showered individually then. All clean and fully clothed in what they'd arrived in; they met Mary Beth on the way back.

"Thanks, guys. Never knew I loved you so much." She smiled brilliantly and went on to the control room to bring the bio back up. Al glanced back. She wore an orange jumpsuit now. *Fine hunk of woman*, he thought.

Chapter 23
Seth Hollister's Finale

At the podium, Arthur leaned on the angled wood as he had done five nights before and every night since. *A sign of how things are changing,* he thought. *We are no longer tied to our cocoon. Living underground saved our lives. We had heat and light and food, but that was the chrysalis and now we must become the butterfly.*

"Ladies and gentlemen. May I have your attention." He waited for quiet. "A brief synopsis first and then we'll get to the heart of tonight's gathering."

Most of the assembly now sat, pretty much like an audience in an auditorium. They'd brought chairs from their cubicles or from the little dining area. The meeting area was large enough to accommodate the entire original population of Biosphere I. Generally over the past five years the area had been given over as a children's play area. Most recently they'd taken it back for meetings. The children had been moved into delightful holding areas in the nearby caves.

The children were all in bed. For the most part they were quiet. Two or three women watched the kids and as sound carried well in the caves they could hear clear enough to understand the proceedings.

Everyone enjoyed the meetings. Not everyone could be topside. Everyone, though, wanted to be a part of creating history. If they couldn't be there physically, they'd do it vicariously.

The hall quieted and Arthur's pleasant, modulated voice began. "A lot has happened. The reactor is repaired and every indication is that it is fine and will continue to be. Al and Frank are okay."

The crowd appreciated that news with a swell of murmurs.

Arthur waited for quiet. "Yesterday our intrepid five equipment caver's discovered fuel for the heavy equipment they'd found the day before. Today they used a miniscule part of the reserve they'd found and started one of the machines, just for a few moments. The equipment is in good shape and is in running condition. Jerry Ells, our frustrated civil engineer is now in his glory. He's got a real job!"

The crowd tittered. A few of the children moved and cried out. The watchers quickly quieted them.

"He's going to build us a town!"

At that the crowd cheered. More children woke up and the three monitors were kept busy for a while.

Arthur continued. "Tomorrow morning, Matt Duncan, Mike Peters, Roddy Brown and Jules Beggin begin a two-week journey beyond our little valley. They have augmented radios with a far superior range over the first radios that were made, courtesy of Ernie Tibbets. They also carry small amplifiers he calls boosters, which they will put in strategic places to carry our signal wherever they go. They are going to try for Ross River, about a hundred and twenty-miles from here. There is little else between but mountains. The closest place where we might find more fuel is in Whitehorse, over three hundred miles away. We wish them all speed."

The four hung together near the back of the big room. Several near them slapped their backs and wished them well.

"On another note, Doc Simmons tells me that George is raring to get out of the infirmary and join us. Not for a while, George. Patience. I promise there'll still be things to discover by the time you are up and around."

Laughter.

"Now to the evening's main attraction, Seth Hollister's diary. As you all know, it covers a period of about eleven weeks and is the last testament we may ever have about the last days on the surface of the Earth. Running from March 15, 2011, the last entry is dated June 6, 2011. In what I previously read, Seth tells about receiving a message from corporate headquarters ordering the construction crew to backfill our tunnel.

"He had a tough time of it. Some of the men were scared and wanted to break into our biosphere. They had radios and knew that things, you know, politics, had turned ugly and more dangerous than ever before. He prevented it and ordered his men to enlarge the equipment depot. They tried to make it safe for them.

"They had plenty of food and drink, enough to last about three months. Seth convinced the men that we were possibly the only people on the Earth with a chance to make it if it all came apart and that it was up to them, him and his nineteen men, to give us that chance. Seth Hollister was a man's man and a hero. Today we can thank every one of those men who sacrificed their lives that we might live. Therein lies yet another reason for us to succeed. We *owe* it to them."

The audience seemed to be holding its collective breath.

"They finished filling our tunnel in sixteen days, three days fewer than it took us to dig ourselves out. How they could have been quiet enough that we didn't hear a thing is amazing. Finally, on April 16, 2011 the bombs went off and *Black Saturday* became reality. Radioactive clouds quickly spread and began to cover the Earth. It took a while to get to our latitude, but it got here. Seth Hollister realized their only hope lay in sealing themselves in. Two days later he gave the order to dynamite the rocky cliff over the cave entrance.

"You remember the diesel barrel crawl space Matt discovered? Seth's diary indicates they decided to do that so they could check and maintain the generator. It had a five hundred gallon tank. If nothing went wrong with the equipment it could operate for a month before it ran out of fuel. The controls were inside so power wasn't a problem. It didn't work the way they planned. The explosions took down more of the mountain than Seth expected and covered the entire cave entrance, including the exit he made. They were trapped, regardless, but they'd filled the fuel tank on the 19th and at least they had lights!

"What follows I will read to you from Seth Hollister's entries. The date is April 20, 2011."

I went and did it that time. A week ago I told Crandall to put a hundred and fifty pounds up and wire it in. He told me that from his inspection of the rock strata it was way too much. I insisted. "Got to put as much in front as we can.

Radiation'll find a way in if we don't." He says, "Gonna find its way in, no matter." And then he spits cud out of the side of his mouth like, "Yuh never listen, yuh dunce!" I don't say anything. My read is we're not going to make it. I'm agreeing with him, but I can't bring myself to say it. Like, survival is trying, even when you know better. Anyway, we set it off this morning. Whole frikkin' mountain came down over the top of us. Who knows, we might not get the radiation, after all. We'll just die of starvation or asphyxiation, one or the other. Neither good choices.

Arthur leafed through a few pages and stopped at another one dated April 25, 2011. "I've read every entry. There is a lot of pretty much the same stuff, day after day. With your indulgence, I'll read what's new or what carries the man's saga along. Everyone okay with that?"

"Sure, Arthur," someone in the front said. No one else responded.

"The date here is April 25, 2011." He commenced to read.

No radiation yet. Not to speak of. Our Geiger counters are still reading pretty low, but they're climbing a little. Stuff's out there. Air still okay. Food holding out. Men aren't, though. They're scared silly and I'm breaking up fights often enough now. Keep telling them, it could blow over. Hold out hope! They don't believe me. Hell, I don't believe me. How do you convince anyone about something you don't believe in?

Arthur flipped ahead. "This is May 15, 2011." He read:

We're still here. Air is okay. This is a big cave. Got a little odor now but nothing anybody complains about. Radiation levels are up but still within the safe range. In here, anyway. Don't think I'd want to go outside any more. Not much to say. We're going to die. Matter of time.

"May 18th."

Generator's fluctuating. I put three guys on trying to break out of our cocoon. Don't know why I bother. Have to keep going, I guess. This is twelve hours later. The guys broke out and Charlie went to fix the generator. Bad filter. Running smooth now. Fuel okay but I'll ask for volunteers to top it off tomorrow. Have to fill some five-gallon cans and drag them out. The guys will be hot when they return. They can shower and hopefully they won't get the sickness.

"June 1, 2011."

It's decided. The whole crew's had it. I can't blame them. It's die now or die later. Boredom is a killer. Our medic made up a nice cocktail from the pharmacy. Put it in a pot and heated it up, quicker, he said. Served every man Jack and we raised our paper cups and we toasted to our world gone to hell, gone somewhere, just gone! Only I pretended to drink and I didn't. And I smiled at the men and told them they were heroes and I'd see them on the other side. I felt like a hypocrite! So fourteen get onto their bunks and lie down and wait it out. It doesn't take long. Twenty minutes. That's it. Now you're here, now you're not. Five of us stay up front. Does it matter where you fall down, long as you're not getting up again? Who cares? One by one they lie down and a couple have some stomach distress. Doesn't last. And they stop breathing eventually, but they're unconscious and don't know it. And now I'm alone. I'll hang around a few days. Just for the hell of it.

"June 2, 2011," Arthur intoned.

"*All alone. Was it cowardice? I don't think so. I have to play this out. Everyone is dead except me. I've gone over to each one and put the sign of the cross over them. Don't know if they'd want me to, but they're not here any more. I feel better. Funny about that! If there is anything else after this life, like all the stuff we learned as kids and gradually throughout life we denied, then they are somewhere else, maybe a good place. If not, what does it matter? I'm this side of death and they're over the other side. Just read what I wrote. I'd better keep control. One thing that'll get to me is loneliness. Midnight now. Guess I'll wander awhile.*

Arthur looked out at his audience. They had never been so quiet.

"Is this bothering you? Want me to stop?"

People looked around at their companions and friends. Everyone seemed to be searching for an answer to that question. A few coughed, but no one moved.

"Should I stop?"

A few mutters, then a kind of ground swell, soft, not demanding, "No...no...we need to hear this. Please, go on..."

"I cried last night," Arthur said. His hand shook. He dropped it to his side and raised it again to the page. He grasped the top corner and looked down to the page again. "June 3, 2011."

I got to thinking about the biosphere today. We buried it beyond the ability of any of us, least of all of one man to get down there and save himself. I gave the order. It was the right one, I know it inside. But how I wish I could call to them, let them know I'm here, ask them to let me in. God, this old survival instinct's got me saying things. No! Made my bed. Now I'm lying in it, all alone. Always did before, but this is different. Wonder if I'm the last man on the face of the Earth. Got to stop thinking that way. Going to walk the perimeter again like I did last night. Took me twenty minutes. Maybe I'll do it a few times. Maybe I can sleep, then.

"That's the end of that one. More?" Arthur asked. They stood there, waiting. "June 4, 2011."

Beginning to wonder what the value of staying alive is, anyway. How do I play this out? Played out already, isn't it? The people below, will they ever get out? Will they find this in twenty-five or thirty years when they can—maybe—dig themselves out? When the radiation's gone. Will they run out of air, just like I will, if I insist on living, on keeping on? Why? Got to think about that. I wandered the cave seventeen times today. Back and forth, back and forth. It's not getting smaller, but it's not getting bigger, and I wonder why I keep doing this. The men are corpses and the smell is ever-present now.

Getting worse. No place to bury them. That's not the half of it. In a few days I'll have trouble breathing the air. My lungs will be breathing the putrefied essence of eighteen men. Better tell what happened with Alfie. Should have before. No, I'm beat. I'll tell it tomorrow.

Arthur looked up again. The silence filled the cave. Not a baby cried. "June 5, 2011."

Alfie Potter. Only man to quit the crew. Only man who ran. Only man I couldn't control. Happened on the nineteenth. I sent him out with five of the guys to top off the diesel reservoir on the generator. They did the job and came back. I sent them right into the showers. Alfie said he'd close up the exit drum. He never came back. Ducked out and must have headed out across the valley for the high pass. He didn't make it, he couldn't. At the time I couldn't believe any one of my crew would run off. But he did. When Alfie didn't come back in, I sent Herb and Justin after him, but it turns out Alfie pulled some rubble down on the entrance and we were locked in again. They came back with a pencil scratched note saying he's sorry, but he just couldn't take the cave anymore. "I know I'm going to die and I want to die outside under the stars." Made me so mad I couldn't write about it then. Now I have to. Got to complete the record. We'd been listening to the radio all packed into the communications room day after day. Like we couldn't miss a word, like we were all hanging from a line off a mountain and it was fraying and we could see it but we couldn't do anything about it and we couldn't get off.

Arthur turned the page.

I couldn't raise the company home office in Chicago after the eighteenth. After a few days we had to search the band for some word, any word. Finally there was only one station left. AM 790. I heard the guy mention Whitehorse. Guess he broadcasted from there. The announcer was a little nuts. He prayed and he sang and then he coughed for a couple of hours and then...nothing. I think that's when it hit me hardest. I spun the dial one end to the other and back and kept on doing it.

Finally one of the guys came over and turned the radio off. He said, "Forget it, Seth. The world's cooked." He turned and walked away. I don't even know who did that. I sat there stupid.

More about Alfie. I've got to get this out. I said we were all plenty scared. News broadcasts had gotten more ominous every day for weeks before. Charges and counter-charges. Just when you thought you couldn't take any more, it'd get worse. The others stuck it out with me. So why did I feel like I'm a failure because of one man's final act of free will. Why? Because he was my responsibility, that's why! I have to stop now.

Arthur didn't ask this time. "June 6, 2011."

My name is Seth Hollister. I'm fifty-six years old. I was born in Des Moines, Iowa. I had two sisters, Laurie and Gail. I loved them. My parents both died within two months of each other four years ago. I loved them, too. Thank God they didn't have to see this. Where is God, anyway? The stench of rotting corpses is strong and I've decided to go for the other side. I saved some of Doc Foure's cocktail. I drank it a couple of minutes ago. It's doing something inside. As my last rational act, I will this diary to whoever finds it. Good luck to you. Don't make the same mistakes we did.

Arthur closed the journal quietly at the podium. He hung his head and everyone saw and closed their eyes in silence. Tears squeezed out of many eyes that night. Finally, in an act of closure, Arthur spoke to the audience. "He said, 'Don't make the same mistakes we did.' Friends, we surely can't afford to, can we? Meeting adjourned."

Chapter 24
A Bit of Exploring

The breakout exploratory party left early. Matt, Mike, Roddy and Jules first stopped by George's bedside and spent some time with him. He was on the mend, but a long way from able. He knew and wished them all "Best of luck and don't fall in any holes." The men laughed and said they'd be careful.

George said, "I'll miss you guys and I'll miss the adventure."

Mike said, "You've had enough adventure for a lifetime."

Jules put his hand on Georges shoulder. "You'll do fine when you're fit again."

George looked at him and then the others and nodded.

They shook hands all around, turned and left without looking back. They didn't see George turn his head toward the rock wall and they didn't see his shoulders begin to shake. But they knew.

Outside, they met Gil Castonguay, assigned as base monitor for this day. They went with him up the tunnel. He sat in the console seat, checked the equipment and turned to them.

"Good luck," he said. He firmly shook each explorers hand.

"Thanks."

"Check your radios."

They pulled them from their belts and did a final radio check.

"Stay in touch."

"Right." They turned their backs and trudged way.

Matt took the lead and headed south. The snowfield at the top of Keele Peak caught the beginnings of day and cast one brilliant facet at the brightening sky. To Matt it looked like a friendly beacon.

The four were dressed in several layers of clothing. They had sweaters and heavy coats, scarves and hiking boots. They were all different, but of bright colors. Matt wore a bright orange parka, Mike's was Kelly green; Roddy wore bright blue and Jules iridescent violet parka jumped out at them. Jules came up with the color-coding idea.

"Make it hard to miss us, guys, and if one of us gets in trouble, we'll know who immediately."

"I like it," Roddy said. The others agreed.

On their backs they carried forty-pound packs with the same color-coding. These included sleeping bag, shovel, a first aid kit featuring tourniquets, bandage tape, antibiotics and anything else they could think of to stave off serious trouble in the event of accident. Each carried two hundred feet of thin but very strong nylon braided rope; a super sharp knife and a curved trimming saw. Matt grabbed an axe from supply so they could share it amongst them and gave it to Mike to carry. Each explorer had a map of the mountains. Matt carried the Geiger counter and the others split out the weight of the boosters.

Jules concocted some miniature flares the night before to put in their packs.

"Just break it in two," he said, "and they will light."

"Not bad," Mike said. "Guess you learned something in Chemistry!"

"Yeah, but that's it. Don't ask me anything else."

Mike snickered.

Each explorer checked the others pack for fit and readiness. The shoulder and circumferential snap-ties they adjusted for maximum comfort so, they could move in multiple ways without their packs becoming burdensome.

They traveled lightly and remained relatively silent for the first hour. Looking around, watching their footing on slopes that became progressively steeper and trickier took a lot of time. Because of the terrain, they lost sight of the cave entrance within a few minutes. Ernie had assured them that the new radio/transmitters would keep them in touch for several miles.

"When you get to the highest point you're likely to find before descending toward the next mountain range, find a place to attach this." Ernie held up his collapsible directional antenna. He fanned it out and showed them the two methods he'd devised for making the installation permanent.

"Adjust it to aim for the spur of our mountain. That's where we'll have the Base antenna. Line of sight is still important in all these mountains. I'll have an omni-antenna up there before nightfall. Try a radio check around six p.m."

"You're a good man, Ernie," Matt said.

"Sure. My end is done," the electronics man finished. "You're good to go."

"Thanks, Ernie, we'll be talking."

"That's the idea."

The use of the expertise within the biosphere went like that. When it got to food, they took a wide range of nutritious freeze-dried stuff the kitchen staff concocted. That made it light and compact. Rations for the two-week hike, which included three extra days of provisions just in case, weighed twelve pounds. They took canteen water, but expected to fill along the way. Water test strips and purification tablets took up little room. An amazing amount of nutrition took an amazingly small part of their packs. Energy transfer needed to go to the legs, circulatory system and heart, not to burden.

They carried maps that showed the Mackenzie Range and points south and west into the Selwyn Range, which ran generally north and south, west of the larger Mackenzie mountains, kind of a sister range. If they got that far, their direction would eventually take them to Ross River. As a destination, it wasn't much, just a small dot on the map. Its main feature had roads that went in four directions. Matt liked that. Also, there would be a road on the other side of Front Mountain, along the bottom of whose northwestern escarpment they slowly moved.

Matt stopped and consulted his map. "According to this, we could hit the Ross River road by walking another twelve miles south-south-east. We have to cross Templar Pass. That'll mean some climbing but it's only sixty-five hundred feet and that's easier than any other pass in fifty miles. My guess is we'll get just below it by late afternoon. We camp and start up in the morning. Any thoughts?"

"Why not go until night and then camp?" Roddy said.

"We could, but it'll be a lot colder above four thousand feet. We have bedrolls but no tents."

"Right."

"We'll play it as we see it."

"Yeah, okay." They moved on.

About mid-afternoon they stopped to eat. The mountainous area was barren of grasses or trees. It looked like the end of the world. They found it depressing.

"Even less above here," Mike mentioned.

"Hope the east side has forests," Jules said.

"Hasn't got tough yet, guys," Matt said.

"I imagine getting over the pass will take some doing. Glad there's no snow up there now."

"If we can cave it, we can climb it."

They littered the pristinely primal landscape with their talk and the little echoes that came back to them. They saw no evidence of life and didn't expect it. They doubted that animals living in this land any more than passed through on their way to green places.

Eventually they struggled up their packs and went on. The land became rockier still as they turned toward the pass that now rose above them.

"We have another hour. Let's make as much time as we can. I figure we'll be up at about four thousand feet by then," Matt said.

Mike had gone ahead. "Watch your footing. Better spread out. Some of this stuff is slipping under my feet and I don't want anybody getting a rock shower."

"Always knew you were a right guy," Jules called from below.

"Just trying to help," Mike smiled.

"Hey, Mike! Like we did it on the back caves, remember," Matt called.

"Oh, yeah. You guys pull off to the side and I'll get above this. Let you know when it's safe." Mike climbed on all fours, picking the best spots on the loose hillside. About halfway he slipped and came down twenty feet with a small rockslide. He hugged the loose stuff until it stopped and then gingerly moved to the side, got purchase and started up again.

Matt looked around for a better spot to climb, but the shale-like hillside extended for hundreds of yards to either side. He decided that Mike had picked the best spot and they'd have to wait on him.

"Another hundred feet, Mike," he called.

Mike didn't answer but moved slowly upward, crabwise. Several times when he felt the rock base start to shift, he lay flat, spreading out his bulk over the widest area he could until motion beneath him stopped. Other times he plowed ahead, the detritus of the mountainside moving downward in a slow moving rivulet, making him look like a ship at sea as it leaves its wake behind. When he got to the top of the jumble, he called down. "Listen, there's a big stick-up rock up here. It's not going anywhere. I'll hook up and toss my rope."

"Right."

After a minute he threw the end down. "Okay, grab and c'mon up."

Matt scurried up the rope with gloved hands, doing a little dance as loose stuff worked out from under his feet, followed by Jules. The labor saving rope helped a lot. When Roddy, last up, finally topped the ridge, Mike collected his rope and reattached it to his belt.

He stood for a moment and looked at the next challenge.

"Good idea we clip on while we climb." Mike unclipped the rope again and handed it off to Matt, who did the same with Roddy. Roddy followed suit with Jules.

For the rest of the hour they climbed steadily. Outcroppings appeared often enough to anchor them to their path. There were no further incidents. Near the pre-arranged stopping time, Jules spied a natural amphitheater another five hundred feet higher. The place where they stood had no cover and a chill wind cut around them, the cold on their faces making it difficult to talk.

"Let's head for there," he pointed. "Looks like a good windbreak."

They were glad to resume their trek. Twenty-five minutes later they entered a cleft between the rocks and discovered a flat area large enough to accommodate all four sleeping bags. Darkness closed in around them. The wind began to whistle and moan around the rocks. Their joints ached and they were glad to stop for the night.

Three were content to sit and relax, but Jules, on a whim, took his flashlight and worked his way back into the cleft. He was gone for nearly five minutes when they heard a shout.

"Hey, guys, look at this!" Jules sounded excited.

The three men got up from where they sat with their backs to the upside wall of the cleft. They grabbed their flashlights and ran toward the sound of Jules voice. The cleft closed in, but before it got too narrow to negotiate, about fifty feet in, it turned and they entered another cave. Roddy, with his bulk barely made it through. After that, it obligingly opened up into a long, clearly geological fault crack. And on one flat wall of the cave they saw...pictures, really old pictures.

Mike said, "I thought all these were in France."

"Me, too," Roddy said. The four stood and looked in awe at paintings that could have been thousands of years old. The animals were reminiscent of deer and bears. They couldn't tell if the surreal aspects they saw were part of the artists design or if these animals were out of the ordinary.

"Untouched." Mike held out his hand but drew it back.

"These aren't right. Something's wrong with them. What's wrong with them?" Jules whispered.

They shined their flashlights closer. The deer-like animals were painted in three colors. The dark, perhaps black outlines they saw could have been carbon from a fire-stick. The red they couldn't guess at, but Cro-Magnon Man's cave drawings in France had red in them. The other color was a kind of beige, like but not like the surrounding mountain colors.

The most arresting thing about the deer was their super wide chests and long tails. The chests were massive, much larger than native deer. And they seemed to have eyes that stared straight out of their faces, not from the side. They gave Jules and Matt a creepy feeling. They knew most about the Cro-Magnon peoples and their cave drawings. These weren't the same.

The representations of the bears seemed similar until one looked at them closely. The bear's eyes were too far toward the back of their heads and the eyes were large. That didn't fit, either. Nor did the length of their limbs, far longer than any bear they'd ever seen. They had tails, too, as long as the deer. It didn't fit.

"Surrealism wasn't Cro-Magnon Man's style," Matt said.

"No, it wasn't. They weren't great artists, but they tried to depict nature as it was. Very strange."

"How far back does this cave go?" Roddy said, changing the subject.

"I don't know," Jules said. "I stopped when I saw this."

"Well, it's interesting, but we're about to lay up for the night and it's a lot nicer in here than it is out there."

"I'd agree."

"I'm going to scout forward," Roddy announced.

"Go ahead."

Roddy disappeared into the darkness.

"Roddy!"

Faintly. "Yeah?"

"Wait up. We ought to buddy. Safer."

"Okay, come ahead."

Jules disappeared after the voice.

"C'mon Matt," Mike said, "let's bring the packs and bags in here."

"Lead the way."

Mike and Matt made short work of it. They heard yelling when they turned the corner where the cleft met the cave. They dropped everything in a heap and, flashlights out, ran toward the sounds.

"What's going..." he stopped. Roddy, followed on his heels by Jules ran out to them, almost running them down.

"Something in that cave," Roddy said and stopped, completely out of breath. As he turned Jules ran into him.

"Oof!"

"Settle down!" Matt yelled.

"Right." Jules got his voice. "Cave opens up big inside, kind of like the depot, but it goes a long way in and a long way down. We heard something flapping and up out of the dark we saw...something...don't know what, but it's alive and it flies and it's big, huge! Scared the beejesus out of us."

"Something alive?" Mike said.

Matt stared. "Do you know what this means?"

"We're not alone?" Roddy said helpfully.

"Yeah...good."

"Wait a minute. How big?" Mike asked.

Roddy looked down the long, black corridor. "Wouldn't fit there."

"That big?"

"Hey guys, we have a decision to make," Matt broke in.

"Stay or go?"

"Uh-huh."

Roddy spoke up. "I don't think the bird or whatever it was saw us, but if it can hear, it sure as hell heard us. I want to go back and take another look."

"You're braver than I am..." Jules said.

"Or more foolish," Matt finished for him. "Personally, I think we should sleep outside. However, more important than that is, we need to stick together. We all go or we all stay. What'll it be?"

"I don't like to get spooked," Roddy said to the three. "I'd like to find out what's there and what it's living on. And my guess is, unless it has some light somewhere down there, it's probably blind."

"Right," Jules picked up the thread, "and if it's blind it probably has radar, like a bat."

"And if it has hearing like a bat, it definitely heard us," Mike kicked in.

"And if it's as big as you say, it has an adequate food source," Matt finished.

All three started talking at once. Matt held up his hand.

"Discretion, gentlemen," Matt interjected, "requires that we get the hell out of here and report our findings to base. Let them brain trust and let them tell us what they think. Then *we'll* decide what we want to do. It's our expedition, but we're letting them down if we go off half-cocked, and I believe Arthur promised everyone no one would, right?"

Roddy seemed angry. He wanted to go back.

"Matt's right, guys. Let's get out of here. Mark it on the map and we, or others will explore another day. Look at it this way," Jules continued, looking at Roddy, "if there are only one hundred adults alive in the world, and if we are four of them, that's a significant percentage. It's four percent of the population and eight percent of the men. Roddy, you seem upset. Imagine how Mary Beth would feel to lose you."

Roddy's face changed. "You got me. Okay, let's get out of here."

Chapter 25
Palaver with Base

"Base, can you hear? Base...over." Matt keyed the radio while being buffeted by some nasty winds. The cold numbed his face and tore at the sleeve of his parka. He turned the back of his hood to face the wind and got some relief. A distant but clearly distinguishable voice came back.

"This is base. Who've I got? Over."

"Matt. Who's on duty? Over."

"Al Parks, Matt. How you doing? Been waiting for your call. Over."

"Hi Al. You didn't answer when we called at six. Over."

"Yeah, I know. Antenna blew over. Had to go up and do it again. What's happening? Over."

"Hey Al, could we get past this 'Over' stuff? You'll know when I stop talking."

"Give it a try. Go ahead."

"Okay, we're parked for the night. We've discovered something alive."

"Are you breaking up or did I hear you say you found something alive?"

"You heard me."

"That's big news. Come back."

"You haven't heard all of it."

"Meaning?"

"It's something we've never encountered before. Huge, bird or bat-like, it flies, lives in a massive cave on the western slope of Front Mountain just below Templar Pass. We have it marked on our map." He stopped. The silence dragged for a few moments; then Al came back on. "I think that's why, 'Over' is needed. So, how big is huge?"

Matt passed the radio to Roddy. "Roddy here, Al. The thing is five feet in girth and the wingspan on a guess has to be twenty feet. Uh...over."

Silence, then, "Repeat that?"

Roddy repeated what he had said.

"You take some of that party fluid with you, Roddy? Something like that doesn't exist."

"You're right, Al. It doesn't exist."

"You're serious, aren't you?"

"Scouts honor."

"Wow!"

"And guess what?"

"Go ahead."

"We decided not to investigate before we called in. How about us?"

"Whaddya know, it works," Al said, almost to himself.

"What?"

"Nothing. I called down for Arthur and other interested parties. They should be here soon. Tomorrow Ernie is going to hook up the permanent base below and have a slave unit up here so we can communicate from both places more easily. Right now we have a radio like yours down there picking up the calls. Works, but tomorrow it'll be better. Ernie is earning his money lately."

"What money?"

"Just an expression."

"Oh...okay, I'm handing this back to Matt."

Matt took the radio and keyed it. "Back, Al. Roddy sure likes to talk."

"Talking's good. Means you're still alive."

"Bunch of comedians," Roddy said.

"Ah, Arthur and company."

"Who's there?"

"Mary Beth, for one, Sue Dorchester. Doc came up, too, when he heard about your discovery."

"Hi to all. Tell Mary Beth that Roddy is behaving himself, barely."

Mary Beth keyed in the mike. "That's my man. Hey, Roddy."

Roddy keyed his own radio. "Hey, Mary Beth. Don't listen to these fools. I'm being good...sort of."

"I liked the 'good' part. Not sure about the 'sort of.'"

Arthur took the mike. "Hello, explorers. Found something, did you? I got it second hand. Could I hear it again?"

"Sure," Matt said and waved Roddy to take it. Roddy proceeded to tell the whole story, from the point where Jules went to explore the cleft and discovered the cave, through the part where he and Jules had gone deeper and made their shocking discovery, then back to running out of the cavern. "Tails between our legs!"

"Smart," Arthur commented from far away. "He who runs away scared...lives to tell someone who cared. Bad poetry, but it carries the message. "

"Anyway," Matt rejoined the discussion, "we are safe and we will all stick together in the future."

"Good idea, Matt. I wonder if the 'something' you saw is mutated from normal Earthly stock?"

"That's frightening. Radiation can do strange things to DNA, but in twelve years?" Mike interjected.

"Seems like a short time, Mike, but we live in a new world. We don't know what we'll find."

"True, but I'm a little less settled now."

"Yes, I'm afraid we're going to have to mull this over. You all be careful, very careful."

"We will, " Matt said. "This one came out all right and now that we know that other life may have survived and even mutated, we'll be more careful than ever."

"Anything else to pass on?"

"No. We're going over Templar Pass tomorrow and we ought to be close to or on the road to Ross River by tomorrow night. Wish we had some weapons."

"A sharpened stick can provide a sense of security," Arthur said, " and it makes a good walking stick, too."

Matt laughed. "Always thinking, Arthur," he said.

"We'd all better be doing that, Matt."

"We know. Better get some sleep. Going off."

Sue and Mary Beth spoke into the mike together, "You boys take care now, you hear?"

Roddy keyed, "We will."

They put away their radios and settled down for the night.

Chapter 26
Breaking Ground

Jerry Ells was up early following his quick eyeball survey of the town site the day before. His job title had changed to Town Planner and Chief Engineer. Hal, Don, Mark and Hans had stayed at the depot to check out and learn how to run the equipment. They'd shaken Jerry's hand and Hal had thanked him for all the good work.

"Not afraid of work. Could watch it all day long and not feel an ounce of fear." He smiled. They cracked up, probably better than the usual groan that old chestnut would normally get. Another way of saying, "So long."

The biosphere had no surveying equipment, but it had a lot of string and stakes were lying all over the place for the taking in the near woods. He took two off-duty plant life specialists with him, first to help lay out the dimensions of the Citadel, their place of safety as he thought of it —just in case. Second, the two women could examine the grasses and grains in place and try to determine how safe or unsafe they might be.

To that end they both brought magnifying glasses and a microscope with them. Al Parks had been asked to use his carpentering skills to fashion a tow-along wagon. He made it from their rapidly depleting store of finished lumber below. It was a box three feet wide and five feet long set on a solid axle. Two long handles jutted out in front at an angle, since they only had people power now. Al promised to readjust the handles when they could get the goats up top and use them.

More than once someone wished they had horses, but the biosphere simply couldn't handle spirited animals larger than dogs. He pilfered some wheels from a broken med cart in Doc's office (he told Doc he didn't need it anyway since everyone came to him) and attached everything with nails and screws. They could see the merchant in him. He guaranteed his work...for thirty days.

The cart carried all the equipment needed for the first day of fashioning a town out of a field. Three thousand feet of strong white string took up some space. They carried a holer, rake, two shovels, an axe and a maul. Jerry carried one of the four Geiger counters the Bio had. It had been decided that a counter should be located in every major area where they started a work project.

"Okay, ladies," he said, "we're going to have an easy day in the fields of New Beginnings."

"We're ready. What do you want us to do?"

Jerry outlined the job. The three, Jerry, Nancy Spiller and Maude Nash moved through the fields and light scrub making paths, digging holes, placing stakes and stringing them. In free moments, they took samples of the various grasses and subjected them to magnified and microscopic examination. They identified them and began a journal of their findings to put together later.

The day dawned beautiful and bright, but the first clouds they had seen since emerging from the "cocoon" began appearing out of the west in mid-morning. During the day they overspread the entire sky and began to thicken. Now and then Jerry would look up and gauge the clouds. It looked like rain, but until it smelled like rain, he didn't call a halt to the day's proceedings. That happened a little after four.

"Ladies, I'd prefer not to be caught out in a rainstorm, not, at least, until I am sure that it's not spitting radioactivity."

"We'll start picking up now," Nancy said.

"Thanks, and thanks for all of your work."

"We're all in this together. I've had a good time. Did you, Maude?"

"Sure did. Call me anytime."

"Well, you might be interested to know that I've taken readings all day in various places and for all intents this valley is no more dangerous than on any sunny day. But I don't want to take chances, so we'll quit for today and we'll come back after this is over. Then I'll take readings again. If they're like today, I'll begin to believe."

"Everyone will."

"Yes, they will. Hal Hasting is doing the same thing up at the Depot."

"The Depot?" Maude asked.

"That's the name that stuck after we discovered the equipment storage place."

"Oh, I hadn't heard."

Nancy told Jerry that they'd collected a lot of data on the plant life.

"Great. That's really important. Okay, let's get back before the rain."

"Want to leave the cart here?"

"Best not. If the clouds rain the wrong thing, it will contaminate everything it touches."

"Of course, that's right. Want me to pull that thing for a while?"

"No, that's okay. It pulls easily enough. I'm fine." They made the trip back in silence. Jerry appreciated the two women, nicely curved, nothing gaudy about them. Maude and Nancy were thirty-four and had graduated from the same college in eastern Minnesota. They'd been lifelong friends. They could be feisty, but generally they were as mellow as bright, industrious people could be and they were fine workers.

Jerry mulled over their conversation. Logic dictated that if the valley was radioactivity free when they broke out, what rain they would be getting on this day wouldn't contain any, either. He decided not to say anything. Better to err on the side of caution until he'd personally seen enough good days to believe in them.

Jerry Ells had not formed a serious relationship amongst the female population of the biosphere. He was a thinker and spent much time consulting his largely unused books on engineering. Now he felt he was doing what he was made for and he silently reveled in it. He didn't want any woman to be too close, but someday, the way things were changing, he might very well change along with them.

The women had taken note of his developing works during the day and they were impressed with how easy he made the entire process appear. Nancy thought he was handsome in an angular way, but Mike was taking most of her time and she felt very comfortable with him. Well, she hoped Jerry would find someone. *I'm sure he will*, she thought. She thought about her relationship with Mike from time to time in terms of children. The old bio-clock kept ticking away, and Mike didn't seem interested in having kids. She wanted kids, yet she felt conflicted, too. Funny how watching Jerry perform so flawlessly should put a lump in her throat.

They arrived back at the cave and interrupted her reverie. The sky had lowered to "seriously threatening" and Jerry realized they hadn't arrived at the cave entrance a moment too soon.

Arthur was there to greet them.

"Hello, Arthur. What brings you topside today?" Maude called.

Arthur gestured out into the valley. Maude turned in time to see the sky open up. Lightning flashed, followed on its heels by thunder. The flash and crash were so close they were one.

"Whew! All of that, Maude. This'll be our first chance to find out what the clouds contain."

"In spades, from the look of it."

"Just what we need." Lightning etched her handsome face and thunder covered her words.

"What you say?"

"Getting chilly," she said. "I'm going down."

"See you later."

Jerry stood to one side, watching the communal by-play and realized he enjoyed it. That was a revelation. He didn't believe he ever thought such things. He turned his attention to Arthur.

Arthur had a Geiger counter and Jerry watched him sweep it slowly back and forth at the oncoming storm.

"Nothing."

"Best news of all," Jerry said.

"I really didn't think it would be problematical."

"I didn't either, Arthur, but it's nice to confirm it."

He turned to gaze across the wide valley, west to east. The sky broke and the rain came down in sheets and torrents. Arthur searched the valley with the binoculars. No one should be out in that and no one was. He watched and waited. Gradually the frenetic pace of the deluge eased into a steady soaking rainstorm. Without the benefit of the old Weather Channel or any other TV station, for that matter, they were set back one hundred years to a time when storms came when they did and you knew it when it happened.

Although Arthur was a scientist, everyone knew he seldom found fault with easier, less complex times, when life was slower and perhaps more meaningful. Introspective, Jerry watched awhile longer, seeing but not seeing, and then returned to the biosphere.

Jerry thought about the work they had done. They'd done well. They'd made a start.

Chapter 27
Templar Pass

"Base?" Matt's voice came over the speaker.

"Gil here, Matt."

It was six a.m. Per the Bio's lottery; Gil Castonguay had the monitor at the moment. To learn the radio equipment and be ready for transmissions from the exploring party was altogether too easy, as the men only came through sporadically. Therefore, monitors brought books on their specialties or on whatever else interested them. The planners made sure a large collection of the world's best fiction was also part of the library. Although unlimited space did not exist, hardcover books as well as audio books on CD were allowed because of their psychological value. CD's were still available as Ernie had kept the playback units operating even after the computers failed, but the were of limited use as the Bio had only three for its population. The women could knit if that was their thing. The sphere's sheep had been producing wool for years. No one among them could sit and do nothing. The depleted world had one motivated bunch struggling to come back.

"Morning, Gil. We're starting up the pass. With luck we should hit the crest in two or three hours. We'll place a booster up there somewhere when we can see the other side, and another beyond to give us omni-directional radio for the next valley chain."

"Got you. I'll mark the log. Anything interesting?"

"Be glad to get away from this area. Creeping us out."

"You weren't bothered?"

"No, not at all, but a couple of us slept with one eye open."

Gil laughed. "Glad you kept your sense of humor."

"It's not totally intact, but it'll come back. We're heading out."

"Good climbing."

The four shouldered their backpacks and made their way around the sheer cliff face. A narrow ledge, uncomfortably negotiated, led to easier climbing. It was then that Jules saw it.

"Guys, up ahead. You see what I see?"

The others craned their necks.

"Bones?"

They made their way to a flat ledge and all stood around Jules' find. Medium boned, definitely human, bleached by years in the harsh climate, nothing was connected now, but the bones hadn't been disturbed.

"Unlikely place for anybody to be," Jules ventured. "I think we've found Alfie."

"Who?" Roddy asked.

"The guy who ran, Alfie Potter."

"Oh, yeah. Probably."

Matt keyed the radio. "Base."

"Go ahead."

"Believe we've found number nineteen. Not gnawed, either no animals near or too sick by the time they came around."

"I'll put it in the logbook and tell Arthur."

"Roger."

"I wonder if Seth is more at ease now."

Matt said, "It's sad. C'mon guys."

The hillside above the ledge had a good angle, maybe twenty degrees. It wasn't very stable, but in time they'd picked their way up. They fell behind Matt's projected timeline and didn't get to the solid high place they needed for a permanent booster installation until about ten. Jules chose the top of a reddish beige vertical monolith that looked like it might stay for another million years or so. Pulling at his chin, Jules decided that normal upslope winds would also keep snow from covering the booster.

"This'll work."

"Good view toward the catcher on our mountain," Matt replied.

"I'll go," Jules said. "Give me a hand up, big guy." Roddy came over and cupped his hands. Jules stepped into the catapult and Roddy quickly lifted Jules up and over the top of the eight-foot pinnacle. Jules eyeballed the home mountain and then his line of sight expanse of the pass, nodded and unhooked a booster to plant on top. He hammered tiny pitons on the legs into the rock enough to hold it. When it was stable, he carefully unfurled the antenna, spreading it out like a Chinese fan and latching it to the metal protrusion on the base.

Looking down, he smirked and said to Roddy, "Knew all that brawn would come in handy some day."

Roddy came back. "You'll get yours."

"Base." Taking his radio out, Jules called, "Give me a strength check."

"Okay. Move it a little."

Jules complied.

"Come back a few degrees."

Pause, then, "Looks good. Button it down."

"Okay." Jules did something to the unit and then went to its other side and adjusted its antenna fan to point through the cleft of the pass.

"Coming down." Jules turned and slid off the rock face. Roddy caught him for a soft landing.

"Whadda team," Mike said.

"Okay, guys, let's see what's on the other side," Matt said. They resumed their trek. Except for a house-sized boulder here and there, the land became relatively flat. They walked easily and fifteen minutes later began to descend. Matt looked back toward the pinnacle where they'd left the booster. He couldn't see it.

"We've got to find a high place with a big view or we'll lose contact."

Mike spied a potential site a half-mile to the right and a couple hundred feet higher up.

He pointed. "We have to go there."

They made the detour; couldn't lose contact with Base. They climbed up and down over land that quite possibly had never seen a human foot. Nothing friendly about this part of the pass, but they eventually arrived at the place. It provided a good back view, but as important, they could see a tiny thread of river several thousand feet below on the opposing side. Even with binoculars, Matt couldn't see the tiny booster on the other side of the pass, but he thought it would be all right.

"Base, copy?"

"Got you, five by. Nice signal."

"This booster should give us this side of the range."

"Roger."

"Jules," Matt said, "You do this well. Want to plant another?"

"Sure." Jules took the booster and mounted the highest point he could find with an open valley view and planted it, this time in a depression filled with red dirt. He used the six-inch pitons for this job, tugged at his installation enough to believe winter storm winds wouldn't bother it and adjusted the booster in the casual direction of the catcher on the other side of the pass.

"You improve on that signal?" he asked Base.

"Don't move it. You're fine."

"Okay. We're heading down."

"How's it look?"

"Rocky here, but good news. Lot of forest way down and we can see a river. We're heading for it."

"Right. Base out."

The reddish rock of the mountain range eventually gave way to hardy scrub and below four thousand feet, trees began to appear.

"The east side seems more friendly," Mike offered.

"We'll see," Matt replied.

Jules started to whistle. They looked with new eyes at old growth. Nothing but pine needles stirred. The land, except for the thickening forest, appeared devoid of life. Another thousand feet down they found growth so thick it became difficult to move easily.

"Stick close, men," Matt suggested.

"Hard not to," Roddy said. The forest closed around them. They watched the ground and the tops of the trees. They tried to penetrate the thickness of interwoven growth with eyesight that failed ten feet in front of them. They fought their way downward for two hours, making occasional radio checks. Suddenly, the trees thinned abruptly and they found themselves facing a huge field a mile wide and maybe twice that long. It descended at a steep angle. They walked out into the field and stopped suddenly.

Mike said, "Do you see what I see?"

"Yeah."

What arrested their attention was a mountain goat, not like one they'd ever seen before. It stood in the middle of the field, half a mile away. They stood in the three-foot tall grass and stared, and even though they were too far away for the animal to hear them, it picked up its head and looked directly at them.

Chapter 28
Dangerous Encounter

Roddy sucked in his breath. "That sucker's big."
At a guess, the goat had to stand seven feet tall. It was off-white and sported the same long, stringy hair found on a normal mountain goat. It showed no fear. It seemed...interested, even intelligent!
"Very strange," Matt said.
And in that moment it began to trot toward them.
Jules keyed his radio. "Base, can you hear us."
"Base, Sue here."
"Jules, Sue. I'm going to describe something to you. Listen closely." He stopped and called to the others, "Hey, guys, better grab some sticks or something."
"Already thought of that, Jules," Matt said as he began to cast around. Roddy and Mike looked around, too. There was nothing nearby that looked solid enough to be used as a weapon.
In the midst of turning back, Mike said, "Whoa, pardner!"
The other three turned. Standing behind them were three more huge mountain goats. How they had gotten within twenty feet of the four none could say, but there they were.
Jules talked excitedly into his radio. "Sue, I started to describe an unusual specimen of mountain goat we saw in the big field ahead of us. Now we're surrounded. These animals should be shy to the point of disappearing. They are not only *not* shy, but they seem to have us boxed in. We don't know what to make of it. We have made no overt move toward any of them. I'd better describe them. They stand seven feet tall, about the size of a Percheron, but thinner, maybe stringy is the word. They have an off-white shaggy coat. Their size and mannerisms are

not what we would expect. If they are intelligent, and it appears they are, we are outmatched. There is nothing here we could pick up to defend ourselves with. We might try climbing these pines, but they could get to us before we could climb high enough. Pass the word. The world is still a dangerous place, and there's life out here."

"I will, Jules. Be careful!" Sue sounded frightened.

Matt happened to be looking at the closest goat when Sue's voice came though the radio. The goat looked directly at Jules when she spoke. The animal seemed startled by the sound from nowhere.

Jules continued, while keeping an eye on the three closest. "If these are mutations, and they must be, they've never seen humans before. I'll try to keep you posted. The fourth one is arriving from the field. We'll know what's in store in a minute."

"Oh, Jules!" Sue was beside herself. "I've called below. They're monitoring but don't have direct voice hookup to you yet. Ernie's working on it. Arthur and a couple of our animal people are coming up with some advice."

Jules broke in. "This is a new situation, Sue. I doubt advice will help."

The fourth mountain goat arrived and stopped twenty feet from them. It stared as the others had. It made no sound, but the other three seemed to know it was the leader. Its coloring was a bit darker and it may have been a couple of years older. The others deferred to the new arrival.

Matt, Mike and Roddy stood a couple feet apart, facing in different directions. They didn't look frightened but they were doing some heavy thinking.

Matt spoke in low tones to the three. "They're looking us over. I suggest we do the same. They might be curious. Our species haven't come in contact before. I think if we appear scared of them, they might make an unhappy decision concerning us. Now, I have an idea. They're big enough to carry us..."

"You mean, ride them?" Roddy broke in.

"They're bigger than horses, why not?"

"Yeah," Jules added, "they'd do for horses, if they'd let us."

"Better," Mike said. "This type of animal is perfect for these mountains. Now we have to find out if they'll let us."

Jules spoke up, "I have an idea, guys. I worked on a ranch a couple of summers during college break. Now, let's see what I learned..." He moved slowly toward the leader. The leader snorted in a very horse-like way and stood it's ground.

"Jules, be careful," Matt called.

"Not afraid, good," Jules breathed. He got to within five feet of the goat when it shied away. "Got my scent, I think. Can't make heads or tails of it. I want to pet its nose and see what that does. This guy is plenty intelligent, though. And blue eyes, too."

He continued to talk soothingly as he looked around. The three other animals stood like statues. They seemed as curious about what would happen next as the men did. The animals were wary, but Jules guessed, had no natural enemies. The goat kept watching him. Jules approached again. His trajectory took him outside of the safety zone, if such could be said they had at all.

"Mike," Matt said, "Key your radio open so Base can hear what's going on."

"Good idea. Base, listen in." He pushed the radio into his belt so the key would stay open and leave his hands free. Just as he did that, the leader goat spun around and put its body between Jules and the others.

"Jules, watch it!" Mike yelled.

Jules spun to stay directly in front of the mountain goat and continued to press forward.

"He's crazy," Roddy breathed.

"No, not crazy, Roddy," Matt said. "He's doing the only thing he can. He's being the aggressor, and it's throwing the animal off. See."

The big goat backed again. Then it twisted sideways and lunged for Jules head or shoulder. Jules wasn't there. The wiry man remembered the lessons learned many summers before. As the goat bared its teeth and lunged, Jules slipped to the other side and put a fist as hard as he could alongside the goat's long face. Off balance from its initial move, the goat went down hard with a squeal no human had ever heard before.

Before it could get up, Jules jumped on its back. Matt, Roddy and Mike stood rooted, voiceless and amazed. What the hell was Jules anyway, Superman?

The mountain goat struggled to its feet and immediately tried to shake Jules from his perch. The man grabbed its sides with his legs, wrapped his arms around the muscular neck and hung on. The other mountain goats seemed to have forgotten the men altogether. They were as engrossed in the action as the men.

The older goat switched one way and the other. Jules hung on. At one point, it dropped to the ground and rolled, hoping to crush the man under its weight. Jules jumped off with split-second timing and was back on before the goat could regain its feet. It got up, bucking, not like a horse, but in goat fashion and it looked incredibly silly. The three watchers would have laughed if the contest weren't so deadly.

The goat tried running next to a tree to scrape off or damage his rider. Jules was quicker. Somehow he seemed to sense just the precise moment to bob or weave, to move or grip tightly. It was a wonder to watch him.

After ten minutes the big goat stopped and put its head down, breathing hard. Jules sat up in his impromptu saddle and stared at the other goats. Then he grabbed the goat's left ear and pulled. Wild mountain goat no more, the creature turned and faced the others.

"They communicate without words, guys," he said. "I don't think its mental, but some sort of twitching movement serves as language for them. They are quite bright. Much smarter than pre-war horses! What I'm trying to do is to persuade the other goats that I am their leader now. If I succeed, you'll all have mounts for the rest of the trip."

Jules went back to staring at the three riderless goats. They began to fidget and to move about. Then one of them started to shake and move just a little. Under him, the former leader goat did some of the same. The goats began to approach the men. Each knelt down on its front legs and made its back available for one man apiece.

Not without great trepidation did they mount, but Jules said it was okay and they would be fine.

"I'm not going to say that these goats have some kind of religion, but they have a well developed social structure. There is a top goat, and it gives counsel to all the others. This one," he pointed down, "has given me the leadership of his 'tribe,' I'll call it, and I get it with all the trappings."

"You are one amazing man, Jules," Roddy said fervently. "I can't believe what you just did."

Just then, Mike remembered he had an open key to Base. He released it and the radio was immediately filled with voices.

Mike keyed back, "All okay, here. We'll have a story to tell, but later. Right now we have to learn how to ride our neo-goats. Think I'll name mine Trigger. Later, out!"

Matt took charge again. "Great job, Jules. Now, how do we make these animals go?"

"Watch!" Gently, with his in-turned heels, he applied pressure to the lower sides of the goat's flank. The goat moved forward. Jules clucked softly and the goat's ears turned back as if awaiting a command. He said, "Left," at the same time placing his right hand on the right side of the goat's neck. The animal obligingly moved left. Jules took the animal through several maneuvers, making it look easy.

"It *is* easy, gentlemen," he said, as if he'd read their minds, "much easier than training a horse, actually. Horses are—were—very beautiful, but not very bright. These animals will be much easier to train. At the same time we will need to respect their intelligence. We have fallen into a race of beings that will become more partners than servants. Fortunately, their social level allows for a respected leader, one they will all look up to and serve. We, the last remnant of humanity, have already begun to ascend. We've taken over another, lesser race. But maybe not that much lesser."

"How do you know these things?" Matt asked.

"My mother told me a long, long time ago that I had a special gift."

"What do you mean?"

"I learned how to feel, maybe it's empathize, with lower creatures. No big deal to me, but my summers on the ranch were something else. Nobody could figure out why I could ride anything they had there, especially Thunder. Kind of why I jumped at the chance to conquer this animal."

"Wow," Mike said, "so why did you become a chemist?"

"Always loved messing around with chemicals. There's a few stories I haven't bounced off you guys."

"Bet we'll hear 'em," Matt laughed, "but right now let's solidify our new position."

"Yeah, sure. First thing you do is talk to your mount. I didn't do that initially because it was him or me. Now we need to become benevolent partners."

"Go ahead."

Jules leaned forward and spoke lovingly into the back-turned ear of his mount. "I'm going to call you Conan. Only a great leader can become a great follower."

Conan listened intently and turned his head as if to say, "I understand." And perhaps he did.

Chapter 29
First Digs

Hal and his crew arrived at the depot early. Today's work involved getting the payloader, small shovel and grader filled and going. All equipment had fuel, but most were near empty. Hans tinkered the electric forklift back into operation, making it much easier to fuel the bigger pieces.

"That's got it." Hans re-hooked the recharged battery pack. He stood on the rear platform and checked over the simple controls.

"Here I go." He moved the joystick fractionally and the fork rose smoothly off the ground. He moved the clutch to "Forward" and engaged it. A lever to its right applied power. The unit proceeded smoothly forward. Hans played with it in the open until he felt confident and then nodded to Hal.

"Grab a drum from over here," Hal said.

The barrels lay on their sides, enclosed by steel uprights. The forks were pre-adjusted to fit on either side of any barrels. Hans turned the forklift on its heel, adjusting the height of the fork to come under one of the partial barrels and lifted it like he'd been doing it for years.

"Easy!" he said to Hal.

"Okay, okay, you've got the job." He laughed. "Take it to the front, over there," he pointed, "and grab a nozzle."

"Got it." Hans stopped the machine, put on the brake and dismounted. The nozzle fit into the end of the drum and twist-locked. The neoprene gasket was in excellent condition. A five-foot hose dangled from it.

"Give me a hand turning the barrel, Hal." They muscled the barrel a hundred and eighty degrees. Now the nozzle sat at the bottom.

Hal stood back and scratched his chin. "Full barrels are going to be a problem. Ah, I've got it. We take the barrel out and set it on the ground, attach the nozzle and then roll the barrel over. One guy can do that. Then you can pick it up with no problem."

"That'll work."

Hans remounted the forklift, lifted the barrel high enough to clear the floor a couple of feet and headed out to the big cave. He came to the payloader first. Raising the barrel above the height of the fuel tank, he inserted the nozzle into the tank and pulled the handle. Fuel poured in. Twenty gallons topped it off. Fifteen left.

Hans made four trips and filled three pieces using partial barrels to empty them first. Now their reservoir held exactly thirty-three full barrels of diesel fuel. Big construction equipment could work all day without refueling, so they could leave most of the stuff at the town site and bring the payloader back to carry fuel to it as needed.

They made short work of starting the three construction vehicles. Being inside out of rain and weather had preserved them perfectly. Several squirt cans of light oil on a shelf in the fuel cave sprayed judiciously in the right places freed up what didn't work well on the get-go and the machines fired up almost immediately.

"Yeah, man!" Don yelled the sentiments of all.

Hans took over the Payloader. He acclimated readily. Mark Cohen and Don Smythe took on the bucket shovel and grader respectively. A half hour of study and experimentation produced "three working dudes," Hal said.

"I'll stay here and coordinate. Don, you grade a big path for the other pieces. I placed a few sticks of that 20% dynamite we found under the rock shelf at the drop-off. Should break it up enough so Don can smooth it off make getting to town easy."

"Okay Hal, let 'er rip," Matt called.

"Base," Hall said into his radio, "We're blasting."

"Go ahead, Hal. Everyone is alerted."

They stood inside the edge of the big cave while Hal connected the leads.

"Now," he called and pushed the plunger. A muffled thud shook everything. Hal went to look. When he came back, he said to Don, "Go ahead."

Don mounted the high seat and cranked his diesel. He moved slowly into bright sunlight.

The red rock had nearly pulverized and Don had little trouble grading. The incline was still steep, but the equipment's low center of gravity handled it.

With a wave, Don set off for the town site.

"You guys head for the work site. Jerry'll be there."

The men fired up their machines and headed after Don. When they arrived Jerry stood by the outside edge of town with a big smile.

"Welcome to New Beginnings."

They looked over the long grassy area. Dotted here and there in an orderly pattern they saw stakes planted at intervals. A long straightaway spread north and south. On the east and west Jerry and his crew had set out town plots with lots of land in between.

"Main Street," Jerry said, looking at them.

"Just like the old West," Mark said.

"Yuh," Jerry said with a broad expanse of hand, a big smile and a suddenly developed western twang, "Down that-a-way is the post office. Pony Express should be comin' through any time. Futher down is the saloon and up heah yuh'll find the schoolhouse. Mighty perty schoolmarm, too. Sheriff's office midway down. Bettuh leave yer shootin' irons on tuh fence, theah. We got a ordinance 'bout thet."

"Pretty good, Jerry." Mark laughed and the other two chuckled. "Ever think of being on stage? One leaving in a few."

Who hadn't heard that one before, but it struck Jerry's funny bone and he doubled over laughing. Finally he got control and said, "Okay you guys, this is what I'd like you to do. Don, you have the grader. We need a street. Can you scrape the first three inches off down along this lane? That should remove the waving grains and give us a start. Mark and Hans, come with me."

Jerry strode off towards the center of town.

Hans called to him, "Hey, want a ride?"

"Nope. Town isn't that big."

The Payloader and bucket shovel drove off. Jerry showed them a large plot he'd staked out. "This is the first order of business, guys. We need to build a place to run to if something bad happens."

"I hate to ask, Jerry," Hans said, "but like what?"

"Precaution, Hans. No one knows. It's just a good idea. Arthur thinks so and for now I agree."

Hans was silent for a moment. "You're right. With our "huge" population we can't be too careful, can we?"

"No."

"Well, we've got the Bio and the big construction cave and in town we'll have this. What do you want us to do?"

"I think this place should have a cellar. The rest of the houses should be okay without. I'm trying to figure a ten-minute run, absolutely max to get safely to the fort. I planned out the town with that in mind. The plots are big enough so we can grow some of the food we eat. The veggie people can deal with that. We have animals and we'll need to create herds. I'm figuring in another ten years we'll be five times the population we have now. Barring accident, most of us can plan to be around for another fifty years. We'll outgrow ourselves pretty quick, if you look at it long term."

"Okay, one thing at a time. What's the rock and ledge situation?"

"This valley's been here for nearly half a million years, best I can figure. Plenty of topsoil and it goes down deep. Deep, it's probably much older, but I'm no geologist. You shouldn't run into rock we'll have to blast near the surface except in rare instances."

"Okay, drop the line." Jerry cut the line and the two men moved into the designated area and jockeyed into position.

"Jerry," Hans called over the roar of the engines, as the engineer started away, "where do you want the residue?"

"Oh, yeah." He pointed to a low area two hundred yards north of them. "Drop it over there. We'll build up some land. We can level it anytime. Just dump it."

"Roger." Hans went to work clearing the perimeter area of the fort.

Inside, Mark's bucket dug deep into untouched valley soil.

Chapter 30
Planning Committee

Inside the biosphere a serious meeting went on...and on. Arthur presided and although the meeting had lasted for five hours already, no one seemed anxious to leave. Certain women designated to watch the children now had a radio on low, so they could hear, too. No one wanted to be outside these discussions as democracy flourished.

Arthur spoke from his chair. He felt profoundly fatigued and wanted a resolution to the meeting, but he hated to suspend by-play because he felt that fundamental things were happening. The new, growing civilization had to get through this, had to agonize, had to agree or disagree and had to air its feelings. In the end the majority would have its way, but Arthur knew holdouts would not pull in the same direction. All must agree intellectually and if not, those with different views had to have wiggle room.

This meeting compiled all the information they'd gathered to date. He'd gotten it all out on the table, fledgling law, religion, the institution of marriage, how far it should go, how much freedom they should allow themselves, the whole thing. Could they rely on reason entirely? What law and what justice? What to tell the children? How to bring them up? Schools, churches, allow or disallow? Within the community there was much division. They'd touched a deep nerve where they all lived. Repressed feelings had no place in the discussions, or did they? If a pure route to the future were to emerge, would they all have to bare their souls? Yet, how did one lose feelings, prejudices, deeply buried secrets? How did one bare a soul hidden within conventions and upbringing, genetic differences and economic stratification, wrong decisions, mistakes, and yes, guilt? How did one do that?

Arthur had said, "We cannot allow divisiveness." But how to prevent it? Everyone knew that to hold on too tight was the easiest way to cause rebellion. These were uncommonly intelligent and well read people. They knew, but they disagreed in that same knowledge. Parameters existed in every individual and in the sense that no one could stand in the same space simultaneously with another, so, too, could they not walk in the same mental footprints as the others. Their roots went back to a destroyed civilization. Those roots ran much deeper than any wanted to believe.

The luminous clock that served the assembly room showed eleven. People were beginning to yawn and their minds turned with more frequency to their duties. Finally, Arthur had had enough and he could see he wasn't alone.

"People, we need to stop. I hate to, because we have aired our arguments with righteous intensity and I feel we are getting somewhere important. Please hold your thoughts until the next meeting, tomorrow night. With Gina's help, I will compile all the material we have discussed, put it into some semblance of order and present it again tomorrow. Write down thoughts uppermost in your minds to preserve it. Meeting adjourned."

"Arthur, are you all right?" Gina looked worried. She knew the time he'd put into this. For him it was nearly a crusade. He wanted to lift himself and the new civilization by its bootstraps.

"I'm tired. I'm fine, Gina."

"You can't do it all by yourself."

"But I'm not. Everyone is participating. It makes me feel proud."

"You are doing too much," Gina said severely. "You are not as young as we are. You don't have the resilience."

"I'm not going to hurt myself, Gina. Don't worry so about me."

"How can I help it, Arthur?" But she backed off. He loved her for it.

They walked along toward Arthur's cubicle in silence. Abruptly, Gina took his hand and led him to the dining area. Several others were there before them. They greeted the two and went back to their private conversations. Gina went to the urn and brought them a cup of tea.

"Let's work here, if we must do any more tonight."

"That'll be fine."

Gina took out her notepad and quietly reviewed with Arthur what she had written. From her numbers, three quarters of the adult population agreed very closely on marriage. They thought it a good institution, but that marriage worked because of commitment, two people deciding that life would be better with each than without, not because the institution was presided over by some deity, or, in fact, even because it was an institution.

Gina had no problem believing that a higher power was responsible for them, but like most, she wondered about how ineffective, uninvolved, and irresponsible such a power might be, that it could sit idly by while the world blew itself up.

It was too hard to accept the old pretext that "God moves in mysterious ways," given their circumstance. She was too bright to believe it, yet her roots were deep. She knew many of the women felt as she did and she believed that she must come to a change in her thinking for the future of their colony to work. How to resolve it? She didn't know.

A harder school of thought, based on reason and aired with vehemence during their discussions, suggested that God in however many forms was a creation of man and that such a creation could be relied upon only so far as it could rely upon Man's own credibility. Numerous examples made their way into the conversation. On its face, little rational argument could be made for the other side, and eventually the few who felt devoutly that God had a plan for humanity ducked behind the veil of belief without reason and stayed there. They would be hard to move.

Arthur broke into the monologue. "It is terribly important we resolve the issue of religion. If we don't, some of us will leave. If they survive, the seeds of new conflict will have been sown and eventually, fifty or two hundred or two thousand years from now, it will be apocalypse all over again. The human animal must learn, and it must do it now."

"Then we'll have to change our nature," Gina said.

Arthur despaired. Human nature must change. But how? The circle closed again. It depressed him.

"Okay, as to marriage, we can probably get everyone to buy in to a civil ceremony at most. At the least, all it should take is two individuals professing their love and life commitment."

"Yes. And there will always be people who won't commitment with any of the other sex. And what about gay? How do we treat that?"

"The psychological profiles of every member of the Bio," Arthur said, "indicate that we are all strongly monogamous and strongly heterosexual. The planners were old fashioned in that regard. But to try to legislate the freedom to be ourselves in all of our complexity would be like asking a teenager to abstain from sex. Young hormones don't allow it. Not only that, but project our repopulation mission a hundred years into the future. Gay is not a choice. It will likely turn up somewhere. Maybe we'd better leave a place for it."

"Guidelines are what we must have, firm enough and loose enough. Driving deeply the values we decide to live with is what we'll have to rely on. What else can we do?"

"I hope we can swing this."

Gina said, "I truly believe we have as good a group as any you'd find. We'll be fine. Let's go on."

"What's next?"

"Law. I think everyone agrees we must have law. The majority will have to negotiate with the minority to totally agree on what it should be. The one thing I got out of it was that there shouldn't be a whole lot of it."

"Right, and I agree. Ideally, we should pick one or two precepts of basic law and make them in all things the only law. Perhaps we should take the Ten Commandments, or the five social ones anyway, and combine them into one single law that covers all. The degree of punishment would be based upon the seriousness of the act or omission."

"What a marvelous idea, Arthur! One law that can be interpreted in all ways as a matter of degree." Gina sounded excited.

"And if we took the Commandments that apply to our new society, those who insist on remaining true to their religious teachings would find it easier to agree."

"Bring that up at the meeting tomorrow."
"Yes, I think I will, but tonight I have to think about what our law should be and how to make the wording all inclusive."
"I'll think about it, too."

Chapter 31
An Unusual Ride

Jules led the group now. Matt still had most say, but as a thoughtful leader he knew he needed to yield to expertise. As resilient individuals in a situation with no precedent, Jules had stepped forward, taken the challenge and won the day. They shied away from thoughts of how it might have come out without Jules.

In the lead, Jules on Conan now rode steeply downward toward the lower forest. As they approached it, a herd of mountain goats appeared where the trees stopped and the grasses began. Conan, head high, looked proud again. The difference Jules felt was slight, but significant. Conan now proudly carried his master.

"Conan," Jules said to his mount. The ears turned back and Conan listened intently. "You need to inform the herd that they are to stay in their feeding ground. Tell them that you are taking your human on a long journey. Tell them to await your return. Can you do that?"

Conan craned his head partially around and looked at Jules with one eye. Then he stood perfectly still as if contemplating the sounds, as if the meaning of this foreign tongue was reassembling into understanding of some sort. Shifting to a position that took in the bulk of the approaching herd, he gave a piercing sound that seemed part whinny and part bleat. Jules believed he'd gotten his message across. The mountain goat herd stopped twenty feet in front of Conan and he started to twitch and shimmy. A ripple of shimmies wove through the herd.

As a quiet aside to Matt and the others, Jules said, "These animals are more than intelligent. I'm sure Conan grasped my idea and he's passing it on to the herd. I couldn't do that."

"But they're not dangerous?" Matt replied.

"It's not something I could explain. How do you explain a feeling?"

"You're the boss."

Jules had another idea. "Conan, tell them to be ready to migrate through the high pass above them on our return. We want them to meet other humans. We will care for you and you will care for us. Tell them."

Again Conan stood in thought, considering the strange sounds. Then he made that sound and the shimmying began again. When it stopped, the entire herd knelt on their forelegs briefly, made the sound and galloped off.

Jules spoke conversationally to the others. "Unusual sound. Believe I'll call it a "blinny." Now do you agree that they are highly intelligent creatures?"

Roddy spoke first. "Jules, I can't tell you how glad I am that you're on our side."

Jules laughed. "I can't tell you how glad I am that I'm out here with you. The lab is going to be pretty bleak when we get back."

"I have a feeling, Jules," Matt said, "that your lab time is about over. Others can be trained for what you do. Managing a herd of neo-goats might take up a lot of your time."

"Yes. I have a real empathy for these creatures. I think I might be able to train them to do a lot in our valley. I have a strong feeling they will cooperate and assist us voluntarily. I think they will pick up English handily. They might teach us a thing or two."

"After what I saw, I can believe almost anything," Mike put in.

"Goes for all of us," Matt said. "Shall we..."

"Yeah."

Four mounted riders atop four unlikely creatures of Earth picked their way toward the eastern valley. As they rode, Matt called Base and gave them the complete story. A legend was born.

The forest below turned out to be much thinner than that above. Their steeds had little trouble negotiating the steep hillsides and deep valleys. As night finally approached, Matt called a halt.

"Will we need to tie these Neos, Jules?"

"No, we shouldn't do that. I don't believe they will run. It's like they've entered into a contract with us. We are their masters, but they are our partners. Understand?"

"Not really, but we'll follow your lead."

"Look, the leader was beaten. That doesn't take anything away from him, not the way he sees it. He has simply moved into a different relationship with other creatures, us. He owes us. And I think that we owe him, because he has put his trust in us. That make any sense?"

"No, but I don't care tonight. If you say handle it this way, that's the way we'll do it."

"Okay. I don't want to beat the subject to death. Incidentally, you might think of names for your rides. Get them to associate you with your mount. You'll make them feel special."

"You're kidding," Roddy said.

"Never more serious, Roddy. We have a unique opportunity to do something really right here. I bet never in your wildest dreams did you think of riding a seven-foot tall mountain goat, but here they are. And you're doing it. And I think it's good for both races."

"Jules has a point, guys," Matt said, because a bright light just went off in his head. "We have to change. We can't be the humans we were. We have to become something else or we'll be setting our new civilization up to fail. Maybe this is our first real opportunity. I say make the most of it."

They set up camp for the night quietly. Before they went to bed, Mike renamed his goat Geronimo. Trigger just didn't fit. Roddy named his Thor and Matt's became Viceroy. At Jules suggestion, they talked to their mounts for a half hour before crawling into their sleeping bags. The four goats grazed placidly nearby, encircling and protecting them.

Jules lay awake for some time after he heard the regular breathing of the others. He had to help his friends really *see* the new relationships, not just go along with him. The next days would be a proving ground.

Chapter 32
New Beginnings Yields Another Treasure

The town hummed. Word got to everyone on the status of the adventurers as quickly as the Base monitors heard anything. Most fell into the new upside-downside routine easily enough and arguments were remarkably few for people who now lived a dual existence. Care of animals and plants in the caves required part of the day and the rest of the time they spent topside learning new occupations to fit the constantly changing face of their new world.

Everyone agreed with Arthur that it wouldn't be appropriate to bring the animals up any time soon. Corrals and pens would have to be built. There still remained potential dangers in the highly energetic weather topside. And now that other life had been discovered...

"These are the only certain animals left on Earth, just as we are the only certain people. Until we find others, they, and we, are precious in the extreme," he said.

Jerry filled the uncomfortable void. "All the animals know is what they live with. We'll keep living on two levels until time to do it differently."

Arthur nodded. A low buzz filled the room. Waiting was appropriate, so they went on to other things.

Now Arthur quietly began a new quest. He needed leaders. He had several already, but the new society needed more. They had to be right thinking and had to buy into the direction the majority had taken. He smiled at the thought, but culling his crop of scientists and technicians to include a few gadflies was as important as having a solid majority carrying the wave. *They'll keep us from being complacent,* he thought, *because it's our last chance.*

He mentally ticked off his list of current leaders. Broadly, men or women satisfied his criteria if others looked up to them. Somewhere along the line, dominance would be found in most of the one hundred, but not all the time and not at specific times. In fact, at least ninety-percent of the group preferred to let others do the leading. He needed people who would create the foundation of a new civilization, a daunting task. Ten percent wouldn't do. Wouldn't do at all.

Time to move. Arthur left the tunnel and walked out to New Road as Don Smythe had named it. His grader did the majority of the work to produce the wide dirt road that now ran between Biosphere I and New Beginnings and he'd earned the right. No one was unhappy with his choice.

He met Sue Dorchester coming toward him in a hurry.

"Arthur! I'm glad I found you so soon. Hans found something with the backhoe this morning. Jerry wanted you to see it."

"What is it?"

"I don't know, really, some kind of rock formation or something. Hans sounded excited. Jerry looked and told me to run back and get you."

"Why didn't you call me on the radio?"

Sue colored. "I was working with some plants and I took it off. When Jerry approached me all excited, I just flew; I didn't think about it."

Arthur laughed. "He could have called me himself."

Now Sue laughed. "Jerry doesn't get all discombobulated often. Bet he never thought about it, either."

Sue turned and headed back. Arthur grabbed her hand and increased his pace. As a youth, Arthur had developed a healthy interest in geology. What did Hans see?

The two covered the distance and soon overlooked the dig site for the new fort. Jerry and Hans stood at the edge looking down.

"Hey, Arthur, look at this." Jerry called. "Something always gets in the way of a building project, doesn't it?"

Hans spoke up from below. "Arthur, look at what I found! Can you identify them?"

Arthur looked down. A smile of delight covered his face. Dinosaur tracks! What a great thing!

"You've spent more time uncovering, I see," Sue said. When she left the site it was a jumble of rock and she couldn't tell what had excited Hans and then Jerry. Now it was very evident what they'd uncovered. She was amazed at the delicate work Hans could do with a backhoe. She noted that a couple of shovels rested carelessly against a large red rock deep in the dig. They'd been doing fine work, too.

A short, makeshift ladder led into the pit. It sat on a flat rock within jumping distance of the bottom.

"Is that thing safe?" Arthur asked, laughing.

"We've been up and down, but how much do *you* weigh?" Jerry chuckled.

"Funny!" Arthur said as he headed for the ladder. He bounced down, belying his years. After a few steps over loose rock he was staring at 65,000,000-year-old prints.

"Hans used to do a little rock hunting," Jerry called down to him, "and, he tells me, a lot of reading on the Jurassic period. He recognized them right away."

Interesting, Arthur thought, *I don't remember reading that in Hans's profile.*

"Eubrontes, I believe," Hans said. "Several others, too. Before these mountains pushed up, this must have been a shallow sea."

"Hans, I'm glad you noticed," Arthur said. "This is a find. The negatives you've uncovered are as perfect as any I've seen. Congratulations."

"Thanks." Hans beamed.

"Looks like I was all wet. I thought the topsoil couldn't be over a half million years. Eight feet down it's a hell of a lot older, isn't it?"

"This top part is a few million years old, Jerry," Hans began, "but the part I hit with the bucket *is* much older. Any ideas?"

Arthur thought for a moment and then said, "I think it's about plate tectonics. This whole region ran up against the Pacific plate and formed the mountains, but this Selwyn Range is far north of the California section. It's been twisting around toward the subluxation point in the Aleutians, so the really old sedimentary rock became covered oddly. That's my guess."

"I buy that," Hans said. Is there anything Arthur doesn't know, he wondered?

"Anyway, Arthur," Jerry began, "I suggest we take some time and uncover whatever else we can to a point, and preserve them as best we can. Maybe we can make a permanent structure to house them in the future. Moving our fort fifty or a hundred feet south won't pose a problem."

"Good. You men did exactly the right thing. This kind of history is worth preserving."

"What should we cover the rocks with, loose stone?"

Hans spoke up. "Straw."

"Right," Arthur said, "Have a couple of guys mow some of the fields out there. Lay the straw out about ten inches thick. That'll keep it from degrading until we can effect a more permanent solution. The only thing that can hurt this stuff is weather. We'll save it so others will be able to look and enjoy it. As our New Beginnings children grow, it will be good to show what our teachers tell them. It'll be our first field trip. Good suggestion."

"You definitely think outside of the box, Arthur. Now I'd better get back to work."

Chapter 33
Interesting Results

Arthur climbed out of the excavation and studied the layout of the tracks, trying to figure how large an area should be uncovered. Likely other prints would turn up in other areas. They couldn't preserve them all, but Arthur's sense of history convinced him that they needed to preserve and safeguard the site.

He'd have to start another journal. He sighed, waved to the men below and started back toward the depot. He grabbed two green strands of wild grain and pulled. They separated from the main plant easily. Looks like rye, he thought. Wonder how the analysis is coming along?

Back at the biosphere, he checked with Nancy Spiller and Maude Nash.

Nancy said, "We have found small changes in the rye and wheat, but we don't think the grains will be dangerous or inedible. We were surprised that more damage to the gene structure of the grains did not occur."

"That's good news," Arthur replied.

"On the other hand," Maude said, "we've tested the pine samples Roddy brought back from his foray across the valley and there are marked differences in what is and what was."

"How so?"

Maude picked up a sample of the material Roddy brought and compared it to samples they took from down under.

"See."

Arthur looked. The samples taken from the far ridge looked malevolent. They were green, tinged with yellow and seemed to have moistness on the periphery. He leaned over to smell them.

Vaguely pine tree like, but they also carried a scent Arthur first identified with lilac. Trees shouldn't smell of lilac.

Suddenly Arthur sneezed. It came quite unexpectedly.

"That's interesting," Nancy said. "We both sneezed when we smelled the samples, too. I wonder if that fragrance is a natural allergen?"

"Some of the other samples have unhappy differences," Maude said, "such as this fern. It's called Adaintum capillus-veneris. It's known in southern equatorial regions where warm, moist conditions are found. It shouldn't be here. This is too far north. I questioned Roddy and he says it was all over the place where they gathered it."

"We're afraid," interrupted Nancy, "that more has happened than just a four degree rise in world temperature. Somehow seeds of this plant have blown far north of their normal habitat and have taken to our northern soil. It's scary!"

"I see," Arthur said. He grabbed his chin and pondered. "Okay, keep up the good work. I'll bring this up at the next bio meeting. Bring some notes on what you've found, will you?"

"Sure."

Chapter 34
Ross River Road

In the early morning the explorers awoke, totally refreshed. The four Neo's grazed nearby. Matt breathed a sigh of relief. Believing Jules was one thing. Seeing it another. Being trained in an empirical system, seeing *was* believing! *Nothing against Jules*, he thought, *this was all him. Next time it'll be easier.*

They stretched and moved to get the ground kinks out of their bodies. The Neo's watched the men, fascinated by movement that didn't seem to mean anything.

"Start with your mounts immediately," Jules said urgently. "Connect with them."

"How do you know that?" Mike interjected.

"I don't for sure, but I told you I have an instinct for this and it seems exactly right to me."

Matt said, "Jules, you are the Neo authority. Go see your mounts, guys."

They each approached their designated mountain goat and started talking to them.

Conan's ears went forward as Jules approached him. "Conan, we are going into the river valley below. Beyond that is a road. A road is a flat place where the vehicles of humans used to travel."

Jules couldn't be certain he'd gotten through to Conan until the Neo began to exhibit signs of nervousness. Wait, no! His eyes narrowed. It wasn't nervousness. Anticipation? Conan couldn't by definition, have met humans before. His species arose after apocalypse. He tried mightily to guess at what Conan might be thinking. It came to him that Conan was doing the same thing. In a master/partner situation, Conan's need was to understand his master. Jules smiled. Wow! More than intelligent, intuitive, too! But what could the animal be thinking?

He sensed getting a handle on it was as important to the Neo as it was to him, to humans. Jules turned to look at his companions. They were talking to their animals and it pleased him. The others had taken him seriously.

Following breakfast, an event of great interest to the animals, they mounted and began the long descent to the river below. They looked over the countryside from the breathtaking height of four thousand feet. Mountains rose ahead of them and slowly receded behind, becoming a deep purple-blue in the distance. Long rills, evidence of age old geological folding and eroding, created stark shadows in the early light.

Conan led the procession, picking his way with delicate precision. Jules remained a presence on Conan, but the animal did it all. As sure-footed as Conan, the other three Neo's nimbly found their way. Following a short shimmy, the others fanned out, not following the leader's direct path but leaving him in front. Matt, Mike and Roddy didn't try to drive their animals. They simply sat.

Jules enjoyed the beauty and simplicity of the order Conan gave. No one animal could dislodge any part of the hillside and bring it down on the ones in front, and neither Conan nor any other Neo could accidentally start a landslide and bring the others down with him.

Occasionally Jules said something to Conan and the Neo's ears went back to listen. Otherwise all four sat in silence, thinking.

It took two hours to descend fifteen hundred feet. The animals had a knack of picking the right trails and the riders accepted their superior finesse.

One incident marred the perfectly comfortable ride. Having traversed a precipitous stretch of side hill, the ground suddenly shifted and Conan began to slide. A broad range of unstable hill immediately separated from the hillside. The other three, although fifteen feet apart and slightly uphill, got caught in the slide. As the rock and surface debris gathered speed, the Neo's worked their way to the edges of the slide with hardly a blink. Their legs danced rapidly on the moving stone in a blazing demonstration of fancy footwork.

"Didn't falter for a second." Mike called. "Great way to demonstrate a couple of important laws of physics!"

Back on stable ground, Jules called to the rest. "If *we* had been on the slide, there is no way we'd have gotten off it. You guys okay?"

Mike Peters goat, Geronimo, and Roddy's Thor ended up on Jules side of the slide. Viceroy found footing on the other side. They waited while Viceroy tracked back up the hill on safe footing and joined them.

"Never seen anything like it." Matt called as they got back into easy voice range. He grinned and patted Viceroy on the side of the neck in appreciation.

By noon they'd trekked over a narrow plateau and could see a small blue trickle a thousand feet below in the hazy distance, the South McMillan River.

"We'll hit the road by mid-afternoon at this rate," Jules called to the others.

"Map says it's a couple, three miles this side of the McMillan. Crosses it some miles down." Matt said.

"Ought to be in decent shape," Mike said. "It's one of the best Canadian highways in these parts."

Conversation trailed off. No one felt like talking. The animals had an odd gait, but it wasn't really uncomfortable. They just had to hang on tight.

The sun crossed the zenith and headed west. By mid-afternoon the sun shone bright over Front Mountain and Templar Pass. In another hour it would go behind the mountain and then shadow would cover the lower hills for a couple hours before nightfall.

The land began to level out and the rounded foothills were easy to negotiate. They ploughed through a sea of grasses and grains, which closed in as they made their way through. The high stepping Neo's left the land almost as they'd found it. The grasses they found in their valley appeared the same as here.

Jules called a halt. The Neo's immediately went to grazing, tearing mouthfuls of apparently delectable grasses off near the roots and swallowing it.

"Let's take five, guys. Good for the Neo's." Nobody argued. They dismounted and stretched out the kinks. "How much further, Matt?"

"We should be right about on it."

"Kind of what I thought." He eyeballed the mountain above and the sun, which had just dropped behind a western peak and left them in bright shadow. They walked around, happy to be off the Neo's spine ridges.

"Jules," Mike asked, "do you think our friends would mind if we made some saddles?" he rubbed his backside vigorously.

Jules laughed. "Maybe later, Mike! Not this trip."

"Afraid of that. Maybe I'll walk awhile."

Roddy said, "Look, we can use our sleeping bags, open them up, tie them on. What do you think?"

"Might work, but let's not rush things. These beings are friends, not beasts of burden. I'm thinking they feel closer to us without something in between."

Mike let out a groan.

"We'll work something out with them, but don't forget, they are not; I repeat *not* dimwitted horses. Please don't make the mistake of thinking that way!"

"Okay, okay!"

"Let's get moving," Matt called.

They remounted, pulled up to the lip of the current hill, and there, two hundred feet below was the road. Mike forgot his chaffed butt. "Let's get there." He started to move.

"Hold on, Mike." Matt pulled up his binoculars and surveyed the road. He could see for miles in the direction of Ross River. Behind them a curve and high cliff barred further seeing. At the limit of the ten-power oculars, he saw a dark dot on the road.

"A car," he breathed.

"Really?" Roddy said.

Matt said it looked as dead as the rest of the world.

"My guess, five or six miles." He nodded to Jules, who told Conan to get moving again. The four Neo's picked their way down a steep trail that looked little used, single file. Finally they reached old Canada Route 6. Its condition reminded them that nature was cruel to roads everywhere, but especially so in the north.

"Matt," Jules called. "Conan isn't happy with the roadway." The goat fidgeted and moved, sidling toward the grassy side.

"What's the trouble?"

"He doesn't like pavement. Hoofs aren't happy on it."
"What do you suggest?'
"Ride the sides."

The other goats hadn't stepped onto the road and didn't seem interested. They turned southwest toward Ross River, a hundred miles away.

Chapter 35
Adding to the Learning Curve

The road stretched out. So they could stay even, the animals took alternate sides of the road. Matt followed Jules. Mike urged Geronimo across and Thor followed the Neo-goat to the other side. The road's shoulders had disappeared years before and grass grew high right to the edge of the gradually disintegrating roadway. In regular places, where the slabs originally connected and frost had buckled the pavement, grass grew tall in the cracks. The road took on the appearance of a single row on a checkerboard.

Conversation floated across and back. The Neo's listened intently. No one could question *their* focus. It slowly dawned on the three who followed Jules lead that the animals were not only highly intelligent but also very special. For one thing, the Neo's needed little guidance. The seemed to read their owners minds.

"It's intuitive," Jules said. "There is no way I can believe they read minds, but they have a special sensitivity and we seem simpatico to it. Like they were made for us, and maybe we were made for them."

"My Thor," Roddy said, "shakes and shimmies a little at a time. These animals are talking to one another, right?"

"Yes."

"Any idea what they are saying?" Mike asked.

"No," Jules replied, "but they are carrying on a conversation as surely as we are."

"Any danger?"

"None at all. They are much smarter than horses *ever* were. They know they could overpower us any time they wanted, but they simply don't want to. They are connected in the best possible way. That's why I said it is important for you guys to come to an understanding of the Neo race and become sensitive to them. They are trying very hard to become sensitive to us."

"Wow!" Roddy let out a whistle. Thor turned his head and tried to look directly at Roddy. The other three did likewise.

Jules laughed. "That's the first whistle he's heard. He's probably wondering what other things his human can do."

Matt and Mike chuckled. It *was* comical. After that, with more to think about, the four continued in silence.

The Neo's covered distance deceptively fast. Matt thought the animal's gait did it. Jules agreed. "The way their shoulders and hind quarters rise and fall is no doubt due to the steep inclines which are generally home to them. It makes me curious about their stamina on a long trek."

"We'll find out," Matt said.

"What would you guess, four miles since we came down the hill?" Roddy called from across the road.

"All of that," Jules responded. He checked his watch.

"That car you saw should be coming up."

"Yeah, that's right..." Roddy said.

Soon the car came into view. They stopped short of the dark blue vehicle to look it over.

"Alaska plate," Jules observed.

"Heading away," Mike said.

"Salesman?"

"Up here? Who knows?"

The Neo's weren't nervous and seemed curious. Mike, who used to know his cars, the model, style, engine size and all manner of other trivia studied it for a moment and announced, "It's a Buick Roadmaster, vintage 2005. You guys know the story about the side ports?"

Matt said, "I always wondered."

"After heat ports were redesigned out of the car—too hot to touch and the builders wanted it to be smoother and more aerodynamic—the vestigial three engine port holes were surrealized. The sense of it was that Buick had to have those ornaments because people identified with them. They were *Buick!*"

"Everybody had a gimmick," Roddy said.

Jules laughed. "Where'd you get *surrealized* from?"

"Picasso?" Mike laughed.

They dismounted to inspect the car. All four tires were flat and rust had made strong inroads on the body, especially around the wheel-wells. The pockmarked front hood had badly rusted as well. The windows were up. A skeleton sat in the front drivers seat. They could see a gun on the seat to its right.

"Trying for the mountains," Jules commented.

"Had to be sick," Mike said.

"Yeah."

Roddy grabbed the passenger's side door. "Stand back, men."

The other three gravitated unconsciously toward their beasts. The Neo's watched intently. Roddy pulled on the handle and nothing happened.

"Stuck or locked." He looked through the car to the inner door on the driver's side.

"Unlocked," he said. He tugged harder. A little rust trickled out onto the road.

"Rusted shut." He hit the door with his foot, hard. A lot more rust filtered out from between the door and the frame. It moved a little. Encouraged, Roddy bulled it through and wrenched the door one final time. It protested, but opened. Roddy stood back as a whiff of dead air billowed invisibly out.

"Leave it awhile," Matt said.

Roddy came over to the group. Now the Neo's were nervous and needed to be calmed. They didn't like the faint smell.

Sensitive noses.

Jules talked to Conan, but also spoke to the other Neo's. "When one of your number dies, the flesh smells bad, doesn't it?" Conan shimmied briefly. It started on the right shoulder, continued upward to the bulging neck muscles and finished with a slight twist of his head.

Jules said to Conan, "Yes means this motion." Jules nodded his head.

"No means this motion." He shook his head.

"Conan, I think you said; we leave for another feeding field."

Conan shook his head.

Matt, Mike and Roddy stood amazed. The intelligence of the animal was clearly close to human. With no prior contact, the ability of the two races to communicate so quickly with such different equipment truly amazed them.

Jules pressed. "What happens to the one who died?"

More shimmying, on the right, then left, then a raised foot.

"This one beats me, guys, but I want to see this through. Conan, I don't understand you."

The Neo repeated the shimmy. Jules stood thoughtful and then said, "You bury it?"

Conan shook his head.

"You eat it?" The idea shocked him, but it might be plausible.

Conan nodded.

"Omnivores!" Matt breathed. He looked a question at Jules.

"No, not for humans, I don't think."

Conan seemed to want to know what had passed between the two men. Now *he* didn't understand.

Jules said to Matt, "We have been totally honest with these creatures. I think it should stay that way. That would be an automatic departure from what humanity would likely do in a new circumstance. Therefore we shouldn't do what people would do."

The other three thought about that.

Roddy said, "I'm as honest as the next man, but somehow I don't think I could do that."

"Why not?" Jules asked.

"Too much past, I guess."

"Remember what Arthur said in one of our meetings? If humanity wants a second chance, it can't be like it was. Something like that."

Mike jumped in. "I know what Roddy feels. To preserve humanity, we have to stop being totally human."

"Not really," Matt said. They turned to look at him. "We have to make clear choices, but they are choices. We aren't pre-programmed to live our lives like ants or squirrels or other lower forms. Choices have been humanity's saving grace and curse since we developed a highly specialized cerebral cortex. We have it within us to change and that's what we have to do."

"So we choose to never tell another lie?" Mike asked.

"What a world that would make!" Roddy flapped his hands and rolled his eyes. The others laughed. Looking on, the Neo's shimmied amongst themselves. Again, Jules couldn't figure what they were saying, but he felt strongly that every exchange between them would bring better understanding.

The others, Matt excepted, seemed content to let things evolve without significant effort on their part. Jules decided to talk to Matt when they were alone. Mike and Roddy had to change, to seriously buy into the new way of doing, at *least* insofar as Neo's were concerned, before they returned to New Beginnings. They had less than two weeks.

After he talked to Matt, he would ask Matt to get on the radio to Arthur and alert him to what they were doing and why. Arthur would understand. He didn't want the entire group to hear that conversation. Suddenly he hit his head with his open palm.

"What's wrong?" Matt said.

"Realization! I did what I've just asked the rest of us not to." He smiled ruefully.

"Tell us," Matt said.

"I just said we had to change, to be honest. I planned to maneuver Matt off to the side and talk about convincing you two," he pointed at them, "to be really serious about getting into your animals, not just going along. That's how I saw it. I just did the thing we shouldn't do. It was deceitful."

"What you're finding, Jules," Matt said, "is that change won't come easy. We are all flawed. We need to overcome our flaws or make them work for us."

"How do we do that?"

"I don't know."

"This is a new thing. We'll try, Jules," Roddy said. Mike nodded.

Chapter 36
Camping by the River

They talked for a half-hour before trying to get into the car. They found it distasteful. Matt got the counter out and checked for residual radiation.

"It's okay, guys," he said. "Let's see if there is anything we might need."

They poked through the car, managed to get the trunk open and went through its contents.

"Lord above," Mike called. "The spare still has air."

They found the jack handle, first aid kit and various rags.

"Think we ought to bury the bones, Matt?" Roddy asked.

"Yes. That's one habit I think we should preserve, don't you?"

"Yeah."

"What about the gun?" Mike said.

Matt thought about it. "I have my answer. What do you guys think?"

Roddy said, "We don't have a gun at the bio that I ever heard."

"Should we?" Jules asked.

"Another thing we haven't given thought to," Matt replied.

"Now's the time," Jules said.

After a few moments Matt broke the silence. "There isn't anyone or thing in this world that would require firepower to repel, excepting that giant bird or bat, possibly...and ourselves The Neos are our friends and partners. They've never been exposed to anything like that. Lightning and thunder are natural things. Neo's understand death and have their own code. We could conger up a defense whenever we need. I think taking the gun would give our new civilization a negative message. I vote no."

There was a chorus of agreement.

Mike said, "The odds of falling into old habits are greater if we take back the ancient ways. Leaving the gun would be a big step in the right direction. For us, I mean. It might even become part of the legend we are creating and serve as lesson for future generations. I can't believe I'm saying these things!"

"What do you mean?" Jules asked.

Turning to Jules, Mike said, "I'm actually beginning to accept responsibility all hundred of us have for the future. It's a real weight."

"Yeah, it is, Mike."

"We're done here," Matt interrupted. "We'll take the first aid kit. The gauze is good. First Aid cream probably not, but maybe, never been opened. Let's move on."

Jules said, "We should bury the gun with the bones." They thought about it.

"Yeah." Roddy unhooked his shovel, took the gun gingerly from the seat and walked a hundred feet into the wild. The others collected the bones of the man, using his shirt, which still had strength as a repository, and brought them over to the hole Roddy dug. The Neo's gazed after them.

When they returned, they remounted. Matt took a moment to consult the map. "Twenty miles to where the McMillan meets the road, then we follow them both for about another twenty. We should be able to cross here," he pointed and tilted the map for the others to see. "Then another sixty, give or take to Ross River. Barring problems, three...four days."

Going was relatively easy and by nightfall they reached the river and began to travel along the northwest side. No longer raging from spring snowmelt, nonetheless, the river ran swiftly and rapids were everywhere, Class Three or worse, Matt decided as they followed the road down a hill. After that, the road descended more gradually.

Finally they came to a long level stretch. Up against the backdrop on a high red cliff they found a wooded area, overgrown, but complete with picnic tables. They didn't seem much the worse for wear at a distance, but up close they saw nature had begun to reclaim the fashioned works of Man. One table was strong enough to hold them, so they stopped for the night and Roddy lit a fire. Fire has always drawn Man's eyes and lighting a fire comes easy. He'd been doing it for a million years. Not so the Neos. They spooked! They ran away in four directions. Roddy stood open mouthed, watching them go.

Jules quick mind took it in!

"Roddy, whistle!"

At Roddy's whistle the frightened animals stopped. They turned toward the men and their fire but didn't start back. Jules walked softly out to Conan, now a hundred yards distant. The other Neo's converged on Conan. They looked fearfully back toward the fire but stood their ground.

"Conan," Jules said as he approached his mount. The others listened. "Fire. That is fire. You have seen it in forest fires, haven't you? Lightning strikes in dense, dry woods. Great fire, killing fire! It can be frightening, but we have it under control. Return to camp without fear."

Jules couldn't guess at how much Conan really understood, but he bet it was a lot. The goat dropped his head and Jules roughed it up. He smoothed coarse off-white hair. Raising his head, Conan shimmied quickly to the other goats and they made their way back to camp. Jules walked beside his animal, occasionally brushing the high shoulder with his hand. Like humans, the Neo-goat seemed to enjoy attention.

"Roddy and I have a lot of work to do, I know, but we'll be serious about it," Mike said as Jules walked back into the fire circle.

"No problem, Mike, Roddy. We'll all get better at it as time goes. Try to understand what they are saying as hard as they are trying to understand us. When you consider the bridge, different species...new species, alien intelligence, mannerisms, all the rest, we're in the crucible and we're all learning fast."

"Glad you're around Jules," Mike said.

"Me too, Mike. I wouldn't miss this for the world."

"Not what I meant."

"It's what *I* meant."

The four Neo's grazed while the men put their supper together and ate. Then they laid out their sleeping bags around the fire and settled in for the night. A little conversation broke the stillness from time to time, and a loud, involuntary "Oooo" followed a bright meteor as it blazed across the sky.

"I used to do that as a kid," Mike called softly.

"Me, too. Probably all of us," Matt said. The others agreed. It made for a couple more minutes of conversation as they roused themselves to pay attention to the sky. At some point they all realized that they were learning more about each other in the best forum possible. The celestial fireworks ended with that bright flash. Conversation ebbed.

Then the stillness was complete.

Chapter 37
The Going Gets Tough

In the morning they ate and quickly packed. Matt brought Base up to date. Then they mounted and were on their way. The Neo's walked beside the road down a long hill. On the left the shoulder disappeared, so Mike and Roddy came back to Jules side and they rode single file.

To their left water cascaded over dangerous looking rapids and several falls. Rt. 6 had caved away slightly without a road crew to fix it. After that the road pulled a few hundred feet away from the river. Soon enough they could hear other sounds. A wind picked up and blew into their faces.

"You smell that?" Jules called to the others.

"Yeah, oil or diesel fuel," Roddy called ahead.

"Yes, that's it. Diesel, I think."

The road made a short, tight "S." As they rounded the corner, they began to see a large, circular tank. The tank had been breached near the top. A heavy diesel smell came from the saturated moat surrounding the tank. Then they saw the mineshaft opening.

"Down, Thor." Roddy dismounted and walked over to the tank.

"It's diesel fuel all right. Tank rusted through. Been leaking for a bunch of years is my guess. Still some in it, maybe six or seven feet. Size of tank, I'm guessing ten thousand gallons? It's a find."

"Must be contaminated."

"Probably, but oil floats on water, so..."

Matt gestured to Roddy. "Take the counter and check it out."

Roddy took it and walked up the moat. "Got a reading, a little high."

"Let's tell Base and go on. I'll mark the spot."

Roddy handed the counter back and Matt replaced it on his belt. Mike called in the find. Sue was on the com and mentioned that they were getting quite sophisticated.

"Got a log book right next to me. Everything goes into it. Already interesting reading," she said. "And listen to this! Ernie's got one of the computers in the depot working. He's going to set it up in a protected spot in the upper cave and we'll be able to record all conversations. How about that?"

"Sounds delightful," Mike said. "Guess you're going to have to clean up your language, Roddy."

"Me? *Me!*" Roddy exploded. "When do I cuss?"

The others laughed. Roddy didn't do that.

Matt keyed in. "Whichever way it goes, I'll enjoy those perspectives when we get back."

Twenty-miles further on they came to the bridge.

"Oh, damn!" Jules said.

The pilings were there, but the fifty-foot steel span lay crumpled a hundred feet downstream and sixty feet below them. The river raged in the narrow gorge. The western side of the roadway ended in an impassable cliff! They'd have to cross here or retrace their way many miles east. Up near the picnic area they'd seen a wide, shallow fordable stretch.

"Damn!" Mike echoed.

"Said that," Jules interjected.

"Okay, guys, brain trust!" Matt said.

Roddy said, "That place back where the river was wide, we could do that."

"Two problems, Roddy," Jules spoke up. "First, the place is more than half a day back. That'll put us behind schedule. Second, the terrain on the other side looked pretty formidable."

"Any more suggestions?"

Mike said, "Jules, bet you could work a lasso and hook the pylon."

Jules looked around. Above him he saw a flat stretch about twenty-five feet up. He could toss from there. "I could, Mike, but how do we get our Neo's over there?"

"That's a problem. I'm pretty used to Geronimo and I get a feeling he'd object to staying behind."

"We're not leaving our friends."

"I agree," Matt said. He took out his map and looked at it critically. The topography was much like the South Dakota badlands, a tough, maybe impossible ride.

Jules said, "Maybe if I can lasso that stanchion sticking out over the river and hand over hand it, I can get the sense of a possible crossing. Over there on the opposite side, I could climb that. Maybe there's a way." Jules pointed to a very steep rocky embankment that rose two hundred feet above the roaring river.

"Okay, Jules. See what you can do."

Jules dropped his pack, got out his two hundred foot section of rope and, looping it over his head and one shoulder, scaled the sharply angled rock to the place he'd seen. Removing the rope, he dropped the coil on the ground in front of him. Picking up one end, he carefully tied a slipknot. Gathering rope with one hand, he let out fifty feet and draped it across the ground, dropping the remainder of the coil well back. The others watched him work. Then, with an odd motion the others didn't get, but that seemed natural to Jules, he started the rope at the slipknot and began swinging it round and round, faster and faster. Completing a final turn over his head, he flung it up and outward. The rope arched over the thundering waters and reached for the other side, nipping but not catching the stanchion and fell into the turbulent water.

A groan from the watchers didn't gain Jules' attention. Totally focused, Jules dragged the rope back, coiling slowly and expertly.

Jules looked down on his audience, smiled and said, "Test throw."

Repeating his first attempt, Jules laid the rope out again and started his swing. This time he swung the rope even faster. When he let it go, they heard a sound like a taut guitar string. The rope arched as it had before, but this time it settled over the stanchion. Jules played the knot closer and closer and finally yanked it tight. Then he pulled with all his might. The metal piece shifted and stopped. He pulled again. It didn't move.

"Hogtied!" Mike yelled.
"Not yet. Mike, you and Roddy put your beef into it."
The two men came over and grabbed the rope.
"Ready, Roddy?" Roddy grabbed a slack piece and ran it around his hand and wrist for purchase.
"Yup."
"Pull!" They pulled. The piece moved a little. The two men took another hold and yanked. With a scream, the section parted company from the foundation and fell toward the river. Mike and Roddy were instantly pulled toward the rough edge of the chasm below.
"Let go! Let go the rope," Jules shrieked.
Roddy eyes went wide as he tried to disengage from it. Mike was pulled off his feet and slammed hard on the ground but managed to let go. Rope whipped through his hands. He rolled to get away from it. Roddy wasn't so lucky. Attached to the rope, the falling member snatched Roddy over the edge. He vanished with a fear-crazed yell!
Standing behind in shock, Matt reacted without thinking. He grabbed at the very end of the rope as it snaked over the side and dove for a small outcropping to his left. The rope uncoiled impossibly, hypnotically fast. He threw his body to the ground and hung the piece in his hand around the nub and held on with a death grip. In the last second he screamed at the other two.
"Mike, Jules, quick!" he called. They saw what Matt was attempting to do and dived for the nub to hold the rope. Just then it pulled taut...and stopped.
"We've got it! Jules, look over the side!"
Jules got up and ran to the precipice. Roddy dangled from the rope three feet above roiling white water. White spray leaped for him and had already soaked his still form. Held by his hand, which looked broken, his head was down and he seemed unconscious. As Jules looked he saw blood spread slowly from multiple parts of his body from contact with unforgiving rocks.
Jules assessed the situation in a split second and called, "Conan! Thor!"
The big goats trotted over. Jules grabbed Thor's rope from the makeshift carrier they'd fashioned for the Neo's.

"I need you both," he spoke quickly to the two, "to hold me as I go over the side. We have to save Roddy. Do you understand? You'll have to pull us both up together."

They shimmied in unison. Jules nodded and looped the rope over both goats' necks, tied it in the center and without another moments thought, went over the side. The goats took the pressure, leaned back and held.

Matt said to Mike, "You okay?"

"Yes."

"I hurt my left hand diving for the rope. Can you take up the slack while I reposition myself."

"Sure."

Matt gradually gave up his pressure on the rope to Mike. It moved slightly, but Mike said, "No problem, get another grip."

Matt shook his injured hand and immediately got familiar pins and needles. He thought and then called to his Neo. "Viceroy! Can you help here?"

Viceroy approached and Geronimo followed. They had been watching the action steadily. Matt could swear they both knew what was happening and would do what they could. He moved between incredulity and something like love.

"So hard to believe, and yet..."

The Neo's stood over their master/partners. Viceroy walked close to the rim of the river canyon and stepped on the rope. Geronimo then stood next to the rope and shimmied at Matt, who caught on quickly.

"Mike ease up on the pressure on your rope. I think Viceroy has taken the rope temporarily."

Mike eased until the pressure released.

Matt said, "My hand's still dead. Loop the rope around Geronimo's neck and tie it."

Mike did as instructed and said okay when he finished.

Geronimo leaned back and Viceroy released the rope from his foot very slowly, picking it up vertically until Geronimo could take Roddy's full weight.

Mike's jaw went slack. "I'll be damned!"

Finally! Realization. What they had in these animals came home to them.

"C'mon, Mike. Let's see what we can do to help."

Mike and Matt ran to the edge. Jules was already at Roddy's level and looking him over. He glanced up. Over the roar of the white water below, he shouted up. "Roddy's out cold. Broken wrist and a lot of superficial cuts. A lot of blood. I'm going to tie my rope around his waist and cut the other one off his wrist."

Jules didn't wait for an answer, but went right to it. Soon he called, "Okay, have Thor and Conan start easing back on the rope."

Matt turned and told the Neo's to pull. They eased back and the rope stretched.

"Stop!"

The Neo's held where they were.

Matt looked over the cliff and yelled to Jules. "No good. Stretching. Can you ease him down anywhere?"

Jules focused on the wild scene below. "No!"

"Hang one." After a short delay, Matt called down again. "Mike is on his way down. He'll outline the plan for you."

"Okay."

Jules seemed to understand instantly. The Neo's! Yes, he'd guessed. In moments two more ropes plummeted toward him. Mike rappelled down one of them.

Mike said, "Matt's idea is to make a basket and tie these strands together for strength. I'll climb back up then. Matt is rigging a rolling pulley that'll keep the basket away from the rocks. The Neo's will pull you two up. All you have to do is to keep the basket away from the rock wall. I'll help on top."

"Got it. Can do. Let's get started." It would work. They formed the basket and eased Roddy into it as carefully as possible. He hadn't become conscious in all the time they'd worked. Jules worried but said nothing. He knew everyone was thinking the same thing.

Jules got between Roddy and the jagged rock wall. "Go!"

"On my way." Mike shimmied up the rope and Matt soon pulled him over the side. They disappeared for a moment, and then two logs appeared, jutting out over the precipice. A third fitted horizontally over the first two and nestled into the crook of two branch stubs. Suddenly Jules felt a tug and saw Matt and Mike muscle the three-strand rope over their apparatus. He heard a command. He and Roddy began to rise.

Jules paid attention to the rocky wall. With his back against the basket holding the injured man and by a series of pushes, he arched the two into space to avoid touching as long as he could. It seemed like hours, but he knew minutes only had passed when he heard Mike's voice close by. He was too tired to see.

"Easy does it, Jules. You're home."

Jules concentration broke and he realized they had made it to the top. Hands grappled Roddy's still form and pulled him over and out of sight. Then, breathing heavily, the same hands reached for him.

Jules lay quietly for a couple of minutes to gather strength. As he rolled over and sat up, Conan dipped his head and blinnied. Jules grabbed the big head in his hands and cried, part relief, part exhaustion. Conan stayed with Jules and the others watched. Something passed between Neo and human. They couldn't see it, but felt some kind of sharing in the exchange, maybe a special kind of empathy.

Chapter 38
Altered Plans

While Jules recovered, Matt and Mike attended to Roddy. They carefully laid him out and checked him over.

"He's alive. Broken right wrist, dislocated left shoulder. Legs seem okay, no wait," Matt carefully felt to the side of a massive gouge, "fibula, I think, yeah, broken leg, too. Right ankle doesn't look right, but it's not broken. Roddy looks like tenderized beef. I don't think he has any internal injuries. He ought to, but best I can tell, he's okay inside. Have to wait 'til he comes to." He pushed and prodded gently.

He murmured, "Glad I paid attention at First Aid classes."

"Shall I call for the Doc?" Mike asked.

"Not yet. Help me strip him, Mike." They pulled off his clothes. Serious gouges and lacerations in seven places accounted for most of the bloodletting. It still bled. Some would have to be packed to slow or stop it.

"He looks like hamburger, Matt." Mike said. He opened the first aid kit and tried to figure out what to work on first.

"Internal?" Jules looked at both.

"We don't think so."

"Okay." Without another word, Jules got off the ground and positioned himself over the big man. Jules grabbed his left arm, thought for a second as if to review exactly how to do it and then swung Roddy's shoulder around. It audibly popped into the socket.

"Nice!" Mike said.

"Better now while he's out."

"I want to look at that ankle." Matt probed and felt. He grabbed his own ankle and felt it over, then went over Roddy's again. "Don't think it's broken, but the swelling is still coming up and definitely at minimum it's a horrendous sprain. Okay, let's stop the blood, then we'll splint the breaks."

They worked on him for nearly half an hour before Roddy began to groan and come to. He tried to move and cried out sharply. Slow awareness came. They waited.

"M...M...Matt?"

"Hey, big guy. Welcome back." Matt's gentle tone masked his pain.

Roddy lay for a few minutes. They watched the confusion leave his eyes. They waited.

Finally, "I went over, didn't I?"

"Yeah."

"How come I'm not dead?"

"We don't know. You pushed the odds some."

"I know!"

Mike spoke up. "Jules saved your hide."

"Not so, Roddy. We all had a hand in it," Jules came back.

Matt said, "Let's finish this up and call Base."

"Yeah."

"Roddy, you hurt inside anywhere? Back? Stomach? Kidneys?"

"Shoulder hurts a lot. Insides okay, I think. Find out next time I pee."

"Thank Jules. Roddy, your shoulder was over the top a few minutes ago."

Roddy's eyes widened. He took his right hand and gingerly felt over the shoulder surface. He winced. "Thanks, Jules, from the bottom of my heart. I've heard dislocations are agony."

"Yeah, they are, Roddy," Jules said.

"Got to call this in. I think we're stopped for now."

Matt took his radio and contacted Base. Gil was on. He radioed down for the Doc and then for Arthur. They connected a three-way. Doc Simmons asked pointed questions with pauses that told the explorers he was writing things down. Finally he said, "C'mon home. Roddy needs attention here."

Matt spoke up. "Doc, Roddy can't ride. What would it take for us to create a shelter for him and nurse him from here."

"What will you do?"

"Don't know. Plenty of wood around. We can fashion something and we'll have the help of the Neo's."

"You're resourceful. Are your first aid kits depleted?"

"Yes. Not completely. We picked up an extra at that car up the road. Don't worry about us."

"I'm not. I'm worried about Roddy."

"Doc, we're going to Pow-Wow. We'll check our options and call in later."

Arthur broke in. "We'll do the same here, Matt."

"Out."

Chapter 39
Pow-Wow

"Gil," Arthur said, "Call a general meeting. Right now. Let's get some support into this. Mary Beth needs to know about Roddy, too."

"Sure, Arthur." Gil broke the private link to Arthur's quarters and flipped the newly installed general call switch, thinking how timely Ernie had been. Ernie and his helpers had strung wire and set up transmitters, pumped up the power on the main console and had now tied everyone into the system.

"Attention everyone! Gil here. There will be an emergency meeting of New Beginnings for as soon as we can get together. Those of you, who can, please come to the auditorium immediately. Those who can't can follow the discussion by radio."

Arthur secretly reveled in the many directions his initiatives were taking. It pleased him even more about the initiatives others were taking. Approaching sixty-eight years of life, he knew that his time, no matter how vital he felt now, would pass much sooner than any others, barring accident. He smiled grimly, "Like George. And now Roddy!"

Sue Dorchester peeked into Arthur's place. "What's going on, Arthur?"

"Roddy's down. He's alive, but badly hurt. Tell you the rest as soon as we get together. Rouse some people, will you?"

Sue looked alarmed. "Sure, Arthur. Mary Beth is on duty. I'm sure she heard the call."

Arthur dressed quickly and headed for the auditorium. He found nearly a third of the population there when he arrived. More streamed in, looking apprehensive. Some turned to neighbors with questioning looks.

"What's going on?"
"Don't know!"

Arthur went to the podium and held his hands up. The podium now had a microphone and was connected to speakers on the sidewalls and through the communications console in the upper cave. Ernie's electronic switching mechanism allowed for any of various means of reaching part or all of the community.

Everyone knew the drill by now and things settled down quickly. "Friends, Roddy has been injured. Let's wait for the rest and I'll explain."

Shock, to some a little relief. The mountain wasn't coming down on them, anyway. Concern on all faces. What could they do? The exploration team was beyond their reach. Some confusion.

Mary Beth came running in from the power station. "What's happening?"

A neighbor said, "It's Roddy."

Mary Beth looked scared. "Is he...?"

"No. We don't know..."

They milled in tight groups. Mary Beth realized that Arthur was about to speak and held back her questions with great effort.

Arthur rapped his gavel. Silence followed instantly.

"Everyone," he said, "Matt has just called in to base. They arrived at the McMillan River Bridge to Ross River using old Canada highway Route 6. They discovered that the bridge is gone. They tried to lasso a stanchion on the far side and succeeded, but when they pulled hard on it to check its stability, the piece broke and carried Roddy over the edge. He has multiple injuries but he's alive and he's going to stay alive. Problem: he can't be moved from his spot. The exploring party is deciding in the field what they must do and we're going to offer any suggestions we can. That's what the meeting is about."

Arthur settled back slightly and the questions came.

Al Parks spoke up. "Can we spare some people to trace their steps and give them an assist?"

"Yes, a possibility, Al," Arthur said.

Mary Beth said, "I want my man back whole, but I can't see thinning us out. Matt, Mike and Jules certainly can do what's necessary. How bad is Roddy?"

"Lacerations and gouges, blood loss, broken left wrist, leg, severely sprained ankle, dislocated shoulder, overall tenderized from what Matt says. Jules popped the shoulder back in. Nothing internal."

Mary Beth let out a slow breath. "Sounds like he'll heal. He's strong."

Murmurs of relief in the crowd.

"Arthur," Frank Billings spoke up. "Not much we can do from here except send out a rescue party and that doesn't sound sensible to me. They'll solve their problems and keep us advised. You're not thinking of a permanent move in that direction, are you?"

"I think you're right, Frank. I felt that showing our explorers that we're solidly behind them was a good idea and I thought between us we could help. Doc?" Doc Simmons stood at the edge of the elevated rocky stage with his hands grasped in front of him, waiting.

Arthur turned to him. "Anything you want to say?"

Doc walked to the podium and Arthur moved to the side. "Yes. First, they are many miles away over terrain that won't be easy to hike. All we could do is to bring them medical supplies and food. Second, and this should probably be first; those four are as self sufficient as anybody in our colony. I believe we picked them for that reason. If Roddy can't be moved, then they'll stay together until he can be. Third, something nobody has mentioned and that I think is highly significant is that they have those mutated mountain goats, the Neo's, which are helping them.

"I find it hard to think of goats as intelligent and resourceful animals, at least the intelligence part, but I think we'd better listen to what Matt and Jules are saying about them and start changing our preconceptions."

He finished and there was silence.

After a few moments, Arthur said, "I think Doc's hit it on the head. Doc can stay in touch for any medical question or request they have. His comment about the Neo's; that hit home, too. There may be little other life out there, but we're not alone."

"Jules said they are like partners, really smart, smart as humans?" Maude Nash called from the group.

"Maybe," Arthur said, "but different smart is my guess. They'll take a lot of study."

Isabella's foghorn voice lifted to the podium. "Yeah, and they'll be studying us, too."

A little chill went through the audience.

"Food for thought. It gives me an idea. Next time we meet, or soon, we ought to talk about those Neo goats. For now, we have work to do. Meeting adjourned."

"Wait, Arthur! Hal here." From a speaker on the podium, Hal Hastings voice came loud and clear.

"Yes, Hal."

"We haven't met in a few days. New Beginnings is going well and we're working our tails off out here. We've been using a lot of our fuel. About half of what we had is gone. Ask Matt more about that fuel source they found. I need to know what we can expect from that tank. Viable? How much; and we should figure a way to get it. Would you?"

"Will do."

"Okay, thanks."

Arthur had a thought. "Jerry?" he keyed.

"Yes, Arthur."

"Word is coming to the Bio piecemeal. I want to tell everybody first hand how it's going up there."

"Sure. We have staked out some three hundred acres now. That's enough for fifty couples with plenty of land between them and room to grow. Two days ago I asked Brian and Thad to make a corral at the end of the valley, the one Jules and Roddy found. That should be mostly complete by now. When they get back I have a couple other chores for them. I want to thank the people who are taking up the slack down below, too.

"Anyway, I want something permanent built up by that hot steam vent. I've thought of some uses for it so that we won't tax our diesel dump. One of them is...I'm thinking that a timber mill could use steam for power. We'll be ready for lumber very soon. Gonna need timber, lots of it. That's all for me."

"Thanks, Jerry." Arthur paused and looked at the assembled group. "You folks know I get out to the digs as often as I can."

Isabella broke in. "You're all over the place."

Everyone laughed, even Mary Beth. Relief traveled through the crowd like a wave.

Arthur laughed. "Ha, ha. Good enough! Now we're adjourned."

Chapter 40
New Plan

"Sorry, you guys. Let you down." Roddy sounded miserable.

"Don't do it, Roddy," Jules said.

Matt said, "We're in this together and we'll finish it together."

"Actually, maybe we shouldn't," Mike spoke up. They turned to look at him. "Look, Roddy's down and he can't be left. One of us stays and the other two go on, find a way across, make it to Ross River, finish the mission. There's not much chance of finding a lot of life ahead, is there?"

Jules said, "Like we found no life behind us?"

"Hang on, guys," Matt said. "We'll talk it over and vote on it."

The others nodded.

"From my view," he said, "the Ross River mission is important, but not important enough to spilt us up. There have been lots of abortive journeys in history."

Jules followed. "Should we cut our strength in half and discover something ahead just as tough to handle as this gorge, or have another injury, for that matter, we wouldn't have the backup we now have. I'm against it."

From the ground, Roddy's voice came up strong. "I didn't plan to ruin it for us, but splitting up is a bad idea, unless it's to backtrack. At least we know what's there."

"That's three against, Mike," Matt concluded.

"You're right, guys. I withdraw my suggestion. I'm aching too hard to see what's over the next ridge."

"Me, too, all of us."

"Yeah."

"Besides, we're brain-trusting this with Base. Maybe they have something."

"Right."

"Roddy," Matt turned to the injured man, "what can we do to make you comfortable?"

"Leave me be. I'm not hurting much now. Do what you need to."

Matt looked him over and then said, "Okay, guys, let's construct a shelter and get ourselves into it. Jules, the Neo's will help, right?"

"I'm sure they will. What do you want them to do?"

"Could they bring some good sized logs to the area and we'll figure out how to use them."

"Hotel McMillan?"

"Sounds good to me."

"Conan, you understand what we need to do?"

The Neo shimmied intelligently, moved forward and walked away with Jules. Pines forested the upper slopes of the nearby hills, but a beautiful grove of aspens populated the lower hillsides. Mike figured there were about six acres of aspen trees. They would be much easier to work than pines. The trees were too big to pull down, so they'd notch them with their hatchets and fell them with the small crosscut saws they carried.

From the height of the sun they'd have at least six hours until dark. They got busy.

Two hours into the work, Base called the group and Arthur told them what they'd come up with. "Basically, it comes down to this, men. We could get a party to you. We could bring you supplies. We could rig something to get Roddy back for treatment, but the bottom line is, and everyone here agreed, you are in the field and you have to make field decisions. You tell us that you can keep Roddy alive and fix him up well enough so he can get back home, then it's the right thing to do."

Matt keyed his radio. "We've talked it over. We stay until Roddy can move, then we head for home. We'll stop at the ruined tank and see what it will yield. We'll let you know and Hal and company can figure out how to get to it efficiently. We'll make another trip later and bring what we need to get across the gorge. That was and still is a goal, but it doesn't have to be done today."

"I thought you'd say that. Okay, men, stay in touch."

"Will do. Out."

Matt turned to Roddy. He looked troubled. "My friend, you know this is going to be it for you for a long time."

"I know, Matt."

"You concentrate on getting better. We'll do the rest. Oh, and don't try to help. We're fine." Matt knew Roddy. He'd try doing something and open a wound. Matt turned his back on him.

"C'mon guys, let's get at it."

In the six hours they succeeded in cutting out twenty-ten inch aspen trees. They stripped them and made a pile for burning near the roadway. Everything that could be used they put in assigned piles. The Neos pulled them into camp with little effort.

Thirty-foot trees easily became a twenty-foot square base for their building. Notched at the ends and fitted, the respectable foundation grew uprights. They cut up two of the two hundred foot nylon ropes they carried into six-foot lengths, which yielded sixty-six ties, enough to lash their log building together with plenty left over for additional bindings.

Mike's mathematical skills came in handy figuring the job and there was little waste. He drew basic configurations in the red sandy earth nearby. The others started calling it Mike's blueprint. By the time it got dark and they quit for the day, the beginnings of a semi-permanent structure solid enough to withstand storms that might roll down the valley at any turn in the weather stood above ground.

The Neos proved their worth time and time again. There was nothing surreal about it. They watched carefully and responded—correctly—when asked. Clearly they understood much of what the humans were about, perhaps more, in their way, than the four explorers could guess of them.

Jules had full confidence in the animals and by the end of the evening the others did, too. Jules breathed a quiet sigh of relief. Now there were truly four of the colony who would support the Neos—as partners.

"Matt, Mike, Roddy," Jules said earnestly, "We need to prepare the rest for these animals. It'll mean not thinking of the Neos as they think of the Bio's goats. They're not the same. Maybe tomorrow we should suggest that the Bio animals be penned at the end of the valley in that place Roddy and I found. I'd keep them there, too. I wonder what our Neos would think of them?"

"Another species of goat? Wonder if we'd have war?" Mike said.

"I think they're too smart for that, but it will be interesting. I wouldn't be surprised if some wouldn't agree to become herders." Matt, as always, gave a considered reply.

"What about the dogs?"

"What about the dogs? That'll take some thought."

The night deepened and with no moon, too many stars shone above, making it hard to easily see the northern constellations.

Exhaustion finally took over. They retired early and, guarded by their silent partners, slept soundly.

Chapter 41
The Storm

In the morning Jules made a cook fire and boiled water for tea. Despite how tired they were, each woke up at different times of the night to check on Roddy. Roddy's sleep was fitful and one or another gave him pain powder and sat up until Roddy dozed again. They'd pretty much locked him into his sleeping bag simply by zipping it. With his injuries he couldn't get out if he'd wanted to.

"I got to go, guys! Get me out of here."

They carefully rolled him out of the bag. With his splinted leg, he couldn't get on his knees. Roll and pee, all he could do. No formality, no privacy.

His face turned gray a couple of times, but he announced that he didn't think anything was broken inside. Then he smiled.

"Ah, relief!"

Matt said, "We'd better stop this and make a privy. Can't have Roddy peeing all over the place."

"Yeah," Mike said, "Whyn't we think of that before?"

"The world is your outhouse when you're on the move and we're not moving," Jules said simply.

"After breakfast we can work on that," Matt said.

They took account of their remaining supplies. They were in good shape.

"We can last right here for a week and a half before we have to head back. Roddy, you be in shape to travel by then?"

"Sooner, Matt."

"I think so, too."

In the east the sun came up, bright and clear. About mid morning they noticed a single puff of cloud slowly move into the open blue western sky. Within an hour little puffs filled the sky. Soon the clouds banked and began to peek between the hills. By noon the clouds moved up and over them, and the sky turned sky steel gray. The Neos began to fidget.

"A little weather coming our way?" Mike called.

"No bet," Jules said and he eyeballed it. "About half an hour, maybe less."

"Let's shore up what we can," Matt called from the lumber pile. They worked faster. The three men completed the exterior frame and began to match the rafters as closely as they could to the overhead lean-to styled roof. They got about half of it covered and lashed down.

"Good angle, Mike."

"Maximum space, maximum rain-shedding."

It wouldn't shed much rain yet, but with rafters every four feet and lashed furring strips running horizontally, they had enough space for the bundles of grass that would finish it off, tied perpendicular to the furring strips. Plenty of grass grew along the edge of the road and ran up a quarter of a mile toward the hills in places.

"Grass hut technology at it's best. All natural ingredients."

The darkness made it hard to see well.

Jules chuckled but was concerned. The Neos were getting exceedingly antsy. "They're nervous. I think we'd better listen to their instincts."

Just then, without warning, lightning struck not fifty feet west of them. The Neos fled in terror. They headed east in total rout.

"Conan, come back!" Jules shouted as the thunder crack followed instantly. The Neo, hazed by lightning and terrorized by the massive thunderclap, led the panicked run. Conan, Geronimo, Thor and Viceroy quickly disappeared toward the east, running madly on the road.

"We have to go after them," Mike yelled. He started running.

Matt shouted as another bolt flashed nearby. That shout was lost, but after the thunder Matt tried again. "No, let them go! Get Roddy under the shelter."

Mike's senses came back. What was he thinking of! Could he catch terrorized Neos? Like, could he fly? He ran back to help Jules and Matt drag Roddy and the mat he lay on, into the partial shelter. They all crowded together just as the skies opened up.

The first thunder seemed a signal. Behind it they heard a roar. A fierce wind raced down the valley between the hills and the rains came with it. Night descended and the wind hit like a hammer. They had to hunch over and hold on to avoid being blown over. The rain came horizontal, cold, biting, like some malevolent force had found them and it picked at them gleefully. They had to bend forward just to breathe.

Lightning played around them, striking, striking, striking; so close at times that they began to get frightened. To many cloud to ground strikes. The four men had donned their rain gear minutes before it began, but it made no difference. They were soaked in seconds. They could do nothing but huddle miserably on Roddy's mat, circling the injured man in the way cows face inward during a storm.

Time after time, they felt an electrical tingling. Bad!

Jules yelled to be heard. "There's a lot of iron around here!"

"We need a floor," Matt yelled back. "If we survive this, we have to build one."

Too close! They'd built on an iron mountain.

"Lucky we built on a small rise," Mike shouted. "I can hear water on either side of us."

The others said nothing. This was dangerous and they could do nothing about it.

Thunder rolled every few seconds for a long time after. Finally—it seemed like hours—they could look up briefly and brave the rain. Occasional silhouettes of trees appeared as stroboscopic flashes in the near distance. It hit them hard and the wind stayed wild. Gradually it became sporadic and at long last the rain became steady and fell straight down. Thunder became muted, following the lightning as it moved east.

"Whew!" Mike said. "Glad I can still hear myself think."

"That goes for all of us," Jules said.

"We need to get ourselves off the ground, guys. Jules is right. A lot of iron around here. We were really lucky today."

"You can say that again."

Roddy spoke up from the ground. "Worst one I remember."

"I'll keep track of the weather from now on, too," Matt told them.

"Not a bad idea. That was a real gully-whomper!" Mike ventured.

The other three laughed and then Roddy groaned.

"I shouldn't laugh, guys."

"Won't be long before you can again, Roddy," Jules said.

"Yeah."

"Where'd you hear that one, Mike?" Jules asked.

"My father used to live in the east. There was this weather forecaster, Hilton something-or-other on a local TV station. Dad loved listening to him. Had a kind of unique style; made Dad smile."

"Interesting."

Chapter 42
The Building Takes Shape

"It's nearly two o'clock. Let's dry off and get to work." Matt said.

"What about the floor?"

"I'm sure we have time for that now. What are the chances of another storm following this one?"

"Don't know. The world temp is higher than before Black Saturday. More heat, more energy," Mike offered.

"More *violent* storms. Maybe not *more* storms?" Matt said, a little hopefully.

"Whatever. Humanity has done for the world and probably changed it permanently."

"Maybe not, Mike," Jules said. "You're familiar with chaos theory?"

They stopped work to look at him.

"Sure," Mike said.

"I have a theory, too. My theory," Jules went on, "is that anything humanity could do was only a shudder in the total dynamic. The earth will snap back."

"Okay," Mike came back, "it probably will. Chaos theory says that the systems it studies are basically disordered. The theory itself is really about finding underlying order in apparently random data. I love the stuff. Edward Lorenz did the first meaningful research while working on weather systems in 1960. Anybody interested?"

Roddy's voice came from inside, ignoring Mike completely. "Didn't I read your theory somewhere, Jules?"

"Maybe. Nothing's new... right?"

"So they say," Roddy returned.

"Who the hell are 'they', anyway?"

"Anybody interested?" Mike said hopefully.

"No!" Three voices ended the subject.

"I'm going to pout!"

Matt changed the subject. "Another time, Mike. Hope you're right, Jules. I wonder where the Neos are?"

"Probably won't see them tonight," Jules said.

"You don't think?"

"The storm blasted them back to their primeval beginnings, is my guess."

"They'll be back?"

"They're bonded to us. They'll be back."

With a collective shrug, they set to work again.

Mike and Matt worked on the big lean-to. Jules decided to go into the woods to cut out saplings for their outhouse. He brought a lot of stuff back, dumped it fifty feet into the woods north of the main structure and piled it high. Looked like a good site. Newly washed out areas from earlier runoff he used as a guide. He picked a place not likely to be affected in any future flash flood.

Using the small fold-up shovel they all carried, he began to dig. The pelting rain had done one good thing. The saturated ground—usually like cement—yielded to the shovel. Before long he had a pit four feet deep. Banking the top section with the excavated dirt to prevent the hole from taking on water, Jules proceeded to lay out the base and build from there. Every so often Mike or Matt would call out to him.

"Is it ready, yet? Gotta go!"

"Go in the woods!"

They smirked. They called plaintively fifteen minutes later. And at the half hour.

They moved Roddy to an out of the way place, but where he could see the work being done and feel vicariously involved. Their running chatter kept him tuned in and now and then he joined it.

By late evening the framing was complete. Jules had created a primitive but useful privy for the group, finishing about the same time.

"Works just fine, guys," he said.

"You tested it, huh?"

"Oh yeah!"

"Speaking of need," Roddy called, "I could use an assist."

"You want to try it?"

"Not out there, yet. Legs weak. Can't lie here all the time. Won't get strength back that way. But I need to try and move around some and I think I can get to that fallen log downwind with a little help."

All three moved to help him up. Roddy's two-twenty didn't make it easy, but they did what they had to.

Matt said, "Surprises me you can move at all."

"I'll get there."

They assisted him back to the comfort of his mat. The effort exhausted him, but Matt felt good about the man's spirit. They took it very easy on the left shoulder and checked his wounds for redness and re-bleeding. All wounds were coagulated and looked acceptably good.

"Pretty sterile up this way. Radioactive bath didn't hurt, unless some microbes have adapted."

"Who knows? I wouldn't bet my shirt that all microscopic forms have left us," Jules opined.

"I'm heading north," Matt said, and left. The path to the outhouse was easy to negotiate and the place looked entirely functional. Soon he returned.

"Nice job, Jules."

"Thanks."

"Think I'll go inspect it," Mike said and set out.

Matt and Jules surveyed the new building. The roof was finished and firmly secured. The sides now had thin verticals lashed to the horizontals. The roof would have to wait for covering. For strength and rigidity, they'd used four-foot aspen sapling branches from the grove to cross-brace the structure. Matt notched the uprights at right angles and Mike cut out an extended section from the saplings, such that when they were matched, a stiff wind wouldn't put a lot of strain on the cording.

Matt made a note in his journal to request nails. They would help. If they had to stay for the entire week and a half before setting out again, he wanted to also suggest they start building an iron furnace and forge and use some of the raw materials they seemed to be sitting on. Maybe they'd make their own. Wouldn't hurt to hone their trade skills.

"Matt," Jules said, "you know, this building sits on dirt right now and that's probably okay, but I had a thought. Why not dig holes on the inner aspect of each upright and plant a four-foot log? The flat top will be an excellent foundation for the floor and tying directly to the verticals will make the lean-to much more permanent."

"Good idea. We should do that tomorrow. One of us can cut grass and bundle it. The other two can build the floor. Can't guess how long it'll be before we get another golly-whomper!" and he smiled.

"Wouldn't be bad if we got started before this stuff becomes cement again, either."

"Yeah."

Night deepened perceptibly. They ate sparsely and went to bed. The Neos had not returned.

Chapter 43
Thor Returns Alone

All four kept a lookout for Neos. Jules said he was sure they'd be back, but they hadn't arrived by the end of breakfast. There was plenty to do at the site, so they put worry away and did what they could without the animals. Mike elected to cut and bundle grass. Matt went into the woods to choose and fell the right trees and Jules started digging.

Making four, four-foot holes was a tough job. By mid morning he'd dug two of the holes and started a third. He longed for a posthole digger, but they existed only in memory so he had to cut the sides wide as well as deep. Matt finished his cutting and stripping job and returned to their temporary homestead carrying two of the logs.

"Made them six feet long. No one will object to a floor two feet off the ground."

He dropped them.

"You look bushed, Jules. Let me take over before you get blisters." Jules held out his hands. Too late! He accepted the help and Matt started digging.

Jules went over to the little pool of water they'd found in a depression by the road. It would be dried up in another day, but for now it was a nice convenience. He washed his hands, grimacing at the popped blisters, but said nothing. Beyond the road, the roar of the McMillan River could be heard, still racing from the deluge of the day before. As he finished and shook his hands to dry them he looked up.

"Conan!"

A Neo approached, walking slowly and limping. It wasn't Conan. There were minute differences in the appearance of each Neo and soon Jules recognized Thor, Roddy's Neo.

As he approached, Jules called, "Thor! What's happened?"

The animal came to Jules and stopped. Jules petted the long face and looked searchingly into the animals' eyes. Thor shimmied an answer and gave a short blinny. Then he started to move off toward the encampment. He blinnied louder.

Jules realized what Thor needed.

"Roddy!" he yelled. "Thor is back, alone!" They walked into the cleared area together. Thor went up to Roddy and nuzzled him. Roddy stroked the face and neck. The look of relief on Roddy's face almost pained Jules. Did he ever know how Roddy felt.

Matt stopped digging and came out of his hole. Mike walked in from the field up the road carrying a huge bundle of grass he'd tied with one six-foot strand he'd separated from three-strand nylon.

Thor looked like he'd been through hell. His coat was matted and blood, nearly stopped now, had drained down his sides. Jules pulled up his right front hoof to look at it. Thor looked at him and tried to remove his foot from the cradle Jules had made with his hands. Jules spoke softly to the goat and Thor relaxed.

In between the cloven hoof he found a sharp stone imbedded deep into the soft tissue. The bottom part of the stone jutted an inch past the hoof. It showed wear. As painful as it must be, Thor didn't let it stop him. The leader had given him a job to do, and he would die before he'd give up.

"Roddy, tell Thor to stay still and I'll work this out. Got to hurt a lot."

"Thor, let Jules help you," Roddy called to his animal. Thor looked at Roddy and seemed to understand. He shimmied.

Jules went to work. The stone was driven deep and didn't yield. Trying to remove it hurt the Neo and it grunted, but didn't move away anymore.

"Matt, did anyone bring a pair of pliers?"

"I did," said Mike and dropped the bundle where he stood. He went to his pack and fished around in it. Grabbing what he felt, he withdrew pliers, and handed them to Jules.

"Why didn't I think of this before we left?"

"I threw them in as an afterthought," Mike said. "Thought we might have to repair some of our equipment and they didn't weigh much."

"Thanks, friend. I'll never be without them after this." Jules became intent. He gently worked the pliers into the flesh, trying not to hurt Thor, but obviously he did. The Neos coat gleamed with something like perspiration and his eyes grew wide from pain, but he let Jules do what he had to.

Gently Jules got a grip on the shard and then he began to work it, side to side, a little at a time. Thor blinnied, but stood.

"Good fella!" Roddy called softly to his steed.

Finally the stone gave. Jules extracted a bloody five-inch stone knife.

"No wonder he couldn't work it out himself!" Jules exclaimed.

"Poor guy," Roddy said to the animal. "Brave Thor!"

"Yes he is." Matt watched the entire process. "Jules, you'll have to give us a few lessons. Looks like we're going to need them."

"You can do any of this, Matt. Any of you can. But these animals, they are marvelous!" He placed Thor's foot on the ground and looked up at him. Blood from the uncorked wound ran freely now but would soon coagulate. "Thor, you're going to be okay. It'll be tender for a few days, but you will be able to run and climb, do everything."

Thor blinnied, then he set off in the direction from which he had come. Still hobbling, leaving a bloody mark with every step, he looked back.

"Wants us to follow him. The others must be hurt or trapped. Drop everything, guys. Bring shovels and rope. And a saw and the hatchet!"

They grabbed everything they might need and headed off on foot. The Neo couldn't travel fast, so they kept pace. After about two miles Thor led them into a ravine that diverged from the roadway. They hadn't seen it before because tall trees at the outlet concealed it, but the deluge of the day before had taken some out. They had climbed the ravine for another mile before Thor blinnied. He got an answering blinny, a very, very welcome sound.

Neo sounds were similar, but as with people, there were subtle differences and Jules heart leapt. "Conan!"

Jules hadn't told anyone how afraid he'd been when he saw Thor return to camp alone. *Matt and Mike must feel just as I do. They're bonded as much as I am, and I told them not to worry, so they didn't. Got to be more open. They deserve it.*

Mike called, "Geronimo!"

Matt followed with "Viceroy!"

Two more blinnies! Relief on the faces of all three! They climbed over a large, fallen tree and looked down. standing in water only inches deep now were three bedraggled Neos. All six seemed inordinately glad to see each other. The humans crawled over the huge pine tree and hugged their animals.

Only then did they look around.

Matt visualized a scenario for what had happened. The first flash and crash had the four Neos racing, panic stricken, away from the iron mountain. More sensitive than humans, they must have felt the electricity in the air and realized they were in great danger. On a primal level they'd reacted, momentarily forgetting their partners. With the storm close on their heels, they'd galloped east on the Ross River road.

Perhaps a lightning strike to their right had caused them to veer into the ravine. They ran wild-eyed into a dry streambed and headed up the rocky gorge. The sides of the ravine narrowed and the walls grew high, but they could do nothing but run. Finally caught by the storm, they entered a solid, rocky floor, barren of trees.

Ahead of the Neos was a wall. They stopped in confusion. The wind and rain broke over them. Trees came down all around them, but the one huge pine that had fallen behind them effectively blocked their exit. Conan led, Matt thought, followed by Viceroy or Geronimo and then by Thor. Thor, to the rear, ran into the tree at the moment it fell across his path. It stopped him short and narrowly missed killing him. Blinnying in terror, he reared, heart pounding! His body broke small branches from the force of impact. Sharp sticks punctured his flesh and blood began to flow.

Bleeding and disoriented and in considerable pain, Thor sat on his haunches, more afraid than ever, suddenly without his fellows and his leader. He stayed that way for a long time.

The wind howled. Rain came down in sheets. Water began to swirl around his legs, climbing fast, higher. He realized his danger and tried to climb the side of the ravine. He managed to get above the flood and stayed where he was, unable to move for hours.

In the meantime, the three Neos on the other side of the windfall cried piteously as water crept up their flanks and the thunder of the once nonexistent waterfall began to build again. Soon they had to swim. Water thundering over the new waterfall added to their terror. A swift current developed and tried to carry them downstream. The mountain goats were impelled into the downed tree. Their legs flailed, caught at branches and exhausted, they hung on. The new river raged around and past them, pushing their bodies hard against the tree limbs, piercing and abrading their skin.

An hour went by but it must have seemed like eternity. Finally the rain stopped and after a long time, well into the night, the water level began to fall. Thor's blinny was encouragement to the three waterlogged Neos. After determining that they were all alive, Thor stayed in contact and helped them not to give up.

When the flash river had quieted and their feet touched the river's stone floor again, Conan told Thor to find the humans and get help. Thor went away, barging through the woods and back to the road. At the bottom of the ravine, just before he entered the narrow strip of grass next to the road, Thor stepped on a shard of rock. Impaled and in agony, he kept on. Using three good legs and the occasional painful use of the fourth, he hobbled three miles to the human camp.

Exhausted near to death, he heard the thin human yell the name of his leader. Then, realizing he was mistaken, called his name, "Thor! What's happened?"

Energy surged and Thor made his way to the Jules human. Jules looked him over and pulled up his foot to inspect the painful hoof. Thor tried to pull away. Jules spoke soothingly to him.

Then Roddy, Thor's partner called to him. "Let Jules help, Thor."

Thor quieted and let Jules work on him. Jules used something harder than rock—the words 'steel' and 'pliers' made no picture in Thor's mind—to remove the stone. He withstood the grinding pain as Jules worked the rock shard out. When Jules tossed the sharp, bloody object away, Thor felt great relief. He shimmied briefly and gave a short blinny of thanks. Then, still exhausted but unwilling to rest, he turned toward his fellows, leading the humans to the ravine.

Yes, Matt thought, it had happened that way. Without knowing, he knew.

All partners, excepting Roddy, were now reunited with their Neos. Mike and Jules trimmed branches away from the center of the tree with the hatchet and Matt began work with his saw. It was a big job. It took two hours to get through the big pine tree. Once through, Matt tied a doubled piece of rope round Thor's chest and asked him to open a path.

Thor dug in and the goat's muscles bulged. His coat began to glisten and sweat ran from his pores. Then the men saw movement, just a little! Slowly the upper half of the tree moved out of the way. The men got their backs into it, too, pushing and tugging. The mountain goats stood quietly, understanding what needed to be done, understanding that they could do nothing and must rely on their people. Then they saw light ahead, a place to push with their chests. They joined the labor. More swiftly now, the big tree moved away and bumped into a lower gully.

"You're free," Mike shouted.

The Neos filed out. As Matt untied the rope, the three Neo-goats approached Thor and shimmied for some time. Then each one in turn laid his head over Thor's back.

"Thanking him," Jules said. "Unbelievable."

Animals and men walked down the hill together. The men wouldn't ride again until they returned to the ravine's outlet.

Finally, Jules spoke, "Okay, Conan, Viceroy, Thor and Geronimo, let's go home." The others could hear the love in his voice. The goats bent onto their front legs and their riders mounted. Thor, riderless and still limping, led the procession.

"We'll sleep well tonight," Matt said. The Neos blinnied.

"They know, don't they?"

"Bet on it."

Chapter 44
A New Configuration

Matt finished his report. "That's it, Arthur. These animals are incredible."

"Thanks, Matt."

"I think another five days and we can start back. Roddy's strong and he'll manage. I want Doc to look at the wrist. It's set and stabilized, but it's a bad one."

"Start back when you can. All for now."

Arthur turned to the interested crowd. "Business as usual. Roddy'll be all right. They won't go forward. Should be back in about ten days, I think."

"How about sending a party out to meet them?" Mary Beth said.

She'd go in a minute, Arthur thought. *Maybe she should.* The atomic pile was stable and she had plenty of backup for potential problems.

"Would you like to go, Mary Beth?"

"Would I!"

Arthur spoke to the fifteen or so who'd crowded around to hear the last message from the explorers. "Do we all agree that things are running well enough here and that we have enough backup to afford to send another party?"

The general murmur said yes.

"What would be our purpose?" Arthur had an idea that had nothing to do with sending people.

Nancy Spiller stood five-six and had a long thin face. Working in the gardens much of the time had begun to bow her back, but she was well muscled—there were few in the bio who weren't physically fit—and bored with the daily routine. Her fingernails had that cast and coloration of impacted dirt and her hands were cracked, but she had nice pale blue eyes, kept herself well and was attractive in a plain sort of way.

"You know, Arthur," she said, "I'd like to get away. Now that we're half moved from one place to another, at the moment I don't have all that much to do. I'd like to see Mike. I'd go."

"Weren't you helping Jerry at the town site?"

"Maude and I marked off a lot of quarters for people, but Beth Howell could finish it and she's a bit idle right now."

"Well, if it's all right with Beth."

"It will be."

Arthur's mind went a mile a minute. He'd never considered letting any of the women go exploring before, but why not? He could think of no reason why any of these intelligent people couldn't or shouldn't make a journey into the wilderness of their new world. An eye-opener of sorts, he calculated it would work. The women of the Biosphere were, if anything, more cautious than the men. That would make up for the lack of a man's physical strength. They had other strengths, stamina, for one.

Besides, Mary Beth was for Roddy and if he remembered correctly, Nancy and Mike Peters had dated casually a few times. What an idea! *These kids grew up in the nineteen nineties,* he thought. *Far cry from my time. Life is change. Think I'll see if the changes were good ones.*

He reflected: Matt saw a bit more of Millie Bainbridge than of the others, although Arthur had more than once heard him profess his love of the single life within his small circle of friends. Five-feet-four inches of naturally blonde Millie wouldn't be bad to send Matt's way.

Just then Millie, apparently reading his mind, said, "Arthur, if Nancy and Mary Beth are going, I want in, too."

Arthur smiled. "Okay, how about a fourth?"

More voices left their reticence behind and clamored for attention. Then, overshadowing all the closer people they heard Doc's voice. "Arthur, I think I had better go, too. It'll cut days out of my assessing Roddy and I can't imagine why I didn't think of it before."

"Good idea, Doc," Arthur said. "Your assistants can handle things here."

"Four is enough, ladies." Something flitted in the back of Arthur's mind. "You'll need a carrier."

Doc looked at him. "What do you mean?"

"Why not take one of our goats?"

Doc stood in thought.

"See if Neos cotton to the real thing, Arthur?" Perceptive Babs Monigan spoke up. Babs largely shepherded sheep but everyone in the Biosphere had more than one job. She knew goats, too.

"What do *you* think, Babs?"

"I think, yes, Arthur."

Doc nodded slowly. "Better to find out before our guys bring in a whole herd of Neos."

"Okay, folks." Arthur keyed his mike. "Matt?"

"Here, Arthur."

"We've decided to send Doc with a party to get to you or meet you on the way. They'll bring a re-supply."

"All right, if that's what you want. Who's coming?"

Arthur lied a little. "We're scrounging up three people who have nothing to do."

The three women tittered behind him.

"Okay. You know the route. The guys will have to take care on the upslope of Templar Pass. Lot of loose rock. After that it'll be easy enough. We'll start back as soon as Roddy can handle it. It'll be awhile. Likely you'll get here before that."

"That's fine. Why don't you plan to stay right there, then? Give Roddy more time and less pressure to be moved. Anything you want us to bring along?"

Silence, then "Yes. Jules wants some testing equipment. I'll put him on."

Jules voice came on conversationally. "Hi all. I want to check out the fuel we found along the way, see if it's good and how much."

He gave a short list.

"We're going to send one of our goats," Arthur said.

"Another good idea," Jules came back. "I'll need to prepare the Neos. Since you're doing that, pack some extra non-perishables and we'll supply our way station right away."

Matt came back. "That changes things. Okay, we'll design a few changes into our structure here. Keep us busy. Oh, more tools, heavier building stuff. And rope, a lot more rope."

"How much?"

"Uh..." Matt looked around as Jules spread his hands wide, "a thousand feet."

"That will tax our home supply."

"We can make more. Matter of fact, we should get a rope making industry going, all types."

"I'll have Gina add that to the master plan. Anything else?"

"Yeah," Jules spoke up again, "I'm thinking about the herd the guys will come across. They've been introduced to us and you shouldn't have a problem, I don't think. Wait, let me talk to Conan." He went off. Jules strode to the grazing area and went up to his mount.

"Conan, we have more of us coming soon. Will the herd let them pass?"

Jules spent long minutes with the Neo trying to fathom his understanding and his answer. At long last, he returned, satisfied.

"I asked Conan if we needed to go back and pave the way for the new group. I think he said that when we entered into *partnership* with them—that's exactly what I believe he indicated—that he'd instructed his herd to treat all humans the same way. Let me talk to base on that."

"Go ahead," Matt said.

Jules relayed the indications and feelings he'd gotten from Conan.

Arthur said, "How sure can you be, Jules?"

"Arthur, this is new ground. I have a sensitivity to these animals that is deeper than I've ever felt for horses or any lesser animals. I suggest you take a loaded gun with you, but under no circumstances are you to use it unless attacked. Give the gun to whoever is least likely to get nervous.

"The Neo's will definitely see you and they will come running. Hold back, stand still, don't show fear; stay together, don't threaten. Wait for one or more of them to make the first move. If they get on their forelegs in front of you, mount them and hold on. Name them, praise them and soon you'll be bonded.

"If they react negatively you'll have to deal with it as you can. I stress that I don't think you will have to."

After a short silence, Arthur came back. "Gentlemen, the consensus is we're going to go with it. We'll take Jules advice, tongue in cheek. Doc will carry the weapon. Nothing seems to bother him."

"Good. When do you start?"

"We'll put it together and start in the morning."

"If there's more we'll let you know."

"Okay, talk to you tomorrow. Out."

Arthur keyed out to a suppressed uproar. He laughed briefly. Joking had become unbridled since they'd left their emotional pressure cooker weeks before. Amazing how they had lived at one level, collectively believing that nothing else could be done. But the vibrancy since leaving the tomb; amazing!

"Let's get busy. Explorers pack. I'll see to the testing equipment. Babs, which goat?"

Babs said, "Hector. He's an old goat, stringy but strong."

"Good choice."

Babs set out for the goat pens.

"Get some sleep. We'll meet at six a.m."

On the general com device, Arthur announced the plan to the population of New Beginnings and retired to his expanded quarters. He picked up his journal and leafed to where he'd left off.

Chapter 45
Doc and the Ladies

The day brightened through the window. Gil, on duty in the com shack, woke to a sky filled with patchy clouds. To the west, more and thicker clouds topped the western Selwyn Range and filtered out behind it. The day had a vaguely unsettled feeling. Seventeen minutes to six. He'd set the alarm for quarter of. He often anticipated it. Gil pressed the stud on top, scanning the bank of telltales and silent alarms automatically.

The "shack," located modestly inside the lip of the upper Bio cave had grown. It contained a bed, three chairs and the com equipment and now qualified as the nerve center for all New Beginnings happenings. Someone, probably Al, had dubbed it "radio shack," and it fit. No doubt in time it would become greater than current labor had created. It would probably move, eventually. Assigned personnel had a highly important job.

Arthur arrived at five minutes before six.

"Hi, Gil."

"Hey, Arthur. All quiet."

Behind him he heard three women and the clop of goat hoofs on the stone tunnel floor. Arthur turned to watch the troop manage the last couple hundred feet of tunnel.

"Morning, ladies. Ready?"

Nancy spoke first. "Ready and rarin'!"

"Where's Doc?"

"Coming."

The three wore backpacks buckled at the shoulders and velcroed at the waist. In keeping with Jules color-coding idea, the predominant colors were intense red, pale orange, pale blue and dark green. Thus all colors between the eight would be readily identifiable.

"I'm comin'! I'm comin'!" Doc called out of the darkness. He materialized with a second goat, a young one named Herman, carrying two bags. One they recognized as his doc bag. The other looked like a fishing tackle box. At its side, firmly attached they saw a rounded pocket that looked more like a quiver than anything else.

Doc answered before they formed a question. "Yes, fishing. We've discovered goats and other life, why not fish? I commandeered Herman here because it was pretty obvious to me that Hector couldn't carry tools and equipment and this stuff, too."

The ladies looked from one to the other.

Another brilliant thought by the builders, anticipating an unlikely need. Half a dozen telescoping fishing rods had gathered dust in the storage room and Arthur had put the idea of their use out of his mind. They were anomaly. To what purpose a fishing rod? He'd never thought of it since, even when the caves opened out to the bio-people. They'd found no water.

"How'd you know, Doc?" he asked.

"I keep medical supplies nearby. Noticed 'em."

"Well..."

Doc turned to the ladies, his intense red outfit rumpling loosely. "Ready?"

"Ready!" He looked at their multi-colored outfits. "Won't lose you girls in a crowd, will we?"

They laughed.

Nancy said, "Won't lose you either, Doc."

Doc tossed an arm over Hector's back. Hector looked back at Doc reprovingly as if to say, "Enough's enough, Doc." The others noted that the tackle box hung comfortably on the right balanced by the med-bag on the left. Doc said to Gil, "We'll call in emergencies and twice a day to update."

"Okay, Doc."

Arthur said, "Don't let on about the packages we're sending along."

Nancy piped up, "Now we're packages?"

"Nicely wrapped, too," Arthur said quickly.

"Why Arthur!" Mary Beth tittered. The others laughed. Arthur had never joked like that. He colored a little.

"Guess I get to do all the talking," Doc said. "You know, the guys will want to know who's coming, probably soon. Want we should pick a few names out of our crowd and fool them?"

"I'm not in favor of lying to our men, but they'll know something's afoot if we don't," Nancy said.

"How far do you want to carry this?" Arthur responded.

"Don't know. I think the men would object if they knew."

"Why?"

"Macho?"

"If they have any true macho in them, they'll have to get over it," he said. "You really think they think that way?"

Nancy paused before answering. Her eyes got a faraway look. She turned to Arthur. "None of us is that far from our previous lives, no matter how noble our cause or how desperate our circumstances. We can do things you can't and you are physically stronger in most instances. I think the men who are off by themselves, relying on brains and brawn without our influence, will very likely revert to older thinking. The race has bred true to date. We can't just ignore it."

The rest of the group stayed silent, thinking. Finally Arthur said, "Maybe. Nonetheless, I'm going to rely on the rigorous testing, picking and choosing the company did before deciding on all one hundred of us. The profiles involved psychological testing of the highest order. As chief scientist my responsibility has been much greater than taking weather measurements and administering to the biosphere. Much of the company's charge to me I haven't mentioned.

"But I think you're right. Now is not the time for tomfoolery. We ought to tell them who's coming. We've had fun with it up to now..."

Doc spoke up. "I'll call them." He keyed in his receiver. "Matt..."

They took it well. The first protests faded when Mary Beth interrupted to dress down Roddy. She did an expert job. Matt, Mike and Jules had nothing to say after the outburst.

Arthur nodded as the three ladies geared up. Doc waited to lead Hector as Nancy took Hermann's tether and led him away.

Babs Monigan laughed at a thought. "One old goat following another."

Doc looked back over his shoulder. "What, I'm no fun at parties?"

Babs tittered.

Nancy took it up. "See, your job defines you."

Everyone laughed. Doc grumped, but he smiled inside.

"Payback will be interesting," he said.

Arthur raised a hand. "People, you'd better get going. You're probably looking at rain right after noon," he said. He squinted at Keele Peak, now surrounded by deepening clouds. "Remember, storms are more energetic. Plan your route and keep us advised. Good luck and be careful!"

"We'll be fine," Doc said.

They started walking. At the turn before they disappeared, they waved and were gone.

Chapter 46
Relaxing by the River

"Roddy's ears are still ringing." Mike said.

Jules smirked. "Didn't know Roddy's face could get red."

Always the leader, Matt said, "C'mon guys, go easy on him. He's still a hurtin' unit,"

They sat on the edge of the short lean-to's drop-off. Roddy lay close to the group on his back. The muted roar across the road and through a stand of piney woods gave sound to the pastoral scene.

"You'd of thought Mary Beth would have a little sympathy," he said.

"You scared the hell out of her, Roddy," Jules said.

"Yeah. I know."

"Woman's got a way of getting to a man."

"No argument."

His face had a tinge of gray. He kept his pain below the surface, but Roddy knew he'd almost died. He knew it'd be a long time before he could do his share again. Lying around killed him.

Work had pretty much ceased, but Matt mentioned that it wouldn't be long before three women and the Doc would be coming and they might start thinking about certain privacy issues he could foresee.

"Might as well keep at it. Place is big enough, whether we pair off or not. Needs a couple more rooms."

"It's a way station, Matt, a place out of the rain...hopefully," Mike added.

"I can't sit around and there's plenty to do."

Jules got up. "Me, too." He eyeballed the sky. "More weather comin'."

"Let's shore it up some."

"Okay."

"Roddy, you do nothing but heal, okay?"

"Yeah, sure." He didn't like it.

They got up, stretched and discussed a plan. With a long stick, Matt drew some designs in the flat area in front of the way station.

"We can add a couple of small rooms to the station here," he pointed, "and here."

Jules suggested they make a compound for the goats to come. "They're aren't at all like Neos. They won't hang around if we don't pen them."

"Good," Matt said. "Mike, would you go to the fields and bring back as much of that hay/thatch for bedding and roof material as you can. We can weatherproof this place a lot better than it is now."

"Sure."

"I'll take my hatchet and attack the forest out back for more stays and braces. Jules, how do you feel about making a privy for the ladies."

"About as good as you would..." he laughed.

Matt smiled. "I think we can use up the rope that we have left. The new crew is bringing more."

"Let's not use it all, Matt," Jules piped up. "They aren't here yet."

"I get you. We'll save one two hundred foot rope and cut up the rest for what we need."

"That'll do it."

They left in three directions.

Chapter 47
Second Team

Doc Simmons personality allowed for levity, but normally he kept to himself. He found it a bit of a strain because it pulled him out of his reading. Medical and pharmacology texts represented far more than a simple need in his profession. He actually enjoyed diving in and engrossing himself for hours at a time. Volunteering for this assignment—he thought of it that way—took him out of his element. He realized that he, of all the party, would likely be the most uncomfortable. He resolved not to let it be.

He knew he had a quick mind and a quick tongue, but he really didn't like using them for jocularity. Nonetheless, he could parry with the best of them. His study of medicine included psychology, a necessary part of the job he'd acceded to when chosen for the Biosphere experiment. He had no illusions about how others saw him and his need to appear accessible to the entire population motivated him to act beyond himself.

He settled comfortably behind Nancy. Nancy held the lead for the moment, but he wagered silently that Mary Beth would make it to the front before long. Doc saw more leader in her than Nancy.

Millie followed Doc and Mary Beth brought up the rear.

They appreciated the newness of landscape their eyes had never seen. No one had a lot to say initially, but gradually conversation became a feature of the adventure.

After a few minutes they were out of sight of the cave. This time they had a couple of watchers high on the south side of their mountain. Eventually, they disappeared, and radio became their only link to Base camp.

The clouds thickened and lowered. Muttering thunder grew as the expected storm swept over them. They searched out a rock overhang on the low side of Front Mountain. Doc thought to yank out his ground cloth and cover them. It kept them from getting thoroughly soaked. Wind driven rain lashed at them all the same. The storm lasted an hour. The out jut proved to be the top of a natural sluiceway and for about twenty minutes, water poured over them.

"Like living under the falls back home," Millie shouted.
"Where's that?" Nancy asked.
"Cranston."
"Really? Never thought to ask before. You go to Brown?"
"Yes."
"Went to Connecticut."
"Storrs? Used to party over there...now and then."
"My, my a party girl!"
Everyone laughed.
"Not that much."

The fusillades began. For thirty seconds—it seemed much longer—thunder crashed and lightning continuously lit the landscape. Conversation stopped. The mountain seemed to move under them. Doc kept looking up to see what might be coming down from above. Finally the storm moved east and the lashing rain became steady. Shortly thereafter the sky brightened over the western mountains and soon the storm petered out. An hour later they took to the trail again.

With a pretty good roadmap, they made decent time. Twilight found them in the sheltered place the first explorers had found. Even though they were fifteen pounds lighter than the men carried on the first trek, the ladies complained more about their loads. The two pack animals handled their considerable loads well and if they complained, no one heard them.

"Who would they complain to?" Millie said to the group.
"Hope they don't sound like us," Mary Beth offered.
Doc piped up. "Hope all that talk keeps you warm, ladies."
"Zip it, Doc," Mary Beth said good-naturedly.
The three women got a kick out of that. Doc smirked.
"This is where Roddy and Jules discovered the monster bat, isn't it?" Mary Beth said.

Doc said, "Yes."

"Anybody want to explore a little?"

A resounding "NO!" came from the others.

"I've had enough for today. My pack got heavy over the last hour," Nancy said.

They agreed. Setting up took little time. Bone weary, they faded quickly, all except Mary Beth. She gazed up through a cleft in the rock at the over-brilliant stars. She felt like a pioneer woman. It took awhile to fall asleep.

Chapter 48
Mutant Meeting

In the morning, Doc, for some reason he couldn't fathom, led again. After a few minutes he dropped back.

"Ladies, do we have a democracy?"

"Sure, Doc," Nancy called.

"Good. Somebody else get democratic and take over."

Mary Beth moved to the front.

"Keep up, Doc," and off she went. Not long after, Mary Beth's long strides got calls from behind to slow down.

"Spoil sports!"

"We want to get there, you know, walking," Millie piped up.

Mary Beth looked back. "Short-legged girls!"

"Sure hope you excluded me," Doc said under his panting breath, but Mary Beth heard him.

"Not to worry, Doc."

Mary Beth slowed. Doc grimaced and plodded along at the slower pace.

Everyone felt exhilarated. They were away from the biosphere, away from their companions, away from comfort and security, far out of their nest. There might be danger, difficulty, maybe even tragedy, but somehow, with each deep breath that took them farther from home base, they felt more alive, their senses heightened and more in charge of their own destiny.

They had less trouble than the earlier party on the loose stuff on the west side of Front Mountain. Templar Pass came and went and by noon they were heading down the east side. They picked their way through dense forest and broke out into the huge grassy field. Before long they got a feeling and, looking around, saw seven-foot tall mountain goats behind them. Neo's moved around the party and they were surrounded.

"Time to take Jules instructions to heart, ladies," Doc called.

The Neo's converged on the humans, the closer ones walking stiff-legged and purposeful. Others galloped in from farther a-field.

"They're so huge!" Millie gasped. Nancy reached out and grabbed her hand. Mary Beth stood stately and still, looking almost regal. Doc's hand searched for the gun and he grasped it in his pocket, but did not pull it out.

The closest goat looked them over and they watched as little tremors moved from one side to the other, the head jerk and legs stomp. The others responded in kind.

Under his breath, Doc said, "I'll be damned! Just like the boys said." *They're the same age as me. How can I say that? Being Doc is different.*

Mary Beth, closer than the other two heard him and without taking her eyes off the herd, said, "You didn't believe either?"

"I do now. Hard to believe things that just can't happen."

"What, like the end of civilization?"

Doc said, "I've had twelve years to get used to that."

"Ain't we all, Doc?"

As the herd closed in, one of the Neo's walked up to Hector and Herman, who looked decidedly frightened. They crowded together and tried to back up. It started to shimmy and make other unlikely moves. The goats quailed. The Neo stood looking at them for a minute, snorted and turned to its mates. Another shimmy session ensued.

The herd grew quiet and then turned to face the humans.

"Faint heart..." Doc started. "I'm going to address this one."

He pointed to the closest one, the one who'd checked out the human's goats. The goat made no move, but gave his complete attention to Doc. Nancy and Millie remained still and Doc could tell they were trying hard not to be frightened. It went against his grain to key his radio and ask for advice. The ladies looked up to Doc and he knew they were thinking the same thoughts. They waited for him.

The Mission

"Say, old boy," Doc began, "You wouldn't like to get on your knees and let me ride you, would you?'

The Neo stared at Doc and cocked his head, rather like his old Cocker Spaniel. *No more of those in the world*, he thought sadly. Then, after a few seconds and to the amazement of all, the Neo edged closer and knelt on its forelegs. *Get on it and ride, Jules had said. What else? Talk to it. Give it a name. Show it that its trust in you is justified. The beasts are highly intelligent. Think of them in different terms*, Doc thought. They aren't beasts. They are another intelligent species, not like us, but smart.

Doc had invited the Neo to allow him to mount. Like any dare he had taken in his youth, he had to make good on it.

"Looks like I put my foot in it."

"Sure did, Doc," said Mary Beth with a short, slightly nervous laugh, "Go do your thing."

Doc hesitantly moved forward and to the right of the Neo's body. The Neo blinnied impatiently.

"Guess that means hurry up. Oh well, what the hell!" Doc threw a leg over and sat on the sharp boniness of the creatures back and grabbed some long hair on its neck. With a lurch, the animal regained its footing. Doc sat tall astride the body of a totally new species.

Three more Neo's detached from the herd and presented.

"Don't be bashful, girls, do what I did," Doc called from high above.

Millie said, "They're scary." She backed a step, but Mary Beth caught her arm and moved her forward.

"C'mon, ladies, you don't want to show the Doc we're a bunch of wimps, do you?" she said.

That got Nancy moving on her own and when Millie saw her, she abandoned fright and steeled herself into doing what she had to.

From on high, but conversationally, Doc said, "We are a superior species, but these creatures are clearly very smart. Jules suggested a course of action. I suggest we follow it. One thing, Millie, do not let your fear show. I don't think that would be wise."

"What do you mean, Doc?"

"I don't think these creatures would—I hate to say it but I'm going to—I don't think these creatures would respect us if we show fear."

"What?" Mary Beth said vehemently, "You think they're that smart?"

"Smarter."

That was enough for Mary Beth. She marched up to the Neo in front of her, threw a leg over and sat. The goat got to its feet and stood waiting. Nancy was next. She managed with no trouble. Still on the ground, Maude accepted her fate. Doc had sympathy, but he didn't let it show.

Millie put a tentative leg over the back of her brute and grabbed hair quickly to avoid falling off the other side as the last Neo heaved to its feet.

"We're up, Doc. Now what?" Mary Beth said.

"Talk to your mount. Let it get to know your voice. And think up a good name for your steed. Jules impressed me with the urgency of those few things. Bond, that's what Jules said."

What followed appeared comical, four humans astride four massive mutated mountain goats leaning over and talking to them.

Doc's baritone, "So how are you doing today, my fine fellow? Eat a lot of grass? Didn't slip on any rocks, did you? Do you have a sweetheart? Why am I saying all these silly things to you?"

Doc's Neo had his ears back, intently listening. Every so often the front or flank would shimmy and that, coupled with a soft snort or a turn of the head, Doc thought, represented goat language. *No, these animals are anything but dumb. They're probably wondering when I'm going to say something intelligent.* He thought about a name.

Meantime, the ladies were up and feeling just as silly as Doc, but unwilling to talk silly talk just to hear themselves. Mary Beth got an idea. She keyed her radio and asked to talk to Roddy. Soon Roddy's voice, weak but all Roddy, came over the air. Mary Beth had to grab for neck hair when her mount started on hearing a distinctly non-female human voice above her.

"Easy there," she called, by the minute becoming master of her situation.

"Hey, Mary Beth"

"Hey, you big lug," her voice was gentle now. "Sorry for my last call. You worried me some."

The Neo settled down. They seemed to get over upset rapidly, another indication of intelligence. *Better than us*, Mary Beth thought.

"I know. I'm on the mend. How soon..."

"We're surrounded by Neo's. I wouldn't call them docile critters, but they've got heads on their shoulders. Finally got mine on straight. What'd you call your goat?"

"Thor. And they're Neos, not goats."

"Sure. Okay, did Thor have a sweetheart?"

"You're asking me?"

"Uh-huh."

"Hang on." Roddy went off. Jules came on.

"Roddy deferred to me. I've studied some mythology. Thor was an Icelandic god, the god of thunder. I've not read that he had a mate, but I have a suggestion."

"Go ahead."

"There is an Egyptian mythical goddess named Thoth, spelled t-h-o-t-h, hard "o" you might consider."

"Thoth...Thoth...I like it. Thanks Jules."

"Any time, Mary Beth."

The riders congratulated Mary Beth on being the first.

Jules came in again. "By the way, how did the meeting of Neo's and our goats go?"

"No violence," Doc said. "I watched closely and my take is that my Neo tried to communicate, couldn't and is now treating Hector and Hermann as retarded cousins."

"Really? I wondered about that. That's great. My guess is that our herd at home will take more getting used to the Neos than the other way around. But they seem benevolent?"

"Yes, exactly the right word, Jules."

"Great! Well, I'll get off now and let you do your thing."

"Right. Out." Doc spoke to the ladies, "Practice with your Neo. The rest of you, any ideas?"

"How about you, Doc?" Nancy called. Her seat wasn't that comfortable, but she could live with it and she felt relaxed on her Neo.

"I'm going to call mine Pan." He keyed his mike. "Jules, what do you think of Pan?"

"Great choice, Greek, god of woods, fields and flocks."

Doc sat smug. "C'mon, girls."

Millie finally spoke up. "Mine is female. I want her to be Crystal."

"Okay, Crystal. Nancy?"

"Mine's a boy. I'll call him Apache."

Doc said, "Like from the days of the old west?"

"I've told Mike he's acted like a war whoop in the past," she said. "He'll get a kick out of it. Yes, Apache. I like it."

"Okay, good enough." Doc keyed his radio. "Jules, we're on top. What now?"

"Conan is the Neo's tribal leader. They have all heard the name. They pick up on things very quickly..."

"You can say that again," Doc broke in.

"Ask yours to find Conan. I think that should do it. Oh, and hang on tight. These animals are fearless."

Doc spoke to his Neo. "Pan, find Conan."

One ear back, one forward, the Neo set off. The three mounted Neo's shimmied silently and then followed. The rest of the herd made way. They headed rapidly down-slope.

"Ouch," Nancy called. "Thought I had enough padding."

"You and me both," Mary Beth kicked in.

"Pipe down," Doc called. "You got a corner on pain?"

It was Millie who made the rare observation. "Would you rather walk?"

The Neo's had a fabulous sense of smell. Unbeknownst to the human riders, they followed the exact trail left by the first four, down and down.

Chapter 49
Another Day Alone

Jules dragged in at sunset. "Privy done, nice path, security, privacy."

Matt and Mike were finishing up the station roof. Mike tossed the last of the bundles up to Matt, who promptly tied it down. He walked off the low end of the building and jumped two feet to the ground.

Jules looked the building over. For a rough woodsman's dwelling, it looked good. Their primary concern was to make it both weatherproof and strong enough to withstand the world's fierce storms.

"We'll see, but I think it'll be okay," Matt said.

Mike the math guy had calculated all the structural elements. Between the three workers they'd created a comfortable enough way station and they were all tired enough to want to use it.

"Wait a minute!" Mike said, as he gazed at the spot where Matt had landed.

"What?" Matt asked.

"Look at the back of this building. What do you see?"

"Red dirt, upslope...ah."

Jules saw it at the same time. He grabbed his little fold-up shovel and started pulling dirt away fifteen feet behind the center part of the way station's backside. Matt and Mike, just as tired but energized by need, pitched in and drew a deep channel diagonally from Jules point to either side of the station. The upslope hard packed, almost cement-like soil resisted, but the shovels dug bit by bit.

"Make it deep, guys," Jules said. The other two grunted with effort and saved their breath.

Twenty minutes later they finished. Now a two-foot deep cut scaled down to the near edges of the station at about a thirty-degree angle. Beveled on the high side, any water that sluiced down the steep upper slope would shunt to the sides.

Jules said, "Mike, you think another cut, up about fifty feet, right over there," he pointed, "would represent insurance?"

"Yeah, I think so, but not tonight. Where do you get all that energy, Jules? No wonder you're skinny."

Matt said, "Let's take a chance for tonight and work that up tomorrow. I'm as beat as you, Mike."

"Getting dark, gentlemen, but you know," Jules said, "I need a bath."

Matt looked across the road at the river thundering beyond the trees. "Too late. We can't chance losing somebody at night. There's a little runoff pond across the way that still has a few inches of water in it. That'll have to do."

The other two were too tired to argue. They trudged off. From a near field, the Neo's looked up from their grazing.

"Wish they weren't so interested in everything we do," Mike said.

Jules looked at him. "Think about what you just said."

"Oh!" He looked a little stricken. "Right."

Jules took the lead, running across the road and flinging off his clothes as he went. As the other two ran to catch up, Jules splashed into the big puddle, which turned out to be a couple of feet deep at one end. He executed a belly flop onto the deeper part and raised a big splash.

Mike yelled, "Hey, cut it out! Leave some for us."

Three naked men cavorted in the little temporary pond. From across the road, the Neo's looked on with an expression that might have been curious.

Cleaner and much refreshed, the three settled in around Roddy. He smiled at them and told them it wouldn't be long before he would be chasing them into puddles.

That night it rained again and the rain tested their defenses.

Chapter 50
Wake-up Call

Nancy woke up with a start, completely disoriented. She felt around and, realizing that she was in her sleeping bag, tried to identify the deep, rumbling sound that had brought her awake. The river, yes, that was it, but it had lulled her to sleep earlier and now it had awakened her.

At the same moment the four Neo's blinnied, quickly walked close to their partners and reached down with their muzzles to nuzzle them. Now Nancy felt wet. It was still pitch dark.

"Everyone up! Water!"

It hadn't rained where they were. Nowhere near. They'd made camp near Old Route Six in a likely looking spot several miles past the old car. The bony backs took their toll on the long ride. The sight of the protected hollow looked inviting and once the shadows came over them in the late afternoon the temperature plunged. The grassy area looked like a good place to bed down for the night.

The women complained to Doc there were things about camping that smacked of deprivation.

"You're not used to it. Think pioneer." No way would he tell them how his butt felt.

"Right!"

"Sarcasm?" the women wouldn't deign to answer.

The low area cut back on the night chill if a wind came up, he said. Late, after they'd spread their bedrolls and crawled in, they heard thunder in the mountains north of them. Too far away to matter, they decided. Nancy found a flat place a couple of feet lower than the rest and climbed in.

They woke in panic. Doc's voice quickly cleared of sleep. "Grab everything and head for higher ground. Get moving!"

They piled out of their bags and grabbed. They got most of it. Hermann and Hector were higher on the hillside staked on short tether.

The Neos led the human party to the side and upward, choosing a path the humans could mount and blinnied softly as the group sought footing.

"Everyone call out!" Mary Beth yelled. Nancy and Millie said, "Here." Doc's deeper voice told them he was close.

"Who has a flashlight handy? Mine's in the bottom of my sleeping bag."

After a second, Millie twisted one out of her liner and flashed it on. They watched the ravine fill frighteningly fast. Their haven, safe from the night chill, not safe at all.

"We'll have to better consider where we sleep in the future," Doc offered.

"You think?" Mary Beth said caustically.

"A master of understatement," Nancy added. As usual, Millie said nothing.

"Anyone know the time?"

"Middle of the night?" Doc said.

"Comedian!" Mary Beth said, again too loudly.

Doc wondered why Mary Beth acted like that. Scared, that was it.

"Look. We're okay. We'll find another place to bed down."

On the edge of rage, Mary Beth, screamed, "Don't make it light, Doc, this is serious shit."

Doc Simons felt decidedly uncomfortable. He'd never heard Mary Beth curse in public.

"I know, Mary Beth. I said that because I'm scared, too."

Mary Beth Holiday, Atomics expert in an ordered world, Roddy Brown's lover, her seriously *damaged* lover, her world creaking, dissolving, her security suddenly undermined by a freak event, her mind slammed hard, forced herself to take a necessary step back. If Doc admitted to being scared, maybe she should admit it to herself.

After a long moment, her breath calming, she said, "Yeah, Doc, we can cool it down."

It took awhile.

After they got back into their sleeping bags—Nancy finished out the night in Millie's bag; hers was soaked—Doc lay awake thinking. Could have been worse, a lot worse. The Neo's had guided the humans in total darkness to safety. That would go into the record.

Chapter 51
Happy Meeting

"Okay, you guys, the ladies will be here tonight, maybe even by mid afternoon." Matt took stock of their creation. Only three days since they'd arrived and so much had happened since the call from Doc. Roddy had come back enough to become a pain in everybody's backside and they loved it. The gray guy they'd lived with since the accident was browning up nicely and Roddy seemed energized in knowing Mary Beth would likely arrive in only hours.

Well wishes flowed like wine from Base. Arthur offered words of encouragement, but no longer made suggestions. He realized that, sink or swim, they were in charge of their destiny. What news came out of the way station site heartened him. They were going to be okay; the whole colony was going to be okay. His throat tightened and he did his best not to show it.

Arthur concluded that the seeds he'd planted were beginning to bear fruit. His family was not long lived. Although his situation was markedly different from those of his parents and close relatives, he had no great desire for a long life. He wanted to live long enough to see the colony headed right, and it seemed that way.

"So," Arthur said to Matt, "they've passed the diesel depot and have fifteen miles to go?"

"About that."

"Great! What a homecoming."

"Jules went up the mountainside and picked bunches of flowers. Mike showed me how to weave baskets. We've made four.

"Basket weaving, my, my."

"I have no idea where he came up with that talent, but they look good to me. Roddy is trying to get up and I keep putting my fist in his face, but he keeps trying."

"I love what I'm hearing."

"We're okay, Arthur."

"I know you are."

"I'll be glad when Doc gets here and checks Roddy over."

"Soon, Matt, soon. Got to go. Talk later. Over."

Matt keyed out and went back to fashioning a chair. Time flew when they were busy. After two hours, Mike looked up from his weaving and shouted, "Riders!"

Everybody came to a complete stop and looked up the road. Barely discernible in the rising heat of mid-afternoon, four shapes melded into three, then two, and then four again. They grew larger by degrees. Matt looked around to be sure the station was presentable. He checked the positions of the welcome displays.

"I have time to finish this chair, I think," he said to Mike.

"About fifteen minutes."

Jules got an idea. "I think I'll line up the Neo's and have them present. I'll go talk to them."

Spirits went up proportionately as the riders loomed larger.

Jules came back crestfallen. "If I got Conan right, they don't stand on ceremony. I'm not going to try and change anything."

"What do you want, Jules?" Matt exploded in laughter. "We meet a new species, get them to like us, name them, ride them forty miles or more, save their asses and they return the favor, and now you want them to learn to bow to our ladies? Haven't you done enough?"

Jules colored.

Mike looked up. "There, finished. Stick some of those flowers in this one, Jules. And Jules..."

"Yes?"

"You're the man, Jules. Got it?"

From behind them Roddy's bass voice came loud. "What the man said, Jules. You should listen."

"Thanks. I'm not looking for that."

"We know," Matt said. "We're just real glad you're around. I'm finished with this chair. How about we mount up and go out to meet our ladies...and the Doc."

Jules slapped his forehead. "Brilliant! And here we sit."

They called their Neo's and mounted quickly. Over his shoulder, but with a laugh, Matt called, "You stay where you are, Roddy. We'll bring the mountain to Mohammed."

Roddy made a rude sound. Thor looked wistfully after the group, but obviously wanted to stay near his partner.

Jules looked back. "I checked Thor's hoof this morning. It's completely healed. That blows my mind."

Matt said, "Interesting. They amaze me."

They rode out rapidly. The Neos seemed as anxious to see their fellows, as were the humans. In five minutes they met. They dismounted and glad-handed and hugged each other while the Neo's congregated in a tight circle and shimmied and moved. They then surrounded the two frightened goats and shimmied some more. Conan bent to Hector and blinned softly. Hector backed and brayed. Satisfied about something that Jules couldn't fathom, Conan took his group away and left the little goats alone. They soon calmed.

Doc, not the hugging sort, shook hands all around. "Aren't we missing someone?"

Matt looked slightly embarrassed. "Yes. Let's get back."

They rode along, the ladies and men chatting happily with one another. At the Way Station, Doc dismounted first. He went over to Hermann, disconnected his medical bag and headed for Roddy.

"How you doing, Roddy?"

"Better, Doc."

"Let me look you over." Roddy submitted to Doc's poking and prodding and answered his many questions. Doc made thorough work of it. Roddy grimaced a couple of times, but never made a peep.

"Jules, you put the shoulder back?" Doc knew, but wanted to acknowledge him.

"Yes, Doc."

"Fine job. Where'd you learn how to do that?"

"Ranching summers. Breaking horses always ended up hurting somebody."

Doc remembered some of the talk. He turned to Roddy. "You're damn lucky. You ought to be dead."

Mary Beth came over as Doc stood and began to put his instruments away. "Doc, let me take over."

She sat down next to her man and started running her hand over the top of his head. "Roddy lover, what do you think of marriage?"

"If it'll keep me from falling over cliffs, I'm in favor of it." He gave Mary Beth a sidelong grin.

"You big lug!"

Ripples of laughter started through the group and grew and another weight lifted.

Dinner was nice. The ladies prepared the food, not exciting, but it always tasted better when they did it, some kind of finesse, the men reckoned.

"Yeah, not having to do it ourselves is what," Roddy ventured.

Doc got to room with Jules. Mike and Matt bunked in the middle one and the three ladies got the third room. They left Roddy where he'd been all day. With walls of stick and straw, they had plenty of unneeded privacy. On beds of straw supplemented by their sleeping bags, they talked until sleep overtook them.

Later still, thunder reverberated through the hills.

Chapter 52
Revising the Plan

Gil Castonguay called down for Arthur. He looked at the time. Almost eight. Unusual, he'd overslept.

"Yes, Gil."

"The explorers want to run something by you."

Arthur rubbed the sleep out of his eyes and said, "Give me a minute."

He sat on the edge of his bed and slumped forward, hands on knees. Taking longer to get up today. He felt a minor pain in his gut and decided maybe he'd run it by Doc. Pain within wasn't something he had. Probably the veggie supper the night before. He'd tried a new spice the kitchen staff thought would add some variety to the usual fare. Not bad, he'd wait.

Arthur dressed quickly and got on the cave console.

"Arthur here."

"Arthur, this is Matt. There are two things we want to do. First, Jules and I will go back to the damaged diesel tank and check it out thoroughly. That's priority. While we're there, I want to check and see what they were mining. There may be equipment, too. If it's copper or iron we should take advantage of it."

"I agree."

"After we call in our findings," Matt continued, "we're going to cross the river. It's wide and fairly shallow up there."

"What do you hope to accomplish?"

"Route 6 is the only way toward Ross River and at some point we will need to continue south. We think we can toss a line to this side and we'll have people to catch it. We'll span the river, rope it tight and rig a pulley to get back and forth. Eventually we can add more rope and create a bridge that will handle the Neo's weight. We need them and we aren't going anywhere without them."

Matt's voice took on an edge and Arthur wondered at it. He knew the animals were bonded to them, but Matt sounded so *possessive*...

Arthur said nothing then. He'd think about it later.

"Base?"

Rather than ratifying the plan, Arthur said, "You're in charge, Matt."

Silence...then, "Yes. That's our plan. Explorers out."

"Base out."

Arthur wandered back to his billet, so engrossed in the revelation he'd just had, that he didn't hear Sue Dorchester call to him or notice until she grabbed him by the arm. Shocked to be so out of touch, he colored.

"Sorry, Sue...thinking."

"I dare say," she responded.

"Something I can help with?'

"Yes, but what were you thinking?"

"Oh, nothing...well, something, but I want to think about it awhile before I say anything."

"Oh."

"So what do you need?"

"It's George. I just visited with him and Duncan came along. He wants out and Duncan wants his daddy. Doc's not around and I can't make that decision for him."

Arthur peered at Sue. "You detect a problem?"

"He's chafing."

"Sue, I'm not Doc, but what would you do in his place?"

"I'd let him start moving around. Build up his strength. Make him feel like he matters, 'cause he sure doesn't feel that way now."

"Sue, you are a bigger part of his life than I am."

He looked at her and shrugged his shoulders. A brilliant smile reached her lips.

"See you later, Arthur."

"Bye, Sue."

Sue headed back to the infirmary. Arthur had directed everything for as long as she could remember, but he'd hedged today. Why? A leopard doesn't change its spots.

Arthur continued to his area and sat in the chair now vacant of unread piles of reading. More pain in his gut. More pronounced. Better lie down, he thought. Interesting, no more aspirin, but the Doc had made remedies from experimental herbs they grew in the caves and they worked as well. He grabbed a pinch of pain reliever from his pouch and downed it with water. There.

In a few minutes the pain eased and he forgot about it. He had more interesting information to consider. The Neos were a force in the lives of the explorers. Mike might be a bit impulsive, but Matt was measured. It's what made him a good leader. Jules had leadership qualities, too, but he wasn't like Matt. Matt had sounded possessive, so he now believed wholeheartedly in the Neos and in his relationship with them.

What had he said at a meeting long ago? We have to change. We can't be like we were before. We have to forge a different path. We can't make the same mistakes again. I wonder...I wonder.

Arthur lay in his bed. What would the morning bring?

Something new, no doubt.

He nodded off.

Chapter 53
The Town Grows

Jerry felt pretty good as he surveyed New Beginnings. His baby. Everything had gone well so far, maybe too well. They'd had rain, but had not gotten a storm of the proportion that came through the valley the first day they were up. They were due.

Minor glitches resolved soon enough. Babs Monigan, taking a break from her sheep herding duties, while working near the brook lower down, slipped on moss and hit her head on a rock. Unconscious, her head slipped off the rock into deeper water. Tim Marining, a Bio cow herdsman and now a designated logger, heard her short scream, raced to her aid and pulled her out in time. She bloodied the water, and Tim made it a point to tell her how much she'd scared him that day. Her scar would cover with hair and she made less fuss than Tim did when she came to. Jerry worked her up on site and decided she didn't have a fracture. He ran it by Doc by radio and gave her the rest of the day off.

"Take something for the headache," he told her.

On her way back to the Bio, Babs wondered why she hadn't noticed Tim before. She knew him, of course, a broad shouldered, shy kind of guy, but never thought of him much, not like she was thinking now. *Never noticed his eyes before. Nice eyes. I'll approach him,* she thought, *after all, he did save my life.*

The dumpsite problem should clear soon, he hoped. Some of that hinged on the explorers' report of a diesel dump on their side of the mountains. They had little need to clear the rubble until he knew if they would have an additional supply. He took one last look and keyed his radio.

"Base, Arthur available?"

"I'll call him," Maude Nash said.

In a couple of minutes, Arthur came to the radio.

"Yes, Jerry?"

"Arthur, you haven't been out this way for a week. I think you should. Got some time?"

"I will in a day or so. Pretty busy here at the moment."

"Come when you can."

"I will. Something I should know?"

"Yes."

"What?"

"Come when you can," Jerry repeated.

Arthur turned to Maude. "Jerry sounded like he'd just had a child."

Maude giggled. "He did sound excited, didn't he?"

"You know what it's about?"

"Couldn't say."

"Or wouldn't?"

Maude gave him a small smile and a "don't look at me," shrug.

"Humm. I'm curious, but I have to finish the revised duty roster. We've agreed to bring up the animals and cut back on plantings and I have fifty-five people to move around." He looked for a moment as though his people were moving too fast on the project. Reducing Bio strength to ten percent two weeks hence went against his grain. What if something bad happened on the surface? Mentally he shook his head. Must be getting old.

Maude said, "Don't worry so, Arthur. It'll be okay."

"You into mind reading, Maude?"

"No, but anybody could read your expression."

I'll have to watch myself, Arthur thought; then wondered why he'd thought it. Good people, smart people. They didn't need him as much as they thought. Maybe that was it. He felt himself growing more useless daily. The five men at the depot were working their butts off on the town project. Hal brought back a daily inventory of the use of the machines and the remaining diesel fuel.

Yesterday he'd asked if Arthur had word about the tank the explorers found. He told Hal that Jules and Matt were going back to check out the site and should be there soon. He'd check with Sue. She ran the communications console today.

Two weeks back he'd released fifteen men to cut a road into the high timber in the north valley. In a couple of days, Jerry began to see logs dragged in by one of the payloaders. Two more men and three women went into the carpentry business and a sawmill had begun to take shape on the south end of town down by the river at the site of an earthen dam under construction.

The deal was to produce power to run the mill's equipment using an old fashioned waterwheel. The mill would be far enough from town, but close enough to satisfy the need for safety. Damming the stream to create water pressure for a gravity feed wheel would produce a lake above it, but it was many feet below the town site and Jerry's active mind thought it might make a recreation source, especially for the children. That took the place of putting the sawmill by the steam vent a couple of miles further. They'd put it on hold as they didn't have enough sheet metal to make a boiler with present equipment. One day, though...

Arthur finally took Jerry's invitation and showed up. Jerry and company's industry amazed him. He could see a dozen buildings taking shape. The fort closed in a large enough area to house two hundred people. In a few years it wouldn't be big enough, but by then other alternatives would have supplanted the original by design. By then they'd know what they had to deal with.

"Nice job, Jerry. Think I'll phase myself out."

"Not yet, Arthur." Jerry made a mental note to talk to a few people about Arthur's unintended vibe. He thought Arthur sounded a little depressed.

Arthur's low-grade stomach pain came back on the way to New Beginnings. He knew something was wrong. Couple days more and see, then he'd call Doc on the quiet and run the symptoms by him. Am I being pigheaded, he wondered? No, it could be temporary. He'd wait.

What an excellent choice he'd made for Project Manager. Jerry saw everything with an engineer's eye and his organizational skills were perfect. The town hummed.

Chapter 54
The Tank

Conan shimmied to Viceroy. The Neo's eyes, set back as they were, allowed them to be watchful straight ahead, but also to "listen" to each other if traveling side by side. Each Neo kept one ear forward and one behind. Jules talked to Conan and Matt did the same with Viceroy. Sitting higher than the Neo's heads, the men had marginally better visibility. They also had a different kind of eyesight and theirs saw with better clarity at long distance.

"I think they're having fun," Jules remarked.

"Seems so," Matt replied.

"You made it clear we're going back to that old mine?"

"I think so. Don't have this Neo language down pat, but I'm learning almost as fast as they are."

"That's discouraging."

Jules laughed. "Not a problem, Matt. My guess is if we could read their thoughts, they'd be so alien that we'd go nuts."

Conan's ear twitched.

"Nothing, big boy," Jules said to the animal. Conan turned the ear forward and swept the landscape. He blinnied.

"I think he just told you to can it," Matt said.

"What, go crazy?" He laughed. Matt gave him a look.

They rode on in silence. When they got to the ravine that had almost cost them their lives, both Neos looked up it and shimmied.

"That I understood," Matt said quietly.

"Yeah."

Several hours later they dismounted at the mine. Matt took testing equipment from the pouch at Viceroy's side and Jules made lunch from rations. They left the Neos near the road munching the long grass. Here the river meandered a quarter mile away. First things first. They checked out the diesel fuel tank. It had held ten thousand gallons at one time.

The tank had rusted through a couple of feet from the top and the only evidence of a spill lay in the thin stain below a small hole, down the outside. Weather had scoured off the fuel but the lubricating value of diesel had left a streak less rusted than the rest of the tank. A darker stain in the red dirt at the bottom showed where diesel fuel had leached into the ground. They climbed the rusted metal ladder onto the narrow catwalk near the top and discovered a round, deeply pitted dome.

"I wouldn't walk up there," Matt said.

"No, but overall, it's possible there's a good bit of fuel in the tank. Diesel floats on water," Jules offered. "Just a question of how much water pushed how much diesel out through the breach."

"There's a maintenance cap over there," Matt pointed. "It's got a swing arm release. If we're careful, we might break the rust free and get a look."

"We can try it."

They worked their way along to the maintenance cap.

"Stuck."

"No kidding, Sherlock. I'll get a rock."

Jules dropped to his knees and grabbed the edge, swung over and dropped to the ground. He searched out a heavy rock and tossed it, two-handed, to Matt. Matt looked over the swing release, gauged it and gave it a solid whack. The tank rang like a ragged gong. He hit it again, harder. Still nothing. Chips of the rock fell below. Jules came back up the ladder.

Steadily, the tank rang with repeated blows. Finally Matt stopped to rest.

"It moved a little and the handle is still strong enough."

"Let me take over," Jules said.

Matt handed him the rock and Jules first knocked it shut. Then he tried again. Rust dribbled over the tank's top. Jules blows rang over the empty countryside.

"Got it." Pushing it back and then forward repeatedly, the handle grudgingly moved an inch and then more. The pile of rust grew. He whacked it back again and went at it. The play increased. At last it unhooked and swung aside. The two men got close and lifted against the rusted hinge.

"Hinge it," Jules said. "On my count...one..." They tugged. "Two..." Again. At five they began to feel the slightest movement. "Down..." They pressed. "Up..." In a minute the cap had moved a little. They kept at it. Sweat stood on their foreheads. When it eventually gave the diesel smell became pungent and they stared into blackness

"Good. Smells right, too. You're the Chemist. How do we measure it?"

Jules said, "It won't be easy to determine. The holes in the top aren't large, so most storm rain would have rolled off. That's the good part."

"The bad part is all the years it's been doing it," Matt said.

"Yeah."

"And the other thing is how much was in the tank when the world came to an end."

"It's at the level of the side leak. Tells us nothing. I'll get a stick long enough to push to the bottom. The tank is ten feet high. We'll tie a piece of cloth to the end and test at different depths when we hit water I hope some of it will discolor the cloth and we'll get a reading on the height of the water in the tank."

"How much college did it take to figure that out?"

"If we had water detection paste, it would be easy."

"Paste?"

"Yeah. It only turns color when it hits water. Tell us exactly."

"So what now?"

"We're not dead in the water. First, the holes aren't large on top, so there's a good chance it hasn't taken on water in bulk. Second, this is a mine. It has to have equipment that uses diesel fuel. Maybe we can get it going. I have another idea if this doesn't work."

Jules went back down the ladder and cut a thin aspen sapling about ten feet long. Matt worked the cover hinge and swing arm back and forth until they moved more or less freely. He blew away the rust as it accumulated so it didn't go down the hole.

A shadow crawled across the top and Matt glanced up. The dark underside of several massive cumulous clouds drifted overhead.

"Couple hours to some weather, Jules."

Jules looked up. "No problem, we can hole up in the mine." He came back with his long pole. He tied a piece of paper toweling to the bottom end with string and said, "Here goes nothing."

He inserted the pole into the diesel fuel a couple of feet and brought it up.

"Okay." He dipped it again, another foot, repeating the process until only two feet of pole remained visible above the fuel.

"Nothing. Going all the way."

His arm disappeared as Jules pushed the stick all the way in. "Bottom," he called. He pulled it out.

"I can't tell."

Matt looked it over. "Me, either."

"Plan B."

Matt looked at him inquiringly.

"Let's go look at the mine equipment."

They closed the maintenance cover and swung the arm to lock position.

"Much better," Jules said. "Before we go down, how about dipping a handful of fuel onto the hinges?"

"Okay." They opened the cover and Matt at full reach got the tips of his fingers wet. He rubbed it over the newly freed hinges, repeated several times and finally satisfied, closed it up again.

"Better than nothing."

The blue sky fast disappeared. They both looked up.

"We better hurry."

"Yep."

They climbed back down and worked their way to the mine. A line of pitifully rusted, narrow gauge tracks ended twelve feet outside the mine entrance at a solid looking stop. Dim doubled ruts six feet lower backed up to the track.

"Loading," Matt mused.

The rust diminished under the overhang. Inside the entrance, hidden in it's own alcove, they came on a skeleton in a chair. The head had fallen off, but the torso, hip and legs were somehow still connected. Rotten clothing had nearly disintegrated, and tatters fell into the rib cage and into gaping holes in his Levis. On closer inspection, Jules saw evidence of gnawing. Small animals or large birds had feasted on the remains. Nature's carrion eaters came in many sizes. At its feet lay a twelve-gauge shotgun. The chair, surprisingly, had weathered its years under the overhang well.

"Doesn't look like he trusted people back then, did he?"

"Here's his head," Matt said. "From the hole, looks like he did himself."

"Better than waiting."

Matt took his magnetic generator flashlight from his backpack and shook it for thirty seconds to charge it up, then shined the light into the darkness. It didn't show anything. Slowly they inched into darkness deeper than the darkening sky, sliding a foot along the rail spur. Eventually they closed their eyes to accommodate and soon they could see the thin flashlight beam play on rock walls, timbers and equipment. The rails continued for several hundred feet before they came to the first branch.

"Far enough for now, Jules. Looks like they mined ferrous oxide. Used railroad ties to hold the ceiling. Interesting no railhead closer than Ross River. Those creosote soaked ties are in really good condition. Let's look at that diesel up front."

"Okay." They acclimated to the dim overcast light quickly. At the entrance they heard the threatening rumble of thunder. In the west clouds piled high and a halo had formed many thousands of feet up. After the glance, they walked over to the aerator.

"Make this quick."

It was beyond repair, but the diesel motor seemed potentially usable. They traced the fuel line to a small box out of which sprouted several pipes, two capped and two with spigots. A test drain with a clear glass bulb below it sat to one side, covered in dust.

"Ah-ha!" Jules exclaimed. Matt watched while Jules wiped the glass and saw the amber color of diesel fluid within.

"Not enough," he muttered. He searched around for a bucket, anything he could run fuel into. He found a dented, zinc coated water bucket in a pile of trash, covered with grass and weeds. Jules shook it out and wiped it clean with a handful of grass.

He looked at the lowering sky and at Matt.

"Only have a couple of minutes, five at most." He opened the sampling spigot and diesel ran sluggishly out for a moment while he cleared the thirty-foot line to the tank. Then he had clear water.

"First foot is water," he announced. Just then lightning flashed nearby and thunder cracked instantly. They ran for the mine opening as the first big drops came out of the sky and all hell broke loose!

"Viceroy!" Matt called.

"Conan!"

The Neos ran to their partners. They didn't want to go inside the mine and reared in fright.

"Conan, it's okay. Come to me."

Matt called his Neo and they cajoled the Neos under the overhang, but not before they were soaked. Conan nuzzled Jules and Jules gently turned the big goat around so he could see outside. The wind swept in and rain followed in sheets with abundant lightning, but none so close as the first strike. The Neos blinnied, but Matt and Jules held their manes firmly. After awhile they quieted and stood beside their humans while the storm raged.

"Wonder how the Way Station is handling this?" Jules said.

"It's pretty tight now. I think it'll stand okay."

"I'd like to know how the sluice behind the station is handling the runoff."

"If the radios will work inside this mountain, we'll find out." Matt keyed his radio. Nothing but local static.

"No dice."

"Let's explore."

"Later. Our Neos need us."

"Right, of course. Don't know what I was thinking."

They settled down to wait, pushing up against their animals, who pushed back.

Chapter 55
Arthur's Dilemma

He didn't think anyone noticed, but they had. Arthur had one characteristic he could never abide. As leader, he'd never wanted it and he spent much time giving his authority away. What he couldn't realize was that his self-effacing brilliance made him a great leader and dear to the hearts of virtually everyone in the Biosphere. In bringing the Bio people out into the light of a new world, he made the perfect grandfather and that is how they thought of him, regardless of personal maturity.

All realized he would deny it, so they deferred to him in subtle ways by accepting his logic and suggestions and making them their own, but not before testing him from their perspectives, to Arthur's delight. Secretly, Arthur would have been deeply disappointed if everyone had said, "Yes, Arthur," and gone about their business.

In his cubicle deep in the Biosphere, Arthur had a sudden urge to tie up loose ends and finish writings he'd let hang. The list of new jobs was daunting, but he handled it with Gina's help. Now, with steadily increasing pain balanced by steadily increasing denial, Arthur began to fidget.

They noticed. Word went around that something was up with Arthur. Everyone decided to say nothing directly. Arthur needed to be first to share what bothered him. They kept a focused eye on him.

Inside with his privacy curtain pulled, Arthur felt a sense of his mortality. Chronologically still a relatively young man he knew that nature sometimes played a trick or two with all men. That night he decided he had to call Doc. Spicy food was not the offender here.

Finally Gina couldn't stand it.

"Arthur?" Gina's voice came through his curtain. He detected strain in her voice.

"Come in, Gina."

She moved the curtain aside and entered.

"What's going on with you?"

"What do you mean?"

"You're not well," she blurted.

"Of course, I'm well. Indigestion, that's all."

"Everybody has noticed. I told them I couldn't ignore it and I was going to talk to you about it. They said you'd decide when to say something, but I said you are too personal and I said you hold things in—you do, you know—and you'd live with a problem so's not to worry the rest of us."

I'm that transparent, he thought? Well, it solves the dilemma. "Gina, I'm not going to be foolish. I plan to call Doc Simmons later tonight."

Gina seemed relieved. "Oh, good."

"Anything else?"

"No, Arthur."

"Then you skedaddle."

Her smile brightened the room and she bent and kissed Arthur on the forehead. "That's from everyone."

With a swish, she left. The warm glow lasted until the next bout of pain.

Chapter 56
The Mine

After the first brief encouragement, the Neos stood in the mine entrance and didn't try to bolt. They shimmied quietly to themselves as the storm blew itself out. Matt and Jules felt their conversation and reflected on it.

"I'm going to study these shimmies and the other motions harder. I'll eventually discover what each means to them," Jules said.

"Help me with it, Jules."

Matt was a convert, definitely. "Absolutely."

They released the Neos to graze and went outside to use the radio.

"Matt to Base and Way Station."

A cacophony of sound came from the small speakers.

"You were gone so long."

"Are you all right?"

"Whoa! One at a time." The noise ceased.

"First," Matt said, "we are fine. We got caught in the storm and stayed dry inside the mine. The mountain is high grade iron and we couldn't get a signal out."

He proceeded to tell both parties about the diesel tank, what they'd found in the mine, how their partner Neos had acted intelligently throughout the storm after their first misgivings and how they were more solidly connected than ever. He asked about how the lean-to, as he described it, stood up to the storm and how Roddy was doing.

Doc's voice said, "All's well here and Roddy's still chafing to get into the swim of things. Had to exercise my authority on him."

From the background they heard Roddy yell, "He's a damn jailer!" followed by laughter. Jules grinned at Matt.

"Now," Matt said after fielding several questions, "we are going to spend more time determining exactly how much diesel fuel there is, then we're going back into the mine a bit further and will report on what we've found there. After that we are crossing the McMillan here where it's broad and shallow and we'll keep you advised on that. Out."

"Thanks, Matt. Base out."

"Same for us," Doc said. They heard him murmur to the ladies before he un-keyed his mike, "You girls don't have anything else to say, do you?"

A chorus of "No's," followed and then static silence.

"We're okay, they're okay; let's get cracking."

They returned to the testing spigot and opened it up, filling several buckets with slightly contaminated water.

Finally Jules said, "Just let it run and we'll watch it closely. We're not going to worry about polluting anything that won't leach into the ground."

"Agree."

After that they sat on nearby rocks and watched for the fluid to change to amber. After an hour it did.

"Okay. Now we know fuel is above the feed. I need to find the water valve. Should be on the opposite side of the tank at ground level." He walked around until he found it.

"Here," he called. "Look around for a pipe wrench."

Matt remembered a toolbox inside the mine entrance.

"Hang."

The toolbox was rusted shut, but a rock solved the problem. He searched through and at the bottom found a large, well-used wrench, which he brought to Jules. In the meantime, Jules had cleared away grass and debris and made a watercourse for the contaminant.

Jules took the wrench and tried the two-inch plug, but it wouldn't budge.

"You didn't see a piece of pipe in there, did you?'

"No, but I'll go back and look. Ought to be something lying around."

While Matt looked for a pipe, Jules searched for a large stick. Soon Matt returned with a four-foot piece that fit neatly around the handle of the wrench. After that it was easy and soon water flowed unchecked into the gully Jules had made.

In another hour diesel began to come out. They stopped the flow and capped the outlet.

"I'll do it," Jules said. He ran up the ladder and unhooked the swing arm, popped open the maintenance cap and tested.

"Five feet of good diesel," he announced. "I'll figure it out when I come down."

"No need," Matt said. "I'll call Mike and give him the dimensions and depth and he'll figure it out in his head. Might as well earn his keep today."

Jules laughed. "Okay."

Mike told Jules and Base that they had exactly 5000 gallons of diesel the color of amber. Hal gave them a resounding cheer and told them it would help immensely.

"Anything you can do to cover the holes in the top?"

"'Fraid not. We'll need plastic or fiberglass. Have to wait on that," Matt said.

"Damn!"

"Hal, there's a lot of rust, but the breaches aren't large. The weather's been at it for at least twelve years with no maintenance."

"Okay, but let's put some covering or repair material on a list for when we get back."

"Sure."

Jules doubled back into the mine and Matt followed. At the split in the tunnel they took the right fork. Their lights showed that the beams were in good shape and the ceiling looked good. They didn't expect anything to be living in the mine, but remembered vividly the huge bat-like creature they'd encountered on Front Mountain.

"Forewarned is forearmed, right, Matt?"

"It is."

So they carried five-foot long aspen saplings Jules had used in the diesel tank, sharpened at the ends. They checked out the tunnel together, buddied up, though they felt the risk was low.

They alternately charged their flashlights to keep the light constant. The right fork took them deep inside the mountain. The track ran true and the gentle downward slope moved in serpentine fashion, following the high-grade vein. A quarter mile in they came on mining equipment and blasting caps. They found the dynamite thirty feet further in. Fifty feet beyond, the tunnel ended. There they found four skeletons. Each had been shot and a pistol lay in rock dust nearby.

"They all knew."

"Yeah," Matt said, "don't beat yourself up about it."

"I'm good. I wonder if those guys were trying to burrow in as far as possible to escape this thing."

Matt eyeballed him, but said nothing.

They retraced their steps to the other tunnel, which branched four times while they stayed to the right. That one ended two hundred yards in. They surveyed the rest. No one tunnel was as long as the first. They found no more bodies, but did discover more mining equipment, old but in decent condition.

"I'll take notes on this stuff. Everything is ours by default, I guess," Matt said.

"A couple of the veins have petered out," Jules said, "but the others keep going. We may want to work this mine again in the future."

"I'll mention that."

"Did you notice how dry it is in here?"

"Yes. I'll mention that, too. Never heard of a mine that didn't drip. Must be a feature of the strata hereabouts."

"When George is better, we'll get him out here to give this place a good going over."

They left the tunnels. The sun now hung in the west.

"Another two hours before we need to stop," Matt said.

"The sun is right. Let's make it across and hole up for the night, couple, three miles south."

"Good."

They called their Neos and alerted the colony of their findings.

"Out."

Chapter 57
Across the McMillan

Viceroy and Conan presented for their men and on a nudge, headed for the river. Although it was Conan's right as leader of the Neos to lead, Jules asked him to stay back so he could study their language. He couldn't be sure Conan understood, but the Neo did as his partner wanted. Viceroy looked back and shimmied, which Conan returned, and then Viceroy took first spot. Jules shook his head as he realized that Conan did understand, without question.

Again they rode in silence while the Neos shimmied conversationally. Passing the day? Did they do such things? Jules tuned into their actions while Matt made for the river. In minutes they were walking alongside looking for an easy crossing.

"There," Jules pointed. Conan now took the lead.

"Figure anything out?" Matt asked.

"Not really, but Conan clearly knew what I wanted. Hope they don't discover they're smarter than we are."

Matt thought about that for a few minutes and then said, "Probably not, and certainly not in the same ways, but I'm impressed."

Jules nodded.

Rocks littering the shore smoothed out and a large, flat runoff sluice formed a narrow ramp. A boyhood picture flashed into Jules mind. His parents took him to a lake near their home as a boy. They'd back their motorboat down the steep cement public access ramp on occasions when his Dad could get away for a weekend. How he had loved that. He'd learned to water-ski on that lake and suddenly realized he still loved it. That was before his horse farm days. Maybe some day things would settle down and survival wouldn't be the *only* thing.

By the way station the river couldn't be fifty feet wide. Here it was a hundred-fifty feet or better and the water ran slow and shallow. Large, rounded rocks jutted above the surface. Jules knew how surefooted the Neos were, but wondered if their cloven hoofs might slip more easily in the water with the men's weight above them because of the change of balance. They were used to their riders. Jules let it go. They'd soon find out.

"Conan across," he said to his Neo. The tilted rock had a crease in the middle, but it led smoothly into two feet of clear water. The rocks below the surface appeared negotiable. Jules gave him his head.

"I have to keep remembering that Neos don't need to be led," he mentioned to Matt.

"I have trouble there, too."

Viceroy followed a half pace behind. The Neo's hooves slipped on rounded rocks, but they balanced nimbly. Viceroy slipped with Matt on a broad, tilted, underwater rock.

"Whoa, big fella," Matt called. Viceroy put both ears back and shimmied under him.

Matt laughed. "I think he said, 'Not to worry.'"

Jules chuckled.

At mid-stream a channel five-feet deep and five feet wide slowed them. Conan looked it over and blinnied to Jules. Conan's hesitation caused Jules to examine the deep watercourse. He thought he saw it, but said nothing, interested in what his Neo would do. Looking around, Jules saw a ramp-like rock twenty feet downstream.

Ah, he thought. "Watch closely, Matt."

"Okay."

Conan gathered and jumped into the cold mountain water. He set a course for the ramp rock, which he easily mounted, putting him back into shallow water again.

Viceroy waited until Conan made it out and then blinnied to Matt.

"Go ahead, fella," Matt said. Viceroy mirrored Conan's move and soon Matt and Jules were side by side again.

"What did Conan see?" Matt asked. "I didn't see anything dangerous."

"Directly ahead were two furrows in the rock at depth. I think Conan was concerned about catching a hoof."

"Oh. Damn, they're smart."

Jules chuckled. "It's hard not to think of them as horses, but they are worlds apart."

They gained the further side swaying to keep their equilibrium as the Neos gyred and gimbaled over the slippery rocks, muscles bulging with effort.

On the south side the grass grew thick and abundant. Still no evidence of bugs of any kind.

Matt commented on that. "My guess is that grasses and trees are less susceptible to radiation death than mobile species."

"That would fit."

"Suggests a study."

"Then there's the Neos and the giant bat."

"Both mutations."

"Why them?"

"Like I say, it suggests a study for when we're a bit more settled on top."

"Thinking of that in connection with water-skiing, too. Being settled, I mean."

"I used to water ski," Matt mused.

They moved inland a few yards to avoid large rocks at riverside and headed southeast.

"Wish we had a camera," Matt said.

"Can't think of everything."

"Should have thought of that one."

"Well, anything that needs description we can call in immediately."

"Digital pictures tell a more comprehensive story."

"Yes, they do. They also run out of power and therefore have limited use. At least we can keep notes."

They picked their way up a low headland and at the top of the rise they could see miles into a valley cleft on their left, invisible from across the river. The perspective along the river was different, too. The going wasn't tough and the Neos ambled along. Shadows gradually crept over them.

Jules eye searched the territory. "Another mile."

"Yes, with the storms, we'd better make a lean-to for the night. I hear thunder in the hills again."

"Yeah. Let's avoid iron deposits and sleep high."

"Right."

Twenty-five minutes later they found the spot. Working quickly they threw a temporary shelter together and finished just as the light failed. They ate cold food from their snack packs. The Neos grazed nearby.

Matt got Nancy at the Way station and Sue at Base. "Pretty uneventful. This side is challenging, but we knew that before we started. We got wet."

"Master of understatement, again." Her voice ended in a laugh.

"Tomorrow we'll get opposite you at the old bridge."

Mike broke in. "Matt, there are some eighty foot fir trees up the valley above us. I've been talking to Doc and the gals and we're going to cut half a dozen, strip them and bring sixty-foot lengths down by the river. Our Neos are very accommodating and seem to want to help. We could do with some bigger equipment, axes and a chain saw, but what we have will work.

"Anyway, I figured a way we can get them across the fifty-foot span of the river here with your help. Laying them parallel, large end, small end and reverse throughout with one foot in between each and the small ends blocked with flat rocks to make the tops even with each would give us about an eleven-foot width and a very strong undercarriage. That's plenty. You'll have to clear the debris and level a spot ten feet wide on your side. After the base bridge is laid, we'll corrugate a road across using aspen saplings, shim it horizontal and fill the gaps with stones and this cement-like red dirt and we'll have a road a herd of Neos couldn't take down."

Matt listened with interest. "How do you plan to tie it together?"

"I can't picture sixty-foot trees moving at all, can you? Regardless, if necessary, we'll destrand our rope. Later, when we can get nails and spikes, we'll buttress it to make it more permanent. We'll put up sides, too." Everyone thought of Roddy.

"Good, Mike. I like it. Jules?"

"Sounds good. When do you start?"

"Tomorrow morning."

"We'll be at the bridge site around noon, I think."

"Don't know if we'll have it all here, but the gals are aching to do something and they aren't afraid of work. We'll have enough to get it started."

Doc joined in. "Looks like I'd better make up some poultices, something for pinched fingers, and for blisters."

Laughter filtered over the air before Matt keyed his mike again.

"Great, Mike. Okay, we're off for the night."

Jules turned to Matt. "Sound like a bunch of pioneers."

"Yes, they do."

Chapter 58
Rendezvous

It rained again that night but the majority of the storm slid off east and south of them, so all Matt and Jules got was a spectacular light show. After it passed and before either man tried to get back to sleep, stars shown brilliant in the clean swept sky.

After a few minutes, Jules said softly, "You still awake?"

"Yes."

"The night sky...I appreciated it on the horse farm—nights I had to be away from the bunkhouse—they were gorgeous...but nothing compares with this!"

Matt's voice was introspective. "I know. Was this night sky worth losing a world?"

"If we've been given another chance..." he let the words die. Matt said nothing, but a kind of tension filled the space between them for a few moments and then faded. There was no going back. They relaxed, elbows raised, hands behind their heads, and the sky faded into sleep.

Five hours later the east dawned and they woke to crisp cold. They breakfasted on coffee substitute and the dry energy concoction the Bio had packed for their exploratory trip. It had enough taste to be enjoyable and they felt rejuvenated by the time they packed and boarded their Neos. They could do the fifteen-mile stretch in a bit over three hours, figuring for iffy terrain and slow going.

Matt drew a map from memory of the territory they'd passed since they got onto the south side of McMillan River the previous night.

Now he said, "Describe that cleft back there, the one with the view before we stopped last."

Jules recalled it. "Sheer rock walls at the entrance, reddish rock with lighter streaks running almost vertically, not high, more like a gate. Spectacular view; could see thirty miles, wouldn't you say? Heavily treed into the hazy distance, appeared to open out into a rill valley, running stream in the center. Couldn't see much beyond that. I'd like to walk through that cleft and see the whole thing."

"Nice." Matt drew as Jules described the scene. When he finished, he held it up.

"An artist, how about that!" Jules said.

"Always enjoyed cartography, but never studied it. National Geographic was my favorite."

"Mine, too. The photography was so great; I only rarely read the articles they came with, sad to say."

"I read a lot and learned a lot. There was so much of it. My dad collected them for thirty-five, forty years. Had every one, even the three-D issues. They were something."

"Really?"

"Yeah. Went back to 1988, December, I think. Really impressed me."

"Must have cost a bundle to produce—in the millions."

"I'm sure. Boom times, if I remember my history."

"That would figure."

Matt folded the map and put it away.

"Ready?"

"Conan!"

Fifty feet away, munching a tuft of green, Jules' Neo looked up. "Time to leave."

The Neo blinnied and he and Viceroy trotted to their partners. They evenly distributed the packs over the animals' rumps on either side. Material was carried on a special heavy cloth with a grain that tended to stay put even with the natural rocking motion of the animals. Neos didn't like cinching and that idea had been dropped very early in their relationships. They seemed to like their riders close to their bodies, an item that caused much discomfort until the men and women became hardened to it.

The unexpected give and take between the original master/partners and the final human/Neo partnerships went more to the side of the Neos. The two intelligences may, in fact, have been near equal in discernment and cleverness and in pure cortical gray matter, but such a disparity in mental processes existed that Jules marveled in the odd fact they had come together at all, that they had found something they needed from the other, that they had bonded rather than being repelled.

In some ways they were animals like goats or horses. They showed little curiosity, except about the immediate area. They didn't seem to have a world view and readily allowed themselves to be led, yet their conversations, Jules thought, were constant and of high order. He tried to imagine, but failed from the sheer alienness of the attempt. How did one contemplate a mind one couldn't know?

It was as if the Neos had evolved rapidly to fill a human need, but Jules scoffed at that. Bonded though they were, needing each other in a fundamental sense, he could not bring himself to accept the possibility that some force beyond his ken had conspired to throw Neos into Man's way. Could they be the element of change humans needed to avoid a recurrence of its failed history in some dim future. Neos had no history to speak of. Jules had not shared any of these thoughts with Matt as yet, but it would not have surprised him to discover that Matt was thinking parallel to him all along. He decided to air them.

The Neos presented and the men mounted and set off. They appeared to walk slowly in their odd gait, but they covered ground. Sitting astride their beasts, the men had a lot of time to think.

"Marvelous animals," Jules murmured. He looked straight ahead for a while but didn't try to guide Conan. The two Neos picked their way.

"Matt..." Jules inflection told Matt he was troubled. Matt looked over. Jules related his silent thoughts. Afterwards, they rode in silence for an hour.

Matt had to struggle with it now. Jules was a friend. How could he not? Had he not had similar thoughts, not as well articulated as Jules', though, he thought wryly. The man had a head on his shoulders, and sensitivity. He couldn't not like him.

"Trouble ahead," Matt called.

"We'll let the Neos figure it," Jules replied.

The Mission

They'd come upon a fifteen-foot wall that led straight into the river. The river level dropped several feet as they progressed, and narrowed considerably. The water here moved right along and white water rapids continued as far as they could see. They'd have to go around or over.

Conan shimmied at Viceroy. They evidently decided to brook a slight ridge halfway up the side. Conan turned his ears back and blinned softly.

"They want us to dismount," Jules said.

"They can climb that?"

"Sure." Conan knelt and Jules dismounted. He grabbed a hank of rope.

"Make sure their load is tight." They checked the straps.

"You can read their minds now?"

"Not quite, but I know Conan and I know what he's going to do."

"I plan to be flabbergasted."

"Watch. Okay, Conan."

The Neo stood back ten feet, ran and with a nimble jump, planted all four on the two-inch ridge. Without hesitating, he jumped to another outcropping and in his third jump gained the top.

"I'll be..."

"Don't underestimate a Neo. Now watch."

Viceroy followed exactly. The two Neos turned and stood. Jules uncoiled his rope and tossed it to Conan. The Neo grabbed the end in his teeth and as he reared back, Jules walked up the steep rocky face.

"I'll be damned."

"Here." Jules handed the rope to Viceroy. Matt grabbed hold and mirrored Jules feat.

"I'm humbled," Matt said as he reached them. "Thank you Viceroy."

The Neo snorted and nuzzled his partner.

"Important to remember that Conan is for me and Viceroy is for you. Neither would allow anything they could prevent from hurting either of us, but they are possessive."

Matt hugged the big head. "I am, too."

"I know. Already we are beginning to change. It's almost symbiotic, our need for each other. Have you noticed the strong goat odor we got at first is no longer with them?

"Yes."

"I believe it's not only a matter of our getting used to them. I think some other factor is involved. I think we are...what...acclimating? Growing together, more similar?"

Matt thought. "Yeah, you're right. Came on gradually, but I'm betting *we* won't smell the same to the folks back home when we get back."

"Or Roddy, or Mike, or any of the so-called "rescue" party, either."

"I'd better make Camp and Base aware of all this."

"Plenty of time for that. Let's map what we can see and get to the rendezvous point."

"Another four miles, I think."

The terrain remained rocky, but now grasses and trees grew thick toward the river's edge. At places they were forced inland around groves.

The sun climbed higher and the day warmed. They shed their insulated jackets and tied them to the supply bundles. About a mile from the bridge they came upon a trail. The Neos lowered to smell and then started to look around. They seemed nervous...or was it anticipation?

"What we got here?" Matt queried.

"Don't know. Neos are territorial, but I think the river has been their boundary before last night. Monster bats and then Neos, now what?"

"Glad we kept those stakes from the mine."

They saw nothing, but became more wary and looked back more often. The McMillan thundered now. The river had fallen over thirty feet below the surrounding land. It wasn't easy to hear. Finally they made a turn and they could see the bridge remnant in the distance. The Neos had calmed and the men decided it couldn't be too serious; that whatever had bothered them wasn't a threat.

Surmounting a last depression, they appeared in plain sight of the Way Station to the waves and cheers of their friends on the north side.

Chapter 59
Building Bridges

Mike yelled across. "Look at this."

"This," were five sixty-foot pine logs shorn of branches and laid out near a low contraption about six feet from the edge of the sixty foot drop-off. They were laid alternately, large end, small end, as Mike had explained by radio.

The noise of the river made hearing difficult, but one of the station's party had fashioned a bullhorn from available material and Mike made himself eminently clear.

"We could almost breach the river ourselves, but the mass and weight of these pieces and the short fulcrum made it too cumbersome to take a chance on losing them to the river, and we've all developed interesting blister patterns on our hands, scrapes on arms, etc."

Looking up the hillside, the south-side men could see two Neos in the distance struggling down a makeshift dirt road with a sixth bridge section in tow.

Mike continued. "What we're going to do is to swing a big end piece horizontally across the river using the rolling pulleys up there," he pointed, " and you're going to have to construct something massive enough to stop it at the right spot on your side."

Matt and Jules instantly saw what Mike needed and began to search the nearby woods for something that would effectively block the momentum of the oncoming log. They went some ways into the woods, but soon they reappeared, dragging a good-sized piece onto the old roadway. They found rocks their Neos could move and inside of an hour, and created a proper stop for the first piece.

"Your turn," Matt shouted.

Mike called to two Neos tied to a jury-rigged turnstile. "Okay, pull!"

Slowly the wheel turned. The end of the huge tree cleared the road surface and moved smoothly out over space, taut ropes near the small end taking the weight. The Neos kept even pressure on the turnstile and Matt and Jules watched while the first section of the new bridge approached on a big horizontal arc. Mike had figured that the south side roadway was a foot lower than the height on the north and factored it so it would arrive almost even with the road on that side. When the piece arrived and struck the stop, Mike called to the Neos to stop and slowly back. The log settled into place.

A cheer went up. The log hung across the chasm leaving five feet on each side. Jules climbed on and untied the ropes.

"Nicely done," a voice came over the radio.

"Base? How did you get into the act?" Mike demanded.

The peal of laughter came from Nancy. "You want to keep this all to yourself, Mike?"

"Uh, no, I mean..." He stopped.

"Arthur here. Since you're doing yeomen's work we're going to create an honorary position for people who work beyond the call. Mike, you are designated Yeoman of the Day."

"Thanks."

Thor pulled the next log into the north stop. Mike tied several ropes to the other end and the pulling began again. By nightfall they had three logs in place, a foot of space between them, separated by six inch tall, flat rocks. They talked by radio now, brought Base up to date and settled down for the night. They had a lot to think about.

Matt and Jules would cut twelve-foot saplings from their side to add to the ones being produced by the larger workforce on the north side. In the morning they would install the other three bridge sections and then begin laying roadway perpendicular to the main bridge undersurface. They'd meet somewhere in the middle. Maude and Doc's job was to gather small stone to fill the cracks to make a useable bridge out of it.

In the morning they started early.

Although Mike had no engineering experience, his math told him the new span would have to be shored up in the center to keep it from sagging. He designed four stays set onto stable rock underneath the span that would arch out eighteen feet on either side and take the majority of the weight.

"The weight of the bridge will hold the whole thing together. The more it tries to sag, the tighter the stays will hold it."

"Seems right to me," Matt said. "Why not I ask Jerry?"

"Sure," Mike said, but he sounded a little hurt.

"Mike, I know you're right, but we're going to trust a lot of people and a lot of weight to this bridge. Maybe Jerry has a suggestion or two."

"Okay, Matt, call him."

"Jerry, let me describe our bridge."

Jerry came back. "You don't have to, Matt. I have the flavor of it. Mike has done a great job, more than he needs. You have what, six logs cut?"

"Yes."

"Let me talk to Mike."

"I'm on, Jerry."

"Okay. You have three over right now, right?"

"Yes, Jerry."

"Spread them out to your twelve foot width. Two outer and one center. Notch the outer ones at fifteen feet. The center twenty feet will carry all right. Measure off the exact distance from a stable rock point fifteen feet or so down the cliff and cut your hypotenuse to fit. You with me?"

"Of course."

"Good. Using the middle log as a working crane, move it wherever you need to get leverage, place the angled pieces to their footing and lash them to the undersides of your outer members. To get a snug, strong fit, raise one end of your outer structure three inches when you place it and the weight will, as you stated, settle in and hold like iron. Do it the same way for all three. After you are finished, return the working crane to center to become a bridge support and your cross members will hold the entire structure together. I promise you, it will be strong enough to take one of the heavy machines in the equipment cave, or a herd of Neos."

Mike laughed. "You know your stuff."

"So do you, Mike. Without an engineering background, you figured it all out."

"You think the four men can get it done?"

A howl came from the female faction. "Hey, we're not exactly helpless, Jerry."

Laughter from the radio. "No, but defer to bigger muscles, won't you?"

"Oh, you mean the Neos?" Nancy said smugly. Clearly heard snickers.

Matt keyed his radio. "Okay, everyone, we all agree we need this bridge, right?"

It became quiet.

"Our purpose has become clouded. The original decision was to get to Ross River and find out what we can. The question now is, do we stop to build a bridge or do we get on with the original purpose. Let's decide."

They stared silently at the little figure across the river.

Valid point.

Mary Beth finally spoke. "We got our whole lives to check out the rest of the world. I say we build the bridge and then go."

Arthur's voice came from a nearby speaker. "I agree with Mary Beth. Small steps will get us where we want to go a lot safer than racing into the unknown and stretching your lifeline too far. This is only my opinion. You decide."

"Al here." They listened. "A quick way back is better than your back against a wall."

"What do you mean?" Matt asked.

"We think the world is empty. Maybe no people, but it's not empty."

Valid point.

"Okay, let's vote. Base, you're out of this. Build, raise your hands."

"Unanimous. We stay."

"Democracy in action," they heard Nancy say.

"Let's get to work."

Chapter 60
Herd Troubles

The Neo herd lived on the eastern half of Front Mountain's steep grassy slopes and valleys. They had never broached the western side, though they knew of Man. They knew that eight tribe members had joined with the strange humans who rode them. Those closest to the transformation, Neo brothers and sisters who had felt the powerful urge to partner but had not been chosen desired it, too, but they could do nothing.

So the Neos ran and played and remained true to their breeding. But a society is a living thing. In every society, there are aggressive members and those less so. With the mutated goats, three Neos in particular were getting restive. None had been close to the original or secondary encounters.

They knew their leader stood a little higher than all the rest. The herd looked up to that one and gave it a kind of fealty. That Neo had the gift of the herd's attention. That Neo gained the responsibility for offering wisdom to the entire tribe.

Conan, acknowledged leader, had been away for days. Although they thought at a very high level, the wisdom of their leader had left them and they needed it. Therefore, they needed Conan.

The herd numbered three hundred and forty-four. Eight had gone. The three began talks with herd members, testing the air, getting opinions. At first, all Neos turned down any thought of going against the leader, shying away from thoughts of disloyalty. But as the days lengthened and they were left to their devices without their source of wisdom, the three disgruntled Neos gained a foothold with the herd.

The situation could be resolved, but Conan must be the one to do so. Confrontation could occur at any time. One older female stood aside and watched the byplay. She had been closest to the first group of Man and had felt the powerful urging, the need to join the strange, new creatures. She had felt the power of them, and she knew what she must do.

Conan, she must find him. He would either return to the tribe and reassert his leadership or abdicate. Either choice was an acceptable response. Dividing the herd was not. When the herd settled for the night, she left it. She followed the spoor easily. It led down and down, through woods and grassy plains, and through rocky land completely devoid of life of any kind, over unstable, shale-like rock that slid at the least provocation.

Arriving on old Route 6, she stopped to sniff the unfamiliar surface, and then plodded along the road's edge, as had the explorers days before. She came upon the car and sniffed it and realized that inside this metal thing had been one like those who had taken their leader. She snorted to clear her nostrils of the putrescence. That one had ceased life. She hoped it had been eaten according to ritual.

She continued the night without rest and at first light arrived at the diesel tank and mine. She did not like the pungent smells, but paused because the old trail was now overlaid with another trail that headed straight for the river. Both carried the leader's spoor. She decided and followed the river trail. At its edge, she stopped. The scent was gone, but worse, the unknown ruled on the other side and it made her afraid. No Neo had ever crossed. What had happened to the leader? The other path, then.

Returning to the road, she picked up the older scent and followed it. Worried that the tribal situation might become dangerous while she was away, she increased her gait into the ungainly Neo trot. She could maintain it while on dirt and grass, but on rock she had to slow. Still, in less than two hours, on an easterly breeze, her sense of smell delighted in the scent of others of her tribe. She ran faster.

In the distance she saw slow moving specks on the road. She blinned. In seconds her sharp ears caught a returning blinny. All work stopped. Little men stood and gazed at her running form. She arrived in a rush and, ignoring the humans, shook and shimmied and snorted her message to Thoth and Thor, while the others looked on. As she finished, Thor tossed his head toward the river and the Neo messenger looked across, startled to see Conan looking at her. How could he be in the land of the unknown?

The leader blinned. Thoth and Thor blinned in tandem.

Jules got on the radio. "We have a situation. This Neo wouldn't have tracked us down if there weren't a problem."

He turned to Conan. "Try to tell me."

Jules Neo, in spite of the distance, had caught much of what the messenger had said. He shook and shimmied for Jules and placed his muzzle in Jules open palms. Then he made like to move away, to head back the way they had come. Impatient. Turned and looked at his partner. Moved away again. Looked back.

"Okay, I got the message." He keyed his radio and announced for all to hear, "Problem with the herd. Conan has to go but he won't go without me, so I'm going. Do what you can without me. This is important. I'll return as soon as I can."

With that, he said to Conan, "Present."

The Neo went down on his forelegs and stood with Jules aboard. Then he turned quickly and raced away faster than any Neo they had ever seen run before. Soon he was behind the near forest and gone. Jules voice came back through the radio. The messenger Neo turned in concert with Conan and ran parallel to him. Soon she, too, disappeared in the distance.

"I'll keep everyone advised. Wish we had more bridge finished. Do the best we can. Out."

For moments, everyone stood stunned at the turn of events. What could be wrong? Another animal, the huge bat preying on the herd? What?

Matt took control. "C'mon everybody, let's get this bridge built."

Chapter 61
Conan's Ordeal

Neo and partner covered the difficult terrain as quickly as possible. On the other side of the river, the messenger Neo turned on all four and started back, keeping parallel with her leader.

Doc said quietly, "We'd better hope that comes out right."

The others nodded. Their social plight now extended to a herd of mountain goats. Strangely, no one thought it odd. The degree of symbiosis hadn't hit them, but Jules knew.

Jules hung on. Conan's reaction was measured, but urgent. When they arrived at the cliff after four miles, Conan stopped, looked the situation over and blinnied to Jules. The man took in the problem and thought of his solution as Conan gathered and jumped into high grass beside the faint trail. All Jules could do was to hang on. Spongy moss absorbed their fall and Jules smiled at Conan's solution. He'd been ready to get off and climb down. What really impressed him was the fact that Conan factored his decision to allow for Jules weight and his belief in Jules ability to take the leap without injury. He filed away another Neo superiority.

They arrived at the broad, shallow riverbed in less than half the time it had taken them to ride southwest. Conan lunged into the river, satisfied that his rider wouldn't come off under conditions bordering on the extreme. The deep area he did differently, making water pressure work for him.

Smart. Jules thought, very smart.

Soon they'd crossed the hundred fifty feet of river and gained the other side. Behind them another Neo trotted into their circle. Conan turned and shimmied to the female messenger. He went over and nuzzled her, stood back and shimmied for a few minutes.

Now Conan and the female picked the smooth dirt roadside and literally ran. The miles flew. At the turn leading to the Neo tribal pastures, they bolted up a draw and climbed steadily for fifteen minutes. Then, winded, Conan stopped and knelt for Jules to dismount. Jules guessed they would be just out of earshot from the ranging herd.

It was mid-afternoon. Jules stood by while Conan recovered his strength. Smart Neo, he thought. No anger, just resignation, a need to confront his problem, but to confront it from a position of strength, not exhaustion. Conan calmly grazed for a half hour. Visibly refreshed, Conan returned to Jules and presented for his partner. Jules mounted. His Neo shimmied briefly.

With a snort, the female began the long climb to the grazing pastures. Conan stood and watched her.

"You told her to announce your coming, didn't you, Conan?"

The Neo blinnied softly. Like royalty. They followed the female a hundred yards behind. The grazing pastures opened out suddenly at the end of the tree line, stretching far in either direction. Just in that moment, the female blinnied loudly, urgently. As they entered the open area, Jules could see hundreds of Neos gravitating to the middle of the field. Others ran awkwardly to it.

Conan moved slowly, looking to the right and left. In the five minutes it took for all to assemble, Conan and Jules arrived and stopped. The Neo blinnied, shimmied and shook. Belatedly, reluctantly, three males separated themselves from the herd. Conan addressed them. Two eventually bowed to their leader. With a bellow, Conan dismissed them and they disappeared into the herd, which made a wide way, as though ashamed to touch or be near them.

Now Conan addressed the third. Jules decided the remaining Neo wanted to challenge Conan for the herd. From his perch, Jules tried to size him up. Big fella, three inches taller than Conan, rangy and like his partner, very muscular. The leader stood and shimmied. The herd tightened its circle around the opponents. Three females detached from the herd and surrounded Conan, after which Conan presented and Jules immediately dismounted.

If he read it correctly, Conan had given Jules over to the three Neos for his protection. The meaning wasn't lost on the herd. Now the three females turned outward in a protect stance, but it wasn't quick enough. With a blinny of rage and before he could regain his feet, the challenger lunged for Conan.

There were rules for Neo combat and Jules saw that the challenger had broken them to gain a quick advantage. The big Neo's teeth dived for Conan's neck as the Neo tried to vault to the side. The battle would have been very short if the female closest to the challenger hadn't put her own neck in the way. The big animal bit hard and blood spurted from a torn jugular. The female went down, blocking the rampaging Neo and he tripped on the body.

Conan had time to gain his feet and turned to engage with a vengeance. He flipped his large head into the side of the contender's snout and blood flew from his eye socket. The action, much too close to the fight, left Jules wondering how he would survive the kicking and twisting. As if the two remaining Neos had read his mind, they nuzzled him away from the combat, while staying between him and the fighters. Jules wondered at how personally the protector Neos took their jobs.

As soon as he was clear, another Neo detached from the herd to provide the tertiary protection he must be entitled to. Now twenty-five feet away, Jules could turn to watch. Conan's move had momentarily shaken the bigger Neo and Conan spun and kicked the challenger in the ribs. Hurt, but not out of the fight, the younger Neo went down, but managed to turn to meet his adversary and as Conan turned for the kill, front hooves aimed at the Neo's neck, with a twist, the Neo bit Conan's right foreleg hard. Blood spurted!

Roaring in pain, Conan spun again in a circle so tight Jules couldn't believe it, and kicked hard at the Neo's head. Conan's right rear hoof caught the other Neo in the right eye and the Neo screamed in pain. The side of his head was now misshapen and blood poured copiously from the massive wound. What came from the animal sounded like pleading. Flipping around yet again, Conan dived again and ripped a hole larger than a fist in the challenger's neck.

The young Neo's legs kicked, but without direction. Now the fight went out of him, soon followed by the light of his one remaining eye. He rolled onto his side, lay out and died. Conan, obviously in pain, hobbled to the dead Neo, reached down, tore a section of flank from the animal and ate it, signaling the ritual feast of the dead. Conan stood away while the herd passed, tore warm flesh and devoured it.

Jules had trouble not being judgmental, but realized that the ritual disposition of the defeated animal wasn't so unlike rituals humans had practiced centuries before the world became temporarily civilized on its way to its own annihilation. He likened it to the ritual, "Ashes to ashes, dust to dust." Interesting, Neo's were herbivorous, but in their rituals they were carnivorous. He knew only bones would be left to bleach in the sun after this day.

The radio! He'd forgotten. He grabbed it and keyed the mike. "Conan lives. He's injured but he is still leader. I can't ride him. I'd try to patch him up, but this is his show and I don't want to tread on his protocols. I'll wait to see what Conan wants to do."

People broke in from the Way Station and Base simultaneously. Finally, Jules asked for forbearance, that he needed to get all the way through this and when he had, he'd give a full report. They reluctantly agreed.

Conan stayed, head high, ignoring the blood that ran freely down his leg. Jules watched it slow, but it was a bad bite and needed attention. The Neo stood for fifteen minutes. The bloody muzzles of nearly one hundred tribe members attested to their tasting of the vanquished Neo.

Jules also saw that the Neo female who saved Conan during the breach in the rules wasn't touched. If anything, they stepped around her in the manner of one revered. Looking more closely, he could see that the blood had stopped. She'd lost a lot. The female hadn't moved since her injury and to all appearances seemed dead. Then he saw the very slow rising of her side. How...?

Finally, Conan blinnied for attention and shimmied for a full minute. Leaving his post, he went right to Jules. Putting his head in Jules hands, he blinnied softly and then lifted his foreleg for Jules to inspect. The blood had all but stopped and a startled Jules realized that his Neo had healing powers beyond his understanding. He tested the leg and discovered it firm and unbroken.

"Well, Conan, you continue to amaze me."

The Neo presented.

"Are you sure?"

Conan snorted. He obviously wanted his rider where he belonged. Jules didn't hesitate, mounted and felt the muscles gather as Conan lurched to his feet. He blinnied. The herd turned toward him. He rose, very horse-like on his back hoofs, while Jules casually held a hank of scraggly mane, and let out a shrill blinny. Then he shimmied and shook and soon similar ripples began in the near Neos and continued through the herd

In perhaps a minute the entire herd faced Conan and presented, almost as one.

"Unbelievable," Jules breathed. He must have sounded excited when he keyed his radio. "Ladies and gentlemen, I have just witnessed a most amazing phenomenon. The Neos bowed, curtsied, genuflected, I'm not sure what, but I can guarantee that Conan has tuned the entire herd to the human frequency. Symbiotic or not, we're all going forward together."

If he expected something more, silence over the soft hiss of radio power from the speaker told him what he most wanted. They listened. They were in awe, not of him, but of a whole new species whose inadvertent entrance into the human pale might, in this one moment, become the true start of Man's new and better direction.

After a long moment, Matt's muted voice came through. "Roger."

Chapter 62
Metamorphosis

At the confrontation Jules learned something he would keep to himself for a time, until he thought it through and decided what he could do with the knowledge, maybe only for as long as it took to get back to his fellows. Then he would share. He must always share. It was part of the parcel.

The rending of flesh had a more important purpose. It disposed of an animal that might regenerate back to health and become pariah to the entire herd. Atomic radiation had finally done a genetically good thing. Rapid regeneration helped keep the Neos alive, especially in the early days following apocalypse. With that and a social structure Neos had developed so incredibly fast, came a social need. Anger and hurt and damage invaded all life. There was a brake somewhere and Jules had found it.

No, they had it figured, Jules thought. They had it figured. He wondered who was under whose wing, although it didn't seem to matter. They complemented each other. It came to him why Conan seemed to respond so quickly and so well. He understood English. He'd picked it up. Jules understood the sense of the shimmy and other movements and sounds, but didn't grasp the language. He would have to try harder. Man needed to learn Neo.

"Head for the way station as soon as you feel ready, Conan."

The Neo whuffed. He wasn't ready. More needed doing before he could leave the herd a second time. His leadership reasserted, all males and females understood that their wise one had returned, and that he would leave again. Conan appointed three Neos, two males and a female to watch the emotional temperature of the herd and to form a reporting line to him in the event he was again suddenly needed.

The sacrificial Neo, still on the ground but breathing more normally now, also appeared to Jules to be almost visibly healing. The jugular had stopped flowing and the skin around the breach had begun to tighten. Two female Neos attended her, not allowing the herd general to come too close, although they tried. Jules marveled at how highly developed was the protective aspect of Neo society. Jules thought it made human solitariness a curse. Neos could teach us things we'd never learned as a species. He fitted another piece into the larger puzzle.

Conan seemed in no hurry to leave. His presence was needed and also his right foreleg needed to heal. It occurred to Jules, who wanted to return with his remarkable story, that Conan decided what needed to be done long before Jules picked up on it. The lithe chemist sat straight on his Neo looking as proud as he felt. He knew then that Conan wanted this picture indelibly etched on his herd.

Tentatively, a few Neos approached. They glanced at Jules where he sat easily. Conan shimmied a high level conversation. Others took their place as they went away satisfied. Jules remained mute, looked around, gathered impressions and stored them for later. The pilgrimage went on for nearly an hour. In that time the challenging Neo had been stripped to bones, which were being gnawed for scraps. In the ritual destruction, an evil the herd could not live with abated. All had been made right.

Now Conan decided his healing was sufficient for him to leave. He walked over to the fallen female and nuzzled her, snorted and blinnied so softly that Jules barely heard it. The female raised her head, her first movement of any kind, save breathing. Jules decided that Conan was honoring her and making, perhaps, a promise for the future. The Neo returned the snort and shimmied briefly, then relaxed onto her side again. Conan lowered his head to her, raised it and blinnied to the rest. Then he turned and headed down the mountain.

Jules thoughts ran parallel to the easy motion of the broad back. It no longer pained to ride the spiny hump. He had adjusted, too.

Chapter 63
Way Station Bridge

"Whoo!" Nancy let out a breath.

"Yeah!" Millie echoed the sentiment.

Arriving from the high woods, they took a break from directing bundles of long poles into the campsite. They had both laughed earlier mentioning that, and Nancy had opined the Neos could do it by themselves. Millie smiled and said she was sure the Neos were content to have their partners by their sides, to which Nancy readily agreed and they'd sent a little love their Neos way.

Jules and Conan had arrived minutes before and after breathless hugs they listened to Jules long account of the saga in the Neo field. Mike keyed Base in.

"Unbelievable!" Unanimous.

"I knew you couldn't wait. My turn. What's happened here?"

With Matt and Viceroy's help on the south side and Mike's newly discovered organizational genius—certainly no one would ever go head to head with him in a math contest, but this...? With no small amount of help on the north side from the Neos, two of the stays had been installed on the east side of the bridge and wedged permanently in the rocky jumble while Jules was gone.

"It's above flood stage?"

"Highest stage I can see is fifteen feet below the bottom of the stay," Mike said.

"Enough safety margin?"

"I think so."

With the help of Thoth, Thor and Crystal, the strange horizontal crane Mike visualized and whose construction he supervised earlier, now sat suspended on the bridge's superstructure, ready to do the west side.

Mike told Jules how quickly the Neos grasped the needed engineering.

"They're really smart," he finished.

"You don't even know," Jules agreed fervently.

They'd pulled and pushed with finesse and it was lost on none that the Neos biggest evolutionary problem lay in not having proper grasping appendages. Doc thought about it from an anatomical standpoint and decided an operation might be possible to allow for muscularly controlled small appendages to be attached near the shoulder muscles, but after Jules comment that Neos understood English and that the humans still had little clue to Neo speech, he decided not to say anything. Later, maybe, if appropriate. He began to tick off reasons why it wouldn't be.

Looking at it from another angle, Doc realized that humans had already become appendages for Neos. Conversely, Neos provided power humans lacked. Humans had used dumb animals for many centuries. This new thing was not the same at all. It didn't take much observation to see how quickly they picked up on anything they were exposed to.

They notched outer bridge horizontals three inches deep on their inner aspect and shaved them to allow placement of angled stays. Much care in cutting the vertical and long angle—accomplished by Mike as he swung from a workbasket fashioned of long grasses—allowed the positively cut joiner to fit exactly. Just before insertion, they lifted the outer horizontal a couple of inches so that when it settled in, the weight of the long beam made the bond solid.

"What about windstorm?" Jules asked Mike.

"Unlikely, but I've asked Al and Gil to come up with some threaded iron bolts."

"Right. Cement for the rock face anchors?"

"Yes, and preservative to paint on the whole thing. I want the bridge to last twenty-five years, at least."

"Good."

With earlier practice, the second stay placed easily. Getting it across was a problem, but they solved it by tying both ends and using pulleys, with a man walking the beam to keep it stable. They anticipated no problem with the western, downriver side. Mike had already marked the anchor points. The trickiest part, measuring the correct length to account for dropping the stays into place, Mike figured with a little headwork. He measured them out on the flat road surface of old Rt. 6 and cut all the necessary angles. Jules was quite impressed.

"Shouldn't you nick the sinking angle a little more at the receiving angle," he asked Mike.

"No. Pine is compressible. I want the fit exact so the stays won't tend to round off or soften under heavy pressure. You see I didn't cut into the carrying beam very deeply. The deeper you go, the less strong the beam. That's got to hold a lot of weight."

"You got me," Jules visualized Mike's concept and couldn't find anything wrong with it.

"I'm happy putting the old brain to work, Jules."

"Yeah, we're all doing that."

When he arrived, Jules saw the large pile of saplings on the roadside meant for bridge covering for after they completed the bull work. He gauged they were about eighty-percent done.

No one complained except for blisters and long hours. Roddy complained, of course. Doc told him he could help by weaving grasses, subject to fatigue and his own pain.

He held up both hands. "I count ten thumbs."

"Never mind, then." Mike said.

"But I'm going crazy. I'll do it." Mike showed him how.

"Attitude is a big part of healing," Doc said to Mike out of earshot. "It'll help. Just make sure the women balance their coddling with a keen eye on getting him up."

"They don't need to be told, Doc," Mike said.

Doc thought for a second and smiled. "I suppose not."

"Mary Beth wouldn't let it happen anyway."

"True."

Jules called to Mike, who turned.

"What can I do? Matt's still across the river."

"If you're up to it, try the bucket and we'll place another stay."

Jules figured it out immediately and while he made his way to the bucket, Mike and Geronimo positioned themselves at the swing fulcrum, fitted the northwest stay to the contraption and

Nancy connected Apache to the turntable. At a word, the big log slowly moved out to the edge of chasm. Calling hold, Mike attached lowering ropes to the log end two feet inside of the end. Mary Beth secured Thoth to her harness thirty feet back of the lip and with a signal to Mike the log went slowly over the edge.

Thoth moved forward step by slow step and the stay descended to the wedge point. Using a little play in the swing, the stay settled into the marked spot. Now Jules, who had watched the process with amazement, could do his part. The fulcrum swung the smaller, carefully angled end to his basket and Jules guided it to the juncture. It was two inches too long.

Now Millie, who sat on a small platform strung between the ropes arced over to the east side to hold everything in place moved to the end of her two-inch sapling and applied her weight to a short fulcrum close to the western bridge horizontal. The horizontal obligingly rose upward.

"Another inch, Millie," Jules called.

Millie pushed harder.

"Got it. Ease up." The main horizontal settled into place.

"Perfect. Coming up." Jules scaled the five-foot height onto the unfinished surface.

"Great idea, Mike."

Mike waved. "One more."

The final stay had been shaped while others were installing the third. To get the last stay across the river involved rolling it over the horizontals in place. They tied four ropes onto the ends, two north and two south, then asked their Neos to push/pull it. Since it wasn't perfectly cylindrical, it took time to get it across without dropping it into the abyss. As with the southeastern stay, dropping it could have been disaster for the entire project, but they managed both with great care and without incident.

Now across, they repeated the process for the other one. Jules repositioned his bucket twenty feet at the southwestern contact point. Matt was ready. Viceroy used the same lowering technique as had Apache beforehand. The sun was behind the western mountains by the time they finished.

Clouds drifted in from the west and the sky started to lower.

"Good day's work," Mike slapped Jules on the shoulder.

Matt came over the radio. "Nice job, Mike and Jules. Ladies, you did a land office business today. We should have a ribbon cutting by tomorrow night, don't you think?"

Millie broke in. "Miss you, Matt."

"Miss you, too. I'd come over, but I'm not leaving Viceroy."

"Understand." Millie wondered if Matt said it for Viceroy's benefit. He understood English very well now.

"Mike, I'm going to make a little supper. We're going to get some weather in a bit. How about you bring Base up to date.

"Sure, Matt." Mike keyed his radio.

Just then, lightning flashed in the mountains.

Chapter 64
Finishing the Job

The storm hit about midnight. Matt took shelter in the tree belt a few hundred feet from the river and wrapped himself up for the night. The Way Station got its first real test for leaks. It rained hard for an hour. Electricity spat upon rock and tree and then, spent, the storm moved off.

The thunderous McMillan roared and shook the very rock upon which they slept. By first light two or three had made the pilgrimage to the edge. Mike got there first, worried about the stays. The rest were up shortly after. They marveled at the roaring water. It had come up many feet as the hills above drained, but nowhere close to the bottommost stay.

Before the sun barely peeked over the horizon, the Way Station was awake, refreshed and ready to finish their biggest challenge to date. The ladies brought saplings to the edge and Jules and Mike tied them down. To make a ramp onto the bridge proper, Doc asked Pan to help bring loads of dirt and gravel to the road and they carefully graded it. On the other side, Matt, with little to do, performed the same task.

By noon the workers had half the bridge covered and were walking on it with impunity. The more weight that piled onto the roadway, the stronger the bridge became. By consensus they decided to wait on tying in the center beam until nails were available. They'd blocked both ends of the center span and Mike said it wasn't going anywhere. They got a commitment from Base for the production of spikes for all covering and long bolts for the major stress areas. They tapped Jerry Ells civil engineering knowledge for the accuracy of their plan. He pointedly gave Mike all the credit and told them they didn't need him.

After lunch, Nancy took Apache back into the hills for more saplings. Her Neo dragged in big bundles of the thin trees. By three o'clock, they had enough to finish the span. The planning was exquisite. At six p.m., Mike Peters walked off the end of the newly finished bridge and formally shook Matt's hand.

"Dr. Livingston, I presume?"

Matt grimaced.

Chapter 65
A Necessary Step Back

Those who stood in for the monumental bridge building project over the McMillan expressly to get to Ross River, to what, they didn't know, were Matt Duncan and Viceroy, Millie Bainbridge on Crystal, Mike Peters with Geronimo, Nancy Spiller and her Neo Apache, Doc Simmons with Pan, Jules Beggin on Conan, Mary Beth Holiday riding Thoth and Roddy Brown with Thor.

Mary Beth surveyed the scene and said with hands on hips. "We've got to put up a plaque, guys,"

"Arthur?" Matt keyed his radio. "Mary Beth says we need a plaque."

The Chief Scientist's delighted voice came back immediately. "Don't give it another thought, Matt."

With the key still depressed, he heard Arthur yell to Al. "Got another job for you, Al."

"Arthur?"

"Yes, Matt."

"Don't forget the Neos."

"No, Matt, we won't."

In a gala celebration that night by the eight and their animals while Base listened in, and whose wholehearted response to the bridges completion—which they asserted was astounding—they all raised a cup of tea high and toasted their success. Roddy couldn't stand, but he could finally sit up and no one had a bigger smile.

Doc insisted on giving the first toast. "To the first pioneer outing of the last one hundred, I salute the solidarity, energy, forthrightness and intelligence of we who are again ascending toward the heavens, no longer alone, but with partners who will leaven us as we leaven them."

The others gave a mighty shout and the eight Neos blinnied. They clearly understood. Another milestone, another element of tightening symbiosis.

Jules, briefly lost in thought, wondered if the exploring and rescue parties weren't getting a bit ahead of the rest of their fellows and what it might mean. He got Matt's attention and shared his private thoughts.

"They have been introduced vicariously, Jules."

"I haven't detected any jealousy or negativism in radio contacts, but Matt, they don't have what we have."

Matt thought about it. "Jules, I know where you're coming from. Let's all talk about it now, but leave Base out until we come to a conclusion."

"Agree."

The Way Station group had been sitting around and chatting and enjoying the warm glow that followed their team efforts.

"Listen up, people," Matt called. Conversation stopped. "Jules is more sensitive to the Neos than the rest of us."

Nods.

"He's thinking we are moving away from the rest of the Bio emotionally because of our association with the Neos. Base knows that we are with them and I think some, at least, Arthur for certain, understand that we are changing, too. We are, without doubt, and I have to think it is a very good thing, but there may be a danger. Jules, tell them."

"Basically, I think we should all go home, right now. Come back and finish our trek, yes, but not, I think, before we bring enough Neos to New Beginnings for every adult, at the very least. I don't think we should spring it on Base, like show up and 'Surprise!' I don't mean that. I just think we're getting ahead of the rest and since we're all in this together, I see a danger in all of us not traveling this evolutionary road together." He shrugged. "That's all."

"Wow!" Millie said softly.

"We need to talk about it," Matt said.

Doc spoke. "How many Neos are there, Jules?"

"I don't know; more than us. Three hundred?"

Doc pursued it. "What would we do? I'm fond of Pan and I share with you all a...need...I think, to be with them. So would we bring all three hundred to the valley and see what happens, or should we bring only those we need?"

"I don't know, Doc. Let's ask Conan."

All eyes turned to Jules' Neo. He asked the question. Conan's bright, intelligent eyes stared at Jules for a moment and then he began to shimmy and shake. The other seven Neos turned and listened intently. Conan blinnied. All eight moved to one side and stood. Conan blinnied again and each Neo moved back to his or her partner.

"Yes!" Jules said, his eyes bright. "Conan says—I believe I've got it—that we are one. We cannot be separated. I think he means that the other Neos will need humans as much as they need us. I think Conan has made our decision. Anybody?"

Seven voices spoke at the same time. They stopped and Matt began.

"That primitive display was handled deftly. I understood it."

"Me too," chorused the others.

"All in favor?"

Eight aye's.

"We'll head back tomorrow. Conan," Matt looked to the Neo, "do we take the herd or just enough to 'fill the positions', I wonder?"

Conan faced Matt and shimmied and blinnied softly.

"Okay," Matt said, "you decide."

"Now," Matt addressed the group, "let's figure what we tell Base."

Chapter 66
Neo Decision

"Matt? Aren't you forgetting something?"

Matt searched his brain. "What, Arthur?"

"What of the one hundred, plus forty-six children? And more to come."

Matt frowned. "Of course."

"There will be logistical problems, naturally."

Doc butted in. "I suggest we let Conan know now. It might change his thinking."

"Yes," Matt said.

"And by the way, it hit me that we are deferring to our Neos for information and for decisions, just like a partner would."

Nancy said, "We humans are so arrogant, aren't we?" She tittered.

Matt said thoughtfully, "We have been and now it seems we are naturally subverting our desire to be at the top, happily and with no hidden agendas. Interesting. Jules?"

Jules came nearer. He nodded.

"How much do you need to pass to Conan?" Matt asked.

"Nothing. He heard the conversation. Conan?"

The Neo stood in thought and then shimmied his answer. Jules likened Neo language to Sign with an added vocal accoutrement. In his pre-apocalypse past he'd worked one summer for a cattle rancher, whose daughter was a deaf mute. A pretty girl and Jules junior by only a year, he'd spent many nights looking at the stars with her on the family's front porch. They used a small, rich field telescope and binoculars to augment their excellent eyes. Every so often she would tug at his sleeve and point to a star or group of stars and gesture. By using a red filter over a three-cell flashlight and pointing with a laser light her dad had bought her the Christmas before, she showed Jules how the sky translated to printed star charts she kept on a porch table, Elvira had taught him far more than he'd known about the stars, but more important, she'd given him a real appreciation for them and for the celestial sphere.

Thinking of it now, it was an epiphany that helped him focus his efforts in college. He knew he was far ahead of the rest in picking up the nuances of Neospeak. It would be appropriate, he thought, to create a text of Neo motions. Light ripples denoted pleasure and harder, more definitive ripples of the same type showed anger or distress. Other human emotions had corollaries, he felt, and he kept his eyes on his Neo as often as he could to extend his knowledge. One thing he knew, the Neos were straightforward animals. They had not learned the human trait of lying, although he remembered the big Neo taking advantage of the leader during the fight and it suggested cunning.

"Conan says his people will treat small humans with greater care. I believe he's suggesting that the many females deal with the youngest, etc."

"Good."

Conan blinnied softly. Jules said, "Conan is curious. Do we eat our dead?"

The others smiled at that.

"Better set him straight, Jules," Millie called from the back.

"Yeah. Conan, humans do not eat their dead. Once life has left the body, we call it a corpse. Our ritual is to bury the dead one or to cremate, which is a cleansing by fire. Do you remember the bones we buried from the dead human in the car?"

Conan nodded his head in a startlingly human way and snorted.

"Time to get moving," Matt said.

"I'll have to get back, but Roddy can't ride," Doc said. "What's the status of the rest? Two ought to stay, I think."

Mike said, "I'll stay. Nancy, stay with me?"

"I'd like to. I cleared my calendar for this, so I'm good."

"I have to get back, Roddy," Mary Beth said.

He nodded. "I know. You coming back?"

"Oh yeah, I'll be back. Got to train my replacement."

"So, I thought Jane was minding the store."

"She is."

"She *need* help?"

"For most things, no, but I know the system best and I can give her stuff she doesn't know well. Also I'm going to ask to be relieved of my duties to the pile when Jane is up to speed. And I've got to help her pick her backup, too."

"You sure?"

"Yes. I want to be with you, lover."

Doc said, "I doubt you can do that, Mary Beth. We all have our place."

"But things are changing, Doc, and I'm not leaving anyone high and dry. I just want a change. You'll want to retire some day. You're going to be in charge of creating more doctors, aren't you?"

"That's another subject for a full meeting. I'll bring it up."

"A lotta cross training comin' up," Roddy interjected.

Matt brought the subject back. "Okay, guys, we get a good nights rest and head back at first light. Conan will probably have to spend time convincing or directing or whatever he does. We should make it to the fields by late afternoon."

The meeting broke up, the fire dimmed. With its millions of stars seeming close enough to touch, the firmament became almost brilliantly oppressive. No rain, no lightning, no thunder, and at the Way Station—a bit of life in a small corner of a burned out world—muted conversation slowed and silence followed.

Chapter 67
The Return Pilgrimage

Excitement pervaded the Way Station. The compliant Neos stood near their partners as all but three packed for the trip.

"Mike?" Matt called down from Viceroy. "You all set?"

"I have a few plans. Nancy and I will get Roddy going. I want to do a little daytime exploring. We'll be fine. I'll keep a weather journal, too."

"You'll be busy."

"Hey, leave me your binocs. Great night skies here. Wish I had some star maps."

Nancy piped up. "I used to know a lot of the northern constellations, but not this far north."

Matt reached around to his pack and tossed the binoculars down. "We'll bring an Astronomy text back. Matter of fact, make a weatherproof library and we'll bring back some reading material."

"Sure. All kinds. And bring lots more rope with the nails, spikes and the lag bolts you promised."

"We will."

"Anybody ask Ernie when the batteries in these radios will die?"

"He said they would last a couple of months with average power drain."

"Okay. I'll use it sparingly."

"Anything else?"

"Not for now. I'll stay in touch."

Matt smiled at Mike and Nancy, waved to Roddy, "Let's go."

Viceroy turned and started east into the rising sun. Soon the Way Station became small in the distance. For the first hour sporadic conversation touched on light subjects and once Doc waxed philosophical on the topic of Neo/human integration. Past mid-morning and nearing the diesel depot, they talked about the mine as a possible way stop for travelers. The sun shone warm, but spotty clouds began to make the scene.

Millie thought a larder should be left there in a safe place in case of an emergency.

"Did you hear the story of what we found guarding the entrance to that mine?" Jules asked.

"Yes," Millie said, "I did."

The company looked over the landscape, as if to keep it firmly in mind. Rugged, reddish rock everywhere, punctuated by green trees and grasses, the wildness and silence outside of their pale affected them all. Behind them, a swift moving bank of clouds overspread the sky from the northwest. The sun dimmed to a pall. Lightning began to strike in the mountains north of them. It was just past noon.

"Lot of iron up there," Matt called to the group. He seemed nervous and started looking around, checking the lie of the land, searching for a place to stop that would maximize their chances. Jules seemed anxious, too, and Doc remembered the arroyo they'd been caught in on their way to the station. Wild country. Beautiful, wild country. Will we tame it or will it tame us?

He called across the road so everyone could hear. "The American Indian believed the land belonged to everyone."

After a short silence, Matt called back. "Paradigm shift! I see where that one is heading. Great thought, Doc." Matt took out his notepad and jotted something down. Viceroy turned back an ear.

The troupe made good time, the way known and now comfortable, each seat hardened to the bony backs. As the thickening gray clouds moved over the group, Jules' Conan looked back at him and blinnied. They peered ahead. At maximum range of the human eye, they made out the curve that led to the mine and diesel tank.

"I think Conan is telling us something. We'd better make for the mine," Jules called. "This storm looks nasty." He urged Conan forward and soon the entire party loped along rapidly. They covered the distance quickly, but not without pain. A

Neo's canter fell somewhere between a jolting trot and a ragged run.

Doc complained first. "Is this necessary?"

"Look up, Doc," Jules yelled. At that moment the gray landscape lit brilliantly as lightning split a tall pine fifty feet behind them. The thunder crack sent the Neos into a panic and carried their riders headlong. Jules hunched over Conan and hoped the rest were hanging on. Not far to the north a tall reddish mountain disappeared behind a curtain of rain so thick that Matt yelled to the party, "This is going to be close!"

They rounded the corner and ahead saw the rusting diesel tank.

"Head for the opening to the left," Jules called. He shouted to Conan and the Neo veered past the tank toward the old loading platform. A stand of aspens made the mine opening difficult to see. Only feet before they ran into it, Conan jolted to a stop. Jules swung down before the Neo could present and yelled to the others.

"Get off and run!"

Now lightning flashed all around them, a frightening display of pyrotechnics that made the ladies scream involuntarily every couple of seconds. Matt pulled Millie off Crystal and they ran for the mine entrance. Mary Beth jumped off Thoth and her long legs ate up the distance as she mounted the steep slope. Arriving last with the galloping band Doc abandoned Pan and ran for the steep slope. The rain deluge caught him, thick and cold. The mine's upslope turned into instant mud and halfway up, his feet came out from under and he slid down the precipitous way just as lightning struck mere feet from him. His world went black.

"Everybody inside?" Matt called. He made a head count. "Where's Doc?"

Millie turned and yelled, "Doc! Doc!"

No answer.

"I have to go out," Matt said.

"No, I'll go," Jules called, "but we have to wait. Nobody should be out in that."

"Doc!" they yelled.

"Damn, I have to go!" Matt, completely out of character, sounded angry.

"NO!" Jules pushed him out of the way and ducked past as Matt lost his balance. He vaulted out of the mine opening. Instantly soaked to the skin, he ran to the side slope and skied down on his shoes, arms akimbo and waving wildly on the muddy slide. At the bottom he tripped over the inert form of Doc Simmons and fell forward.

The cold rain shocked Jules back to action. Getting up, he discovered Doc face down. Water ran down both sides of his face. He grabbed a shoulder and turned the doctor over. Jules felt for a pulse, but couldn't get one in the raging storm. He tried to hoist Doc into a fireman's carry, but the man slipped away. Realizing time was running out, he trumpeted out a call to Conan, perhaps nearby, but obliterated from view by the savage storm. In a few moments from the aspen stand, Conan appeared and blinnied.

"Conan, Doc needs help. Can you take him to the mine entrance?"

The Neo blinnied again and started to nuzzle the doctor. Jules raised the man up by the shoulders and dumped the limp form over the Neo's saddle as Conan presented. Conan turned his head and blinnied again.

"Yes, I'll get on, too. I have to hold Doc. Okay, up, Conan."

The Neo struggled to his feet under the double dead weight of two passengers, turned back fifteen feet and got a running start. Conan's partner felt the hard muscles gather and then they flew up the slope, barely seeming to touch it. Matt exploded from the mine entrance and grabbed the two as they slid from the Neo's back.

Millie stood in the downpour aside Matt. Together they managed the inert form onto dry dirt.

Jules gasped, "CPR, Matt," before he collapsed from exhaustion on the red dirt floor.

Matt went over the downed man, pulled open his collar, turned him over and prodded him for broken bones, and began chest compressions. Millie knelt and began rhythmic mouth-to-mouth ministrations, matching five compressions to one breath, according to the manual.

Mary Beth said to Millie, "I'll spell you. Tell me."

Millie acknowledged with a nod. Mary Beth stood ready.

Minutes plodded. Nothing. Then, when Millie could hardly gain another breath, Doc coughed. Turning him to the side, Doc lost his breakfast and water streamed from his nose. There followed a scene no one wanted to think about for a long time, but gradually Doc came back.

Later, distant rumblings from the retreating storm on the verge of hearing, the party sat closely together inside the mine's cave entrance and gathered warmth from the drying air. Most of their clothing hung from anything they could find.

Doc raised his hanging head and said simply, "I owe you my life, all of you."

Matt said, "Nothing you wouldn't have done, Doc."

Tears welled in the doc's eyes. "No, Matt, I can't say that. I don't know if I would have had the personal courage to do what you three did. Around me I had constructed an orderly life. Around me I had carefully built insulation, the Doctor, source of wisdom, the healer. What I realize in this brief foray with death is the extent to which I had re-programmed my fear of making a mistake, my fear of being different, my fear of being inadequate."

He sat and his shoulders shook. Millie put a hand out and touched Doc's shoulder; let it rest there. Some of her warmth passed into him and he stopped shaking. His hand came up and grasped hers. Finally, he took his hand down and looked at her. "Thank you, Millie."

Mary Beth, Matt and Jules looked on and watched Doc Simmons growing epiphany.

Chapter 68
A Stop on the Road Back

"I don't think we need to talk to Base or the Way Station about this today," Matt said quietly.

Jules nodded and Mary Beth said, "It'll keep."

Jules got up and brushed dirt from his shorts. He walked to the mine entrance and looked out. The sun had returned and the five Neos grazed not far away in a heavily grassed area. He was relieved to see that the animals were okay. He'd had to deal with life and death a short time before. He called softly, "Hey, Conan."

The big Neo raised his head and blinnied as softly. His four companions looked up and snorted briefly before returning to yank and chew. Jules turned back. Mid-afternoon; they still had time to get to the Neo herd before dark.

Pasty and still recovering, Doc shrugged off spending more time in the mine. The party looked at him askance, but went along. They remounted and kept a sidelong eye on Doc. He mounted slowly, but Pan seemed to sense Doc's infirmity and brought him up carefully. Pan kept an ear behind the rest of the way along Rt. 6 and when they finally turned to head up the mountain, Pan blinnied and stopped. Conan and Jules turned back and the leader shimmied and snorted for a few seconds. Pan shimmied back and turned his head almost behind himself, enough for one eye to behold a pale, somewhat listless man. The animal's staring eye seemed to snap Doc out of his blue funk, for suddenly he sat up straighter and spoke softly to Pan.

"You can't read my mind, Pan, but your concern is evident. I was feeling sorry for myself and my mind got stuck in it. I'm okay now, boy. You can go on."

Pan snorted and nodded, and began to climb the grassy precursor to the mountain facing them.

"I'm okay, everybody. Really," he said.

The silence that pervaded the last couple of hours broke, too, and normal conversation began again.

Matt said, as he realized that everyone had fixated on the near tragedy. "I don't think we helped much,"

"Understandable," Mary Beth offered sympathetically.

Slowly they mounted the steepness, marveling at the mutated mountain goats unerring steps. Always watching his Neo's motions, Matt thought the human method of climbing would have been as certain, but slower and more tentative, and would probably have included inventive ways to mount objects and scale slippery rubble, something the Neos were born to. He quite enjoyed his perch.

Before the sun dipped behind the nearest northwestern mountain, the long grassy fields came into view. At long distance, perhaps a half mile, Conan spied a lone Neo and blinnied loudly. The Neo's head came up. It turned quickly and sent the call eastward and then leisurely strolled in the group's direction. The party proceeded down a dip and then sidelong up a seldom-used path. Soon they ascended the slight rise and could see the main herd. As they approached, Neos appeared in groups and then in hordes. Blinnies came from many areas within the herd. They were clearly glad to see the leader return.

Conan stepped higher and increased his pace. The other Neos and riders matched him as they trouped into the center of the milling herd.

"Don't dismount," Jules called to the riders. "Conan will let us know when it's time."

"Wouldn't think of it," Mary Beth said.

Matt made an observation. "We can smell the herd, yet we can't catch the odor of our mounts. I wonder if there is a chemical link to our symbiosis?"

Millie and Mary Beth looked contemplative and Matt took out his notepad and scribbled quickly.

Millie said, "I wouldn't have given it a thought, but you're right."

Conan let the herd in close around the five as if deliberately letting them sense and smell their magical partners. Jules didn't say anything, but he was certain Conan was acclimating his herd to the humans as he had after the fight. He sensed that the closer his brother and sister Neos came, the more easily they would accept crossing Templar Pass and be more readily exposed to the race of Man. The developing bond between them needed this for it to rub off or seep in. Some sort of invisible process existed and Conan was promoting it. After a few minutes, Conan led the explorers to another area of milling Neos and went through the same silent ritual.

After two hours sitting, Mary Beth complained. "My butt isn't doing well on this bony back." She looked at Matt. Matt looked at Jules.

"I think this is important. My guess is, our little troupe is putting something like a whammy on the entire herd by its proximity to us. Bear it. We're almost done, I think."

Mary Beth groaned but sat. Thoth flicked an ear back.

Fifteen minutes later Conan blinnied loudly. Dismissed. The herd dissipated under a brilliantly starry sky. Conan shimmied under Jules and Jules said to the group, "We can get down now." Conan obligingly got down on his knees and the other Neos followed suit. Dismounting slowly, they were all stiff from sitting, they gathered in the middle of the huge sloping field.

"We can make camp here for the night. No fires," Jules told the group.

"Cold ticky-tack. Yum," Doc said.

"What time is it?" Millie asked.

"About ten."

They set about bedding down. Their sleeping bags were warm and the cold night air was perfect for sleeping. The herd had moved several hundred yards downrange and grazed peacefully.

"No storms tonight," Matt said.

"Glad to hear," Mary Beth said. "I think I'd climb a tree with all this life around in a thunderstorm."

"I better call Base."

"Can't wait 'til morning?"

Matt hesitated. "Yeah, it can wait."

"Then lets get some sleep. Maybe my butt will heal by then."

Laughter.

Chapter 69
Roddy

Roderick Quigley Brown, Roddy to all, didn't like his first name and hated his middle name. The psychologist who interviewed him all those years ago was a sharp individual, graying at the temples and with an easy demeanor, exceptionally keen hearing and expert at reading body language and he'd picked up on resentments Roddy tried to hide from the interviewer. Conversely, his burning desire to be part of this experiment shone like a flag waving. In his report he stated that Roddy was conflicted, but would fit within the colony. He noted Roddy had directed a small part of his childhood anger to his father for insisting on Quigley as a middle name. The man suggested his middle name need not surface within the biosphere. Arthur had kept that buried in Roddy's personnel records.

In his contacts he asked to be called Roddy. The Bio respected his wish early on and unknowingly avoided the storm within. His mind drifted back. In the beginning, it was all science and horticulture and farming methods and ancillary things. Kind of stiff, sort of quasi-military-like, they all believed it had to be. Roddy professed to be okay with "Whitey" as he was caught mumbling on a few occasions. Some residual from his youth kept him distant and it took a lot of time for the ice to thaw. Eventually he discovered he had few things in common with the three other blacks in the Bio group. Instead, he discovered that three of his white fellows, Matt and Mike and George liked what he liked more than the brothers. He began to see through his veil and eased up.

He didn't work near Mary Beth then and it wasn't until he became a noted spelunker that she caught his eye. She was a looker, but tight and he didn't approach her because Roddy had to admit it to himself, he was shy. Another serious about life person, Mary Beth had charge of the atomic pile and she lived her purpose. She had much less trouble assimilating than Roddy did, but he didn't see her much because she only dealt with a certain few people aligned to her specialty. *Or maybe just a woman thing,* he thought.

Only after the caves opened up and something more than the mechanical necessity of putting one foot after the other just to exist did real friendships form. Roddy thought that was pretty general throughout the Biosphere. In the longer view, nearly all Bio people got to like one another. Arthur said the psychologists had picked wisely and they had. Twelve years he lived in a tomb with lights, air, even entertainment, but it was both tomb and salvation and he could see no other way of looking at it. He felt the tomb part loomed large and crowded out salvation most days. He did come to terms with it by necessity.

Lying back in his woven hammock in as much comfort as the exploring party could provide, Roddy had a lot of time to reflect. It didn't come easy. Roddy was a physical being in mind as well as body and although he had enough natural talent to end up with this group of people, he wasn't particularly cerebral. So Roddy watched his friends do everything else and still do for him and he fumed inside. Occasionally it slipped out. Now five of the party had left to meet the Neo herd and go on to New Beginnings. He knew Mary Beth had to go, but he didn't have to like it. They had claim on one another.

She dealt her final card just before they left. She'd said, "I want to be with you, lover." It left no doubt and the memory made him smile. Feeling swelled in his chest. He loved that rangy gal. He'd marry her if she wanted, but he didn't think that kind of trapping mattered. Knights of old used to jump over their swords, didn't they? Good enough. Some of that talk Gina had with Nancy about going with religion or not he'd caught from a few conversations. He didn't care much. He'd go any way Mary Beth wanted. The poor family he'd been brought up in went to church a lot and he went, too, but he never saw the sense of it. Goin' to be a hassle at some point.

He glanced up the hill behind the Way Station. Nancy and Mike had taken a picnic lunch into the hills to see what was there. He gathered that compared to what they'd find uphill, the slopes above *him* were gentle enough.

The itch came back. He scratched his left wrist lightly like Doc had told him. He wanted to hit it with a hammer; it was so, like inside. Doc said he's healing. Well, yeah!

He had to take a leak. With some effort he repositioned himself so he could aim for the nearby hole Jules had pounded into the hard ground. Jules was clever, and Roddy got on with it easily. He'd punched the hole straight down about a foot and then made a narrow cut to a point fifteen feet away into a cleft amongst some rocks that dipped away from the station. Then he carefully laid small sticks horizontally into the declivity about eight inches down and covered them with aspen leaves. Using much of the dirt he'd dug out, he filled the hole and poured water gently on the top. It quickly hardened into the almost impervious material they'd had so much trouble dealing with when putting in the Way Station posts. Viola! Makeshift pee pipe. Front-loading twa-lettuh. Ha!

Roddy finished his business and wiggled carefully back to his comfort position. Most of the effluent ran into the cleft far enough to avoid the annoyance of odor. Drinking a lot of water, his discharge didn't have much chance to concentrate and it aided healing, he knew. Getting better at it, he told himself, aware that nothing hurt like before except the shoulder. Doc said don't bother wishing, it takes a long time for a shoulder.

Mike had told him not to exert himself while they were gone. Well, you gotta go, you gotta go. Besides, he'd been flexing every chance he got when he thought they weren't looking. Made him feel like a kid. Do this, don't do that, what'd they think he was, three? They couldn't see lying around was driving him crazy? Pretty soon he'd be well enough to hobble around and then things would change.

His brown eyes looked out over the bridge and cut of the river. The far side held a thick aspen grove. Lot of that up and down the river. Decent building material. Nearer to him the road cut a narrow ribbon to the east. West it went over the bridge and disappeared around a curve. It was a nice scene, rugged and wild, but he'd seen it so many times he hardly saw it anymore.

The Way Station sat on the side of a not so gentle albeit manageable foothill. The guys had engineered it well, planting the posts deep in the hard soil, digging a wide, deep sluice that had so far carried off the majority of water from several vicious storms. The wind and rain that hit them was proverbial, time and time again hitting them full force nature. He didn't have any hand in it, except weaving things. Getting good, too. Beyond their hill rose the mountain. He couldn't see from where he lay, but they'd told him. The foothill was heavily treed, mostly aspen and fir and pine, hardy stuff, liked the cold; *about all you get this far north*, he thought. Trees covered the mountain for several hundred feet further upslope and then petered out leaving wild, reddish jumbled rock; moonscape in red. That's where Nancy and Mike went.

Sick of this. When those two get back I want to get hiked to my feet. Sick of being invalid. He tested his leg and decided he could get on that, kind of light. Now if the shoulder will cooperate. Damn!

Thor stood nearby, closer than earlier, as if he needed to be close for some purpose Roddy couldn't fathom, but inside he liked it, like sitting with an old friend.

"Hey, boy."

A blinny rumbled gently from his Neo.

Roddy grabbed the chair he'd been weaving over the framework Mike had made yesterday morning. His immobilized right wrist didn't hurt much and he had the use of his fingers, about as much as his pain would bear.

He started looping and tying.

Chapter 70
The Upper Hill

"You think Roddy will stay put?" Nancy said after they were out of earshot.

"I expect he'll try, but he isn't ready. He won't risk much. Those crutches I made for him are a symbol. No way he can get on them yet, but if he tries, he'll know right off."

Nancy grabbed Mike's hand and mounted the steep slope slowly. They had all day. At their request, Geronimo and Apache stayed behind, but found separation difficult. The air smelled wonderful and no clouds marred today's sky. Each carried a staff of good length. The pointed end helped them in their stride and they had something if anything threatened. She looked up at her beau. Good-looking man, she thought, chiseled features, ready smile, very cerebral. She shivered inside. Funny what turns a girl on.

Mike had proved much more on this exploration trip than she'd seen at New Beginnings. She decided she liked him even more. He was resourceful and strong, and although he deferred to Matt as expedition leader, he thought on his feet more so now, she imagined, than in the past. This trip's been good for my Mike. She gripped his hand tighter. He looked at her and smiled. Good to get away. Maybe this recreation will prove more interesting than she thought. She warmed to the idea.

They left the Way Station about eight a.m. By ten they'd crested the foothill and gotten a new perspective on the backdrop mountain at whose foot they lived. The trees were thick, but every now and then on the way up they came to a clearing. Mike examined each area and invariably they were the same. No evidence of animal life, thin topsoil, short grasses, boulders abounding, but the soil simply couldn't support trees.

Where they stood now, the hill ran downward and cleared the view. Mount Bliss, his map said.

"Looks like we have to go down to go up," he said.

"Oh, Einstein!" she exclaimed.

Mike swung around to smack Nancy on the butt, but he wasn't quick enough. Instead, she swung her staff at the backs of his knees and suddenly Mike was on the ground. He reached out and grabbed her leg and down she went. Soon they were rolling down the gentle slope laughing and giggling. Mike rolled into a shallow hollow and pulled Nancy after him. With a twist he was suddenly looking down at her. Their hike momentarily forgotten, he examined her face above the collar of her light jacket. He kissed her, gently, and then again, harder. Nancy responded quickly and her eyes closed and Mike lost track of the woods around them. And Nancy had only eyes for the face of a handsome man outlined by blue sky.

"You thinking what I'm thinking?"

"Uh-huh."

The sun climbed a couple of degrees higher before they became aware of the forest again.

Mike straightened Nancy's pack as she zipped her jacket. Hand in hand, they picked their way down the short hill and began a steeper ascent.

"Umm," Nancy said, a not so mysterious smile pasted to her face. "Makes a girl feel good."

Innocently, Mike said, "What's that?"

She swung her stick again, but this time Mike grabbed her shoulder and pulled close. The stick went flying.

"Oh, that..."

"Stinker!"

Mike twirled her around and kissed her roundly.

"Much better," Nancy said when she got her breath back.

Mike grabbed her hand and squeezed. Why did the day seem brighter, the grasses greener, the sky bluer?

Soon they needed both hands for balance. Their destination, an outcrop they could see with binoculars from the Way Station, loomed a tenth of a mile and five hundred vertical feet ahead. Earlier content to climb together in silence, now they didn't have breath for conversation.

"Let's," Nancy gasped, "not turn to look until we get to the top."

"Sure."

The trees turned to scrub and disappeared rapidly as they gained height. The last three hundred vertical feet required care. They had staffs, but no rope. The way was rutted and not difficult if taken slowly. The last part took an hour. Finally they arrived at the flat spot they'd seen from the Way Station.

"Ready?" Mike said.

"Ready."

They turned together. Wild and breathless beauty spread before them. The ribbon of old Route Six wove in and out among the trees below. The cut of the McMillan was a wide gash in the earth within which, in places, they could see white water. Here the river and the road ran mostly parallel, and both disappeared in the distance toward the east. At the bridge, road and river branched out and went their separate ways to the edges of the hikers' vision. Except for the ever-present mountain, they could see for miles in every direction. Fluffy clouds, picture perfect in the striking blue sky, contrasted delightfully with partially treed reddish mountains stretching to a hazy horizon. The air, clean and sweet with a hint of piney woods, excited them.

Nancy held Mike's arm.

"Wow!" she cried.

Mike said. "It's beautiful." He came around behind Nancy and held her, arms gentle but firm under her breasts. "I remember reading about the chances people took building homes up against the Rockies in Colorado. One person they interviewed who'd lost part of their home to a landslide said, 'Sure we'll rebuild. Look at that view!' I can see what prompted them to say it. Years ago I thought they were stupid."

"I know. It's almost magical. I'd been to a lot of places before I was accepted for the Bio. The Grand Canyon impressed me so much." She stopped and started to shake. Nancy turned into Mike's chest and cried. Mike swallowed the lump in his throat and held her head gently until she got through it.

After a few deep breaths, she said, "Sorry."

"Don't be sorry, Nanc. None of us will ever totally disconnect from our past...it's our past. But looking forward is the only direction that has merit..." Now Mike struggled to hold it together, "anymore."

"I know," she said, and laid her head against his chest, and she could feel his heart's strong beat.

"So how about lunch."

"Oh, dessert, now lunch?" she said playfully.

"Too much dessert could change your figure."

"Would that disappoint you?"

Mike shook his head. "No, Nanc, not at all."

"Is it the mountain air?"

Mike looked deep into Nancy's blue eyes. "Uh-uh."

They removed their packs and set out the food. Nancy carried light conversation while Mike looked and listened. After they ate, Mike took out his binoculars and scanned the three hundred and thirty some odd degrees of view thoroughly, missing nothing.

"No evidence of mobile life anywhere." He sounded disappointed. Something about a scene he panned past brought him up short, he refocused on it, and a cold chill ran down his back.

"We've discovered Neos and nothing else," Nancy said.

"Well, the giant bat or whatever it was, but it's odd."

"Yes, I know. Like if one life form made it, even mutated, there must be more. There just has to be more out there."

"Stands to reason."

"We haven't been out for very long and haven't covered much territory. I don't think we can assume anything yet."

"Umm," he replied.

"What now?"

"Soak up a little sun and head back. I'm going to look around some more with the binocs."

Nancy lay back and closed her eyes. "You do that."

Mike started scanning the area that bothered him minutes before. Dead flat valley maybe half a mile diameter, sloping sides and...he studied the areas carefully. Something manmade? Crumbling evidence of what? The points on the ground were nearly round and exactly equidistant as measured by Mike's mathematicians eye. Extrapolating for distance, the points were roughly twenty-five feet in diameter, quite round and dark in each center. He figured about three hundred feet between each leg. Why did he think leg? Some sort of construct? What made those marks? Why? The rest of the valley looked perfectly natural.

"What do you suppose that is down there?"

"What?" Nancy opened her eyes and sat up.

"Down there." Mike pointed toward the valley. Nancy got up and came over. She gave it a long look and said, "I don't see anything."

"Here, look through these."

Nancy adjusted the binoculars for her eyes and studied the land below. After a few moments she handed them back. "You mean those marks in the field down there?"

"Yeah."

"Beats me. Another mystery for the young and the restless." She smiled and pulled at Mike's arm. "C'mon, bridge builder, let's go home."

The sun had crept past the meridian and was now solidly in the western sky. They policed used plastic packaging and stowed it away. Mike gave their picnic lunch area a last gander and started back the way they came. He led, picking his way and Nancy followed mostly in his steps. Mike didn't talk much. They cut a half hour off their ascent time, but it remained slow going because of loose rock. Coming through the trees near the Way Station two hours later they saw Roddy and shouted.

"Hey!"

Roddy looked up from his weaving.

"Look at what I made." He held up the nearly finished chair.

"Nice," Nancy said.

"Help me stand. I got to stand."

Mike said, "A little early yet."

"No, Mike, I got to stand."

"Okay," Mike said, resigned. "Your ankle can't take weight any more than the leg. Put the crutch under the shoulder and we'll help you up."

The crutch lay beside Roddy, so he grabbed it and put it gingerly under his injured left shoulder.

Roddy's face paled, but he didn't stop. Nancy and Mike got on either side and on his signal, hoisted gently. Using his right leg and relying heavily on Mike's strength, he got into an upright position. Leaning into the crutch, he bore the pain while he kept his left foot just shy of the ground. His heavily bound and splinted right wrist dangled.

He teetered briefly, bore up under it and said, "You have no idea how good that feels."

"Bravo," Nancy yelled.

Roddy showed her the brightest smile she'd ever seen.

"One more thing."

"What?" Mike asked.

"The chair I worked on, it'll hold me fine. I want to sit."

"You got him, Mike?" Nancy said.

"Yes."

Nancy took hold of the chair and set it out in front of the Way Station on a flat surface a couple of feet from the big man. She scuffed the ground until all four legs sat solidly. Then she came by his side and helped Mike turn him toward the chair.

"Sit easy," she said.

Roddy sat with a groan and said, "Thanks. I couldn't lie there another second."

"Looks like I'd better get started on a table," Mike said.

Chapter 71
Conan's Move

The sun rose in a dazzlingly clear, cold dawn. Dew covered everything, including the sleeping forms dotting the small area in the vast field they'd taken for the night, like the entire sky had settled to the ground, leaving everything clean and fresh. Jules opened his eyes, lay still for a minute or more listening, and then rolled to his side. The others were beginning to stir. Brand new day, very like most others, but this one would be different, he thought.

"You awake, Jules?" Matt called softly.

"Yeah," Jules responded.

"I kind of feel that this is the big one."

"It's important."

Millie joined in. "You don't have to talk quietly. Everybody's awake now."

"I was thinking of the Neo herd. They have excellent hearing," Matt said.

"This far away?" she asked. She glanced downrange.

"What would you hide, anyway?" Jules said to Matt.

Matt was silent.

"We need to guard against that."

"Wow," Millie finally said. "How subtle is our training."

Matt unzipped his bag and stood up. Millie sat and gave him her hands. He pulled her up. She shed her sleeping bag like a cocoon and walked out of it.

"Everything's wet," she complained. "Cold, too. Brrr..."

Jules looked around. "We can dry everything over there." He pointed to a few straggling adolescent pines twenty yards away.

Matt said, "Grab some rocks and we'll build a fire-pit for breakfast."

"Better wait, Matt," Jules cautioned. He turned and whistled. Conan's head came up. He turned and with a snort and some shimmying aimed at four Neos who seemed to be listening intently to him, trotted over to Jules. Jules ran the question by the Neo. Conan seemed to consider for a few moments and then snorted and chortled to Jules. With a hand gripping the Neos mane, Jules turned to the full camp; they had all turned out by now with some stretching and yawning.

"It gets easier all the time," he said, his face lit with a smile. "I believe Conan wants the herd to see us make fire. That'll settle the skeptics amongst them. And I'd swear he just laughed."

Millie laughed. "I was going to say that; maybe ask you if that's what I thought I heard."

Mary Beth chose the moment to break silence. "Me, I heard it, too. What have we *got* here?"

And Doc, standing a bit to the side wondered if it might be a tiger by the tail, but he said nothing and kept his face neutral.

"Let's build that fire-pit." Immediately the group searched for rocks and encircled an area a couple of feet wide. Matt put it together while Jules stood by Conan. Millie, Doc and Mary Beth found some fairly dry wood and piled it next to the fire-pit. Matt contributed a dry sheet from his notebook, crumpled it and put it carefully in the center of some thin wooden strands. The rest of the wood they laid around the perimeter. It would dry as the fire got going.

Conan wheeled and blinnied loudly. Soon, from many areas of the slanted mountain field Neos ambled over. Soon the humans were the center of a large herd. Another, still larger group stood uphill where they could see the small party from above.

Jules said, "Time for a demonstration."

He removed a pack of matches from a front pocket and struck one. The flame flared briefly and settled down. Neos nearby snorted and appeared nervous, eyes wide, muscles tense. Jules put the flame to the paper and it caught. Slowly the small flame grew and its smoke drifted into the herd, which caused more nervous milling. Primal fear grabbed them, but they watched the leader closely and didn't move from their spots. The leader stood stock still, head high. The herd caught on quickly and calmed. The idea of controlled fire they had never seen before. And it came from the magic of the strange two legged animals the leader had introduced them to.

Jules smiled inwardly. *Very politic, Conan.*

When the fire blazed brighter and became hot enough for cooking, Mary Beth grabbed the wire cooking-grate from their pile of jumble, pulled its legs out and placed it carefully over the fire and then pushed the four posts into the soft ground. Millie produced their pot and Matt filled the pot halfway with water from his canteen. Tea appeared from a side-bag and soon another aroma wafted into the surrounding herd. A few noses wrinkled at the strange scent.

The novelty wore off quickly and soon the herd drifted back to grazing. The point had been made. Conan briefly nuzzled Jules hands, and then he too drifted off. It wasn't time yet.

"One smart critter," Doc said.

Matt looked after the retreating back of the big Neo and nodded.

"Breakfast!"

They gathered and quietly discussed what they'd seen as they ate their ration. After breakfast, they retrieved their mostly dry sleeping equipment and packed it into the side bags. The bonded Neos, grazing nearby, saw their humans had broken camp and walked over to them. Side-bags tossed over their rumps, they all presented for their partners. Once aloft, Conan made for the center of the herd. He took center in a small circle, blinnied and shimmied for several minutes, turning slowly to face various parts of the herd.

The essence of his instructions passed rapidly through the herd to the last Neo. The herd funneled behind the five riders and the migration began. Doc felt momentary shock at the biblical simile to Moses.

Matt keyed his radio, "Good morning, Base."

"Al here, Matt."

"Al, we're on our way."

"How many?"

"The whole blinkin' bunch."

"I'll get on the horn. Anything we need to know?"

"Tons, but we have all day."
"Come ahead."

Chapter 72
Return Through Templar Pass

More than three hundred Neos on the trail reminded Jules of a cattle drive. The Neos didn't kick up any dust to speak of, not in the woods and not on the rocky ground that followed. They trudged a lot of forest before the mountain's stark aspect became the norm. *It will be interesting to watch the nimble footed Neo herd as it crosses into unknown and dangerous territory*, he thought.

The sun climbed higher and the day became warm. Conan picked his way deliberately, instinctively deciding on the safest way upward. By noon they began weaving their way across Templar Pass. Jules called a halt for lunch. Little existed for the Neos to graze on, but they didn't seem bothered. He suspected that if necessary they could go for long periods without.

When they arrived near the second relay device, Jules stopped and asked Matt to hoist him up the sheer face of the rock. He looked the device over and pronounced it stable and well anchored. He didn't touch it.

"Opportune time," He told Matt as he jumped down.

Matt nodded. They rode on. The herd didn't travel any faster than the explorers had on their way through the mountain divide. The rolling expanse between Front Mountain and its southwestern sister, Brak Mount focused the moving animals and the herd strung out not quite in single file, but there were so many Neos that the head of the column began to descend before the last Neos were out of sight of their home ground. While they moved placidly, Matt pulled away and picked a vantage on high ground to watch the procession.

He knew they didn't have telepathy—it would have scared him to think that—but they had a sense about them, a herd sense, he thought, that promoted order while protecting individualism. He marveled at the evident fact that some genetic mechanism, perhaps just the right amount of radiation wafting across the region, coupled with the right place to live and the right food, had produced these marvelous creatures from the small and stupid mountain goat. Its predecessor had no thought processes to speak of, not compared with humans. He chuckled at the conceit of his race, but he knew it was true enough.

Jules stopped once more to check the original directional amplifier, found a foot loose and refastened it.

Matt resumed his silent deliberation. Where did the intellect come from? In twelve years? Could there have been an isolated herd of mountain goats that had started to change, to grow into intelligent animals because of some background radiation in the hills? Could this have started long ago? The area was very isolated. Might humans never have discovered this place? It didn't seem likely, but twelve years? And to be in close proximity of humans buried inside of a mountain? Coincidental? What were the chances? Hard to believe, but no other evidence had surfaced. And what about their affinity to humans? It stretched his imagination, and he'd been involved with these creatures for longer than all but Roddy, Jules and Mike. He turned Viceroy back toward the head of the funneling herd. He'd talk to Jules, maybe to Conan and Viceroy, too. An hour and a half after entering the pass, the last Neo cleared the more or less level ground and began the steep descent toward the valley below.

Matt, now riding behind Conan again, said to the group, "I'm going to check in with Mike."

He tried but got no answer. Doc said Mike might be preserving his power.

"Later, then."

The explorers talked to Base off and on during their return and Arthur and company were up to date on everything Matt thought germane to the arrival of the herd late that evening. Arthur got on the horn and suggested that they perhaps should have one more layover so they might arrive in the morning.

"I don't think so," Matt said after conferring with his fellows. "There's little to nothing for the Neos to eat until we get close to our valley. We should arrive around eight p.m. We'll turn the herd loose in the north pastureland a mile south and east of the stream. I'll ask Conan to pass a message through the herd—they are quite incredible about information transfer—to bypass the human ways for tonight and put up for the night there. Only our group and our partners will come into the Bio area."

There's that partner thing again, Arthur thought. He didn't worry, but wonder filled his mind. He greatly anticipated seeing these unique creatures, which had bonded so naturally to the exploring party. He also worried that perhaps not all humans would get along with all Neos, but that would be addressed when, no, *if* it happened.

He grimaced. That stomach pain he'd felt a few days before almost disappeared, but tonight it came back, sharp and worrisome. He'd collar Doc as soon as they got in. He was glad Matt refused to stop for the night.

"Okay, Matt. We'll do it that way. I'll pass it on to the Bio."

"Good. We're picking our way down the west face now."

Conan picked a different route down and the explorers watched with chagrin at how much easier they found it. Every Neo picked its way down-slope carefully. Every so often a Neo would start a small landslide. There would be that rapid tap dance and then the animal would go on without breathing hard. Perfect adaptation. In sharply steep areas and where loose stone presented a serious hazard, they went single file, always on the upslope and no Neo was ever in danger from another.

Matt and Jules rode side-by-side much of the way, but there was never a time when it seemed that Viceroy led. Doc, Mary Beth and Millie ranged on either side. Finally the steep slope gave to gentler terrain and then they were at the bottom. They followed their trail back over the foothills, ever closer.

Mary Beth said, "This way will look like a road when these Neos get through with it."

The rest laughed and nodded.

At long last they spied a light in the distance. Nostalgia gripped them. They didn't think they had missed home, but they did, deep down in the gut.

Chapter 73
Home

Conan increased his step without Jules urging. *Talk about reading my mind,* Jules thought. When the leader did that, a quiet shimmy went through the herd and it moved more quickly. As Conan neared the cave entrance to the Bio, he stopped and let the herd catch up. The area Conan chose encompassed a broken field of waist high grass large enough for the herd to mingle. Where Conan stopped Jules noted a mild rise. The Neo stepped to its crest and faced the herd, patiently waiting until all assembled faced him. Then he blinnied loudly and began to talk to the herd.

With foot work and shimmying —Jules had no illusions about Neos eyesight—Conan told the herd that they would bear off at the next turn and follow the lie of the land to a new grazing ground. He made it clear that only Neos with riders would continue to the hive of Man. Jules thought "hive" more correct than "herd," although he would not have associated either term with humanity. It pointed up the necessity of being flexible with free interpretations between the partners.

Conan then turned and resumed his march up the last of the little hills below the Bio cave.

Matt, Jules, Millie, Doc and Mary Beth moved in almost stately fashion toward as large a crowd as the natural shelf beyond the cave entrance would allow. As they came into sight, an audible gasp traveled through the crowd. To hear about these strange creatures was one thing, to see them up close and personal was quite assuredly something else.

Conan stopped at the trodden area below the shelf and presented for Jules and the other Neos did the same. The five explorers dismounted easily, like it was the most natural thing in the world. Then the Neos stood, but stayed close at their partner's sides. Arthur stood at the fore and held his arms out in welcome.

Jules said to Conan, who faced Arthur but gave him an ear, "This is Arthur, our leader."

Conan bowed, straightened, shimmied and the other Neos immediately did the same.

Sensing an important moment, Arthur said, not looking at the explorers, but directly at the Neos, "We welcome the Neo race to our home and invite you to stay. I have the sense that neither the race of Man or of Neo will ever be the same again. I sense that it is good."

Conan bowed again. *Perfect*, Jules thought, *just perfect*.

"Now we wish to celebrate a homecoming with our fellows." He looked at Matt and the others and said, "How will this happen?"

"Our Neos can graze in the field below," Matt said. "Give me a moment to explain to Conan and the others that we will go into the mountain, but that we will return."

"Conan, Viceroy, Thoth, Apache, Pan..." Matt described the Bio they had come from and how they were going in to talk, but that they wouldn't be gone long. Viceroy seemed a little nervous, but Conan shimmied briefly and he calmed.

Matt nodded at Jules and Jules said to Conan, "See you soon."

The big Neo snorted for attention. Jules turned back. Conan shimmied and moved.

Jules stared, piecing together what he'd seen. "You will join the herd and return in the morning?"

Conan nodded. Jules came back to his Neo, grasped the big cheeks and laid his forehead against the Neo's snout. Conan snorted softly. Jules released and the Neo joined his fellows.

Arthur turned as the procession stopped and witnessed the bonding. *My God*, he thought.

The five headed up ten steps newly carved into the shelf above and entered the Bio cave. The Neos watched them and then moved off down the hill. To Arthur, the whole pageant impressed him more than ever. He wondered if many of the hundred questions in his head he would get answered, but he would ask them. A pain hit him and he grayed with it. Maybe he'd let the explorers acclimate for a few minutes.

"Doc?"

Doc Simmons moved over to Arthur's side and looked at him keenly. "We need to talk."

"True enough," Arthur replied.

Gina watched the contact and gratefully put her arm through Mark's. She couldn't get her conversation with Arthur of days ago out of her mind. Now she could.

The company walked down the tunnel. Not surprisingly, it was set up for a party.

Chapter 74
Infirmary

Doc followed Arthur into the tunnel and neither spoke for a couple of minutes.

Arthur grabbed Gina, the nearest person to him, moments before they exited into the Bio proper. "I want to talk to Doc for a minute. Don't hold up the festivities, okay?"

"Sure, Arthur," she said.

Doc and the Chief Scientist peeled off from the main group and headed for Arthur's quarters. Quizzical looks followed them, but they all filed into the large area, started to mingle and quickly forgot the strangeness. Gina headed there, too, but had no story to tell. Arthur would let the Bio know in due time what, if anything, was amiss. She went over to one of the converted tea urns and drew a glass of golden liquid. Others lined up behind her. The party began.

Out of sight of the crowd, the two headed for the infirmary. Semi-ambulatory George had moved out to Sue's quarters days before. She could tend his needs while he exercised and gained strength. Inside the now vacant infirmary, Doc rummaged around for Arthur's chart, found it and began scribbling notes. He motioned Arthur onto the examination table.

Doc's face still in the chart, he murmured, "Strip to the waist, Arthur."

His patient did so. Doc wrapped a stethoscope around his neck and got out the familiar hammer and thumped in familiar places. Reactions normal, heart, lungs, normal. Upper abdomen under sternum, pain slightly left of center, stomach soft to touch and palpation, slightly distended.

"How long has this bothered you?"

"Couple of weeks I've felt a little strange, but I thought it was probably our creative chefs new spice. Pain where you are pushing, deep inside, sharp, but not overly so, easy enough to live with. Took some of your pain powder a couple of times and it went away. Haven't had to take any for a couple of days now, but it came back harder today."

"Bowels?"

"About what I'm used to for my age."

Doc consulted his chart. "I gave you a complete physical four months ago. Found nothing. I need an x-ray."

"When?"

"Right now. I'll get the tech."

"Anything to worry about?"

"You'll be second to know." Doc hung Arthur's chart up and left the infirmary. He came back with Charlie Brentin, who'd trained as x-ray tech and Doc's nurse. Charlie stood six-one, almost as tall as Roddy and nearly as heavily muscled, but with finer hands. Doc found his strength needful on occasion; injuries involving animals, careless spelunkers and rock fall accidents, that sort of thing. To date there weren't many. A great sense of humor if drawn out, he carried an encyclopedic knowledge of drugs, reactions and antidotes, but stayed to himself and appeared to get pleasure out of watching others enjoy themselves. He'd had a thing for Beth Howell for a while, but it cooled and they remained friends. Everyone liked him except Isabella Gratinelli, and she wouldn't say why. Since nothing appeared to need correction, it stayed that way.

"Hello, Arthur."

"Hi, Charlie."

"Lie back on the table and I'll get the machine over you." He consulted with Doc, repositioned it and threw a lead apron over Arthur's privates. Charlie flipped a switch and the machine began to hum. He made a few adjustments. Doc left and Charlie went behind a screen. The x-ray machine buzzed briefly.

"Couple more, Arthur." All efficiency.

"All done. Going to the party?"

"Wouldn't miss it."

Doc returned, wearing an inscrutable expression.

"Have fun tonight, Arthur. Don't worry about a thing."

"Doctor's advice?"

"Yes."
"Then I won't."

Chapter 75
Mike's Revelation

Matt called to Gil, presently on the Base com. "Anything from Mike?"

"Yes," Gil said. "He called in just as that big goat…"

"Neo, Gil. Don't think of them as goats. They're not."

"Sure, Matt. Anyway, when that big Neo turned and addressed the troops, that's when."

"Yeah. I turned my radio off. All okay? We haven't been able to get him all day."

"No problems. He wants to talk to you."

"About what?"

"Didn't say, just asked me to have you call him."

"Okay. I'll call him now."

"Whatever. I'm going to the party."

Matt smiled. "I'll be there."

Odd, Mike must have something he wants to say before the rest know. Guess secrecy would always be a part of the human condition. He disabled the circuit into the Bio.

"Mike, you there?"

"Hi, Matt. You alone?"

"Yeah."

"Can you cut out the general circuits for a minute?"

"Already done."

"Good. Nancy and I went up the hill to the out-jut for a picnic today, the interesting one we could see from the Way Station. Great view, see for miles. In a valley on the other side it's dead flat and there are some regular, what I'll call footprints that form a pattern about equidistant from any hilly terrain. Maybe somebody built something there years ago, but I can't think what and I pictured something pretty huge landing there.

I'm probably all wet, but I wanted to run it by you and get your take."

"Mike, okay. Look, we can't do much right now. Maybe it's something we can investigate when we get back. Right now we have to deal with assimilating over three hundred Neos with our crowd at Base. That'll take a few days. I suggest you don't go prospecting on your own. Roddy needs you more for now."

"I'm chafing, Matt."

"Bad move, Mike. You're reading too much sci-fi. We have all the time in the world. I will give it some thought, though, and I'll talk to Arthur and look in some books."

"Okay, Matt. We'll do it that way. But I'm chafin'."

"Wait. We'll do this right. Okay?"

"Sure."

Matt turned the Bio connection back on and went down to the party.

Chapter 76
Assimilation Begins

Not a few pounding heads woke to the Bio morning.

Isabella mumbled, "It was worth it...it was worth it...it was worth it."

Arthur lay on his back, hands under his head, thinking about how Doc Simmons professionalism had broken down after the exam and x-ray. Not broken down, actually. Arthur searched for the right term; he was more transparent, more sensitive, less clinical. A change since his return. Yes. Arthur knew something had happened to effect a change in this man everyone thought could handle anything while maintaining his cool and his distance. It would gnaw at him, but he wouldn't ask; he'd wait it out.

Doc gave him more pain powder and told him to use it as needed. At the moment he felt good.

Matt sat on the edge of his bed and looked at still sleeping Millie. She'd giggled when he told her he couldn't even pretend to not want her there. Too much had happened and they'd become really close, past friends, much closer to commitment. He turned and studied the floor, thinking about what Mike had said. Mike's excitement said he wanted to believe in a visitation. The world was a strange place now. Who could say?

No, impossible! But what's impossible? The end of the world? That's not possible, right? Matt went out to look up Arthur.

Jules woke early, the Neo herd the only thing on his mind. He'd had a good time at the party, but he didn't overdo it as some did. What first? He walked to the community shower. Several ladies were up, including Maude Nash and Mary Beth.

A couple of men getting off animal night chores were scrubbing away.

"Wash anyone's back?" he said brightly.

The women tittered. "Wash your own."

Jules got busy with his toilette and cleared out as soon as he could. He wanted topside. The plan included getting the entire population above, and then mingling with the Neos. He believed that all humans resonated at some sort of frequency and that Neos did, too. If so, the right matches would almost inevitably occur. New ground, but he was convinced it would happen that way. Better see Arthur and get the ball rolling.

Matt and Jules met at Arthur's door.

"Hey," Jules said.

Matt nodded to Jules. "Hi Jules. Arthur, are you up?"

"Yes, come in, Matt." They both walked in. "Hi, Jules."

"Hi, Arthur. Ready to get this show on the road?"

Arthur laughed. "Let's talk about the 'show' first."

"I came to talk to Arthur about something else, but I'm glad you're here, Jules." He proceeded to recite his conversation with Mike of the night before.

Arthur said, "I find that incredible, but I'm closer to accepting outlandish theories than ever before. Occam's Razor aside... What do you think, Jules? Are our Neos from outer space?"

"No," Jules started, "but that scenario would answer some big questions. Suppose, just suppose some ET watched us destroy Earth from the safety of space? After a few years they land. They find an isolated band of mountain goats in a protected valley. They do a little genetic engineering and grow seven-foot tall new goats, or Neo goats. By playing with goat genes, we now have highly intelligent animals adapted to the world they face and with the capacity to improve it. Maybe? That's where the theory breaks down. They have no appendages that allow for the making of tools and creating technology. They couldn't have known about us."

Arthur broke in, awe in his voice. "Why not?"

Matt sounded excited, much of his reserve gone. "Yes! How coincidental is it that we find emotionally compatible animals a stone's throw from our Biosphere experiment? What are the chances?"

"God, Matt?"

"That or some ET so far above us that they saw the need to create another way for humanity to evolve. Think about it." His eyes glowed.

"We need proof," Arthur said. "Jules, you are confident that the Neos need to bond with the human population?"

"Yes."

"Small steps, then. Let us begin," Arthur reached for his link to the communications console. He keyed it in. "Who's on Com today?"

"Sue Dorchester, Arthur."

"Please make a general call for everyone to assemble out beyond the mouth of the cave. Call in Jerry and his crew. Get Hal and his men. Everybody is to meet there in one hour."

"Okay, Arthur."

"Jules, why don't you hot-foot it up and collect the herd. Bring them over."

"On my way." Jules literally ran up the tunnel and burst out, startling Sue.

"Where you going in such a hurry, Jules?"

"Watch."

He left the cave entrance and walked to the edge of the apron. From there he let out a piercing whistle. Across the stream, grazing Neos raised their heads. Jules saw Conan work his way front. He raised his arm and motioned. Soon random commotion became ordered movement and the herd began to cross. They moved deliberately, not rapidly. From the town, Jules could see little dots moving toward the Bio cave. Pretty soon he knew Hal and his men would come over the rise and converge on the cave. He couldn't hold down his excitement. This was it!

Voices behind him. A procession led by Arthur came out of the tunnel's gloom. Everyone, Arthur said. Yes, even children, even babies. He would have to be watchful, especially of the younger ones. Must prevent panic. Big animals, little children. It would be a day to remember.

The two groups converged slowly, elegantly, gracefully, as in a dance. Something in the hesitancy of the humans gelled with the ungainly, almost laughable gait of the Neo herd. At the Bio party the night before, Arthur had interrupted them with a final caution about Neos. "They are gentle beings, people, but their size can be daunting. Fear is normal, but put it down. It will help. Jules has assured me that their first interest is in bonding. Some of you may not wish to bond, or think you don't right now, but I want you to mingle...mingle without expectation."

Arthur thought as he stood slightly apart from the others. Now we'll see. Jules closed with the leader. He hid a smile. He knew Neos would also be doing the mingling.

Conversationally, Jules said, "You too, Arthur."

"Oh no, I..." but he stopped, nodded and made his way down the steps into the rapidly growing crowd of humans and aliens. Others looked at Arthur and, especially amongst the women, Jules felt a palpable element of tension subside. Even now, after so many years, Arthur had no idea what effect his grandfather image had on Bio people.

It's all over but the shouting, Jules thought, remembering his Dad's favorite expression. The big animals were very careful around the humans and Jules knew whom to thank for that. He searched out Conan and headed for him. The Neo saw him and came to him, pressing his head into Jules chest and then presenting. Jules got on. He could see that the Neo had a plan and soon Doc was aboard Pan and Mary Beth had mounted Thoth. Looking around the wide field, Jules saw Crystal present for Millie and in another part of the field Matt climbed onto Viceroy's back. All that, it seemed, was anticlimax, because a big, "Oooo" and a few gasps followed a small commotion near the outer edge and almost immediately, Gil Castonguay rose above the crowd. Excited jabber focused on the place for a couple of minutes until another, "Oooo" came from somewhere in the middle and Isabella rocked to her perch on a small but muscular female.

She shouted, "Yah-hoo!" which did more to startle those around her than was good, but calm restored swiftly and Jules decided it probably didn't hurt a thing. There was much the Neos would have to get used to right along with people and no time like the present.

He wondered if the Neos would like to race, as in alien horseracing. Something to think about.

Gil and Isabella kind of broke the ground, because more and more people, or Neos, found compatible partners. *Like mixing two a-similar compounds whose chemistry would ultimately produce a totally new thing,* he thought, *and it's like a dance, yes, it's beautifully dance-like.*" The Neos were the vehicle and the humans were the ingredients by which the vehicle would operate. Horse and carriage, yeah, like that old song Mom used to hum sometimes as Jules came home from school. For a moment the pang of remembrance caused him to squeeze his eyes tight. He didn't want to think that far back.

By mid morning few adults were without Neos. The animals snuffled babies but seemed to decide that they were too primitive to be worthy. Children under six years were handed a similar fate.

"Let's talk to Arthur," Jules said to Conan. Perceiving what Jules wanted, Conan searched out the leader.

Arthur was talking to Al Parks and moved his Neo to the side so Jules could join them.

"I was telling Al here that a new pattern is emerging."

"That's why I came over. It was foolish to think every person would bond and that would be that. Apparently kids under six aren't for any Neo and since we only have four six-year-olds we'll have to diagram this out."

Arthur said, "I guess it's good. There weren't nearly enough people for the Neo population. What use can we get out of the unbonded animals? Do you think that will be a problem?"

"No, I doubt it. Keep in mind that the Neos will be talking this over, too. Perhaps they will be wondering the same thing on a different level, that is, what use they can get from unbonded humans. I'm going to have to spend a lot more time trying to decipher their language. They understand us—our language, I mean—far better than we do theirs. I could use a couple or three with specific sensitivities to learn it too, and then teach it. Everyone will have to be good at it eventually. I'm serious."

"We'll have more meetings."

"All well and good, but you are going to find, even today in the short time we've been inflicting ourselves on the Neos," he smiled at the dry pun, "that humans and Neos will not want to be separated for long periods of time. I'm thinking that we will have our meetings together, somewhere like right here and maybe even in the construction cave."

"I didn't think of that. Do you think Butterscotch here would take unkindly my going down the tunnel tonight?"

Jules smiled at Arthur. "Good name. He'd let you, but you would feel the pull, as he will. What's yours Al?"

"Carpenter."

Arthur laughed delightedly, "Your trade namesake, why not?"

"Kinda how I felt." Al Parks grinned back.

Chapter 77
An Element of Secrecy

"Doc, Gina suspects something is wrong with me and I get sidelong looks from a few others. I don't know what to tell them. And Butterscotch will worry." *Now why did I say that,* Arthur thought. *Jules is so right, yet I find it so hard to accept. The scientific mind won't give up its old chestnuts without their being wrenched almost physically away. I'm more pliable than that, I hope.* But he knew he wasn't.

Doc didn't seem to notice Arthur's strange statement. Arthur waited for a rebuttal or at least a "Pooh-pooh" but it didn't come. The chief scientist sat on the examining table being checked and probed and whacked and Doc even took blood this time. Arthur withstood the indignities. Doc said little until he finished.

Then, with a little smile, he said, "Don't tell them anything at all, Arthur."

"Why not? The people should know."

"You are right, of course, but hold off for a couple more weeks, would you?"

"If you ask, but now I'm curious."

"In the two weeks that I have been back the Bio has assimilated with a strange and alien creature, who, for all we know, was genetically altered from a stupid mountain goat into these wonderful creatures by something vastly more alien. I have been quietly going about my business, making notes and careful observations and...I can't tell you what I'm seeing, but I am seeing something. Don't ask me any more questions on the subject, Arthur. When...if...a pattern appears, I will alert you immediately."

What a long speech.

Arthur shrugged. "As you will, Doc." But he left the infirmary troubled. His pains had abated. Slightly, to be sure, but his condition should be progressing from one pain level to a higher one and it should be growing exponentially. He knew what he had...didn't he?

He went looking for Butterscotch.

Chapter 78
Catching Up With Mike

"Matt here, Mike."

"Hi Matt. How's it going?"

"As well as can be expected. How are Geronimo, Nancy, Apache, Roddy and Thor?"

"Fine. What are you driving at?"

"Not sure. Just wanted to get you off by myself and resonate. I took the com and turned off all but our direct link."

Silence. Then after a few moments, "I feel different. Newer. Geronimo and I are inseparable, nearly. Sometimes I think I can hear what he's thinking, but our minds are so different I can't be sure. Nancy and I are the human equivalent. She's beside me now and the Neos are within fifty feet, which seems to be the comfort zone. They don't like to be further away, like they have pangs of loneliness. What's happening, Matt?"

"Not sure, but it's happening here, too. Even the unbonded and the children, even the babies have an affinity it's impossible to miss. We're changing, Mike. Becoming something else. That's what I know."

"No bad vibes?."

"None."

"Guess we're good to go. When are you heading back this way? Roddy's raring to go. He's up and around, quicker than I can believe it should happen. I swear his wounds are healing faster than they should. You can almost see it happening. You've noticed how quick Neos heal?"

"Sure."

"Thor's been hanging close to Roddy for the past two weeks, I mean real close. I'm thinking, maybe our proximity to them is rubbing off that amazing quality onto us. What do you think?"

"I'd about come to that conclusion, too. You don't have a mirror there, do you?"

"No."

"Check out your reflection in a pool of still water."

"Why?"

"Changes…" Matt sounded like he wanted to say more, but left it hanging.

"I don't see anything different about Nancy." He left the mike keyed and turned to her. "You see anything different about me?"

She shook her head. "Nothing here."

"I know, but take a look at yourself. You'll see what I mean."

Puzzled voice. "Okay."

"You go for rides?"

"All the time."

"How is that bony back?"

"Not a problem. Actually, never a problem."

"Interesting."

More silence. Mike was doing some heavy thinking.

"Viceroy and I will be heading back your way in a couple of days. Bringing a new crew, much food, nails and spikes, tools, and a few instruments."

"Who's coming?"

"Mary Beth and I with six unbonded Neos, loaded."

"Good. Storms are bad. Bridge holding well, but I'd feel safer with more shoring."

"You'll get it. Would you like Al Parks over there to help out, too?"

"Sure."

"He said he'd like to come and see what a bunch of rank amateurs threw together."

"Sweat is pouring off me…" Mike said in a plaintive voice, and then, "Oww! What'd you do that for?"

Matt heard Nancy in the background, "You know why."

Matt chuckled into the mike while he shared their moment. "Time to go. I'd better turn up the systems in case somebody wants to call in."

"Okay, Matt. All is well here. Come quick. Getting tired of Roddy's ugly puss."

"I heard that." Evidently Roddy wasn't asleep.

"You can't catch me...yet," Mike called to Roddy.

"Soon enough, keep that up," Matt heard Roddy say.

"Okay guys, out." Matt wanted to talk to Arthur and to Doc Simmons. As he thought, the Bio was too large a control group to test the subtleties of what was happening to them. He also thought that it was far too late to try and change any part of the direction they had taken.

Who'd want to?

Chapter 79
Cohesion

Before returning to the Way Station, Matt took a tour with Arthur to town, and to the lumber mill in the deep woods near the dammed up stream and the valley's new lake. It wasn't operational, but in the weeks since Arthur had found time to first check out the new area, it had grown immensely. The Bio people's industry had always impressed Matt. Moving south on Viceroy and Butterscotch, they visited the steam vent. Nothing had been done with it yet, but Matt could see the possibilities Jules suggested on his first trip through the area. Doubling back they visited the Construction cave. It had been completely civilized, power providing light in the huge cave and even three of the four computers running again. The fourth was covered.

"Keeping that one for backup," Hal told them. "We can use them, but we'll play hell trying to manufacture new parts."

As they left, Arthur said, "Hal, you and your crew have done a great job here."

"Thanks, Arthur."

"What would you think about a couple hundred Neos cluttering up the place?"

"No bother." Hal's Neo Seth grazed nearby. Hal gazed at the animal affectionately.

Out of earshot, Arthur said to Matt, "How different that would have been a mere three weeks ago."

Matt smiled. "Fitting name for his Neo."

"Lot of that going around."

They rode silently for a while. The warmth of the noonday sun soothed and helped their sense of well-being. Arthur told Matt things were going swimmingly, but he didn't need to. Progress and the pioneer spirit showed everywhere. Matt hadn't had much time to be out and about during the past few weeks. He didn't miss it, really. Millie was handy. Reading progress reports and working around the Bio and near areas were plenty enough. He spent as much time with Viceroy as possible. *It's not like love,* Matt thought, *like I feel about Millie, but it's powerful like love.*

"Matt?" Arthur glanced his way.

"Umm?"

"Al approached me the other day. He's talked it over with Mary Beth and wanted an opinion. I have mine, but I want yours."

"Sure."

"It's about the atomic pile. You know Al is involved in maintenance and emergency work."

"Yes."

"Well, he asked me about the feasibility of running a cable to the Construction site to provide electricity, take the pressure off the diminishing supplies of diesel fuel."

"If we have heavy enough cable to run that distance without significant voltage drop and heating, why not?"

"That's what I thought, but we don't have much cable of the gauge we need. I brought this up because the pile should be good for at least fifty years—they overbuilt considerably in that area—but that it's not doable with what we have."

"You're thinking about Ross River?"

"Yes."

"I'm going back to the Way Station tomorrow. Now that we have a bridge, I can't think of any impediment getting to Ross River. I'll want another two men to accompany me and I think if Al comes along and Roddy's sufficiently on the mend, and after we shore up the bridge against all possibilities, maybe we can head out in three, four weeks?"

"That would work."

"I'll do some more thinking on what else we might need from there, too. Maybe I'll take fifty unbonded Neos along. Hmm." Matt stared unseeing while his brain geared up for changes in plan.

"No reason we couldn't run insulated cable underground to town, too."

"Sure. What is the capacity of the 'pile'?"

"I don't keep the specs in mind, but I have them and you're welcome to look them over. My impression is it could run a second Bio and still not be at max."

"Okay, priorities on diesel fuel and high voltage insulated cable. If Ross River doesn't have enough, Whitehorse is a couple whoops and a holler further along."

Arthur smiled at that. "Could you come back with all terrain vehicles?"

"What's wrong with Neos?"

Arthur looked stricken. "Yes, of course. Old thinking."

"Been partnered longer." Matt softened it with a smile.

"Neos all right?"

"Perfectly acclimated."

"Well, let's get back. Paperwork."

"Yeah, got to pack and I want to talk to Jules and Conan about cutting out a group for the Ross River trek. I'm thinking we'll only take a big group when we're ready to go for the long haul."

"That's smart."

"How soon before we can move into our places in town?"

"You saw the progress. The places need furniture, beds, kitchen utensils, etc. The exteriors for most of our population are done, just basic housing, fix it up the way you like it. Maybe another four to six weeks."

"Don't see signs of complacency yet," Matt said.

The two men guffawed.

Chapter 80
Again Templar Pass

In the morning, Matt said goodbye to Millie. "I'll be gone a week, max."

"You bringing Roddy back?"

"Yeah. Be good for him. Mike says he's healing fast now. He thinks it's Thor. Mike says he hangs around Roddy, close, except for a couple hours grazing."

"I think it's Thor, too. Natural healing empathy? Any such thing? Seems to me everybody is healing from whatever, faster than ever."

"Yeah, I agree. Better head out." He bent down. Millie grabbed his muscular shoulders and planted one on him.

He looked over the five unbonded Neos that had volunteered as pack animals, and then turned to Don Smythe, mounted on Ramrod and Al Parks on Carpenter. Don's work at the Construction site and on the town's main road was pretty much done and he wanted to get away for a while. He had no relationship and nothing to hold him to New Beginnings, so when he volunteered, as important as his work and effort had been, he was the easy second choice for the trip.

"Ready?"

"Yup. Let's get going."

With a wave they started down the trail and were soon out of sight. The ungainly Neo gait no longer bothered anyone, either physically or aesthetically. All Neos were weighed down with whatever they could carry. This load would service the Way Station with food, materials and other supplies designed to make it permanent and relatively self-sufficient. Modifying his perception to fit a time more than a hundred years before, Matt, through slitted eyes, visualized a fully laden mule train making its slow way amongst rocks and twisted terrain on its way into gold country. Only this time gold was diesel fuel and first aid material and long shoring spikes and nails.

Don and Al looked around with great interest. This new territory created changing, fascinating perspectives. Ascending Front Mountain toward Templar Pass, the Neos took the way. Their sharp eyesight avoided dangers the men only later could appreciate. Leave it to the experts.

They stopped for the night in a place now familiar to Matt.

"This where that big bat lives?" Al asked Matt.

"This is the place."

"We have more light than before." He referred to the high intensity flashes they now carried.

"And you want to spend an hour looking in the bat cave?"

"Anything wrong with that?"

"No, but we buddy, okay?"

"Sure. I'm interested and I have a digital camera that works since Ernie figured out how to build a transformer that recharges Ni-Cad batteries."

"That's good news. How come we didn't know?"

"I gave Ernie my old camera, but never expected to get it back all charged up this quick."

"Oh."

"C'mon, Don."

"Ask your Neo first," Matt said.

"Oh yeah, sure," Al said. "Carpenter, I want to explore in yon cave. Okay?"

The Neo didn't look willing, but after a moment nodded his head. Don did the same with Ramrod, who was ever more reticent. Don talked to him in low tones for a couple of minutes and finally the Neo relented.

"I want to go, too," Mary Beth spoke up. "I'd like to see that sucker."

"Everybody be really careful," Matt called as they worked their way into the narrow crevasse. "We don't know anything about what it can do. You all got knives? I'll stay here with the Neos."

The three disappeared and were gone for ten minutes when Matt heard yells and screams, muted by distance and the rocky entrance.

It sounded like abject terror.

Chapter 81
Tragedy Strikes Twice

Suddenly the Neos became agitated. Matt was overcome with dread. He started running toward the fissure but Ramrod muscled him out of the way. He seemed frantic. The big Neo ran into the fissure and immediately got stuck. Matt yelled for him to move back, but the Neo began to make crazy crying sounds and continued to lunge at the small opening. Matt's dread deepened. He'd never seen it first hand, but intuitively he knew Don Smythe, Ramrod's human was dead.

The other Neos crowded up to Ramrod, and they made strange, comforting sounds.

Mary Beth's screaming got louder and louder and she burst from the cave mouth, ran blindly into the fissure and into Ramrod's chest. The Neo whuffed and stepped back. Mary Beth bounced around the big animal and into Matt's arms.

"Mary Beth, get control," Matt yelled into her face. He couldn't slap her into comprehension. He couldn't because he knew why she was terror stricken. He held her tightly. When she realized she was safe again wild panic gradually left her. As reason returned, she broke down sobbing. She sagged, but Matt's strength held her.

"What happened, Mary Beth?" he asked loudly, urgently, but the woman still couldn't talk, couldn't get her breath, couldn't stop sniffling and crying.

Over Mary Beth's shoulder Matt again saw movement. Al Parks dashed out, running into the rocky crevasse and bouncing off it as blood ran down his mutilated face and into his eyes. The top of his head oozed dark red from two deep gashes somewhere in the hairline. They continued through his right eyelash and laid open his right cheek. Blood blinded the eye. His right arm hung slack and oozed blood. It had a peculiar, wrong shape. Al's blood welled quickly and dripped steadily from tattered skin. Oddly, his camera still hung from its string on his right wrist. The eye he could see from peered wildly ahead without comprehension. He looked scared and sick and in serious pain. His breath came in gasps and his eyes were wide.

"What happened, Al?" Matt called, but he knew. He knew. Don didn't follow and somehow Ramrod had sensed a moment when the invisible tether parted and he was alone again, his life link with his partner severed.

"Don," he gasped. "The beast...so big...razor sharp teeth, and the tongue...the tongue..." he fell to his knees and moaned and Matt's stomach made a flip-flop and he hoped he would never again in his life hear such a sound. He didn't know what else to do so he held onto Mary Beth and she didn't resist.

Then another part of his brain kicked in and ratcheted up. Suddenly, his analytical mind vaulted above the scene and he could see the Neos crowding up against Ramrod. He saw the wild eyed, pathetic attempts the Neo made trying to get into the cleft in the rock to get to his partner. He could see Viceroy and Thoth nudging Ramrod and he could feel them supporting the Neo's sudden loss. They were trying to keep the Neo from making a tragic decision.

"Mary Beth," he said quickly, "Al needs attention!" He gently but firmly disengaged from her and she let him. Tough minded woman that she was, she looked around and saw Al as he began to slump.

"Help me with him," Matt called. "We have to get him away from the Neos and lay him down."

With something to do, Mary Beth quickly became sane. Between them they caught Al before his face hit the rocky ground. Dragging him by his shoulders to a sheltered flat place, they gently laid him out on his back. Quickly helping a sleeping bag under him, Matt went over the visible wounds.

"I need the first aid kit!"

Mary Beth anticipated him and handed hers to him, holding it open. He reached in for gauze.

"Deep marks, probably a claw on the top of his head, right down to the skull. Get me some water on a towel." Mary Beth wetted a towel thoroughly and handed it to Matt.

Matt sopped the blood carefully away from the face and with a sigh of relief said, "His face is intact. His eyes are all right. Very, very close. The gash extends four inches down his cheek, but the orbit is okay from what I can see. He's still got both eyes."

"Oh Matt," Mary Beth started to lose it again.

"Later, Mary Beth." Matt glanced at her and held her gaze for only a moment, but it brought her back.

"Okay, I'm okay."

"I need you." He went back to work, packed the bleeding head and pulled a latex skullcap gently over the wounds.

"Now, the arm." Lifting it only an inch, he disengaged the camera and laid it out of the way.

"Broken. I have to pull it straight. You have to help me." He repositioned himself so that the arm lay in front of him. "Get around behind and hold as tight and steady as you possible can. When I say 'Now!' pull and put your weight into it." The woman nodded and assumed the correct position.

Matt felt along the ridge of the broken bone and then felt below for the end of the fracture. Getting set, he called, "Now!" and Mary Beth pulled, holding Al's torso as tight as she could. Matt, sweat standing on his brow, pulled suddenly and hard and when he released, he felt the bone go back into place.

"Whew."

"Matt, you're wonderful."

"First Aid classes is all."

"No, it's not," she said.

"C'mon, let's splint him and then we have to talk."

"Yes, Matt."

They made quick work of it. Al remained unconscious the whole time. Matt took his pulse and respiration and made him as comfortable as he could.

"Weak, fluttery, all I can do," he said, but his expression said more. His expression had more pain than she'd ever seen in a man.

"Matt, no matter what happens from here, no one, Doc included, could have done better than that."

"Thanks, Mary Beth."

"What now?"

"I'm very much afraid about Ramrod. I don't know what I can do. I think we have to go back in and see...what we see," he finished, not wanting to say it.

"No, Matt. No!" She was aghast.

"I have to do it for Don, Mary Beth, but you can help. Tell me as much as you can."

She gulped and turned around and put her hands to her head. Matt waited. Finally she turned back and her eyes were wide and watery and she said, "Al was first in line with Don slightly behind and to the right. The first things we saw were those old drawings and we stopped a couple of minutes to look at them. They were pretty wild, really. Then it was like the guys wanted to explore, they just had to do something we hadn't. We walked along the cave path, checking our steps, alert, listening. It started down pretty soon, but it was gradual and after awhile it opened up and got pretty wide. Then it like dropped off and we shined our lights and they didn't shine back and we knew we were close to the big bat's place."

She stopped and took a few breaths. "We were like on holiday and we made noise for sure, but for some time all we saw was black and then Don moved in front and said, 'Take a picture of me, Al' and Al said sure and the flash went off and it dazzled all of us and like we couldn't see for a couple of minutes and everybody stood still to get their flashlight vision back and that's when we heard it. It made a heavy flapping sound and then it was close and suddenly we knew we made a big mistake and we turned to run but that tongue came out and knocked Don down and then Al and I ran for the tunnel to get away and then the thing wrapped that tongue around Don's leg and started pulling and dragging him and Don screamed and Al turned to fight it. I couldn't believe it but he pulled out his knife and went after the beast and that's when it raked his head and then he had no more fight and he staggered back out of range of those huge claws and..."

She relived it for a moment and sobs wracked her and she couldn't go on.

"It's all right, Mary Beth. Stop." He reached for her again, but she waved him off.

"No!"

Matt waited.

Another deep breath. "I ran, Matt. I ran. I couldn't stop. I never felt so panicked in my life. Even when Roddy...and I thought..." She began to cry again. Matt gathered her in and she let him hold her this time. Finally she took slow, measured breaths and in a couple of minutes she struggled to straighten up again. Matt disengaged.

"I don't know, Matt, but I can't go in there again, not ever."

"Okay, you don't have to. But I do." With that he took his flashlight and strode past the anguished Ramrod. Mary Beth called to him. There was real fright in her voice, but he didn't stop. She couldn't see his tension and he didn't want her to. He hadn't been in the cave before. He had listened to Roddy and Jules and their account last time and just hadn't gone in. Now he had to. He had a mental picture of the place. Jules described things well and he knew that the only dangerous place would be in the big, open area where the rock dropped away into the cavern. No way would he go that far, but he had to know. He had to know because it was life or death, not just for Don, but for Ramrod.

The fissure opened into the cave and he walked hesitantly to the paintings, shining his light everywhere and then briefly on them. He pulled out his knife, held it in front of his body, and his flashlight glinted on the metal. Carefully, slowly, he stepped forward. About fifty feet into the cave it began to widen. Remembering the size of the beast as related by saner minds on the first trip, he went as far as he dared, and as quietly as he could move. Up ahead where the cave widened expansively, he saw blood trail and beyond that he saw a remnant. Clothing? He hoped he wasn't looking at an arm. He'd gone far enough. He had his answer.

Dejected, but certain, he backed slowly away from the deadly place of feeding. He left the cave to rejoin Mary Beth and the animals.

Hoping that he could do something to help Ramrod, he went up to him and put his hand on the side of the Neo's face. Viceroy stood back now and Thoth needed her partner and stood by Mary Beth.

Matt said, "I'm so sorry, Ramrod."

It didn't matter. He knew. He had known. Matt simply confirmed it. With that, the Neo reared and with the saddest blinny Matt ever heard or hoped to, galloped into the descending night. Frantic calls from the two remaining Neos and from the two humans reached out to empty air.

They knew Ramrod would do the only thing left to him.

Chapter 82
Sad Report

"Matt here."

"Base. This is Hector."

"We've lost Don. We have injuries and we've lost a Neo."

The bored sound at Base disappeared. "Come again, Matt."

"Two deaths and injuries. We're camped outside the bat cave. I need Doc on the line and better notify Arthur. Better get Jules, too."

"Omigod! Hold a moment."

Silence except for the whistle of wind rising up the mountain's steep slopes. Matt waited. He didn't want this conversation, but it must be. Mary Beth lay listlessly in the crook of Matt's arm while he made his call. One hand lay across Matt's chest. She looked exhausted and emotionally drained. Thoth stood above her and dipped her head every few moments to brush her partners shoulder with her soft muzzle. Mary Beth's hand involuntarily went up to the big face and stroked it. Viceroy stood by Matt's other side. He was calm, but every so often he would shimmy briefly and then turn and walk to the edge of the short plateau and he'd stare for long moments into the darkening evening. A soft blinny escaped him then and Matt knew he was grieving as deeply as any sensitive being could.

Doc's voice came on. It was a little breathless, but collected and professional. "What happened, Matt? Wait..." Matt held. Arthur and then Jules came on the conference call.

"Okay, Matt," Doc said. Matt began an account of the past half hour and when he was through—it didn't take long—Doc said, "Al still out?"

"Breathing normally now. Blood flow has stopped. I set the arm. Think it's good."

"I expect it is. How's Mary Beth?"

"She's right here. In shock. Grieving. She saw it all."

Uncomfortable silence, then, "We're sorry."

Jules broke in. "Ramrod gone?"

"Yes."

"I don't know how to tell Conan." Almost to himself.

Doc intervened. "Matt, you need to come back with Al."

"I know. We'll stay the night and head back in the morning. I think he's stable enough and I wouldn't move him until he's conscious."

"Your call."

Arthur said, "This is a tragedy. Don will be missed. We'll talk further and arrange for a memorial. For now we have to pause and regroup. Try and get some sleep. When Mike calls in we'll fill him in."

"Thanks, Arthur. We have to finish setting up camp now and we'll keep watch over Al, too."

They signed off and Matt said to Mary Beth, "I can do this, but it will help to be busy, so let's do it together."

Mary Beth stirred off Matt's chest and nodded. She worked dispiritedly at first but soon increased her pace and he watched her come out of it. Finally, as the last peg found a place to hold the tent, she said, "Thanks for being there for me, Matt." She turned and kissed him on the lips. There was no ardor in it. It was a kiss of deep friendship. Matt smiled, a little.

"Think you can sleep?"

"I doubt it, but I'll try hard enough."

"Let's get Al under wraps." They had built a two-man tent next to his feet and they carefully slid him into it as protection against the prominent night chill at altitude. Mary Beth would sleep next to him for the extra body warmth and be available if Al came to. Matt bundled up in his two-man. The Neos weren't bothered by the cold anymore than any naturally clad animal. They stayed close to a sheltering rock wall.

For an hour there was only the wind. Until Al woke up screaming. Two lost hours later they had him calmed and a part of the world again.

Chapter 83
Soldier's Rest

The three managed fitful sleep during the night, but both Al and Mary Beth had more than one nightmare and Matt thought Doc's psychology training would likely play a part in their lives for a while. It was hard not to be edgy when they got up at first light, but Matt needed to be calm and that calmed the others. They repacked the Neos and headed for home base.

Radio talk in the early hours assured them that all was arranged. Doc spoke to Al and got his take on how he felt. Could he ride? Yes, but Mary Beth would ride behind him, distributing her load to the other Neos.

They headed out, each with their thoughts and Matt not without feelings of guilt. As expedition leader, he had the authority to allow their trip into the cave and perhaps also to prevent the tragedy. Mary Beth, once back on her own track realized that Matt might think that way and blame himself. Before they turned in for the night, she gave him a talking to, and he responded at the right junctures.

This morning she wasn't at all sure she'd gotten through to him. Although he appeared in charge, little signs, furtively looking around, especially at the fissure that led to the cave mouth, his dejected slump, and how his mood seemed to affect Viceroy. The constant turn of the Neo's head told her he bore a heavy load and she hadn't done enough to help him lift it.

Tension filled silence ruled on the trip back. On arrival, the injured man was whisked away to the infirmary in Doc's company. Al was pale and he didn't speak, but an occasional tear leaked from his eyes and he stared straight ahead as if in the throe of a bad dream he couldn't shake. Doc decided Al would need a lot of work.

While on their way back to Base, the Construction crew cut out a simple obelisk of stone six feet long, four inches on a side from a nearby seam of straight rock and placed it into two feet of good earth next to Seth Hollister's marker in the cemetery. They would carve Don's name into the stone. There would be some kind of service, but later.

The plot designated as a cemetery for New Beginnings coming ages lay on a slight slope near the top of the hill not far from the construction depot before it dipped toward the new town, and seemed the fitting place to mark all passing. The place could be seen from far below, a revered place, a place to reflect, a physical spot that allowed for expressions of sadness and memory. Most of all, a place where every inhabitant could begin to understand the pain of loss and Man's need to go on.

At an early meeting of the Bio people, shortly after they came to the surface and rediscovered their world, they had to a man ratified a human need for physical remembrance of those gone before. Even the significant few who believed that at death nothing followed, accepted it as a needful thing. Hal Hastings had picked the spot and everyone agreed that to commemorate a passing he'd found the perfect place.

At the extraordinary meeting Arthur called to discuss the tragedy and loss of two of their own, and while he waited for all to congregate below the Bio-cave entrance, he reminisced about how he felt less pain with each succeeding day. He deliberately hung with Butterscotch as much as he could. He didn't understand it and only half believed that he'd taken a turn for the better; that Doc's diagnosis might perhaps have been in error—but he knew in his heart it wasn't. Intuitively, he felt that close proximity to his Neo helped him, that the strange attraction existing between the two acted curatively as a physical bond, that the odd empathy Neos had for humans imparted itself to Arthur as a physical force. He saw people smile as they went by, even when Arthur walked with rather than rode Butterscotch, and he knew they felt the same ethereal force in bonding with their animals.

Finally all had assembled. They spread out more than before because most kept their Neos by their sides. Arthur had no trouble projecting to the larger area.

"My friends," he said, "in a few minutes I am going to ask everyone who is free to do so to make a pilgrimage to our cemetery to honor the memory of Don Smythe and Ramrod. We as a group have been exceedingly lucky. Until this time in the growing history of New Beginnings, excepting two miscarriages several years ago, we have not had a death involving a Bio member. Today we honor the inseparable two who have fallen. In death, to be remembered by the living flows such immortality as any of us can expect.

"Don, until Ramrod partnered with him and therefore became part of him, worked with animals in the Bio and as a laborer in the gang led by Hal Hastings. His record, which I opened for this occasion, shows that he graduated high in his class at Montana University, and that he showed a high mechanical aptitude. He was chosen for the Bio for that and for his secondary talent, working with animals. We were proud to have him as part of our Bio experiment. Don was responsible for grading all the major roads we now think of as our town of New Beginnings. He didn't talk a lot but he was liked by all and loved by a few. His life was cut short, but what part of the short life he lived he lived with quality. In the sense that we are all soldiers, all warriors of a new age, we must now put him to rest."

Arthur paused. Don Smythe and Ramrod's eulogy was ended. The pregnant pause that followed told them the subject must now change.

"Al Parks has been physically and mentally damaged by what happened, as has Mary Beth. She will be okay and so will Al, but healing for Al will take longer. Please be natural with him. We are his stabilizing force. All we have to be is ourselves. Sympathy for a loss is fine, but we are the rock upon which we all stand.

"Enough of that. Let us all pass by the stone that now represents the life of Don Smythe and his partner Ramrod. Think on it and then return to your responsibilities. Thank you all."

The quiet crowd set foot on the well-worn path and gravitated away.

Chapter 84
Way Station

"Mike?"

"Sorry about what happened, Matt."

"Not more than me, buddy."

"I know, but it wasn't your fault."

"Everyone says that, so why do I keep thinking I could have said no."

"Matt, we're all mature people. You led the expedition. No one holds you accountable. It's not your fault."

"Yeah."

"Look, Nancy and Apache and Roddy and Thor and Geronimo and I miss you. We all need that supply shipment you were bringing. How about getting another bunch together and heading this way. You don't need anything else on your mind. Hear me?"

Matt left the mike keyed and Mike heard him take a deep breath. He knew what Mike said made as much sense as what everybody he'd come in contact with had said at Base, but somehow he *heard* Mike. From the others, as sincere as they were, he heard platitudes.

"Yeah, Mike. I read you. I'll get it together again and we'll head your way. Mary Beth has to come. I have to get her near the bat cave again, not in it, but close enough. I ever tell you that when I was a boy I almost drowned in the community pool at home?"

"No."

"Well, I was ten and trying to be smart. I couldn't swim, but I got into the five-foot pool and standing on my tiptoes I could bounce across from one side to another. It felt good. I felt big, bigger than I was anyway. Then some clown dived in and upended me. I came to on the cement deck with people looking down at me, and water running out of my mouth. I was afraid. I wanted to go home, but I remembered something my Uncle Howard told me. 'If something happens and you almost drown, go right back in the water or you'll be afraid of it for the rest of your life.' Well, I went back in and I think the same thing applies to Mary Beth."

"You'd be right, Matt."

Back in gear, Matt said, "So I take Mary Beth and the same unbonded Neos as before. I'll ask around to see who wants to make the trip with me. Thanks, Mike."

"Sure. Now get your butt back here."

"Couple days."

"Good enough."

Mike keyed out and squeezed Nancy's hand. She'd heard the exchange and turned to him, smoothing her hand alongside his several weeks old beard. "You done good, bucko."

Roddy called over from the last chair he'd made and now sat in comfortably, some several feet from the Way Station's front porch, an improvement Mike and Nancy worked on to avoid boredom. Thor grazed close nearby and looked up when he heard Roddy speak. During his weeks away, Roddy had become as astute a chair maker and weaver as Mike and now he sat contentedly weaving a hat.

"They're coming again?"

"Yeah, couple days."

"Good." He got out of his chair and walked with hardly a limp to Thor and grabbed his ears to pull the big head down. They nuzzled each other. It was then that Mike remembered what Matt had said about looking for changes and he saw for the first time what Matt meant. Roddy normally looked very dark, but standing by his Neo he looked lighter. A trick of the sun? He didn't think so and wasn't Roddy's face a bit longer? No, he's been sick; just loss of weight. Not worth saying anything. He'd glance from time to time. Besides, it didn't seem important.

Mike glanced up. A sky filled with puffy clouds and beginning to thicken told him another storm was coming. He gauged it. Probably another two hours. The nexus from Mike's diary of weather conditions seemed to be north and west of the station and historically that was where the most violent storms appeared.

"Gonna have another bad one this afternoon," he said.

"Mike Peters, weather forecaster," Roddy said.

"Yup, that's me. I'm going across, check things out." He called Geronimo and the Neo came up. Mike mounted and they headed for the bridge.

"That extra red sand we've been putting down is hardening like a road," he told his Neo. The ear fluttered and a short shimmy under him told Mike the animal understood.

"Still want to put up sides." The Neo said nothing. They stood at the center of the bridge and looked up and down the river. The familiar scene gave Mike a bump of pleasure. On the other side he dismounted and crawled to the edge to check out the stays. They were good.

He remounted and walked his Neo to the Aspen grove east of the bridge. He identified several tall, thin trunks he wanted to use as railings, firmed them in his mind and then headed back. He looked down the road to Ross River and briefly wondered why neither he, nor he and Nancy had gone past the curve in the road. All that uncharted territory. He really didn't want to go beyond the curve before they had a party ready to head there. Saving the adventure? Not wanting to sully it with pre-knowledge? Probably.

"Everything looks fine," he called to the two sitting in front of the station.

"Mike, help me work out a little," Roddy said.

"Sure. Arm wrestle?"

"Nah. How about a walk up the road and back?"

"We'll all go," Nancy pouted. "I need exercise, too."

"An hour tops," Roddy said.

"Sure."

They headed up the road. The Neos followed at a small distance. When they got to a relatively flat place not far from the Way Station, Mike said, "This is where Jules and Matt and I ran naked into the water after a storm. Very refreshing."

Nancy looked at it with a careful eye and said, "Why couldn't we excavate a little over here and over there and make us a pool?"

Mike said, "Never thought of it. Why not?"

"I'd like it," Roddy offered. He gazed at the river's edge and listened to muted thunder for a minute. "Fifty feet, I think."

"Sure. No worry on that account."

"I'll make a note. We're about out of things to do."

"Right. Yeah. Out of things to do in about a hundred years."

"You know what I mean. But it reminds me. I'll make sure Matt brings some portable excavating equipment."

"Shovels?"

"Yeah. Sure. Bigger ones than what we have here. And hoes and garden rakes and bags and picks and whatever we'll need. Dynamite, maybe."

They were back in little over an hour. Roddy's ankle scarcely bothered him. *Neo medicine works*, he thought.

Chapter 85
Third Time's the Charm

George Handy had a long conversation with his soul mate, Sue Dorchester. She wasn't keen on seeing her mate go on an adventure without her, but she had watched him heal for a long time and knew that his interrupted life required getting him back in the swing. She acquiesced and that gave George his ticket to ride. He searched out Matt when he got wind of the return trip.

"Hey Matt, remember me?" George was all smiles and Matt, who hadn't seen George for a few weeks, said, "Hey, George. What's doing?" Matt grabbed him by the shoulders and gave him a hug.

"Matt, I want to go."

That stopped him. Never thought of George.

"George, you want to go to the Way Station?"

"Doc's said I'm good to go, and *do* I want to go!"

"Well, sure. Doc knows it's not an easy ride."

"Complete bill of health."

"Great. What about Sue?"

"Headed her off at the pass last night. She's okay with it. Gotta be careful, she says."

"Smart idea."

"Figured I'd try not to fall into any holes in the ground this time."

"That'd work."

"So, okay?"

"Okay by me."

"Great. What can I do?"

"Get a pack. It's been standardized for exploring parties. There's a list posted near supply."

"When do we leave?"

"Tomorrow morning early. Be at the cave mouth at six."

"I'll be ready. Who else is going?"

"Mary Beth and Beth Howell. Al is out of it and Beth Howell asked to go."

"That's good. Bethy is good people."

"Yes, she is. See Jules around anywhere?"

"No, but he's out with the Neos most times, I think."

"Okay. Gotta finish my list on what to bring. Mike called in last night and wants a bunch of stuff. Hal wants us to pick up a few hundred gallons of diesel fuel on the trip back. Guess the fuel situation needs attention. I'm going to take ten unbonded Neos instead of five. We have plenty and I get the impression they enjoy it."

"Okay, see you."

"Wait." Something just came to him.

George turned.

"I hadn't asked you because I thought you were still down, but you're a metals engineer. Do you think you could whip up some light, thin, flexible carriers for diesel fuel. Like, fit them along either side of a Neo's back for easy carrying?"

"Take awhile."

"Mark Cohen is an engineer. If he's free to work with you, would that help?"

"Yes, absolutely. What can a Neo carry?"

"Don't know, but they were loaded up for the abortive trip to the Way Station and they had no trouble. I'm thinking they can handle at least a hundred pounds on a side. I'm about one-eighty and they have no trouble with me or what I'm carrying, for that matter, it's another forty pounds. On the way back that's all they'd be carrying."

"Figure about eight pounds per gallon," George stopped to calculate, "about thirty gallons per animal, fifteen per side."

"I know the Bio has a stock of sheet steel we've never had call for. Would that work?"

"Dunno. I'll get with Mark and see what we can come up with. Doubt I can get it done overnight."

"How about if you had until the morning after next?"

"No promises, but that sounds better."

"I'll put off starting an extra day."

"Okay. I better get going." George headed back down the tunnel.

Matt ticked his list off on his fingers. Better call Mike.

On the second morning George, Mark and six commandeered people from below worked their way up the tunnel with ten custom made, hollow, clanging metal carriers, which they strapped to a couple of Neos for the journey. They were ungainly, but Matt could see that when placed correctly, they would cover the flanks of ten animals on the return trip and wouldn't likely chafe.

The "Mule train," Matt liked to think that, but didn't say it out loud, assembled just before six and headed out, promising to stay in radio contact a bit more often than usual. Evidence of industry could be seen this early out toward the town and smoke curled from a couple of chimneys. Soon Base disappeared and no one looked back. By noon they were climbing and Bethy had started to complain about her Neo's seat. Mary Beth chided her, telling her that she'll not only get used to it but she'd probably take on a different gait when she was "broke in."

Matt felt good. The repartee didn't have any strain to it, but they were a long way from the bat cave. Solid woman. She's coming along.

At the forty-five hundred foot level they camped for the night. No one wanted to go into the cave and Matt was relieved to see Mary Beth glancing at the fissure from time to time, which he interpreted as good. It reminded him of his swimming story. He stopped worrying.

In the morning they decided they'd slept well and were anxious to hit the pass. There had been a light covering of snow, but it didn't hold anything up and they made the transfer through the pass without incident. As they descended into old Neo territory the pack Neos began to get excited and the Neos under the riders had to admonish them. They stayed together, gradually making their way to the lower mountain passages. Soon enough tall pine forests replaced vast Neo fields.

Because they could make better time with Neos than on foot, and because they knew the way, before long they were on the Ross River Road and headed west. In the late afternoon they dropped the diesel containers at the mine. By nightfall

Matt figured they weren't any more than five miles from the station and asked if everyone would like to continue or stop for the night.

Go for it, they said, so they stepped up the pace and when they could see a dim light in the distance around eight o'clock, they started shouting. In moments the fire jumped in brilliance. They whooped and hollered all the way into camp. Their Neos felt the excitement and shimmied under them, no doubt wondering more about these strange beings.

Glad-handing and hugs and much happy noise and confusion signaled the re-supply train's meeting with the Way Station group. Roddy sought out his lover and Mary Beth melted into his arms and they squeezed each other so tight Matt thought one of them might squeak. Bethy Howell marveled at the intensity of feeling.

Matt heard her murmur, "I gotta get me some of that!"

Chapter 86
Chats

Sitting by the fire pit where they'd built it near the road, in basket weave chairs mostly made by Roddy during his long recovery, light conversation turned to a review of what the Bio people had accomplished in the nearly two months since their emergence from the mountain. Matt had an overview; he and Arthur had made the rounds most recently. Still, Matt asked Bethy to talk about the Bio and where that stood. She related that most of the Bio was above ground now and only the children, a few monitors and the original animals were being kept below. That would only be for a little while longer, she said. The plan was to get everything up with the exception of the atomic pile when the town was sectioned off completely and the closure at the end of the valley was complete, a matter of days, she thought.

"Mary Beth, you gave up your maintenance of the pile to Jane and that transition has been made. Anything you'd like to add?"

"Jane is up to speed. We'll keep the Bio warm and livable as a safe haven in the event of any unforeseen catastrophe. There's talk of running electricity to the town, but I believe we don't have the length or gauge of wire needed for that. I heard something about getting on to Ross River to see what we can take from there. It's all free. I'll spell Jane if she needs it, when I'm around, but I am officially detached and I go where my man goes. That's it." She looked fondly at Roddy, who sat next to her casually holding hands.

Matt took it from there. "The town is amazing. Jerry and company have put together live-in log cabin units for everybody and the "fort" as he calls it is coming along fast. Up in the forested side hills, a half dozen men are building a sawmill not far from the steam vent. They figure on using it, and I'm sure that will happen. That's a change in plan. Jerry wanted to put the sawmill at the end of the earthen dam we're putting in, but I forget who suggested the present location for the sawmill and suggested that a flourmill would be good near the dam. Nobody had a problem with that. The sawmill building is in and they are custom making the equipment. Making a forty-inch saw to handle the big stuff is a problem, but they'll solve it. They're cutting and splitting with axes and what saws we have and it's looking good. Arthur and I went to the end of the valley and I can say that the animal compound is nearly done." He glanced at Bethy.

"Getting to the situation here, we have all the tools and equipment available, nails, spikes, Mike and I've tried to think of everything. There's fuel at the mine and we'll resurrect some of the equipment there and start mining iron again. We'll make a smelter. The Bio will keep the library, by the way until the waterproof library is completed at the fort. We have more information on making things than we'll probably ever need. We can start tomorrow on the bridge sides and additional shoring. After that's well on the way, Mike has interested me in something he discovered in a valley over that mountain," he pointed, "which may give us some answers about our Neos and maybe other things. I'm sure you've all heard rumors."

"I haven't," Bethy said. Mary Beth shook her head and even Roddy looked quizzical. Mike wouldn't look at him.

"Sorry, guys," Matt looked embarrassed. "I thought it had leaked out."

"So give, Matt," Mary Beth said.

Matt told them of his conversation with Mike and then with Arthur. "We talked about it, but we need proof."

"How do we get proof of an extra terrestrial landing?" Roddy asked.

"The only thing we can do is to examine the site Mike found and see what we see. Arthur and Jules and I were together to talk about it the morning after Mike's call and we came up with some interesting thoughts. For one, there is the proximity of the Neos to the Bio. Now there is the proximity of the markings Mike found to both Base and the Neo grazing fields. How true it is, is a guess, but if someone out there watched the world come to an end by its own hand, is it so impossible to think that they might have identified the last one hundred humans alive? There's the problem of the Neos themselves. If mountain goats lived in a valley protected enough from prevailing winds and therefore from radiation poisoning, what's to say ET managed to tinker with their genes enough to grow a whole new species of the animal? How is it that they are so smart and how is it that we and they immediately discovered an affinity for each other? I'd think it far-fetched if not impossible if I hadn't seen it for myself.

"All the world's former species were like oil on water. They evolved to survive, but they also evolved away from each other. The variety on earth was phenomenal. Suddenly we are all alone. If someone out there has been monitoring us for a few hundred years—is that so hard to accept in view of everything that has happened in the past twelve? It wouldn't take much for me to believe that they knew us, and if they knew us, they would know that we are a suicidal race. We proved it, didn't we?"

"What about the giant bat, Matt?" Bethy asked.

"I don't know, Bethy. I really don't, but suppose they shined or radiated something at our locale, something not nuclear, and it caused an unintended mutation in bats while mutating the old mountain goats? It seems coincidental, but couldn't the bat have mutated separately from the Neos. Who knows? What if there's pitchblende in the mountains around here? What if that mutation has been going on for a long time?"

"It's getting more like science fiction all the time," Mary Beth said. She sounded part irritated and part scared.

Matt turned to her. "I'm not trying to build a scenario we can believe in. I'm only trying to throw out thoughts and I'd very much like it if someone else would contribute."

Mike spoke up. "When you were running through all that, Matt, I got to thinking that a lot of questions about what we're living with right now are answered by your conjectures. What if ET came to the same conclusion that we did? What if they picked up our general trend toward destruction tens or hundreds of years ago and started playing with certain animals' gene structure? What if they anticipated we'd wipe ourselves out and began planning early? What if they decided that a lot about our species was worth saving if the race did itself in? What if they decided if humanity intended to do it again—I know this is far out—and they figured we might be worth it, but expected it would eventually play out the same way, so they threw the Neos our way so we couldn't help but change? That's what we think we have to do, isn't it? It's a decision we came to on our own, right?"

And now breathless, Bethy interjected. "And to let us know we are being watched, they leave us a calling card."

Roddy jumped in. "But they don't want to get involved. Maybe they can't. Maybe Earth wouldn't support their type of being."

"Maybe they are benevolent?" Mary Beth threw in.

Matt held up his hands and laughed. "We're freaking ourselves out. We have no answers. Day after tomorrow we'll head up the mountain and look for ourselves, okay? Get our work done here first and head up. Maybe it's nothing and we're making up stories like children at a campfire."

George had been silent for the whole evening. "The Neos are real, and our resolve to repopulate the Earth is real," he said quietly. "We're going to do it, regardless."

"Don't you want to know, George?" Mike said.

"You know, Mike, no, I don't care, not a bit. I healed and I've got my life back, that's enough."

The fire had gone to embers and rumbles of thunder sounded through the hills and mountains north of them. The excitement of the evening calmed and they decided they were tired, tired of the long day and tired of talking and tired of thinking.

That night the rains came again and the Way Station shook with wind and lightning flashed through closed lids and thunder woke them periodically and they snuggled and listened, but then the storm abated, and they slept the sleep of the weary.

Chapter 87
Doing What They Oughter

Aromatic smoke from the cook fire and the rattle of pans woke the last sleepers to a beautiful and fresh new day. They got up, moved slowly and then faster and the day brightened and the sun, a great orb down low in a valley between two massive mountains peeked through the trees and it felt good to be alive. By seven a.m. they were finished and Mike had given out the assignments for the day. First order of business: cut aspen saplings for the bridge rail. Bethy and Mary Beth got the chore, while George, after swearing he was tip-top got the job of hanging from the basket and driving spikes to make the bridge more secure. Mike would work above him and pass George what he needed.

Roddy and Matt took the other end of the bridge, doing virtually the same things. Roddy passed and Matt hammered.

An hour of that shored up the bridge to Mike's satisfaction.

"Good enough," he said. "Now for railings."

No one questioned the wisdom of this project. Wind funneled down through the pass from the west and could easily have blown an unwary worker into the white water below. Although here was no wind at the moment, Mike insisted they tie themselves to something strong while working. Nobody questioned that, either.

Mary Beth and Bethy used the small curved saws in their packs to cut trees Mike had marked days earlier. Matt doled out hatchets and an axe he'd brought. They stripped the branches and asked Thoth to drag them onto the bridge. They were quickly tied to the four-foot high uprights the men worked on earlier. To further aid safety, they then strung and tied rope to the posts, creating netting thin enough to allow wind to pass without resistance, but comprehensive, too. The explorers paid attention and worked hard. Their Neos worked along side of them as needed and if not they were content to graze.

At the end of the day they gathered at the fire-pit again and Mike pronounced the day a success. As the Neos grazed nearby, Bethy began to sing in her sweet soprano. She sang old show tunes from The Fantasticks and Oklahoma. Mike tried to join and George turned out to have a fair baritone voice. Matt waved them off with his hands and a laugh.

"You wouldn't want me to send you screaming across the McMillan, would you?"

"Oh, c'mon," Mary Beth said with a friendly smile, and she joined in with her high alto. Matt sat and enjoyed the serenade as much as if he had participated. They sang for perhaps a half hour and one or another, deciding that bed was an even better thought, drifted away.

At long last only Mike and Matt sat looking into the diminishing fire.

Finally, with a shrug of his shoulders, Matt stood, leaned down and grabbed Mike's hand and shook it.

"What was that for?"

"Nothing. For being a friend."

Mike looked into Matt's eyes and nodded.

"Look at your reflection, Mike?"

"Yeah. You don't see changes on others, but your image isn't what you have in your mind. Are we really changing, physically, I mean, Matt?"

"I don't think so. I think we are reprocessing our images of ourselves, changing within."

"It's okay?"

"Yes."

Chapter 88
A Perplexing Dilemma

Matt had responsibilities so this trip he couldn't head for Ross River. He'd content himself to gaze into a flat valley, maybe go there and see it up close and personal, rummage around, climb back up the hill and report on what he thought he'd seen. Analyze the data. Form an opinion. Roddy couldn't climb yet and Bethy didn't have any desire to, but George, Mary Beth, Mike and Matt all were too curious not to, so the next morning they set out and by ten a.m. they were on the plateau looking down a thousand feet at the scene.

Mike's binoculars brought the view ten times closer and Matt had to agree about the regularity of the marks and their strange shape. His heart began to pound a little—Mike had something—and he headed down through the sparse forests that grew up the steep hillside with Mike by his side. Before leaving, Mary Beth and George had a turn at the binoculars and wanted more, too. They followed down the steep slope, grasping a tree trunk here and there to keep from going headlong out of control. In half an hour they were at the edge of a vast field more level than it looked from above.

Matt headed for the closest anomaly a hundred feet ahead. They swished through the tall alfalfa, making an easy path to follow. When they arrived, Matt stood for a long time, his eyes searching what appeared to be a round area twenty feet or more in diameter. He remembered that Mike thought the number was twenty-five, but he'd gauged it from a long way off. The area was, even after years of nature overcoming, pretty much a perfect circle. He bent down and felt the ground. Some grass had reestablished itself after all these years, but the character of the ground was more like disintegrating glass, like something very hot had sat there for a time and burned it.

Mike bent down, hands on knees.

"Yup."

"I agree this is unusual. Let's check out a couple more, minimum."

"Okay."

They paced off in the direction of the next round spot.

"The same," Matt confirmed.

"Yup."

Moving off at the same precise angle they'd taken to find the second spot, they found the third one exactly where they knew it would be.

"More burned ground," Matt said.

"Want to bet they are all like this."

"No."

"If these are the marks of a ship's landing gear, you realize the ship must be more than a quarter of a mile in diameter."

"Yeah, I know."

Mike bent down and scraped a handful of the glasslike material into his hand.

"This stuff's sharp. Wish we'd brought a plastic bag."

"Here." Mary Beth took her first aid kit apart and handed Mike a vinyl glove.

"Brilliant."

George and Mary Beth watched closely and kept quiet, taking it all in.

Now George said, "What do you suppose made the burn marks?" He didn't have any questions about their size.

Matt stared at George. "Who knows? Magnetic resonance? Some sort of cold fusion? Flame from a hot exhaust? Except that the burn path would be wider and diffuse. One thing I do think. This wasn't caused by what we think of as fire. Much to regular and precise."

Mary Beth said to Mike, "You're a mathematician. What do you make of it?"

"About the same as Matt, Mary Beth. I couldn't begin to calculate how much power it would take to land in Earth gravity and take off again with a ship over a thousand feet in diameter.

Way beyond me but we'll analyze this stuff when we get back and see if it tells us anything."

"So someone landed and took off and suddenly we have Neos and mutant bats and a chance to repopulate our planet but only if we change and become what we aren't, because if we didn't, we'd destroy ourselves again down the road and maybe next time for good, right?"

"Couldn't have put it better myself," Mike said, and he leered maniacally at Mary Beth.

"You don't scare me."

Matt broke in. "Hey, guys, we have a lot to think of. Let's stay sane while we do it."

"You're no fun," Mike said, but the playful look came off his face.

"Let's get some opinions," Matt said. "Mary Beth?"

"I don't know. It's weird."

"George?"

"I'm closer to believing than I was after supper last night."

"Mike?"

"I don't know either, but the marks are unnatural. They are huge, implying something large. They were produced by something very hot. Takes a lot to fry rock. They are regular. We could see that from way up there," he pointed. "Also, we are in a very remote place and for the life of me I can't guess at why some person or persons would come up here and make them. To what purpose?"

"I agree with Mike," Matt said, "What does this prove? Empirically, nothing, but attached to the observational data of proximity, of new life—our Neos—of the strange and unlikely aspect of our being attracted to these alien creatures we have found on Earth, of life which has never been seen before and doesn't react or think as we do and yet we willingly and completely empathize with and it with us, it would be awfully easy to accept it as prima facie evidence of another life form tampering with us."

"For good or ill?" George asked.

"I don't know, George, but I think, benevolent."

"Yeah, me too."

"Well, let's take it back to camp."

They began to climb.

Chapter 89
Radio Meeting

It took until nightfall for the explorers to get back to the Way Station and they were exhausted. Nancy, Bethy and Roddy had supper ready to heat and the returning troupe was grateful they had nothing to do. They badgered Matt about what they had seen, but he asked them to wait until they could eat and regroup, so facts and opinions were thrown out over the meal by the other three.

"Matt has to call it in, so how about if he only does it once?" Mary Beth said.

They got off his tail, but were otherwise irrepressible.

Stomachs satisfied and the fire burning merrily, and with the exploring party reenergized, Matt called in. He'd had time to think about his presentation and decided to make it fact based and let other minds sort it out and come to their own conclusions. Matt keyed his radio and called Base. Arthur was on.

"Thought you'd call around now, Matt," he said.

"It's been a most interesting day, Arthur. Can you record the facts?"

"Sure. We're set up for it now. Shoot."

Matt started with the trek up the hill and what they visualized from the plateau, briefly described the descent and spent time on a description of the huge, flat area of grassland. Then he went into detail about the circular marks they'd found and the composition of the ground at each site, the specific angle that brought them to each of the three sites they'd examined. He told Arthur and listeners that the explorers and the Way Station people had discussed it at length, but that he didn't want to say anything in this conversation.

"Why won't you say now?"

"I'd rather leave all conjecture out of this until the Bio has sunk its teeth into the facts in evidence. Then I'll give you my opinions and the others will offer theirs. We talked it over."

"You're saying this is too big for the rest of us to be guided by one area of thinking."

"Yes."

"I'll accept that. When are you coming back?"

"The bridge is shored up and I can't believe it will come down in any storm. Tomorrow we will ride back to the mine and fill our custom diesel tanks with fuel. We'll head back then. We'll likely get as far as the Neo field and camp there. I think the unbonded ones would probably like to kick up their heels on the old home ground."

"No doubt. Okay, Matt. Thank you for all you do."

"That's not necessary, Arthur."

"Yes, it is, Matt, but it's not just you, it's all of you. I think it's time for me to tell you all that I'm proud of you and I couldn't hope to have a better group of people to work with."

"Thanks, Arthur," he said, but he sounded a little embarrassed. He added, "We're very tired. We'll talk again in the morning, okay?"

"Sure." It was Arthur's turn to sound embarrassed.

Not long after, all was quiet.

Except the wind.

Chapter 90
Roddy Rides

No rain in the night. It happened now and then. Morning dawned like crystal. The dew evaporated as the camp stirred. Briskly they moved about to counteract the chill. Roddy stood over near the scrap woodpile. He reached down and grabbed two fairly heavy ends—they would go into the fire that night—and began to exercise with them.

"How you feeling today, Roddy," Mike called from the fire pit.

"Good, Mike, real good."

Matt looked over at Roddy. The man looked pretty good, but hadn't been tried for stamina yet. The healing process time for humans was far from met, but with Thor hanging around like a poultice or a good luck charm, Roddy was much further along than he had any right to be.

He said, "How would you feel about going back to Base with us?"

"Would I? Sure."

"You feel that healed up?"

Roddy came over and took off his shirt. The gouges were all but healed. Slight depressions in the worst of them barely showed. He walked on his broken left leg like he might a year past the accident. No sign of the ankle sprain, even though he knew such a severe sprain shouldn't be healed. His right wrist obviously felt good or he wouldn't be holding that heavy scrap.

"I know why," Matt said, "but I'm still amazed."

A murmur from the others agreed that something miraculous had occurred.

"I've been thinking," Mike said. "There's no reason for any of us to stay here. It's not like we have to protect it from anybody and we've weatherproofed as well as we can. Why don't we all go back to the Bio?"

Matt thought, *why not, indeed.*

Nancy, who hadn't much to say, spoke up. "I'd like to go back. It's been weeks and I loves my big guy here, but I have friends I'd like to see."

"You're right. We don't need to keep this outpost manned. Besides, we'll be back again soon. Ross River is still on the agenda."

"More than ever," Mary Beth said. "We need heavy wire."

"Okay, we'll load up and go."

They broke camp immediately following breakfast with Matt's list of things to do in his shirt pocket. They mounted, seven riders on their Neos with ten unbonded. They rode the twenty miles back to the mine, filled the containers and discovered a problem. Getting the carriers strapped to the mounts under weight wasn't all that easy. They wouldn't be deterred and solved the problem using the old tanker drive-up platform and a hoist Jules jimmied from good timber inside the Mine. Ropes did the rest. At first the Neos were skittish and concern about chafing stopped them for a time. Then Jules suggested they open their sleeping bags and use them as horse blankets. That worked fine and the carrier Neos stopped complaining.

Matt kept a log on things that needed changing for future trips. Noting that inanimate material seemed a whole 'nother thing to the animals, he scratched a quick note, "Neos *need* human contact, close as they can get, but carrying fuel is only bother."

Once loaded, the caravan moved past the lonely rusting car, now only a mile marker on their trek.

"Another five and we start up."

"That a landmark now?" Roddy said, indicating the car.

"Of a sort."

They found their trail easily and commenced to ascend the mountain. By late afternoon they came to the Neo field.

"Long way to go yet," Matt said, "and last time we camped in the middle of the field." He looked up at the lowering sky.

"Gonna rain and those thunderheads are piling up big time. It's going to be another bad one."

George spoke up. "We'd do well to get closer to the trees. We'd better get all that metal off the Neos."

"Damn! Right you are."

"Let's move it along toward that stand where Jules said Conan got into it with that big Neo challenger," George said.

"I remember. Okay, let's head for it."

Thunder cracked and rumbled high above them. Black clouds swept at them. The clouds seemed in a hurry. Neos and riders stepped up the pace.

Nearing the little stand of short trees, they dismounted and hurriedly pulled the fuel containers off the Neos. Lightning sizzled and struck in the field not far away. One frightened Neo bolted. Matt had no name for it, so he called, "Come back! Come back!" but the flash and crash were too close and Matt's voice went nowhere. The panicked Neo dashed away with thirty gallons of unloaded diesel. Now lightning struck all around them. They cringed under their rain slickers, hoping that the runaway would be okay, but just then a fat bolt struck the panicked Neo and it stumbled and fell and hit a rock. Suddenly there was fire all around it and they could only watch helplessly as it screamed and died. The storm kept them flat and made them hide frightened for an hour. When it let up, Mike, Roddy and George went to the place where the Neo had been. They came back immediately.

"You don't want to see it," they said.

The women shuddered. "Poor guy," Bethy said.

"I doubt it could regenerate from that."

"They're amazing," Matt said, "but probably not. Anyway, we're here for the night and we need to set up."

The group worked together, loosed the Neos and got camp set up.

Oddly, the Neos didn't go to grazing as they had every time in the past. Instead, they all, even the partnered Neos walked slowly over to the badly charred body of their companion and began a keening, whistling sound over the inert figure. The humans wondered, but stayed out of it.

I have to run this by Jules, he thought. It occurred to Matt that they were losing their solitary independence. But they were becoming interdependent so fast, he wondered if it was good.

Chapter 91
Neo Medicine

Matt stared at the blackness under his rain gear as lightning cracked and sizzled around him. Should they have run into the field and tried to save the Neo?

After the storm he keyed his radio to talk to Jules, but then he released the button.

He knew what Jules would say. He wouldn't know either. "Humans respond differently from Neos." That he would say.

To see in the herd a highly developed social structure was one thing, but to understand the subtleties of it, especially when their only reference point came from an element of humanity they no longer trusted... It didn't solve the equation. If anything it made things worse, because all the Bio people felt as drawn to their animals as the animals to them. He recalled that the Neos had acted selflessly to help humans on more than one occasion.

In the morning George put it succinctly. "We had our heads down and tried to be small in that storm. What else could we do?"

Matt nodded and understood, but his guilt didn't diminish.

"The Neos are still milling around over there. I'm going over."

"I'll come," George said.

Mike joined them. They walked the hundred or more feet to the site of the lightning strike and subsequent fire and when they arrived, they caught a collective breath. The injured Neo still lay on the ground, but the badly burned carcass of last night had disappeared and in it's place lay an animal breathing shallowly, but breathing. New, healthy hide had grown during the night and even hair had begun from new follicles. The unbonded Neo would survive. When Jules had told his story at a different campfire about the female protector whose throat was ripped out, they couldn't visualize his excitement on seeing the healing process. Now they did and the revelation of Roddy's amazing healing meant something more.

"George," Matt said, "if you had the closeness of a Neo when you were injured, you'd have been long healed by now."

"Clifford's going to be a constant companion, I can assure."

They walked back to the camp. The ladies were up and sufficiently made up to satisfy themselves.

"What'd you find," Mary Beth called as the men entered the perimeter.

"The Neo's coming back. It's going to live."

"Wow! That's great."

"I'm going to call Arthur. I'm thinking we wait for the Neo to recover, that it's more important for us to be solid with the Neos than it is to get back in a hurry."

"You don't need Arthur for that. We're staying."

Bethy and Nancy nodded.

"Case closed."

He called Base. Already he could see the magic visited upon the human contingent by the Neo species. Their priorities had radically shifted. Where would it lead?

Chapter 92
New Subject

By the following day the Neo was fine. The three men inspected and stroked the animal. He seemed grateful for the attention.

Mike said, "It seems to me that this old boy doesn't remember what happened."

Matt stroked his chin, a habit he'd begun recently. "You could be right. A lot of trauma must have come the way of the herd in the past twelve years. Forgetfulness could be coping."

"Especially when you consider their method of disposing of tribe members when they aren't wanted anymore," George said.

"Yeah," Matt said. He brushed it aside. "We need to get back. Let's go."

The other two said nothing, but led the newly repaired Neo back to the camp and got things started. Before long the unbonded Neos were reloaded—George had come up with a way of disconnecting the fuel tanks and by using two humans to restrap them in the *present* position, it worked well. With camp broken down and riders aloft, they plodded over Templar Pass and down the other side to yet another welcome back. Mike, Nancy, and Roddy were celebrities. A number of men and women circled Roddy and demanded to hear of his adventure first hand.

He tried to pooh-pooh it, but deep down he felt the rush.

Matt moved away from the gathering. He'd heard it before.

"Matt!"

From behind him came a little thunderbolt. Millie ran into Matt so hard he barely kept his feet.

"Whoa!"

"I'm so glad to see you."

"Me too, you," he said back.

She bear hugged him and his arms naturally enfolded her and it felt good, good!

Millie heard it all but wanted it again, close up. Matt smiled down at her and kissed her roundly.

"That's better," she cried. "Much better."

Arthur came in from town. He'd installed himself in a small cabin near the fort and told everyone he felt more like a pioneer than ever. Matt looked him over and decided he looked arguably more fit than he had when they left only days before.

"Life has gone on," Arthur announced, "and our industry is phenomenal, as you will see. Most of the houses aren't totally finished, but they are all livable. They have furniture and a degree of comfort and they await the finishing touches. It has seemed reasonable to suggest to everyone that a move consistent with a change of town take place and that is in progress. Dwellings have been assigned, but they remain flexible, so let's ride to New Beginnings and you may choose your own, if you care to."

Matt couldn't believe it. Only another week gone and so much more accomplished. Mike, Roddy and Nancy were simply astounded. Nancy clapped her hands in delight.

"It reminds me of an early American frontier town. It's beautiful. It's wonderful."

Jerry Ells came up and gave Nancy a hug. "Thanks. It's a germ from which we will grow a better civilization."

"What about the Neos?"

"We never planned for it, but there's plenty of room."

"Good."

Mike took Nancy's hand and said, "Let's go to town."

They started off, hands swinging. Geronimo and Apache walked along behind them, shimmying occasionally.

Hal on Seth cut out the unbonded Neos laden with his precious cargo, and with a warm smile said to Matt, "Got a place for these. C'mon guys." Seth shimmied briefly and the Neos followed. Matt thought silently that everyone he came across acted in concert with their Neos. How marvelous.

"Matt," Arthur called. Matt turned. "Let's sit down and talk."

"Sure."

Arthur led Matt to a row of three picnic tables and sat on one. Matt took the other side, leaned on his elbows and said, "What's on your mind, Arthur?"

"We're moving. In connection with that I want you to be aware of what we are leaving in the Bio. I've ordered a security lock on the entrance to the tunnel."

That startled Matt. "Why?"

"It's not for now, but for a few years down the road, when the kids are big enough to be curious about the atomic pile and might want to fool around in the caves."

"You're sure it's necessary? They'll always be somebody there, won't there?"

Arthur smiled. "For the most part, but Ernie is going to run a remote station hookup in the upper cave so important readings can be monitored above ground. That way the works will only need inspection about once a week. I suppose we could start a superstition about ghosts or something to avoid misbehavior."

"You know, I never gave it a thought. I've been outer-directed for weeks, but if you must secure anything, it ought to be only the tunnel to the pile. I could see that, but I could also visualize the caves as a kind of training ground for children. What a good way to offer exercise and mountain training in a controlled surrounding. I'll bet Roddy and probably George would be willing instructors. I wouldn't mind a turn at it myself."

Arthur stared at him for a long moment. "How shortsighted I was. That's a great idea. I'll put it on the next agenda and introduce it."

"And I have another idea, Arthur. If the steam vent on the lower end of the valley is reliable enough and could be engineered to give steam power to the town, wouldn't that be a better power source than atomics. The pile won't last forever."

"True." Arthur's mind was off on another path. "Plenty of wood to heat for the winters, plenty of wood for building homes."

"Why couldn't the pile be shut down altogether, once we have another source of power?"

"It's been with us for twelve years. We had a problem only once in that time and you'll recall it was only weeks ago. That could be the start of aging problems, but the pile could also last for many years to come. Eventually we would collect a lot of radioactive debris we couldn't get rid of. Your idea has serious merit. We'll talk about it at the town meeting."

"Then there are the Neos. It's natural to want comfort as we knew it, but we have our partners to consider. My picture of the new civilization is pastoral."

"All we do from here on considers Neos with it."

"Only way."

"Thanks, Matt."

"How did our Bio friends do considering the evidence we discovered, by the way?"

"Yes, we'll talk about that, too."

Chapter 93
Fitting the Pieces pt.1

In keeping with the general move, the central fort became the obvious new meeting hall. Jerry engineered it to hold two hundred people, more than enough room for the almost one hundred adults, including nearing fifty children. In the basement level he constructed a small meeting room and a much larger children's playroom and gathering place. Al Parks—before he left with the Way Station party—and Gil Castonguay had been hard at work with two others, Glenn Bates and Rollie Burbank, recently underemployed in the Bio's planting department. They took to hand making furniture for various individual houses and particularly for the fort, anticipating a need.

Although presently open to the sky, a heavy gate attached to massive vertical timbers reminiscent of early colonial American stockades made it easily defensible. The gatekeeper left it open for all. With the Neos, they felt even less at risk. Plans to roof it against weather were in the works. Some upper-story framework, basically floating rafters, tied part of the structure together. It gave townspeople an inkling as to future construction.

After Arthur's inspection of possibilities, he suggested a small raised platform and a podium, which Jerry arranged immediately. Three steps brought any speaker head and shoulders above the crowd. Gil Castonguay, sole carpenter after Al left with the last Way Station party, had finished the podium only that day.

Jules walked up the steps after Arthur gave his overview. It filled everyone in on various projects.

"Any questions?" There were few, which he answered or fielded. Finally, a voice from the back of the crowd asked *the* question!

"That you, Murph?" Arthur got a wave. "Okay, we're saving that for last. I want to call Jules up next to hear how his work on the Neo language is coming."

Jules mounted the steps and faced the assembly. "Friends, my study of Neo language is going well enough. I'm a chemist and I am neither English scholar nor Neo professor. Matter of fact I profess to very little these days." A ripple of laughter went through the crowd.

He continued. "The best way to pick up an understanding of Neos still lies with one-on-one contact with your Neo partner. The animals are empathetic and that is why they pick up on anything we do. They see our body language and associate it with the words we speak. Understanding is right there for them; hence they understand us whilst we agonize over flank motions connected with head motions, and how different the meaning may be when one or the other is absent, etc. You know what I'm talking about. I can help you a little. I have compiled a group of universal symbols dealing with various common motions and sounds that will be available to all of us tomorrow. We're printing them tonight. I've asked for pocket-sized editions we can all carry with us.

"Neos speak one language, but to avoid misunderstanding on our part and misdirection to our Neos, I have one rule I recommend we follow. When in doubt, *let the Neo decide.* In virtually any situation they will choose the right path. It's Occam's Razor, the simplest solution is usually the best one. Their brand of simplicity has developed in their genes, so trust it. That doesn't mean they are smarter than we are in experience or history or even in the gray matter department, but they do possess an innate ability to choose, that transcends synaptic response, and you may rely on them to choose correctly. They are literally betting their lives on their decisions. You heard the story about Don and Ramrod. I'm sorry to bring it up here, but it is illustrative of the empathy and the rightness of Ramrod's decision, despite the tragedy that followed."

Jules didn't speak for a few seconds. No sound rustled in the hall.

"Also remember that you are as precious to your Neo as the life they possess within and that your mistake could be fatal to your Neo. You are bonded and that means two separate entities that must be near each other to be complete. You feel it. So when push comes to shove, let them decide. That's all. Any questions?"

Astoundingly, the audience clapped. Jules reddened, but waved, looked at Arthur, who nodded, and Jules left the stage.

"Excellent. Now Jerry."

"Hi gang." A few "Hi's" came back. "This is just review. Most of you have seen it all. What you see is a frontier town of the rudest simplicity, which is the way any self-respecting civilization should start, in my opinion. Using modern engineering practices, we have succeeded in moving our new town roughly back to 1650."

Everyone laughed as they saw the simile.

"We have to crawl before we walk and so on. Our knowledge is currently being used to create tools. From them we will manufacture better and better things, although for the first fifty years I expect we will be basically a pastoral society living on grains and what else we can grow. We will use wood until we can enter the Iron Age again and from that will come next steps and ones beyond. Rebuilding civilization from scratch, notwithstanding the advantages we currently have, will take time. All we have is time. Any questions?"

Someone at the back of the assembly shouted, "What's the plan for the steam vent, Jerry?"

"We can't do much until we can get a small iron smelter together and make heat resistant tanks, but it's in the works. No ETA, though."

"Okay, thanks."

A question from the front. "Jerry, how's our diesel situation?"

Jerry looked at Arthur, who said, "Hal is next."

"Anything else relative to the town plot?" Jerry asked. He waited. In a few moments he said, "I'm done."

Arthur waved to Hal Hastings, who moved toward the stairs and mounted the stage.

"Hi all," he said. Greetings came from around the crowd. "In a nutshell, we're at twenty-percent of the diesel we found in the cave. Matt came back with nine, forty gallon containers of decent diesel from the tank on the River Road. The tenth one was lost, as you have probably heard, when the carrying Neo was struck by lightning. The animal healed and survived, but forty-gallons was lost, so our net addition to our reserve is three hundred and sixty gallons. In total, then we have a tad over seven hundred gallons. We could do with more and I would like to request four trains of fifteen Neos be outfitted for another run to the big tank. That'll fill nearly all the barrels and leave something over a thousand gallons of diesel at the mine. Matt said they want to try and get some of the old mining equipment going and we know iron is going to get important pretty soon. As I told you all before, the equipment has stood up well enough and we've been able to fix what's broken so far. That's all I have."

Hal turned to leave and Arthur thanked him. Gina wrote furiously.

"Okay everyone," Arthur said. "We're in good shape overall. Hal didn't mention it, but we'll be using less diesel fuel from now on, since the major excavating and grading is largely done and also since we have the Neos willing to work anywhere we need them. Having a large supply of diesel on hand in the cave is just to keep handy."

"What about Ross River?" someone shouted.

"In a minute. That's the last item on the agenda."

"Okay."

"Next, clothing and food. I think we're ahead of it on that point. The cottage industries we started six years ago for the caves will be moved to the town into a building Jerry designed especially for the manufacture of clothing. The building can be sectioned off to plan for other industries we will need as they arise. Jerry has tried to plan for the next fifty years, insofar as he can."

He looked down at his sheet.

"Last item, Ross River. We will use the exploratory party who first went over Front Mountain. They have requested it and I couldn't refuse. Matt, Mike, Jules and Roddy will make the trek. George and Sue will accompany as far as the Way Station and stay there to await their return. They will set up additional booster relays wherever they can get line of sight for the Ross River people. Millie, Nancy and Mary Beth have decided to wait in town for their men to return. The first diesel train of fifteen Neos will go as far as the mine under the leadership of Hector Bertrand and will return as soon as loaded. Other trains will follow. Any other questions?"

It had been a long meeting. Everyone seemed content. Democracy working...in the extreme.

"Meeting adjourned."

Chapter 94
Preliminaries pt. 2

Neo trains were getting common. The animals seemed as interested and excited as the riders. Enough canisters had been made for the fifteen Neos and by the time they returned, more would be available to replace broken or lost ones. A small group of townspeople showed up to see the combined troupe away. They left with a wave, four explorers and three with other jobs to do. The sure-footed Neos made the trek easy and safe and the largest part of the train halted at the mine. They gave Hector a hand filling the canister tanks and saw him off. George on Clifford and Sue on April stopped at the Way station, resupplied it with non-perishables and eyeballed likely sites for radio boosters.

"I can't get over it," she said. "You did a wonderful job. Everything is so solid." Sue couldn't get over the Way Station and bridge constructed across fifty feet of raging river.

Mike looked proud and Matt said little, as usual. Roddy tried to wax eloquent and failed, but managed to astonish Sue with the history of the place. George listened in. He'd seen it all but remained dutifully, and honestly impressed.

"We'll stay the night and get an early start," Matt said. "In the morning, George, why not follow us a bit to see the lie of the land for the boosters?"

"We'll all go, Matt," Sue piped up.

"Sure."

They built a fire and settled for the night. After the embers died, in the dead blackness of night, a firmament of brilliant stars called for song and for a while the Way Station resonated to harmonies from ages past.

Chapter 95
Extending Communication

The sleepers didn't have to dry out morning dampness. The Way Station had stood the tests of time and no longer represented a challenge. Soon it would be relegated to the background, a thing accepted and relied upon, a platform from which newer challenges could be launched. After breakfast, about seven, they mounted up and a few minutes later crossed the McMillan, glancing down many feet at the wild, white water. Roddy wouldn't look down. He kept a bead on the aspen grove on the south side of the river and let Thor bring him to it. Once there they stepped up the pace, filing along the unfinished, somewhat pebbly edge of the road in the manner the Neos liked. Entering the first curve, the one that made mystery of the terrain beyond, they found seriously rough topography. Nearly sheer cliffs on both sides about ninety feet high of the same common reddish rock provided so little space at road's edge for Neo footing that they were forced onto a road in need of more than average repair. The Neos weren't happy about it.

Jules, who saw everything while appearing to look straight ahead, only occasionally glancing this way and that said, "Blast marks," and pointed. Only Sue seemed interested. From then she kept an eye ahead for the nearly vertical, cylindrical marks made by diamond dust drills.

Mike, quiet for a time, said, "Considering the type of rock hereabouts, it surprises me some of that hillside didn't come down with the world tremors." The others glanced briefly at the speaker, but only Geronimo appeared interested.

A quarter mile past the cleft the road opened out again. Rolling hills to the left and escarpment to the right would make it difficult to surmount, but George eyeballed it and told them the hill above it probably would be a good site for a booster.

"From the lie of the land, I'm going to bet that somewhere on the northwest side we'll find a view to the Way Station or a few hundred feet above it. Either way I'll bet we'll get a good twenty or thirty miles of seeing to the southwest."

"Have fun, George."

"Me and my girl, we'll do it together."

They said goodbye and "luck." Four drove on while George and Sue looked for a way up. After a couple of minutes, Sue spoke.

"George, why don't you ask Clifford?"

George smacked his forehead. "Dumb me!"

The Neo turned his right ear back as George explained their plight. Clifford gazed at the hills and snorted. Then he followed after the Ross River crew—they were a quarter mile ahead—for a few hundred yards, saw an opening and walked into it. George expressed his concern quietly to Sue. "He's got to be kidding."

"Don't bet on it."

The Neo stopped and gathered.

"Hang on," Sue called. Then she watched as Clifford made what they both would have called an impossible leap up the near sheer cliff-side. His hoofs grabbed where they couldn't see anything but red rock and before George decided he didn't want to do this, they were standing precariously on a ridge five inches wide, which Clifford nimbly and most nonchalantly walked for fifty feet before it made a blind turn into much easier going. George realized he hadn't taken a breath in the meantime and snatched a grateful gulp. Clifford turned back an ear. They finished the turn and walked into a widening crevasse heading upward.

"Sue," he yelled, "This is unbelievable!"

"Don't yell. I'm right behind you."

George twisted fully around and his mouth dropped open. "I didn't even hear you."

She giggled. "I had the benefit of watching the impossible accomplished with ease. I told April okay and off she went."

"These Neos are amazing."

"That's such an understatement."

When his heart stopped pounding, he picked up a view of the territory. Clifford plodded along, not particularly interested. The Neo no doubt thought, "How can anyone be interested in rock?" When he occasionally checked out the land he did so to reorient his upward path. Finally the two came out on a large, windswept plateau. Ahead of them a rocky nub stuck up toward heaven.

"Present." Clifford let him off.

George got a booster and his pick and hammer and climbed the nub to stand staring at the surrounding mountains. He didn't have binoculars, but his excellent eyesight noted four Neos and figures too tiny to see clearly somewhat more than five miles down the road. The view excited him, because the road stretched pretty straight until it came to a point in the distance. Thirty miles at least!

"I see them," he called.

"Oh good," Sue returned.

In his three-sixty turn George couldn't see the Way Station, but he could see the plateau he'd been on the day they'd checked out the strange markings on the flat plain below it. That would do.

"I have the landmarks, Sue."

"Great! Button it down and let's go back to the station."

"Give me a couple." George made quick work of it. He attached the booster to the rock face with small pitons, adjusted it by eye to the termini of the road. The receiver side he pointed at the plateau.

"That should do it." He bounced down the steep slope and went directly to Sue and kissed her.

"What was that for?"

"I should take it back?"

'Well, no, but..."

George grinned. "Let's head back."

Sue shook her head. George wasn't demonstrative. But she could live with it.

The sun was almost overhead by the time they arrived back at the Way Station.

"How about a little lunch and then climb to the plateau with a booster? I want to test out that uphill link we planted as soon as possible."

"Okay."

They ate hurriedly. Afterward George went rummaging around the Way Station.

"Aha!"

"What?"

"The extra set of binoculars."

"Oh."

"If the mountain link doesn't work, we have to go back up tomorrow. We'll need 'em. They'll help me point the plateau link, too."

"Where does that one hook up?"

"Mike showed it to me earlier. He set it up for the Way Station, but I may have to move it so I can catch line of sight to both the mine and plateau. I'll figure it out."

They disposed of their trash and headed up the hill.

Chapter 96
More Upset

"About thirty miles, I'd say," Mike guessed, "maybe a bit more."

"We'll camp over there," Matt pointed. An aspen grove grew out near to the road and plenty of space between trees promised easy camping.

"My butt's sore," Roddy complained.

"Gotta toughen you back up, Roddy," Jules said with a chuckle.

"Tomorrow's another day. Long way to go yet," Matt said.

"Yeah." Roddy quit griping.

"Mike, before you settle for the night, will you climb that roundish jumble over there and find a permanent spot for a booster?"

"Sure, how do we look?"

"We have a clear view to the top of that point George headed for. Aim for that."

"Okay, Matt." Mike checked his pack for boosters and equipment. Satisfied, he urged Geronimo up the hill. Soon Mike and his Neo were small creatures moving against the backdrop.

The jumble Matt referred to included a lot of shale-like red stone. It rose a couple hundred feet and was probably the tallest thing in the area. The terrain had flattened considerably and the McMillan, which they could see from time to time, meandered and glinted a few hundred feet away. The road construction people had straightened the road out a lot and more of the same ran ahead of them.

"Boring!" Roddy said.

"We're here to see what's at the end of the road, not what's here, Roddy."

"Yeah, yeah."

Jules observed, "He enjoys complaining, Matt."

"I know."

Just then they heard a rumble from the direction Mike had taken. Startled, they looked up in time to see Geronimo sliding downward, feet dancing. They watched him automatically move toward the unmoving part of the slide and he almost made it when Mike seemed to jerk atop his Neo and then he fell down into the small avalanche and disappeared from sight. A thin yell came to them before they could move.

"Mike!" they shouted, three voices mingling into one. In a second they were galloping toward the mound. They passed scrub trees barely hanging onto the rocky ground, down a slight dip and then they were on the hill.

"Matt, Roddy!" Jules held up his hand.

They stopped their headlong race. Jules motioned and the other two spread out. They knew to be careful on this type of terrain, but they had to balance that against their need. Geronimo had made it to safer ground and stood staring at a spot on the now quiet hillside. He blinnied softly.

"Mike!" Matt bellowed.

A voice came from above. "I'm okay, Matt. Couple of scrapes, nothing, but I'm flat on my back and I think the hill will move again if *I* do. You need to get above me and toss me a rope. This side is unstable and maybe the other, too, I don't know. I think Jules and Conan should search for a better way up and toss me a rope."

"Jules, got that?"

"On my way." Jules and Conan started to round the corner. Roddy walked Thor back to where Matt waited and worried.

"If anybody can do it, Jules can," Roddy said.

"I know."

Once out of sight Jules keyed his radio. "You should be able to hear me in the short distance, I think."

"So far, so good."

"Conan has picked a path I can't see. I'm hanging on."

Couple of minutes. "Sliding...sliding..."

Conan danced his way out of it. "Okay, now."

Matt and Roddy wiped sweat. More minutes. Jules voice began to break up.

"Nearing the top. Getting better..."

Another minute. Through crackling and fade they thought they heard, "Conan, present." Evidently Jules had left the mike open deliberately.

Five minutes went by, five of the longest minutes they'd ever spent. Now and then one of the listeners thought they heard heavy breathing. Then, clearly, "Okay, I'm on top. I see Mike. Hey Mike!"

Silence. Then, "Mike, I'm going to throw this over your chest. Don't grab for it until you're sure you can get it. That whole hillside looks like it wants to come down."

Silence. Then, "He's got it, guys, and I've got him. C'mon up, Mike."

Relief.

It was Mike's turn to dance. Red shale slipped under his feet and large sections of hillside started and slid, then stabilized, then slid again, but he doggedly bounced over sliding rock that seemed intent on burying him. Gradually, Jules played him like a fish up the hill. Near the top he gained purchase. Jules held out his hand, Mike grasped it and the two heard a shout from the bottom of the hill. Mike waved.

Mike joined Jules on the stable top and waved down at Roddy and Matt.

Mike said, "Thanks, Jules, man of the hour. Uh-oh!"

"What?"

"Forgot my booster. Better go back down for it."

"Smart ass."

Mike looked wry. Jules held out a booster from his kit.

Mike took it. "Oh, guess I can use this one."

He found a place and secured it.

"This is good. I think we'll be able to see that prominence a long way. I set it up to cover a big portion of the road for travelers, too."

"That'll work," Jules said. "Now, you go down on the rope and I'll go back the way I came."

"Right."

Mike started down staying as light on his feet as possible while attempting to stay in the most recent mini-avalanches, hoping they'd be more stable.

An hour later they were together again, Geronimo and Mike nuzzling each other.

At eight p.m., Matt tried the radio to Base. Worked five-by.

Chapter 97
Tying It Up

"Stop and think. We've been too lucky." At the moment, the four rode two abreast. Matt and Mike were in the forefront.

They entered a long stretch of straight road; level fields of grain marched away in both directions. They'd been quiet for an hour, looking around and enjoying the beauty of the early day. Mike rode left of Matt and Geronimo and Viceroy occasionally shimmied under the riders. Neos greater peripheral view helped the animals not only in language, but also in overview. They could nearly see behind themselves without turning their heads. Therein lay a disadvantage. Jules' eyes, facing forward, could discern better and he had noted that immediately on meeting Conan in battle. His quick brain adjusted for it, and Jules took the advantage before Conan could do anything about it. Jules hadn't mentioned it to the others; it was subliminal with him. No doubt he thought the others would notice the animals physiology and if they didn't it didn't mean anything, but it certainly accounted for the development of their strange language.

"You know I don't believe in luck, Mike." Matt woke out of his introspection.

"You believe you make your own, right?"

"You know this."

"Of course. My point is, planning, being careful and checking out each step before taking it is all well and good, but things happen you can't plan for and it seems to me something or somebody is watching over us. Maybe just watching."

"Mike, that's ridiculous." Matt turned to his friend and Mike faced him.

"Matt, one thing a lot of time doing nothing does for me fires up my brain. I've been thinking."
"What?"
"About the many coincidences."
"I know. Okay, let's hear it. Let's all hear it."
"Sure." Mike raised the volume. "Hear me okay?"
Two voices from the back, "Sure."
"Okay. We've hashed a lot of this out and questions remain."
"Always questions, Mike," Jules called ahead.

Mike went on. "I'm on brain strain, guys. Look, the country is vast, yet Neos popped up right on our path to the only road toward civilization, like somebody...or thing...knew we'd eventually seek. How's this for a new scenario? Alien ship lands before humanity destroys itself. Like I say, this country is pretty much uninhabited. They grab a few goats, large animals who live off the land and who have genetically evolved to endure as a species. Up they go, alter the animals on their ship, grow a few and maybe six, seven years ago pop down to the surface and drop them off on Front Mountain to acclimate. They are prolific and by the time we bust out onto the surface, they're a free ranging herd of hundreds with a social order and amazing powers of regeneration. That would fit with the enhanced radiation levels at this latitude, an ability to outlive essentially destructive radiation? We live in a cave, blind and deaf to the upper world. We are protected, but we are blind. We know nothing and they don't want us to. I figure they don't want to mess with the little band of indigenous intelligence left on Earth, but they sure as hell know we're there.

"C'mon, how much technology would it take to watch us from space constructing our Bio? We had that before we blew ourselves up. Granted, what they could do with genetics is way ahead, but any space-faring civilization would likely have technology that would appear magic to even us, right? Once we got past the huge egos we humans have carried for a few thousand years we could accept that, you know? And they would have had a great handle of the world political situation and the risks humans were taking. They saw it coming and now it's here and they did something incomprehensible to us little humans. They offered us another path, one we would never have taken, one we couldn't even guess at, yet something that works, is working."

He stopped. No one spoke. He patted Geronimo's neck lovingly.

Moments of pregnant silence, and then, "Mike?"

Mike glanced at Roddy. "Yeah?"

"Something that's been bothering me since we met the Neos."

"Go ahead."

"Like, what you say makes sense, but why did Jules have to fight Conan, right at the beginning, if some ET wanted to help us?"

Mike brought Geronimo to a halt and turned to face Roddy across the roadway. "Maybe, Roddy, maybe they wanted to see if we were worthy."

"Worth the trouble?"

"They know what humans are and what they have been, and maybe they're conducting an experiment. Does what's left of humanity have enough stuff, enough intelligence, maybe enough empathy to become something else and leave behind the destructive creature Man is? So they test us right off the bat. We, through Jules, prove we can rise to the challenge. Then they leave clues we will likely find. And we find some, but we are skeptical. The unwillingness is to believe in something because we've never seen it before, or because it doesn't fit our tight set of parameters. It's so human to reject a new thing, to have our idols smashed, isn't it, guys?"

Attuned to this one voice are three humans and four Neos. There are no words and no shimmying.

"Right now this is brainwork and wild guesses. But maybe we'll find other clues on the Ross River Road, because it's natural for humans to seek out others, even if there are no others. They know we'll go this way. And one other thing. They don't believe we can do it without help. When we realize and accept that, then we'll believe, won't we?"

They rode for more minutes. Finally Matt broke the silence.

"Mike, I think we've all been considering these things. I don't think we have any firm answers, but we're on the same page. I believe the Neos have understood you, too. Let's test it.

Viceroy, did you understand what Geronimo's human was saying?"

Viceroy nodded his head and huffed quietly.

Jules spoke to Conan. "Conan, do you understand what race memory is?"

The big Neo didn't answer right away. Then he nodded.

"How far back does your memory go?'

Again the Neo walked on, as if in thought. He shimmied and the other three answered him. Conan blinnied.

Roddy jerked upright. "What's that mean?" he asked.

"I don't know," Jules said. "I'm going to guess he can't find common ground to answer. Remember, the concept of year is an abstract, but four seasons are less so with enough repetition. I'll try that."

Conan turned back an ear as Jules phrased the question differently, first describing seasons. The intelligent animal stopped and tapped his right hoof twenty-eight times.

"Not bad brainwork, Mike," Jules said appreciatively.

"Thanks. I think I'm going to have to go some to stay up with the Neos."

That brought a chuckle all around. They resumed their trek. By noon they were fifteen miles down the road. At a lower altitude they found the old road in pretty good shape and the preferred sides were wide and easy on Neo hooves. By evening, as the light began to fail, they had covered twenty more.

At camp, Matt called in their progress and told Base they'd probably make Ross River by nighttime tomorrow or during the early part of the day after. They ate cold rations and crawled into their sleeping bags. Heat lightning without thunder flashed at them, but rain in the mountains didn't bother them.

Chapter 98
Ross River Connection

Next day they made time as best they could. The little town was in their sights that night, but they elected to stay out until morning. Brilliant stars overhead, temperature in the thirties, a small fire smoldering toward ruin and another long and uneventful day behind them, tired of sitting and tired of riding, sleep came gratefully.

During the night a storm blew in from the west and they were glad for the little tents. Lightning flashed cloud to cloud and the light show augmented by rippling thunder made little impression on the group. The Neos stayed close.

Morning. Taking a deep breath of the clean air invigorated them and they dressed quickly, tended their needs, ate quickly, policed their area and mounted. They closed the last three miles in good humor and high anticipation. In the first mile they came upon a small house. The lawn had long since turned into a wild field and grass grew right to the closed front door.

"Roddy, want the honors?" Matt said.

"Sure." He asked Thor to present. Roddy dismounted and walked through the grass, his hands splayed, lightly touching the tops of the grains. He pushed on the door and it fell inward as it disconnected from rusted hinges. Roddy walked in, surveyed the dim interior and came back in a moment.

"Old furniture, no one home," he said. "Indian artifacts."

"A large population of Inuit lived hereabouts," Jules said.

"Let's go on, then," Matt called. He jotted something in his notebook.

Several hundred yards further they saw their first telephone pole, a thin power wire sitting atop the bakelite insulator. Looking beyond they saw more poles that led into the little town.

"There's our wire, Matt."

"We'll collect as much as we can to carry back when we're through looking the place over."

Ramshackle houses, not pretty but functional came more rapidly now and the four looked this way and that. Streets merged with Old Route 6 and the little town, except for the silence, seemed to be waiting for something.

"Us," Roddy said. They glanced at him. They felt it, too. They moved slowly to the center. Main Street anyplace always had a look about it and they knew they'd come as far as they needed.

"We're here," Matt said to the group and asked Viceroy to let him off. The others got down, too.

Low buildings had begun to show the ravages of wind and rain, the only thing that lived, now that human, tame and wild animal had passed.

"Wonder what we should expect?" Mike asked.

"What you see," Matt said. He pulled out his Geiger counter and checked the area. Low-level radiation, higher than normal background, but well below danger level. "We're safe."

Jules patted Conan's face and the Neo moved his big head into Jules' chest. "Let's wander."

They split up. One took the trading post and the others went to other businesses to look around. They searched for an hour, looking for anything interesting and compared notes. Roddy found a clothing outlet. Matt noted it and the contents of the hardware store Mike inventoried. Jules and Conan went to the church. He told them it remained pristine inside. "Outside won't take much before it starts leaking in. Place needs maintenance."

Matt traveled furthest. South of town he saw the top of something regular and investigation yielded another ten thousand gallon diesel tank. "Probably for the farms nearby. It's rusted up, but it's got fuel in it, maybe half a tank like the one at the mine. The tank's okay. Hal will be happy."

"Think we should suggest to Base we move wholesale here or Whitehorse?" Roddy asked.

"I don't think so," Matt told him. "I think our valley is the catalyst for the new civilization. But we'll give them what we have and all decide."

They encountered no bodies, although they eventually found a mass cemetery past the west end of town. One grave lay open, its sides caved in by ruthless weather. A skeletal leg jutted from the dirt.

"Last man, I guess," Matt said.

"Must have been awful sick by the time he got the last of them buried. Not very smooth around here," Jules interposed.

"I wonder why," Mike said. "Could have just left them out."

"Might have still feared bears or scavenging animals, whatever."

"Maybe religious thing. The Eskimos had their own brand of beliefs."

"Doesn't matter, does it?" Matt said.

"No," Mike said, "doesn't matter."

Chapter 99
Tidying Up

"Base?" He waited. In a few moments, he heard a woman's voice faintly.

"Matt?"

"You're pretty hard to hear."

"Come again?"

He raised his voice and got right next to the mike.

"That's better. How's it going?"

"Well enough. Not a good signal, though."

"Hang a moment. I'll turn up the gain and hook up to the new PA system."

"Ernie and his guys got it working, huh?"

"Okay, Matt, go ahead."

"We're in Ross River and we've gone through the town. Not much here, but enough, and we found more diesel. We also found a store with farming equipment and machinery. We found wire. We can use it all at New Beginnings, I think."

He went on to describe the things they found and finished by saying, "We hoped to see more evidence of our visitors, but there's nothing here. I think they want us to survive on our own. If we can."

"How soon will you head back?"

"We'll stay another couple of days and check out what we haven't seen so far, pick up anything useful we can carry and gather as much wire as we can. I want to look for a cart we can pull and we'll fill it up. That'll help." He looked at the guys and they nodded. "Exploring party out."

They spent the rest of the day identifying what New Beginnings could use and setting it aside. They slept in town that night and disconnected power line the next day. Then they made plans to return to the Way Station. They found a farm wagon behind the store in a shed in nearly new condition, but with flat tires. Somewhere in the store Roddy came across a bicycle pump and they found an adapter to connect to the valve stem. It took considerable time to pump them back up. Mike and Jules cobbled up a harness for a Neo tow. They made sure it disconnected easily so all Neos could spread the load.

That evening Matt notified Base and promised a volume of notes to pour over when they returned. They slept peacefully in their final night because they knew that home beckoned and home was New Beginnings. Humans and Neos alike felt the pull. Early next morning they said goodbye to Ross River and astride their inseparable Neos, pointed east and north with farm wagon in tow and packs bulging with useful artifacts that might in the future line a wall or two in the New Beginnings fort. Matt wrote in his notes that a museum should be constructed to preserve the important beginnings of their new civilization. Now was the time for things like that.

Chapter 100
Homebound

Occasional chatter, attention called to a feature or other thing, a break for lunch and a break later in the afternoon in a particularly rich field of young grass. The riders stopped because they knew their Neos would be pleased and want to graze; these things encompassed them. A bright fire late became the embers one gazed into during a solitary time when each man thought his own thoughts or fancied that which he hungered for, yet days away, and it kept them quiet and introspective, but not distant. They had grown so close in the days together that many of their thoughts and gestures became similar. And oftentimes one or another would finish a sentence begun by another and none thought it strange. And that was strange.

Then, as they rounded the final break in the mountains cut by the old Canadian road that had served them so well, the Way Station appeared and Sue and George, astride April and Clifford waved and shouted from the middle of the bridge and the Neos blinnied and were glad to see them. And backs were thumped and hugs went around and kisses were planted exuberantly and Neos got together not far from their partners and spoke to one another and the feeling was of coming together, of completion. But they weren't complete, not yet. In a few more days they would again surmount Templar Pass and be reunited with their kinfolk and then the splinter of New Beginnings that had gone exploring would assimilate into the whole of what Arthur had called the embryo of a Human/Neo species. They now traveled in a direction that could no longer lead to humanity's destruction.

Over time, the symbiosis would weld into an unbreakable emotional connection and from the germ of New Beginnings, joyous life would once again spread over the face of a beautiful and accepting world. Earth's occupants would come to thank an unknown race they could never hope to see or meet for its intercession. Perhaps they would call it God.

CPSIA information can be obtained at www.ICGtesting.com
Printed in the USA
BVOW071712200812

298294BV00001B/8/P

9 780982 242421